THE DEAVYS

THE DEAVYS

ALAN DEAN FOSTER

WITHDRAWN

OPEN ROAD
INTEGRATED MEDIA
NEW YORK

Cover design by Jesse Hayes

978-1-5040-1589-9

Published in 2016 by Open Road Integrated Media, Inc.
345 Hudson Street
New York, NY 10014
www.openroadmedia.com

THE DEAVYS

Someone had stolen the Truth. It had been kept in a bottle on a high shelf in the very back of Mr. Gemimmel's drugstore on South Harrison Street. No one in Clearsight had seen who had taken it. Or *what* had taken it. In a town like Clearsight, Pennsylvania, you could never be sure whether something that had been sneaking around was a *who* or a *what*.

The theft had left poor Mr. Gemimmel terribly distraught. His extended family had been in charge of the Truth since the time his very-great-indeed ancestors had found it. They'd been holding a village parley on the beach fronting the Neolithic settlement of Skara Brae in the Orkney Islands, some several thousands of years ago. Since then, a lot of the Truth had been spread around. Quite widely, in fact. But its essence had always been contained in one place—in a simple but very nicely made stoppered bottle of pale blue. It had been handed down from generation to generation, of which proud lineage Mr. Gemimmel was the latest incarnation.

And now the Truth was gone. Out.

Simwan Deavy knew that in the wrong hands, the Truth could be extremely dangerous. It could even be extremely dangerous in the right hands, if those hands didn't know how to handle it properly. His mother, for one, was highly sensitive to it. It was through her dreams that the Truth often passed into the world. Though he'd once seen the Truth for himself, contained in its innocuous glass bottle on the shelf in the mysterious depths of the drugstore, he had never dared to handle it. Now, relaxing in his room with the afternoon light from the open bay window burnishing everything inside in late autumn gold, he wondered who or what had stolen the Truth—and why.

A nimble feline shape materialized on the windowsill. Though his room was on the second floor of the house and the wall outside was flat and vertical, the svelte russet-and-black–hued figure that was now silhouetted in the sunshine had made the leap easily. But then, Pithfwid was no ordinary cat. Or as he himself would have *prefurred* to have it restated, "No cat is ordinary." Simwan sat up on his bed and turned to face the window.

"You heard?"

Licking one forepaw until it was nice and soppy, Pithfwid proceeded to groom his face as he replied. Like agitated stars, small bright sparks crackled from the tips of his toes as those furry digits slicked down the strands of his sable-smooth coat.

"I heard. Gemimmel ought to pay more attention to his inventory instead of spending so much time up front watching the register and helping customers. He ought to pay more attention to things that belong to others, that he has been charged with guarding."

"Too late now." Stretching slightly to see past the cat, Simwan contemplated the untouched virgin forest that backed up to the Deavy property. "I wonder if this might have something to do with the new development?"

Pithfwid paced off a double circle before settling himself on the sill. "How do you mean?"

Rising from his bed, the lanky teenager ambled over to the window. Resting both hands on the sill, one on either side of the contented feline, Simwan gazed out at the woods. Somewhere within the tangle of branches, blue jays were squawking like sportscasters competing for ratings. Carrying an acorn in its mouth, a squirrel took a quick look around before dashing up the trunk of an ancient, brooding sycamore. A stew of wind and small things unseen rustled leaves that October was turning gold and maroon, crinkly and crackly, amber and umber. And as if this business of the Truth disappearing from Mr. Gemimmel's store wasn't serious enough, All Hallow's Eve was approaching.

In the Deavy household, Halloween was more serious than fun, candy, and costumes.

"You know that not everyone in town realizes what the development would mean."

One cat eye opened to squint up at him. At the moment, it was the only part of Pithfwid that moved. "What's that? Humans not understanding the true meaning of things? I'm shocked, Simwan. Shocked!" The eye closed.

Familiar with the cat's moods, the teenager ignored the pointed sarcasm and continued. "The Ord adults can't stop talking about all the new jobs it will bring to town. They don't see that it'll also mean the end of the woods." He nodded toward the trees. "Most of this will get cut down so condominiums and big-box stores and the new mall can go up. They'll dig up the burrows and drain the ponds, channel the creeks and pave over the bogs."

If that catastrophe came to pass, where would he relax in summer, dig through leaves in autumn, toboggan in winter, and frolic in spring? Where would he and Josh and Esteban and Leroy swim nude, dodging the eels and chasing the fish? Where would they sit and discuss the prospects for the Steelers and the Pirates, or the possibilities of buying a car since they'd just gotten their driver's licenses, or the intricacies of the latest video game, or whether Carrenna Fitzhughes from Beeker Street would go out with any of them, if someone somehow mustered up enough courage to actually ask her?

With a sigh that suggested he knew he was not going to be allowed to enjoy his nap, Pithfwid opened both eyes to regard his human companion. "What do Martin and Melinda Mae have to say about it?"

Simwan made a resigned noise. "In their time off work, my parents are trying to rally the townsfolk. But we're the only non-Ord family in Clearsight, and neither of them is strong enough to conjure up a Sway-Spell that would push-persuade a majority of registered voters. Mr. Gemimmel could help, but Dad says he's so upset over the loss of the Truth last week that he can barely summon up enough enthusiasm to open the drugstore." Simwan looked worried. "And Mom . . . Mom's not feeling so good right now. You know how sensitive she is to the Truth."

Rising, Pithfwid arched his back, yawned, and stretched, the movement flinging tiny sparks into the air, as if someone had being rubbing a wool sweater in the dark of night. "What about bringing in outside help?"

Reaching down, Simwan caressed the cat's back. Pithfwid began to purr contentedly, only shifting into a growl when the teen showed signs of stopping. "I've heard them talking about it. Because of Mom's deep attachment to the Truth, Dad knows it has to be recovered soon. They talked about having Senester Balthrop come down from New England to help, but he and the Providence Coven are all tied up trying to sort out the big fraud trial that's been going on up there. Meanwhile, Mom says the New England Masters organization is snowed under with much bigger problems." He stared out at the trees. "Leastwise, they're bigger problems to them."

Pithfwid made a sound like Balthrop, which in Feline would be translated as "contemptuous spit."

"Well, they're *our* woods, and I for one am not going to see them cut down, channeled, drained, or paved over. Where would I hunt? In the smelly thickets of the Gap? Beneath the gnarled roots of Walmart? When I sit myself up on a fence post lit by the full moon and wail, it's ratty boots and thoughtful curses I want flung at me, not glittery high-heels and hundred-dollar sneakers. Feed my soul with old soles, not new ones." Violet eyes peered at the worried teen. "If your parents can't deal with it—"

"Dad *does* have a job," Simwan protested, feeling compelled to defend his well-meaning, if all-too-often-preoccupied, father. "He can't fight the developers on his own, all the time."

"—then we'll have to do it ourselves," the cat concluded decisively. "You and me . . . and the coubet, of course."

Turning away from the window, Simwan made a face. "Not the girls! Can't we leave them out of this?" Throwing up his arms in disgust (but leaving them attached to his shoulders), he stomped peevishly around his room. From the walls, muscular sports stars and models in skimpy bathing suits watched him closely. "You know how they'll be. They'll want to question everything, they'll want to run everything, they'll keep giving me orders and asking me to do stuff for them and embarrassing me if I see a girl my own age I was even thinking about maybe wanting to talk to."

Doing a glissando down from the sill, Pithfwid started across the room. The girls' room was down the hall. "And maybe they'll save your life."

Trading an expression of disgust for one of sudden concern, Simwan frowned at the cat. "What are you saying?"

Halting, Pithfwid looked over his shoulder and up at his friend. Just to show how serious he was, he promptly changed color from black and russet to gray with white stripes.

"Who, or what, do you think stole the Truth?"

"I dunno. Isn't that one of the things we have to find out?"

"Indeed," confirmed the cat. "Hapkin Gemimmel might not be the brightest drugstore proprietor in the world, or the most able dispenser of spells, but he's no fool. I've been through his store, hunting mice. Everything on the backmost shelves was protected with serious, solid spells. Whoever took the Truth knew how to break those spells, and how to do so without getting burned." Whiskers twitched suggestively. "I think it's safe to say anyone who can penetrate a professionally installed enchantment

8

of protection is equally capable of defending himself, or itself. A successful thief is a dangerous thief, Simwan. Don't forget that." Turning, he resumed padding toward the door. Responding to an impatient glance from the cat, the knob turned obediently without being touched.

"Now set this silly adolescent-male nonsense of yours aside, and let's go explain things to your sisters."

Also located on the second floor of the big Victorian house, the room that had been set aside for the girls was much larger than Simwan's. That stood to reason, since there was only one of him and two of them. Or rather, not quite three of them. Or perhaps more accurately, two-and-a-half of them. Or two-and-a-something. The correct term was a "coubet." A coubet of Deavys. *Coubet* was a very, very old French word, Simwan knew. It referred to the thing that the Deavy girls were.

One thing they certainly were was twelve years old. And identical. Identical twins-and-a-something. There was Rose, who might just have been just a little taller and a little smarter than her sister Amber. Then there was Amber, who just possibly was a just a smidgen shorter and a hairsbreadth less sharp than her sister Rose. And lastly, there was N/Ice. The almost-third Deavy sister was exactly middle of Rose and Amber in height, and precisely 'tween them in smarts. But that was only when she was there, which wasn't all the time.

As you can imagine, when dealing with Ords and Ord authorities, this situation presented no end of problems for Mr. and Mrs. Deavy. "How many daughters do you have?" was a question that Ords often asked. "Two-and-a-half" was not a response they were capable of understanding. But Martin and

Melinda Mae dealt with it, usually through roundabout but sometimes by magical methods. For example, they explained to the educational authorities that N/Ice (whose useless and true name for Ord purposes was Niobe) suffered from a non-lethal but frequently recurring disease that required her to stay at home for long periods of time. They could have simply home-schooled her, and the rest of the Deavy brood for that matter, but they felt that even though the children came from a long line of non-Ords, it was important for them to have the experience of dealing with Ords on an everyday basis, since they were living in a largely Ordinary world.

So the sometimes-there N/Ice, who had acquired her real name because sometimes when she was around she was nice, and at other times she was like ice, was just as much a Deavy girl as Rose and Amber and just as identical. For his part, Simwan was pleased with her exactly as she was. Two-and-a-half younger sisters were more than enough. No need for three.

As he and Pithwid advanced down the second-floor hallway, the portraits and photographs that lined the walls called out a cheery, if understandably faint, howdy from the hereafter. Simwan never failed to respond with a polite "hello" or "good afternoon" of his own. He was always glad to acknowledge a greeting from his ancestors. It was reassuring to know that they were around, if only in a two-dimensional sense. As full of them as the house was, with their various portraits hung here and there and everywhere, no burglar or bogeyman could sneak in unobserved. Or was likely to linger for long.

The coubet's room was located at the end of the hallway. Simwan didn't mind being relegated to a smaller space, but he did envy his sisters' high-peaked ceiling. It allowed room in a room to roam. As he and Pithfwid approached, a dull rumbling could be heard.

"Oh great!" Simwan slowed as he approached the door. It appeared to be vibrating ever so slightly. "They've got the stereo cranked again. I'm surprised Mom hasn't said anything."

"Melinda Mae isn't here to hear. She went to the grocery store." Pithfwid's gaze narrowed as he studied the trembling door. "I don't think it's the stereo."

Simwan looked down at the cat, who for the moment had gone purple with pink polka-dotting. "I bet they're listening to that new boyband." He sniffed derisively.

"Tsk," Pithfwid sniffed. "Typical male adolescent jealousy. I always think better of you, and I'm so often disappointed." As he glanced up at the knob, it turned smoothly. The door swung inward, granting them entry.

Though exceedingly localized and modest in size, the tornado that greeted them had lost none of its power. Simwan immediately felt himself swept up and hurled sideways. A small, azure-blue, furry shape went whizzing past his head. Front paws crossed, tail switching irritably back and forth, an impatient Pithfwid yowled his outrage at the unexpectedly windy greeting.

Caught up in the boisterous storm, man and cat found themselves accompanied in their swirling by a plethora of unrelated objects: furniture, games, loose clothing, books, a half-empty pudding box, a stream of vanilla-filled cookies that had aligned themselves into the shape of a dull yellow snake, tiny stuffed bunnies with floppy ears and bushy tails, beds and bed linens, and much more. All of it, with the possible exception of the trio of Shetland pony–size unicorns, was recognizable as belonging to the room in which they found themselves.

Simwan frowned sternly. "All right, that's enough! You know what Mom says about playing around with dangerous weather spells."

A graceful, pre-adolescent figure whose curly blond hair extended past her shoulders promptly popped out of the storm to confront him. It was Rose (he was pretty sure). "It's not a dangerous weather spell!" she pouted. "It's just a spell of dangerous weather."

Simwan was not dissuaded. "She doesn't like you playing with semantics, either."

A second figure blew past, caught herself, swam back to join them. "Do you know how long it took us to conjure up this storm, not to mention keep it contained?" Amber was wearing jeans and a crop-top embroidered with teddy bears, baby chicks, ducklings, and a brace of snarling merlantathoids. "We've been working with it for *hours*!"

"You mean *playing* with it. If it isn't homework, it's play." A dresser whipped past his head, forcing him to duck slightly to one side. "Call it off. Call it off now!" Taking a deep breath, he assumed his sternest Big Brother pose. "Or I'll tell Dad when he gets home. Besides, there are important things to talk about, and I'm not going to keep shouting above this wind."

"Oh, all right!" Pivoting in midair, Rose cupped her hands to her mouth and yelled, "N/Ice, Simwan says we need to talk! Turn it off!"

A third figure appeared, borne by the howling winds on the other side of the storm. It looked just like Rose and Amber:

blond curls, slender pre-adolescent figure, and peaches-and-cream complexion. There was one way to differentiate between the three girls. N/Ice had eyes of glacier-blue, while Amber's were golden-brown and Rose's were the exact color of Gramma Deavy's lavender bath soap.

The last Deavy sibling to arrive was wearing a plain green dress with a too-short hem and sandals with high straps. On her left arm was a tiny temporary tattoo of a peculiar yet handsome humanoid accompanied by the words "Joey Entropy, I luv u" alongside a small heart that was disintegrating as bits of it fell into the accretion disk of a black hole. Her mouth flashed a slash of pale pink lipstick. N/Ice always had been partial to too much makeup, a habit that had forced Melinda Deavy to remonstrate with her sometime daughter on more than one almost occasion.

Coming toward them, N/Ice halted in the center of the storm. Absolutely motionless in the midst of deafening chaos, she hovered perfectly still, spread her arms, and tilted her head back until it was almost touching her shoulders. Rose and Amber did likewise.

"*Memnez tessray sordonn hellephant!*" N/Ice sang out, adding for good measure, "I love you, Joey Entropy, wherever you are!" While Simwan doubted this last bit had much of anything to do with tornado talk, it did seem to add a little spice to the roaring cyclonic convection that was dominating the room.

There was a sharp crackling on a descending note, as if all three girls had opened a box of aluminum foil and were balling up pieces of it with their fingers. The tempestuous howl slumped to a moan, fell to a whoosh, and crashed to a whisper. As the winds decreased, room decor found its way back to where it belonged: the three beds to their places under the windows that looked out over the woods, the dressers back against the far wall, toys and pictures and TV and stereo and miscellaneous objects settling down in the exact spots where they had been situated prior to the frantic meteorological invocation.

Then all was still—but with two-and-a-half twelve-year-old girls in the room, only for an instant. Rose jumped up onto her bed, landing with a contented thump that caused the mattress to bounce her several times. It was a friendly mattress, delighted to bounce. Simwan had tried it himself, several times, much to Rose's displeasure. Amber settled herself nearby: half her attention on her brother, the other half on some teen music magazine. The pages turned without being touched as she studied them avidly.

Rose glared irritably at the third member of the trio. "C'mon, N/Ice—quit flexing in and out!"

On the bed next to hers, a third shape lay on her stomach with her feet in the air and her chin resting on her hands. Simwan kept blinking at her because sometimes he found himself looking right through her.

"In and out of what?" N/Ice teased.

"You know." Rose sighed. "Reality."

"Am not," N/Ice objected innocently. "I'm always in reality. It's just not always *your* reality, nyah, nyah!" She stuck her tongues out at Rose. All three of them.

"Look," muttered Simwan as he moved further into the now quiescent room and toward the three parallel beds, "this is really important." Behind him, Pithfwid lay against the base of the door, blocking it from being opened from the other side as he groomed himself. "Haven't you heard about someone stealing the Truth from Mr. Gemimmel's store?"

"Oh, wow, no," Rose responded. Suddenly serious, all three girls turned their full attention on their brother. Amber even closed her magazine, and N/Ice densified herself to the point where she looked as solid as her sisters. They all knew how important the Truth was, especially because it was so tightly bound to their mother.

"How did it happen?" Amber asked.

"Who took it?" N/Ice wanted to know.

"The truth of it is, the Truth has gone missing, and Mom and Dad are worried that without it around, people will start to believe what those developers who want to cut down the woods are saying, and vote for the project to go ahead."

"They can't do that!" a thoroughly alarmed Rose exclaimed.

Amber looked equally shocked. "They can't cut down our woods!"

"That's for sure," N/Ice muttered loudly. "If they cut down the woods, where will Joey and I go to—" She broke off, suddenly aware of the expressions on her sisters' faces. "Well, what are Mom and Dad and the Ords doing about it?" Amber asked.

"Not much." Simwan leaned against the wall, not wanting to divert his sisters' attention or incur their rage by sitting on one of their beds. "They keep muttering about bringing in outside assistance, but everybody and anybody who could really help seems to be busy with other, more important projects. And since the Truth was taken, Mom hasn't been herself. You know, there's a lot of Truth in her, and a lot of her in the Truth."

"Nothing's more important than the woods," Rose asserted

firmly. "Or to Mom, the Truth." But her tone was uncertain. "What can we do about it, brother?"

"What can we do?" Amber echoed plaintively.

Straightening as he pushed himself away from the wall, Simwan walked to one of the windows that overlooked the backyard and the first trees of the forest beyond. "You know adults. They'll bicker and argue and try to find the best way to do something. What we need is the *quickest* way. So if they're going to delay, I guess we'll just have to find out who took the Truth and bring it back ourselves."

"We'll do it!" At the foot of Amber's bed, the figure of N/Ice suddenly expanded to a height of twenty feet. Head scraping the apex of the ceiling, eyes blazing with fire, lightning crackling in the depths of the dark nimbus that swirled about her flowing locks, she thundered: "WOE UNTO THE FOOL WHO TOOKETH THE TRUTH, FOR WE SHALL SMITE HIM INTO ASHES!"

"Calm down!" Simwan told his sister. She immediately shrank back to her normal size, though a faint odor of ozone remained clinging to her blond curls. "First of all, we don't know who took the Truth or where they took it. If it's out among the Ords somewhere, we can't go around flinging magic every which way while blazing and roaring like Titans. That would be an unforgivable violation of the Prime Codex and you know that sort of thing just isn't done." He glared at N/Ice. "Secondly, *tooketh* isn't a word."

She looked properly abashed. "Oh, Simwan." Her expression reflected her uncertainty. "*Taketh?*"

"It doesn't matter," he told her impatiently. "If we're going Truth-hunting among the Ords, we have to control ourselves at all times. Otherwise we could unleash Chaos, upset the natural order of things, unsettle the World of Man, and our parents would probably cut our allowances."

"Right," Rose agreed somberly. "We have to be careful."

"So what do we do?" Drifting off her bed, Amber joined her sisters in crowding around their big brother.

"How do we get started?" Rose asked intently.

"Where do we begin?" N/Ice added, silently admonishing her hair for momentarily transforming into blond serpents. Having assumed the job of doorstop and turned a disarming puce, Pithfwid looked on approvingly.

Actually, Simwan hadn't thought that far ahead, having focused on first convincing his sisters to join him. Now that they were asking about a plan, he realized he had better come up with one. Fortunately, a safe and always reliable source of advice and assistance was close at hand.

Television.

"On all the cop shows, the first thing everyone does is examine the scene of the crime." Checking his watch, he turned and started toward the door. "We can ride our bikes over to the drugstore. There's still time to get there, talk to Mr. Gemimmel, and make it back before Mom has dinner ready."

"Let's do it," barked N/Ice. "The quicker we get the Truth back, the sooner everyone will see what a bad idea this awful development is." She added more somberly, "And the less Mom will be affected by its absence."

"Right," agreed Rose as she approached Amber. "But I'll have to ride double with somebody. My bike has a tummy-ache. I don't think that last patch Dad put on its front wheel is holding, and neither does the bike."

"I'll take you," her brother told her. For once, a matter of real importance outweighed the danger that some of his friends might see him riding through town with one of his sisters balanced behind him, her arms around his waist.

"It shouldn't take long to fix this," was Amber's appraisal as the four of them filed out of the big room with its bright wallpaper and lace curtains. "We'll just locate the Truth, explain the situation, and get it back from whoever took it."

Pithfwid followed, causing the door to close behind them, and said nothing. They were only kids, he reminded himself, with three of them not quite in their teens, and one of them not even always there. They couldn't be expected to *know* the truth.

Much less realize how hard the truth could be to find.

– II –

Leaves like shards of gleaming electrum spun lazily around the Deavy children as they rode into town. Whenever Ords approached them on foot or in cars, they kept their feet on the pedals of their bicycles. But when the winding, hilly road was devoid of pedestrian or motorized traffic, they relaxed and let their bikes do the work. The bikes were glad to do it. After being cooped up in the garage, they were happy to be let out to roll. No one who saw the four children power their way into Clearsight's small, funky downtown shopping district had the chance to wonder how the wheels of their bicycles kept turning steadily and smoothly when the sneakered feet of the four riders rarely touched the rapidly spinning pedals.

Mr. Gemimmel's drugstore was located in a historic two-story, nineteenth-century structure fashioned of yellow brick. The second floor was home to overflow storage, Mr. Gemimmel's apartment, and a minor displaced fourteenth-century Indian potentate known as the Pukran of the Phu. As the Deavys pulled up in front of the pharmacy, Pithfwid leaped lithely from the wicker basket mounted on Amber's handlebars and padded confidently toward the entrance door. In response to his approach, the front doors promptly parted to admit him. This in itself would not have been remarkable save for the fact that the entrance to Gemimmel's Pharmacy was not equipped with an automatic door opener. Certain cats, however, are. Simwan and the girls followed.

Inside the pharmacy, both of Mr. Gemimmel's clerks were helping customers. Simwan and the girls made their way to the back of the store, where the dispensary was located. This meant they had to walk past the old soda fountain. Even though it was closed for the day, they couldn't keep from looking in its direction, knowing full well of the wonderful treats that were concealed behind the granite-faced counter. Nobody knew quite how Mr. Gemimmel managed to obtain flavors like *acajou* and *cupuraçu* and *maracuja* and other tropical specialties that could be found nowhere else in eastern Pennsylvania, but given the old-fashioned prices he charged, none of his customers cared to probe. Besides, his bestseller was always the vanilla, with real vanilla-bean specks. If you knew how to ask, he would sell you vanilla with Mexican jumping–bean specks, which tickled with every swallow that went down your throat.

Approaching the back counter, they found him busy filling a prescription for Dolores Hopkins. "Oh, hello, Deavys." Capping the filled plastic bottle, Mr. Gemimmel placed it in the basket marked with a big H–J and turned to face the children. He tried to smile, but Simwan could see that the old man was not feeling well. This was hardly surprising, considering what had been taken from him. "What can I do for you kids? Nice to see you too, N/Ice. Is everything okay at home? How is your mother doing?" He ignored Pithfwid as the cat jumped onto the counter and disappeared among the shelves of pills and powders and salves and liquids. Pithfwid would cause no trouble and make no mess. Besides, the druggist knew better than most that the Deavy cat went wherever it wished no matter what anyone said.

"Everything's fine, Mr. Gemimmel," Simwan told him. "With us."

"We know what happened." Peering over the pharmacy counter, Amber tried to see where Pithfwid had gone. "We know about the theft, and we want to help get back what was taken."

"*Sssh!*" Leaning over the counter, a nervous Mr. Gemimmel peered toward the front of the store. Both of his employees were busy doing their jobs. Neither they nor the customers they were helping were looking in his direction. "That kind of talk can be bad for business, Rose. Your mother left that bottle in my care."

"I'm Amber," the girl corrected him patiently. "Why the worry? Even if the Ords knew about the theft, it wouldn't make any sense to them."

"You never know. Customers can be funny when they start overhearing words like *stolen*."

"Can we have a look around, Mr. Gemimmel?" As always, Simwan felt funny looking down on an older man from a greater height. Having shot up significantly in the past year, he was discovering how altered height could change a person's perspective on many things. In a matter of months, he had gone from looking up to people to looking down at them. But not, thanks to his upbringing, down *on* them. "Please? We won't tell anyone if we see something, and we just want to help."

"I know you do. I know about the close bond between your mother and the Truth. Everyone just wants to help—but they can't. I'm afraid this sorry business needs the attention of an expert." With a sigh, the apothecary lifted up the counter barrier and stepped aside, using his other hand to brush at his nearly hairless skull. Toward the back of his head but near the crown was an interesting birthmark that to enlightened and educated eyes might have resembled a snake curling around a staff. "You might as well, I suppose. It can't hurt—and who knows, you might see something I've missed." None of the customers, nor the two busy clerks, saw the four children file into the dispensary area at the rear of the store. Not that it was against any law for Mr. Gemimmel to let them back where the drugs were kept, but in a small town like Clearsight, people with nothing better to do tended to talk about things that were really none of their business. Mr. Gemimmel had a potion for dealing with that, too, but was very careful about how he dispensed it.

Behind its protective white walls and ranks of floor-to-ceiling shelves, the dispensary area was a lot bigger than it looked from the outside. Thousands of vials and bottles and packages filled the shelves, and the farther back one went, the odder and more peculiar some of those containers became. Not only the containers, but the shelves themselves betrayed steadily increasing signs of age. Fluorescent lights gave way to older incandescents, then to oil lamps, and finally to candles seated firmly in holders of graven granite and schist. Occasionally, something dark and swift went rustling off into the increasingly gloomy distances as they worked their way deeper and deeper into the depths of the dispensary. The visitors didn't ask the pharmacist about it, and he didn't volunteer an explanation.

After what seemed like a hike that ought to have taken them all the way to the edge of town instead of just to the back of the drugstore, they reached the very last shelves. Each of these had been hand-milled from a strange mottled gray wood. Several of them were so old that they had collapsed or crumbled to dust. Taller than Simwan or Mr. Gemimmel, the ones that still stood were packed with jars spun of fine porcelain, their once-intricate, bright glazes now cracked and yellowed with age. Other containers on the surviving shelves were of dark green and red and blue glass. Some were still stoppered while others stood with their vacant mouths open and sucking at the damp, musty air. A few shelves held boxes meticulously fashioned of wood, or ivory, or semiprecious stones, or carved cinnabar from the Orient.

Near the very back wall, which appeared to have been hewn from the raw bedrock of Pennsylvania itself, a middling high shelf was notable for an obvious gap between two large, stoppered clay jars.

"I don't suppose either of those holds anything like the Truth, Mr. Gemimmel?" With a hand, Amber indicated the two large vessels.

"Oh no, certainly not!" The pharmacist was indignant. "They're perfectly ordinary amphorae from Athens. A little old, though. Seventh century BC, I believe. Medicinal gifts some Greek gentleman named Mantiklos intended to give to a temple of the god Apollo, along with a little bronze statue." Raising a slightly shaky finger, he pointed toward the gap on the shelf between them.

"That's where the bottle holding the Truth was kept, and now it's gone. One of my back-office homunculi noticed it missing when he returned to work after being away for the weekend." His small, delicate hands formed into tight fists. "Who could have taken it? For no good purpose, I'm sure. In the wrong hands . . ."

Smiling encouragingly, Rose put a hand on the old man's arm. "Don't worry, Mr. Gemimmel. We'll get it back. Simwan and Amber and I, and sometimes N/Ice, are good at finding things. Why, one time we were playing hide-and-seek and we found where N/Ice was hiding even though she'd hid herself on a different plane of existence."

N/Ice folded her arms and pouted. "You cheated! You ordered a pair of my shoes to come and find me, and then you followed them. You didn't find me, my shoes did."

Amber grinned. "Never try to keep a girl from her shoes—or her shoes from the girl."

Ignoring them, Simwan had stepped forward to inspect the shelving that until the previous weekend had held the Truth. He tried to remember what he had learned from watching the relevant TV shows. Sometimes a thief would leave clues behind. Maybe a fingerprint. Or a tentacle print. Or a piece of clothing, or a telltale claw mark. Straining on tiptoe, he reached up to run the tips of his fingers along the empty length of shelving. To a trained eye, even dust could be revealing. Of course, his wasn't a trained eye. At least, not in that way. But there had to be applicable forensic-analysis spells in the big books his parents kept at

THE DEAVYS

home in the den library, or on the part of the Internet that only non-Ords knew how to access.

"Look out!" a sharp, hissing voice warned him. Yea and verily, sometimes a thief would leave clues behind.

Or a booby-trap.

The mass of bristling fur that hit him in the face struck with fang and claw retracted, so that it was like being hit by a large, fuzzy fastball flung by a relief pitcher for the Phillies. It hit him hard and soft simultaneously, just forcefully enough to send him staggering backward, arms flailing as he fought to retain his balance. Almost instantly (the *almost* was critical), something shot through the space where he had been standing a second before. It attacked with mouth agape and teeth positioned to tear his face off. Letting out a simultaneous scream, Rose and Amber jumped in opposite directions, while N/Ice simply went sheer. Mr. Gemimmel threw up both arms to protect his face.

As soon as Simwan had stumbled safely clear of the immediate attack, Pithfwid whirled, leaped, pushed off his friend's face without scratching him, and threw himself at the attacker. Letting out a scream of frustrated fury at having been thwarted in its initial assault, that creature hit the shelving opposite, did a complete back flip, and bounded in the opposite direction. Dust bunny and yowling cat met in midair.

Composed of lint and grit, slime and grime, the dust bunny had formed itself wholly only when Simwan had reached for the empty space on the shelf where the Truth had been stored. All bits of gray gunk held together by lashings of darkly enchanted goo, it had blazing red eyes, a mouthful of razor-sharp teeth, claws hooked like those of a small owl, and big floppy ears. They

25

were so bound up in a furious fighting clinch, it was difficult for those looking on to tell where cat ended and dust bunny began.

Pithfwid tore into it with a ferocity that would have stunned anyone who had only seen the big tomcat sleeping peacefully on the front stoop of the Deavy house. Bits and fragments of dust bunny went flying everywhere: big chunks for every hair that Pithfwid forfeited. But no matter how much of itself the attacking creature lost, it retained every bit of its viciousness. Though determined, Pithfwid was clearly beginning to tire, while its spellbound antagonist was not.

"Do something!" Rose was yelling as she stood off to one side, wanting to help but uncertain how to go about it.

"I'm thinking, I'm thinking!" Amber shouted back. Next to her, N/Ice was fighting to return to reality.

Simwan thought frantically. Stored among all these special potions and lotions and such, there had to be something they could use against their attacker. But what would be appropriate? If they employed the wrong application, it might only make things worse. Whatever they chose, it had better be something soon. Pithfwid's exhaustion was becoming plain to see.

Of course, he thought.

"*Taredon menzies, fluton forth*—I call thee!"

The broom that came tearing down the aisle that led back to the front of the store was moving as fast as if it had been summoned by a First-Level witch. Except that there was no witch present, it wasn't a riding broom, and it looked just like what it was: a broom that was used to sweep up when the pharmacy closed for the night. But a broom was exactly what the situation called for. Steadying himself, Simwan held both hands out in front of him, one above the other, palms extended. The broom handle slammed into his waiting fingers with enough force to stagger him—but that was what he wanted. This was no task for a feeble old broom that was already shedding its straws.

Gripping it in both hands, he stepped as close to the squalling, hissing, mewling mess of dust and cat as he dared. "Pithfwid—get out of there! Pithfwid!"

Eyes flaring, ears flattened, the cat rolled clear. Shaking its head and ears, the snaggle-toothed dust bunny scrambled to its feet, cocked its powerful back legs, and leaped.

"*Immaculatos!*" Simwan cried, and brought the broom down as hard as he could.

The shock of contact traveled up the handle and quivered his arms. There was a brilliant flash of dark light and an explosion of dust. The girls staggered backward a step or two and even Mr. Gemimmel had to reach out with one hand to brace himself against the wall. As he recovered from the shock of contact, Simwan prepared to swing the broom again. There was no need. Lying on the floor between them was a small pile of grime from the center of which glowed two small, intense red eyes. Breathing hard, muscles tensed, Pithfwid approached the pile, drew back his head—and sneezed. Quite deliberately, and with intent aforethought. For an instant, those twin glowing orbs lying within the grunge looked frightened.

Then they were gone, as the cat sneeze scattered the dust in all directions.

Sitting himself down, Pithfwid licked one paw and began to groom himself. "Very nice, Simwan. What better to fight dust with than a household broom?"

"Not quite a household broom." Letting go of the handle, Simwan watched as the seriously strained sweeper settled itself, a little unsteadily, against the supportive shelving. "One of *Mr. Gemimmel's* brooms." Turning, he examined the empty shelf anew. "What do you think? Is it safe now?"

"Let me check." Rising from the ground, N/Ice elevated until she was hovering at eye level with the shelf. "Looks clean. Sparkling clean, in fact."

Simwan was disappointed. "That means no clues. Or if there were any, they've gone with the sneeze."

"Not necessarily. Let me have a look." Gathering himself, Pithfwid cleared the distance in a single effortless jump and began prowling the length and breadth of the shelf between the two ancient amphorae.

Simwan felt a hand on his arm. It was Rose, backed by Amber and N/Ice.

"You're usually a pain in the behind, Simwan, but for a big brother, you can be pretty cool sometimes."

"Yeah," agreed Amber. "I wouldn't have thought of a broom."

"That's not surprising," sniffed N/Ice, "since you usually act without thinking."

"Oh so?" Amber turned on her sister. "I didn't see *you* coming up with any suitable enchantments!"

"Yeah," added Rose pugnaciously. "In fact, we almost didn't *see* you at all!"

While his sisters fell to arguing loudly among themselves and Mr. Gemimmel tried his futile best to calm them, Simwan watched as Pithfwid paced back and forth, back and forth along the length of the shelf, looking for—what? As it developed, the cat wasn't using his eyes as much as he was his other senses. Cat senses.

When he finally halted, it was as sharply as if he had been struck by another homicidal dust bunny. But in this instance, he had only come up hard against a revelation.

"I smell a rat."

"We *all* smell a rat, Pithfwid," commented Mr. Gemimmel patiently.

The cat turned to his humans. "No, I mean literally. A real rat. *Rattus rattus*, only more so. *Mucho* more so."

Simwan found himself eyeing the nearby shelves uneasily, searching for tiny, beady, reflective rodent eyes. The girls edged a little closer to each other. Having certain magical powers and abilities didn't mean one was not afraid of anything. On the contrary, it was just that kind of special knowledge that made one afraid of more things, because there were more things to be afraid *of*.

"What do you mean, 'more so'?" Simwan asked the cat.

Pithfwid replied while actively sniffing the floor around the base of the shelving that had held the Truth. "I mean I smell not your ordinary rat. This is something special. Something uniquely foul. Nasty rat. Rat it out, I say." He drew back his head sharply, raised a paw, and sniffed again of a certain spot. "There's a scent here that was spilled by no ordinary rodent. Not by a cricket's whiskers, no." He looked up again, first at Simwan, then over at the wide-eyed girls. "I think it may be the spoor of the Crub."

Simwan swallowed hard and the girls set to talking animatedly among themselves. Even Mr. Gemimmel looked concerned. Simwan had heard of the Crub. Just like he'd heard about the

Demon King, Agraloth, the Scimitar of Sarakined, and a host of other significantly unpleasant deities that budding sorcerers and sorceresses were required to know about.

Of all the creatures that plagued mankind, fantastical and phantasmagorical, earthy and Ord, none was more common, more potentially dangerous, more intelligent, or more relentless than the rat. And of all the world's rats the king, the emperor, the worst of them all, was the Crub. Though few had seen him (or at least lived to tell of the encounter), he was thought to be the smartest, cleverest, wisest, and most heartless of all his kind. Which raised the obvious question.

What would the Crub want with the Truth?

Nothing good, Simwan knew. Nothing good at all. He thought of their mother, Melinda Mae, who was so closely bound to the Truth, and a lump formed in his throat. Now more than ever, it was clear that they had to get it back—and quickly.

Lowering his head and his paw once more, Pithfwid sniffed at a tiny lump of dust that was still intact. But this time he didn't sneeze. Instead, he leaped back, let out a sharp-voiced yowl of surprise, and bottled his tail.

Something was emerging from the dust.

It got big fast. A writhing torso sprouted arms and legs. A head emerged from lissome shoulders. The body was clad in a clinging gown of what looked like spun silver, and an argent disc balanced atop a head crowned with long black hair. Dark eyes blazed with outraged realization.

"*You!*" the figure declaimed. One arm rose and an index finger pointed first at the cat, who was backing away, and then at each of them in turn. "How dare you insult the fount of wisdom and fertility to whom I have often prayed! How dare you threaten him and his works!"

"Time to go, I think." With that, Pithfwid was off and running. Though his natural inclination was to try to talk things out, Simwan saw the wisdom of the cat's reaction and took to his heels. The girls and Mr. Gemimmel were right behind him.

And the glowing, flaring apparition was right behind *them*, pursuing them around shelves and down increasingly bright corridors. "Die, die, all of you! For your insults, you deserve to be slain where you stand!" From the silver disc atop her head, bolts of fiery white light reached for the fleeing figures. One made contact with Pithfwid's tail, sending him racing past the humans, smoke trailing from the tip of that appendage where the lightning had struck.

As they ran, the Deavy children tried to think of a proper spell with which to counteract the pursuing harridan. But it's hard to think when you're running for your life, pursued by a person as deadly as she is beautiful. Surprisingly, Mr. Gemimmel kept up with his much younger companions, muttering to himself all the while.

"Dear me—have to quash this *now*—will be Hell to pay if she gets out on the street." Like an electronic grocery store scanner, his eyes flicked over every shelf and every container they raced past, identifying the contents, searching for something specific.

They were halfway back to the front of the store when he suddenly skidded to a halt, grabbed a small, thick glass bottle off a shelf, and pulled the stopper. Not even bothering to utter a supporting hex, he turned to confront the shrieking, threatening, oncoming wraith. Simwan and the girls slowed and gathered behind him while Pithfwid took shelter among the larger boxes.

"Die, DIE!" the creature howled, lifting one arm to strike directly at the elderly apothecary.

"I think not," he responded primly. Drawing back his own arm, he flung the contents of the bottle in her direction.

The powder struck the specter square in the midsection. She halted immediately, gazing down at herself in puzzlement. To Simwan, tossing nothing but a little powder seemed a particularly ineffectual gesture on the pharmacist's part.

Straightening, the apparition raised her arm anew, once more preparing to strike. Then a strange expression came over her beautiful but tormented face. Her eyes bulged slightly. She coughed: lightly at first, then harder, doubling forward as the hacking fit overcame her. In fact, she doubled over so hard that her head went all the way into her belly. And kept going until she was no longer doubled over on herself, but tripled over, then quadrupled over. And then, with a brief pop and a modest flash of light, she was gone, having disappeared right inside herself.

"That," declared Mr. Gemimmel firmly, his lower lip curling up over the upper, "is how you deal with an infection. Biowarfare, indeed!" Turning, he resumed walking toward the front of his store. "Even the conjured should know better than to mess with a druggist."

The girls were still discussing what they had just witnessed when Simwan moved close enough to their host to ask, "An infection, you say?"

Mr. Gemimmel nodded somberly. "Like the carnivorous dust

bunny, a thing deliberately planted by the thief, this Crub creature, to deal with anyone who might try to trace its evil deed."

"So what did you throw at it?" Peering back over his shoulder, Simwan tried to remember if he had seen a label on the bottle full of powder. "Antibiotics?"

"Not this time. The infection was site-specific. I had to use antinilotics, since the infection took the form of a vengeful Egyptian deity."

Overhearing this, the girls interrupted their conversation. "Which deity?" Amber inquired with evident interest.

"Well now." Mr. Gemimmel smiled as they approached the outskirts of the pharmacy storage area and the front of his store. "Based on the evidence that most discerning feline Pithfwid discovered, who else would you expect but the goddess Rat-taui?"

Pithfwid nodded agreement. "This little episode should give you some idea of what we're up against, children." Simwan bristled at being called a child, but said nothing. It did no good to argue with Pithfwid anyway. The cat continued. "The Crub is the end-all of every rat that ever spread a plague or stole the last portion of a starving man's food or bit a baby on the toe. It's big and mean and hateful: a bundle of pure evil wrapped in brown bristles and tipped with teeth at one end and an obscenely naked tail at the other. It's the master of rat magic as well as rat knowledge, and it controls entirely too much of both." Whiskers quivered. "We're going to have to be lucky as well as smart to catch it."

"We don't need to catch it," Rose argued. "We just need to get the Truth back from it."

"I'm afraid those goals will wind up being one and the same,"

Pithfwid told her resignedly. "Remember your mother. There's no time to lose."

By the time they reached the pharmacy counter, the number of customers in the store had multiplied, what with only the two clerks to handle all the business. After making good on his promise, Mr. Gemimmel plunged in to help his employees deal with the customer backlog. That left cat and kids to walk out the front door and return to their bikes, which were waiting for their owners right where they had been left.

"So, what do we do now?" Rose looked at Amber. Amber squinted hard enough to see N/Ice, who wasn't quite all there. N/Ice reached out to her brother, made a face when her hand passed cleanly through his arm, and shut her eyes tight until she had reconstituted enough of herself to grab him firmly.

"Yes, big brother. What do we do now?"

Simwan looked up South Harrison. It was getting dark. They couldn't do anything else until tomorrow, and he said as much. "I think we ought to let Pithfwid sniff a circle around the outside of Mr. Gemimmel's store." He smiled down at the cat. "You smelled the Crub inside the pharmacy. Think you can smell it outside as well?"

"If it left any kind of trail, I'll find it." Pithfwid leaped up into the basket that was attached to the handlebars of Simwan's bike. "Since all rats leave trails, the Crub ought to leave one ten times as distinctive. And as you know, cats also have a nose for the Truth. But it's getting dark, and I'm hungry, and we should be at our most awake and alert when we attempt this."

"You don't think it's still around here, do you?" Rose found herself peering anxiously up and down the street. "The Crub, I mean."

"Anything is possible." Resting his front paws on the side of the basket, Pithfwid stood up and pointed. "It came here looking for the Truth, and when it found it, it stole it away. It's taken it off somewhere, no doubt to do something disagreeable with it, so we've got to try to pick up its trail as soon as we can. But not until tomorrow. Dust bunnies and a vengeful goddess of the Nile are enough to deal with in one afternoon. I'm starving. Let's get moving. Don't you want to get home before dark? Or do you want to wait around and see if the Crub left anything else behind to confront those who might be foolish enough to try following him?"

-|||-

They said nothing to their parents of the confrontation in the drugstore, nor of what they had learned. Upon hearing such, Mr. and Mrs. Deavy would most likely have forbidden their children to pursue so serious a matter any further. Which, of course, was exactly what Simwan and the coubet intended to do. So they ate dinner quietly, and worked on their homework afterward. For Simwan, that meant digging into Early European History, Algebra, and Intermediate Malfeasance; for the girls, American Government, Seventh-Level Spelling (of the word kind), Fourth-Adept Spelling (of the hex kind), and Beginning Potions II, the latter involving learning the recipe for baking cookies that included both chocolate and brimstone chips. Before going to bed, they were allowed two hours of television, video games, Internet, and consensual thaumaturgy. The evening proceeded normally, and their parents suspected nothing.

The next morning, they waited for Martin to go off to work and Melinda Mae to head for town hall, where she was working with a group of local activist Ords to organize protests to try to stop the development. Simwan noticed with concern that she was moving much more slowly than usual. Once they had the house to themselves (thank goodness for their school district's special October break), the Deavy progeny were on their bikes and racing furiously for town once more.

Unsurprisingly, it was Pithfwid who picked up the trail outside the drugstore. Not only was his sense of smell more acute than theirs, he could go nosing about drain pipes and cracks in the sidewalk and the tops of weeds without drawing attention to himself. Every time Simwan or one of the girls wanted to do the same, they had to keep a lookout for passersby. Clearsight was a small town, and word would spread quickly if someone saw Amber, for example, down on all fours and with her pert nose shoved into a clump of broomweed.

Whiskers wrinkling in disgust, the cat pointed one paw due east from the back of the building. "The beast went thataway."

"You're sure?" Rose asked as her siblings gathered around.

The cat nodded. "The spoor is unmistakable, and still strong. It can't be anything else. Nothing normal would linger this long." The paw bobbed. "Due east, it headed."

"Can you tell if it had the Truth with it?" Amber had her head back and was sniffing the air for herself. Yes, there it was: a faint but definite stink, not unlike the stench that had come from the Deavy garbage disposal when Melinda Mae had put some bad eggs down it one morning and had forgotten to turn it on, leaving them to fester there for an entire day.

Eyes agleam with expectation, Pithfwid shook his head brusquely. "No, I can't. Now, if the Crub was packing lies instead of the Truth, it would be different. It would smell like those sessions the developers keep holding at the town hall." Turning, he trotted to Simwan's bicycle and jumped effortlessly into the basket that adorned its handlebars. "The smell will last a long time, but it won't last forever."

Poplar Street gave way to Lincoln Lane, and then to Ainsworth. This narrow, one-lane road dead-ended at the top of a short drop-off. From there the scent trail led downward into the dense woods that surrounded Clearsight.

"We'll have to leave our bikes here," Simwan declared as he dismounted. While his mountain bike could handle the slope, there was no telling where the trail led, and it would be better to position their transportation where it could be found quickly and easily than risk breaking an axle or throwing a chain somewhere deep in the forest. With Pithfwid in the lead, they clambered down the embankment. It wasn't steep, but the covering of fallen leaves made it hard to see the rocks beneath.

"Keep an eye out," he warned his sisters. "It's possible the Crub booby-trapped its trail like it did the shelf in Mr. Gemimmel's store."

"I don't think so." Pithfwid glanced back. "From the way its odor is starting to skip forward, I think it must have accelerated when it got to this point. Maybe as much as twenty miles an hour."

"Pretty fast, for a rat." Rose ducked beneath an overhanging branch.

Pithfwid could reach that kind of speed, but his humans

could not, so he was forced to moderate his pace. Occasionally, N/Ice would go ethereal and dart on ahead, the leaf carpet parting beneath her with the speed of her passing, but each time she was compelled to return and rejoin her siblings. When she wanted to, she could travel faster than any of them, but there was no point in doing so. Without the cat's discerning sense of smell as a guide, she could get lost.

Two hours later they were deep in the forest. The mist had lifted, to be replaced by scudding clouds around which the sun occasionally peeped as if spying on them. If they kept going this way, Simwan knew, in another hour or so they would hit State Highway 32 He wondered if the Crub's scent would persist on concrete, or if someone even as sensitive as Pithfwid would lose track of it among the swirling fumes of diesel and gasoline. He asked the cat as much.

"It's possible." Contemplating the prospect, Pithfwid slowed. "The Crub stinks, but so do cars and trucks." He looked around, gazing into the stands of high trees. "Before we hit the highway, it wouldn't hurt to make sure we're on the right track. I'm almost sure that we are, but it's possible the Crub could have laid down a false scent trail and then doubled back, just in case anyone tried to track it by smell."

"That's a good idea. I'll see if I can scare up some locals," Rose responded.

"Don't you mean 'scare away'?" N/Ice couldn't resist sniding.

Her sister made a face. "Be nice, girl, or I'll pull your ectoplasmic self inside out." Turning, she faced away from her brother and sisters, cupped her hands to her mouth, and began to cry. Not a sad cry, or a lonely cry, but more of an inviting one.

No hawks responded, however, nor any eagles, nor circling falcons or dozing owls. After a few tries, she reluctantly conceded their absence. "Not hunting time, I guess. Or else everybody's asleep, or just nesting."

Amber stepped forward. "If your birds aren't around, then their prey ought to be." Kneeling and pulling up the sleeves of her sweater, she pursed her lips and began muttering much softer sounds. Some of them were actually below the range of human hearing—but not Deavy hearing.

For a moment they thought Amber's efforts would prove as unproductive as had those of her sister. Then Simwan heard the first of several slight, barely audible, skittering noises. The gorgeously colored dead leaves that carpeted the forest floor like bits of weathered bronze began to shift and crackle in places, disturbed not by wind but by things moving beneath them. More and more movement accompanied the persistent rustling. Like a collapsing ring, the motion centered on the sweater-clad children, until it finally revealed itself in the form of dozens of small figures who emerged in unison from beneath the leaf litter.

They were mostly brown, though some flaunted patches of black or white on chest, belly, or tail. There were field mice, and dormice, and pack rats, and voles. They gathered themselves in a neat semi-circle facing the visiting humans, preening their nervous whiskers, twitching their tiny noses, eyes like matched black pearls considering one another with as much interest as they did those who had summoned them. Simwan dropped into a crouch, the better to be nearer eye level with them, and said nothing. Amber had called them forth, and Amber would know best how to talk to them. Amid all the soft squeaking and chirping,

Pithfwid resolutely remained where he was. He could not, however, keep his tail from switching back and forth at the sight of
the assembled, and when no one was looking he would raise a
paw to swiftly and surreptitiously wipe a curl of drool away from
the corner of his mouth.

Amber greeted them. "Thanks for answering, people of the
forest floor."

One mouse, slightly larger than the others, stepped forward
and stood up on its hind legs, whiskers quivering as it regarded
the much bigger human.

"When one who knows how to whisper the right whispers
emphatically, we always come. What is it you need?"

"Someone has stolen the Truth from Mr. Gemimmel's drugstore. We need to get it back before it can be used to work mischief. We're pretty sure it was taken by a relative of yours, and
that it was brought this way."

"The Crub," Simwan put in, so that there could be no
misunderstanding.

Mention of that name caused a commotion among the assembled, though since it was a congregation of small rodents it was
a very quiet commotion. Some of those who had responded
whirled and fled in terror, disappearing among the leaf litter and
the roots of the silently watching trees. But a few—bold, determined, or both—remained.

"We have nothing to do with the Crub. It and its followers cast
all our kind in a bad light," the stout mouse exclaimed forcefully.

"Did you see it come this way?" Amber asked. "We're following its scent trail."

At this, a dozen of those in attendance promptly dropped

41

their own sensitive nostrils to the ground, and not for long. "So that's the source of the awfulness we've been smelling around here," the rodent spokesman muttered. "Now it makes sense. No fakery in this, then. It's the Crub itself for sure." One tiny paw rose and pointed. Eastward again, Simwan observed. It was reassuring to know that Pithfwid had been following the right track all along.

"Not a diversion?" he inquired, just to be sure.

The mouse speaker shook his head vigorously, small round ears quivering. "Not a chance, man. The stink is too strong." The paw swung around accusingly toward the shape of a large yellow and purple cat who was struggling hard to feign indifference to the gathering. "And tell your friend to stop looking at me like that. This is a called conference whispered by you, and I won't have him looking at me and thinking of mouse mousse."

"Pithfwid!" Putting his hands on his hips, Simwan glared over at the cat. "They're trying to help us."

"Sorry." With great dignity, the cat turned so that his back was to the semicircle of concerned rodents. "I can't help it. Sometimes instinct trumps intelligence."

One thing the mice couldn't tell them was how far ahead the Crub might be. Given how fast it was moving, they were unlikely to catch up to it until it reached its intended destination. As he strode through the woods, Simwan wondered where that might be. Where would something as vile and conniving as the Crub choose to hole up? Tarrentville? Maybe as far away as Lordsburg? He supposed it all depended on just what the Crub intended to do with the Truth, now that it had it. He checked his watch. If they didn't catch up to their quarry by one or two o'clock, he and his sisters would have to turn around and head back. Otherwise they wouldn't get home until well after dark.

On the other hand, if they managed to make it as far as the highway, they would know exactly where to pick up the trail again tomorrow morning. They could mark the spot, and wouldn't have to spend half a day traipsing through the woods in search of it.

But they never got to the highway. Long before they could even hear the first hornetlike whiz of passing vehicles, they found themselves confronting a thoroughfare of a different sort. It brought them to an abrupt halt.

Though he carefully sniffed of both sides of the singing, swiftly running stream, Pithfwid couldn't pick up the Crub's trail on the other side. It was as if the thieving rodent had deliberately and thoroughly and cleverly washed himself clean of scent in the cold, fast-moving water.

"Or maybe he swam downstream and then came back out," Rose ventured. At her suggestion, they all found themselves looking in that direction, to where the water wended its way noisily and deliberately through the flanking trees.

"He could have gone upstream, too," Simwan pointed out. "Swimming where he could and walking on the rocks where the current was too strong. Not only is there no way of telling how far he might have gone before he came back out onto dry land, we can't even tell which way he went."

Rubbing up against Simwan's right leg, a presently puce Pithfwid growled in frustration. "No question about it—the reek stops at the creek."

"If he crossed the stream, maybe a stream-dweller noticed his passing," N/Ice pointed out. She immediately crouched and began inspecting the moist earth that rimmed the stream. Bending low, her sisters commenced examining the slick rocks that lay both in the water and onshore. Opting for a higher vantage point, Simwan chose to search while standing upright, with the sharp-eyed Pithfwid riding on his shoulder. It was important to look from as many different angles as possible, because you never knew where the sun was going to strike. And if you didn't look at just the right place at exactly the right moment where the sun happened to be hitting, you could look right at a skippl and never see it. Which is what most people, and all Ords, invariably did.

This is because skippls look just like the sparkles of light that sunlight makes on water. Gaze at the rippling surface of a lake, his dad had told Simwan and his sisters during one summer outing, and you'll see dozens, hundreds, of golden flashes of light on the water. Reflections of the sun that will make you squint your eyes and squeeze out tears. The one reflection that doesn't do that is a skippl. They're closely related to the gneechees, Martin went on to explain, which are the creatures you think you see out of the corner of your eye, and when you turn your head to look straight at them, they're gone.

"Hey!" Letting out a shout of recognition, Pithfwid rose up on Simwan's shoulder and pointed. His cry brought the searching sisters running in their direction.

Simwan stood by the side of a small cascade, staring at the smooth rocks that formed the upper ledge. The waterfall was no taller than he was, but among the numerous glints of light that filled the falling, he thought he could just make out several half-foot-high columns of sparkle that didn't appear to conform to the rest. They were moving more slowly, persisted longer, traveled in a slightly different direction, and if you looked really, really hard, you could make out what appeared to be arms and legs fringed with lissome, transparent fins.

Rose arrived first, panting excitedly. "Where?" She stared into the waterfall, trying to locate the source of her brother's excitement.

"Up higher," he instructed her, "and more toward the other side."

"I don't—oh, there they are!" Bending slightly at the waist to get a better angle, she pointed out the golden shapes that were behaving slightly differently from the other glints of light that filled the falling water.

"Good spotting, brother," Amber complimented him as she, too, tracked the now decisively identified creatures.

"It wasn't me." Reaching up, he stroked the cat clinging to his right shoulder. "Pithfwid found them."

"That's only logical." The cat purred as it lifted its spine against the caressing hand. "After all, they are living in a cataract."

"Hi there," Simwan called out, extending a hand outward, palm facing up, as he had been taught to do during a period of home-schooling whose subject matter had nothing to do with ordinary chemistry or biology. "If you don't mind, we need to talk to you for a moment."

For a few seconds, lights with legs seemed to coalesce into a hovering ball of shimmer. Chancing upon the intensely bright phenomenon, an Ord would have shaded his eyes and moved on. Simwan and his sisters knew better. The skippls were considering their request.

Separating itself from the center of the glow, one shard of light sliced in their direction, dancing delicately across the water from ripple to ripple, until it stood gleaming in the steady flow. Then it performed a short but impressive hop to land neatly in the middle of Simwan's proffered, outstretched palm. Once removed from the water that was its home, it was much easier to make out the skippl's twiggy, delicately feminine limbs. Set apart from the distortions caused by sunlight, her face now stood out clearly. Like the limbs, her features were narrow and minimal, as if someone had taken a pencil and sketched a few short, quick lines of face onto a beam of sunshine.

"Whatdoyouwant?" Her high, musical voice reminded Simwan of the upper reaches of a piccolo. He had to strain to make out the reply. Skippls talked almost as fast as they moved.

"Something stinky this way came," N/Ice told it. For good measure, she made herself go an ichorous shade of green, like pea soup that had been left out too long in the sun.

"Something ferocious, fat, and full of evil, bearing with it stolen Truth." Pithfwid punctuated N/Ice's colorful effort by taking a deep breath and making himself turn a color that might best be described as that of chromatic vomit.

Words and color-cues had the intended effect. Glistening like a melting bracelet painted by Dalí, the skippl nodded, turned, and pointed. Light flashed in two different directions at once. It was an impossibility of physics—but then, so were skippls.

"Surenoughsawitpass. Wentthataway, movingfast. Biguglyug. Redeyesfullofawful." The slight shiver in the skippl's voice as she spoke was more full of meaning than any lingering spoor could have been.

Despite the lowing cloud cover, there was still enough glare off the surface of the stream to force Amber to shield her eyes as she peered across the creek. "Was it still heading east when you saw it?"

The skippl moved to the very edge of the water, beyond whose cheerful supportive gurgle she could not long survive. "Theywere."

Close by Simwan's right ear, Pithfwid muttered softly. "'They'? There were more than one?"

Light flickered and flashed: the skippl's way of nodding. "TheCrubwasnotalone. Travelingwithescort. Nastythings." If light could be said to shudder, the skippl certainly did. "Smelledbadthey. NotasbadasCrub. Hurttolookatthem."

Straightening, Simwan stared off into the forest, wondering exactly how much farther it was to the highway. "If the Crub had company, the trail should be stronger."

"Truthyouspeak." The skippl prepared to return to her watery home. "Overhearwaygoing. AllwaytoNewYork."

"New York?" Amber swallowed hard. "You mean, New York *City*?"

"Yes," the skippl responded. "Theytalkingaboutit. Whilepassthisway. GoingNewYorkCity. Theysay. Crubhome."

And to think, Simwan mused, that he had worried about how they were going to find the Crub if it had holed up somewhere in the vicinity of Clearsight. But if it had gone to New York . . . Even an oversize Truth-thieving fiend like the Crub could find a place to hide itself in New York.

"It doesn't matter," declared Rose, breaking the silence that followed the Skippl's revelation. "We have to find it and get the

Truth back, no matter where it's gone to. We have to for Mom's sake. We promised Mr. Gemimmel. We promised ourselves."

"Besides," added Amber, "it's the only chance we have of stopping the development. People have to know the truth, and for them to know the truth, it has to be around."

A daydreaming N/Ice had to be reminded not to let herself drift off into the trees. She came back to reality, and the ground, with a thump as her feet once more made contact with the earth. "So, all right, then. We'll go to New York. If that's where the Crub has gotten to, that's where we'll have to go."

"Uh, N/Ice," Simwan reminded her, "you girls are just twelve." He didn't add that he was only sixteen. "Mom and Dad might not want us traipsing off to the big city, much less on a potentially dangerous hunt for the emperor of all rat-things."

Rose and Amber and N/Ice exchanged a tripartite look before turning back to him with what could only be described as expressions of sisterly pity. "Big brother," Rose told him gently, "you didn't *really* think that's how we were going to put the request to Mom and Dad, did you?"

"Well, I . . ." he hesitated.

"I believe," Pithfwid murmured from his perch on Simwan's shoulder, "that your sisters have something of a more feline bent in mind."

"If you mean sneaky, shifty, and devious—" N/Ice began.

Amber cut her off. "Leave it to us to think of a way to get permission. You're going to have to act as chaperone, at least in name, so I suppose we'll have to let you in on it."

"Once we have whatever *it* is," Rose concluded confidently.

"Notathingtochase, istheCrub," exclaimed the skippl worriedly as she listened to their conversation. "Becareful, youngsolidones. Blessingsofwater, maytheycoverandprotectyou." With a hop and a slide and a jump, the skippl was gone, returned to the cataract from whence she had emerged.

Simwan glanced skyward. It was getting late, he realized. And looking more and more like rain. They might as well start back, especially now that they knew the Crub's destination. He'd only been to New York once in his life, and that was when he had been about the coubet's age. Now it appeared that he was going to go back, but this time in the company of his sisters and not his parents. And Pithfwid, of course. To find and bring back the stolen Truth.

If they all caught cold, standing out in the damp and the wind, no one would be going anywhere, he knew. "Let's get moving. You guys can tell me all about your plan on the way back." He started off along the trail they had made.

"Plan? What plan?" exclaimed Amber innocently. "We don't have a plan, brother. But we will by the time we get home, won't we?" Rose and N/Ice chimed in with equally chirpy confidence.

What they didn't know as they left the stream and its apprehensive cohort of skippls behind was that the always-chary Crub had done one last thing as it had hurried on its way toward the big city accompanied by its noisome band of escorts.

It had been careful to leave in its wake something considerably more dangerous than bad smells.

-IV-

I'm cold."

Simwan looked over at Amber. During fall and winter, she always seemed to suffer more than any of them, while expanding like a flower in the sun come the warming balm of summer. With a sigh, he slipped out of his flannel shirt and draped it over her shoulders. She smiled affectionately up at him.

"You know, big brother, most of the time you're just a big pain. But not all the time." In the absence of his shirt, her words warmed him.

Hugging herself against the rising chill, Rose studied the surrounding trees. The slowly setting sun and the darkening clouds overhead notwithstanding, this early in the evening it still seemed colder than it ought to be. Humidity began to condense around them, uncertain whether to assume the aspect of fog, mist, or actual rain. A bunch of Ord kids might easily have found themselves lost in such surroundings, but not the Deavy offspring. Whenever the path forward threatened to become uncertain, they simply relied on N/Ice, who could see the Way Clear even in the midst of a roaring nor'easter.

Moisture finally made up its mind, and it started to rain.

"Rats!" muttered Rose, drawing the collar of her sweater tighter around her neck. Seeing the startled looks on the faces of her siblings, she hurriedly corrected herself. "I mean, darn. Or damn. Or diamondiferous."

Simwan frowned at his sister. "What has that got to do with anything?"

"Nothing," she shrugged. "I liked the alliteration, and if I also happened to accidentally hit on a near-spell, who knows—I might conjure up a diamond." For emphasis, she scuffed at the damp earth with the toe of her left sneaker. This action exposed a single earthworm, suitably outraged, but unfortunately no diamonds.

Amber found herself shivering, and wasn't sure it was from the cold.

Riding high on Simwan's shoulder, Pithfwid was sniffing the air intently. His eyes were open wide, the pupils expanded, and his ears were cocked attentively forward. From time to time his head would jerk to one side or the other, like a gun turret trying to home in on a target. Except for his violet eyes, whose color rarely changed, he had gone entirely gray to match the weather.

"Relax," Simwan told him. "I'm getting wet, too. It's not raining hard, and I don't recall that the weatherman last night said anything about a chance of heavy showers."

"Isn't that," the cat replied. "I sense something else heavy."

Simwan went into immediate alert mode. Pithfwid was no hypocondricat. If he felt something was wrong, it usually was. "Where?"

"In the woods." Feline eyes searched, searched.

Simwan made a disgruntled sound. "That's not real helpful, Pithfwid. *We're* in the woods."

"Tell me about it," murmured the cat. "And we're not alone, I don't think."

Wordlessly, the girls clustered closer around their big brother. At such times their innate sarcasm took a hike and they were much more his trio of little sisters than they were their usual irritating, know-it-all selves. It was also at such moments that he wished he really was bigger.

On his shoulder, Pithfwid did get bigger, as his gray fur bristled. "Not far away now," he hissed. "Not nearly far away enough. Keep vigilant, be prepared."

"For what?" an increasingly sodden and somber Amber wanted to know.

"I smell a Furk a-lurking."

Cat eyes were not the only ones that widened at Pithfwid's announcement. As he scanned the dark, dripping trees that suddenly seemed to press closer in all around them, their bark peeling away like flayed skin, Simwan struggled to remember the right words that were to be used when encountering such an apparition. Glancing around, he could see that his sisters were doing likewise. Their lips moved as they recited incantations they dearly hoped they would not be called upon to declaim. Rose was rummaging around in her jeans for suitable charms.

Her actions induced Simwan to check his own pockets. The

resulting inventory was less than encouraging: a couple of left-over chocolate bites, three quarters, the Leng army knife his cousin Terious had sent him from Nepal, a paper quip (for binding together several otherwise unrelated words into one smart-ass comeback), a surplus of laundry lint, and some brightly hued rubber bands. Looking down briefly from his scrutinizing of the surrounding woods, Pithfwid examined his human's puny available resources without comment.

"Oh!" Pulling up so suddenly that Amber nearly ran into her, N/Ice went half ethereal as one hand went to her mouth and she pointed with the other. At least, Simwan realized as he took up a defensive stance just in front of his sister, they no longer had to worry about the Furk stalking them.

It was right in front of them.

If N/Ice hadn't pointed it out, they might have walked straight into it, Pithfwid's efforts to safeguard them notwithstanding. This was not because they hadn't been paying attention, but because a Furk is so extremely hard to see. Found only in forests, Furks are the dark spots that fill up the places between the trees. They're big, and shadowy, and like trap-door spiders, they know how to sit in one place without moving while waiting for their prey to stumble right into them. Furks are the reason why the phrase, "The forest just swallowed him up" was invented, only these days most people have forgotten the why of it. Or, at least, the Ords have.

Realizing it had been recognized, the Furk let out a roar and charged. Well, not a roar, exactly. The sound that emerged from the opening that appeared in the exact center of the onrushing, dynamic shadow was more of a groan, the sound a breeze makes when it's been stabbed by an appalling metaphor. In place of arms and legs, the Furk reached out with puffs of gloom. One brushed Amber's back, causing her to break into a wild sprint. She knew for sure now that what had been chilling her had been a different kind of cold.

"Pithfwid!" Ducking to his left, Simwan saw the cat spring at the onrushing Furk, twisting in midair to avoid a slashing arc of dreary. Landing on all four feet, he flashed sparks from the tips of his ears and paws as he spat a challenging hiss at the lumbering creature. Fully enfurryated, the cat had become a streak of bright yellow fur striped with black: a giant bumblebee with indigo eyes. It was a startling sight.

Startling enough to momentarily draw the attention of the rampaging Furk away from the scattering children. Whirling, it struck downward with surprising swiftness. Swift as the blow was, it wasn't quick enough to catch Pithfwid, who darted to one side. Roiling darkness struck the ground. The rounded depression it left when it drew back was filled with dead grass and one cluster of murdered wildflowers that had not been alert enough to get out of the way.

From three sides now, the Deavy coubet was flinging every imaginable kind of spell at the amok Furk. It was the sorceral equivalent of the shotgun effect: blast the target with enough of the right kind of bullet, and accuracy was rendered moot.

"*Fellay tarmagent oot!*" Rose was shouting, her hands writhing over her head in serpentine choreography complex enough to please a plethora of pythons. Coils of purple smoke, impervious to the lightly falling rain, traced a helix around the lumpen mass that was the Furk.

"*Serseshawn peretel prestilong!*" squealed Amber as she flung at their attacker handfuls of mud gathered from near her feet. Where the intentionally addlepated dirt struck the Furk, anti-smoke began to rise from the dimness that was the body of the creature itself.

"*Take a hike, fart-wart!*" screamed N/Ice in a voice that was half choir-girl soprano, half thundering pillar of doom. The vibrations alone were enough to cause the Furk to halt in its tracks and turn away from the cat and toward the coubet.

While he continued to dodge and dance and make impertinent faces at the creature, doing his best to distract it from both his sisters and Pithfwid, Simwan marveled at the skills of the cabalistic choir that was the Deavy coubet while at the same time desperately trying to think of a way to tender some real help.

"Pithfwid!" he yelled again.

On the other side of the Furk, the cat was leaping and pouncing furiously: darting in when the creature's attention was distracted by one of the girls' spells, skittering backward when it returned its attention to him. What with the drumming of the rain on earth and forest, the uncoordinated but enthusiastic spell casting of his three sisters, and Pithfwid's hissing and growling, it was hard for Simwan to hear himself. Straining, he just did make out what the frenetic cat was trying to tell him.

"Your pocket! Use what you have in your pocket!" As a fist of doom descended toward him, the cat sprang to his left, struck the underside of a tree branch, did a complete backflip while changing color from black-striped yellow to dark blue with gold highlights, landed on his feet, and tore at the Furk with one paw. Ripped away, a puff of solid dark, like congealed pudding gone bad, spilled to the ground. The Furk howled in pain and tried to corner the cat against the base of an especially large oak, but the continuous chanting of the coubet kept it distracted.

Pocket—what was the cat talking about? Simwan still didn't know how to use his Leng pocket knife effectively. Even if he did, the tools it contained seemed far too puny to do any damage to something the size of the Furk.

Of course—the three quarters! Silver. That had to be it. Digging them out of his pants, he approached the Furk from behind, measuring his step while madly wiping rain from his eyes. Where to aim? At the eyes, surely—except that the Furk had no eyes. At least, none that Simwan could see. Where then? The mouth seemed the most likely target. With luck, the creature would swallow the poisonous currency before it was aware of what it had done. But he'd have to be fast, and get in dangerously close to make it work.

Seeing his human maneuvering for position, Pithfwid surmised Simwan's intention. Almost daintily, the cat side-stepped another downward blow and darted to his left, toward the crouching, weaving teen. Simwan held his ground, hoping the Furk would continue to focus its attention on the cat. Sure enough, it gauged the distance between them—and lunged. Pithfwid waited almost too long. In the cat's defense, it's hard to estimate the speed at which something that's made of little more than nothing can move. A few tail hairs were lost as the creature's upper appendages slammed together right where the cat had been standing and bristling a nanoinstant before. The frustrated Furk let out a muted howl of exasperation that echoed through the woods.

Seizing the resultant opening, Simwan let fly with the quarters. He had the great good satisfaction of seeing them soar right down what passed for the Furk's gullet. The vaporous mouth shut sharply, with a dull, damp *thump*. For an instant, the creature staggered back on its hindquarters. A smile appeared on Simwan's face.

It disappeared quickly as the Furk whirled and swung wildly at him.

He ducked, stumbled backward, nearly lost his balance, and found himself standing next to the wrathfully chanting Rose. "I don't get it—it was a perfect throw!" Collecting itself, the enraged Furk turned toward him and his sister.

Something small but solid bumped up against his legs, bounced away like a pinball off a high-score bumper. "Not the currency, you dolt!" Pithfwid yowled. "The chocolate, the chocolate!"

Dazed and confused, blinking and bemused, Simwan didn't stop to ponder the apparent absurdity of the cat's command. Reaching into his pocket, he brought out the couple of pieces of chocolate. Dark chocolate, as if that had anything to do with it. Should he unwrap them first, or just remove the outer paper and leave the inner foiling on?

"Throw it, throw!" Pithfwid was screeching. Looking up, Simwan saw the Furk all but towering over him, both of its massive if seemingly insubstantial upper limbs raised high above its head preparing to strike downward and smash him and his sister into the earth as if they were nothing more than a couple of loose twigs.

He heaved the chocolate.

It struck the Furk high up, right between its upraised limbs. There followed a brief instant during which absolutely nothing happened. Then a dark brightness appeared at the juncture of the Furk's arms. They rocked back and forth but did not descend. Having snuck up behind it, Amber and N/Ice were casting spells at it as fast as their lips could move: all to no avail.

The dark brightness spread, sliding smoothly across the Furk's form as slickly as spilled Kool-Aid on a glass tabletop. The Furk began to tremble, then to shake. A high, mystified moan rose from somewhere deep inside the quivering monstrosity. With a sound like bubbles crying, it burst, shattering in all directions and covering everything within twenty feet with fragments of wet, slimy Furk.

"Eewww!" Amber began picking pieces of burst Furk off her damp but otherwise unblemished sweater. Her equally dismayed sisters were doing likewise.

Panting hard, clearly tired by the effort he had expended in distracting the creature, Pithfwid sidled up to Simwan. Using one paw, the cat flicked a piece of Furk off his small, pink nose. "Blech. Filthy stuff. Exactly the sort of being one would expect the Crub to enlist on its behalf."

"But . . ." Simwan was staring at the lumpy mess that occupied the place where the Furk had been standing, "chocolate?"

"Chocolate is nothing but sweetness and light. As a human, you, of all creatures, should know that. And if there's anything a Furk can't abide, it's sweetness and light. Not to mention the complex bioflavinoids and other powerful chemical compounds that chocolate contains. Fortunately, those leftovers you swiped from your parents' last dinner party were *real* chocolate, not the fake stuff that's just made with cocoa butter." He licked his nose. "Seventy-one percent cocoa, I'd say."

"Huh?" Simwan commented succinctly.

The cat sighed. "Never mind. One day you'll understand, and be the better for it." He glanced skyward, blinking away a raindrop. "We'd better get moving. I don't think this storm is going to get any worse, but I am sure it's not going to get any better. If you all come down with colds, it'll make catching the Crub even more of a difficult experience, if not a deadly one."

"Congratulations, big brother!" Amber was standing on tiptoe to give him a kiss. The other girls had also crowded around him.

"All right, all right!" he exclaimed, shaking them off like so many clinging hothouse flowers. "Pithfwid's right. Now we're going to have to really hurry if we're going to make it home before Mom and Dad."

"Yeah." Rose spat in the direction of the mass of Furk mess. It was slowly being dissolved and washed away by the rain. "I *hate* having to fight beings of insubstantiality. Regular spells just do not work right on them. Can't get a proper purchase." Suddenly, she remembered her sister and turned to smile at N/Ice. "No offense, sis."

"None taken," the one who sometimes wasn't entirely all there stiffly replied, at the same time contemplating how best to slip a little itching powder into her sister's new bra.

Soaked and sodden but reasonably well pleased with themselves, they made it back to the house a good half hour before Melinda Mae returned from her daylong meeting with the opponents of the proposed urban development and well before their father returned from work. The children held the planning meeting in the coubet's room, not only because there was more space, but because Simwan had a thing about having girls in his room. At least girls who were his sisters.

Having set their respective tablets to start the homework they had missed completing, they considered their next step. Though most excellently enchanted, the tablets were not capable of completing class assignments on their own, only of organizing and beginning them. No spell could compensate for the absence of creativity and originality, both qualities that were prized by the local teachers. N/Ice had been trying to figure out a way to enchant her machine to achieve this. Each time she failed, and it ended up costing her a grade or two on the paper in question. She had been reduced to grumbling and complaining while being forced to actually read books and do some honest work.

"Okay," Simwan told them, "so we'll find a way to track down the Crub once we get to New York. We can ask in the right places, and we can ask in the wrong places, and once we've run it to ground, we'll take the Truth back from it. It's not going to be easy, and it's probably going to be dangerous, but we have to find a way to do it. One step at a time. The first step is how to convince Mom and Dad to let the four of us—"

"Five," Pithfwid reminded him.

"Sorry . . . the five of us, go to New York? Without adult supervision?" Straightening, he stood a little self-consciously taller in front of Amber's closet. "I mean, I consider myself an adult, but . . ."

"It must be lonely," Rose mused solemnly, "to be the sole holder of an opinion."

He glared at her. "I suppose you think you're more mature? More grown-up? And that they would let the three of you go without me?"

"Of course they wouldn't," N/Ice pointed out from where she was bobbing gently against the ceiling. "But they're not going to let us go and stay there with just you to watch over us, either. Even if Pithfwid comes with us."

Amber was sitting cross-legged on her bed. Or rather, an inch above it. That way, she didn't mess up the covers. "They'd let us go if we had adult supervision while we were there."

Simwan and her sisters turned to her, and even Pithfwid perked up at the possibility a worthwhile suggestion, as opposed to the usual young human nonsense, might be forthcoming.

"Who do we know in New York who'd let us stay with them, who'd have room enough, and who wouldn't try to keep an eye on us all the time and report back to Mom and Dad every five minutes?" Rose demanded to know.

The mischievousness in Amber's voice formed a small pink glow in front of her mouth, as if she was blowing cherry smoke rings. "Uncle Herkimer!"

Rose looked at N/Ice as her sister descended excitedly from where she had been hovering near the ceiling. "Of course! Uncle Herkimer wouldn't mind. I'd think he'd be glad of the company."

"If I were him, I sure would be," N/Ice readily agreed.

"I don't know." Simwan was less enthusiastic. "Staying with Uncle Herkimer presents problems of its own. You know how he is. I don't know if they'll go for it."

"Sure they will." With a soft plop of welcoming linens, Amber settled down on her bedding. "He has plenty of room, or at least he used to, and he'll be gearing up for All Hallow's. We can help out with the decorating." She was all but bouncing with excitement. "That gives us a place to stay, with supervision, but with somebody who won't be looking over our shoulders all the time. Besides," she added, "I *like* Uncle Herkimer."

"Me too," added Rose. "If we run into trouble, he might even be able to help us track down the Crub without telling Mom and Dad about it. You know Uncle Herkimer: He can inveigle lines of communication even Professor Fotheringgale can't access." She indicated her own computer, which was busy working on her homework, compiling a list of states along with their most important products. "Or the Web. You can't google Uncle Herkimer."

"Not anymore," added N/Ice knowingly. "I think it's a good idea."

A gleeful Amber jabbed a finger in Simwan's direction. "You're outvoted, brother! We're going to New York, we're going to stay with Uncle Herkimer, and we're going to find the Crub and bring back the Truth so people will realize why they should vote against this stupid development!" Her voice dropped to a more respectful tone. "And so that Mom won't be hurt."

Any additional concerns Simwan might have wished to express were drowned out by the cheering and yelling of the freshly energized coubet. Besides, it was hard to focus a query on any one of his sisters when all three of them were bouncing from bed to bed while shouting and giving loud voice to their expectations.

Rose started it, delightedly squealing something loud enough to cause her body double to appear in midair. Only, her body double was a perfect replica of the Statue of Liberty—if one discounted the glitzy earrings, tattoos, and noticeably shorter skirt. Amber had chosen to conjure the lights of Broadway, with every one of the plays starring her favorite boyband singers. Detached from theater fronts, the neon, fluorescent, and LED signs spun and bounced around the room in a blinking luminescent ballet of flashing fonts.

N/Ice's contribution to the chaos of expectation (or the expected chaos) consisted of more soberly conjured renditions of the city's other major landmarks: museum fronts, Rockefeller Center, the USN (United Sorceral Nations) building, and especially Central Park with its unique assortment of ambient charms. There was certainly a lot to look forward to besides just catching up with the Crub, Simwan had to admit.

Distractions all, though, he reminded himself firmly. They weren't going on a vacation. They were going after the Truth, something that was difficult enough to find in New York at the best of times, even when it wasn't in the possession of an evil entity like the Crub.

To an outsider it would have looked as if the dinner table was consumed by chaos, but for the Deavys the frenetic rushing to and fro of bowls, platters, pitchers, glasses, dishes, and silverware was perfectly normal. The Grand Table Spell (which Melinda Mae had learned from her mother and which was passed down from one generation of Deavys to the next) kept everything in a constant state of convenient motion. Conversation was facilitated because no one had to ask anyone else to pass this dish or that;

the dishes took care of the passing all by themselves, leaving the family members free to talk about other things.

"How did the meeting go today, dear?" an obviously concerned Martin asked his spouse.

As he spooned up salad, molted malted fairy wings adding a nice crunch to the mix, Simwan could tell from the look on his mother's face that it had not gone well. She didn't look so good, either, he thought worriedly. The essence of her was too tied to the Truth, and its absence was starting to affect her health.

"Honestly, Martin, some of these people . . ." Tight-lipped and visibly worn, she broke off for a moment, shaking her head. "Don't they understand that if they let this project go ahead, not only will we lose the woods, but it will affect the zoning for the entire county? Once the floodgates are opened, they're almost impossible to close again." She made an effort to pit an innocent olive. "That Mrs. Pendergast—sometimes she makes me so mad I just want to turn her into a toad!"

"Don't be too hard on her, hon." Martin forked up a small bale of spinach and onion. "After all, her husband's in real estate and they stand to benefit considerably if the development goes ahead. She's only doing what she thinks is best for her family. Besides, you can't expect the Pendergasts or anyone else to understand what's really going on. Not in the absence of Truth."

"Hmph." Melinda Mae dug absently at the remnants of her salad. She had taken an unusually small portion, and seemed little interested in that. "I'm beginning to wonder if that particular theft might have been engineered by cronies of the developers, just to further confuse people. The whole business has the smell of the Black Arts about it."

Simwan looked at Rose, who glanced significantly at Amber, who nodded just once at N/Ice, who rotated in her chair until she was sitting right-side up like the rest of them. But no one said anything. As weary as their mother appeared to be, the last thing they wanted to do was agitate her further.

As dinner progressed, Simwan kept sneaking looks at his sisters. They, in turn, flashed him one restless glance after another. It was clear that no one wanted to be the first to broach the subject of their proposed trip to their parents, because if the initial asker fouled up the request, that individual would never hear the end of it from the others.

Main courses gave way to dessert, which consisted of spiced cream topped with meringue. The quartet of spiders who had agreed to spin the meringue (in return for having the run of the kitchen and all the wandering cockroaches they could catch) took several minutes to top off the frozen cream, at which point they were so exhausted from the effort that Martin had to tenderly carry them back to their home beneath the sink. Tonight's meringue was pistachio, Simwan discovered with one dip of his spoon.

They were running out of time. Something sharp struck him beneath the table and he turned to see Rose glaring at him. The expressions her sisters wore were no less intense. Clearly, they expected him to raise the subject.

Well, he was the oldest. Who should he ask first? Given how exhausted his mom was looking, he decided to query both of them simultaneously.

"You know, it's been kind of boring around here lately."

"Oh?" His mother's reaction was noncommittal, while Martin,

having returned from the kitchen, remained focused on his dessert and his visibly faltering wife. "How so?"

"Well, we're all caught up on our homework, and we—the girls and I—were kind of wondering what we were going to do next week since we're still off from school."

He plunged onward. "The girls and I, we were thinking of maybe doing something different this year. After all, we're all a lot older now."

"Yes, dear." Melinda Mae slowly dabbed a napkin at her spice-stained lips. Her essence might be faded, but there was nothing slow about her wit. "One year older than last year, to be precise."

"I take it, Simwan, that you and your sisters have something specific in mind?" His father was staring at him. To the average Ord, Martin Deavy came across as a pretty ordinary guy. To someone in the Knowledge, however, he was considerably more. Ords couldn't see the fire in Martin's eyes. Simwan could, all too easily.

He was intimidated, but things had progressed too far for him to back down now. "We, uh, thought we might spend the week in the city."

"Oh," Melinda Mae said conversationally, "you want to go over and spend the week with the Clarendon kids in Marksburg? I certainly don't see any problem with that."

Another sharp pain in his right leg. Throwing Rose a brief, murderous glare, he forced himself to smile as he turned back to his parents again. "Not exactly, Mom. We kind of think it's time we learn a little more about the wider world. You know: museums, life on the street, national monuments—that sort of thing." He took a breath and plunged ahead. "Actually, we were thinking of spending the week in New York."

Melinda Mae put down her napkin. She might be suffering from the absence of the Truth, but she was not insensible. "New York? For a week? *By yourselves?*"

"Out of the question," Martin Deavy murmured quietly and without rancor.

The girls' desperation burst through as Amber took over from her brother. "Please, Dad, Mom! We'll be careful. We know what to do."

"And what not to do," a restless Rose added earnestly.

"And how to behave," Amber added.

"And how not to behave," N/Ice put in gravely.

"I'm sixteen," Simwan pointed out quickly. "I'll take care, and watch out for the girls."

"You'll watch out for *who?*" Rose snapped back at him. "More likely it's us who'll be looking out for you!"

"You're twelve, Rose dear." An unusually pale Melinda Mae was gentle without being condescending.

"I know," her daughter agreed, "but we're a coubet. That means we're really thirty-six!"

"Not exactly, sweetheart," Martin Deavy corrected her patiently. "We don't recognize the math of multiplied expectation at this dinner table. On the other hand, it's true that you're not an Ord twelve, either."

His wife looked mildly shocked. "*Martin.* You're not actually thinking of letting them do this?"

"Well now, hon, I don't know." Scanning their pleading, anxious expressions, he smiled fondly at his offspring. "I think it's admirable that they want to experience the big time on their own, and that they believe they can deal with it. I'd rather see them spending time in Times Square, and Times Rhombohedron, and the museums, and Central Park, than sitting in their rooms for a week doing nothing but playing video games and watching TV." More softly he added, "And it would give you some peace and quiet, a chance to rest until this Truth business can be resolved."

"Yes, but Martin—New York? By themselves?" She eyed her son appraisingly. "I agree that Simwan's very experienced for his age, and the girls quite mature, but still . . ."

"What," Rose ventured quickly, seeing that her mother was weakening slightly, "if we agreed to stay with someone responsible? A grown-up. Someone who you know wouldn't let us get into trouble, someone you trust completely?"

"Well . . ." Melinda Mae hesitated. Having to think was exhausting her reserves of strength. "That might make a difference, I suppose. Who were you thinking of staying with?" She contemplated possibilities. "There's cousin Volkermann's family, but they live all the way out in the Hamptons, a long way from the city. And his wife and kids are Ords, which could present problems of a different kind."

"No, not him." Amber's expression matched the distaste in her voice. "We were thinking that we could stay with Uncle Herkimer. He lives right in the city, down where the Fulton Fish Market used to be." She smiled broadly, proud of remembering how fond their uncle was of seafood.

Melinda Mae exchanged a look with her husband, then smiled regretfully at her daughter. "I would certainly trust Uncle Herkimer to look after you, Amber dear, except for one small impediment. Uncle Herkimer is dead."

-V-

The girls exchanged a glance. Simwan, having initiated the discussion, sat back and let them run with it. With their soulful eyes and beseeching voices they stood a better chance of convincing their parents than he did, anyway.

"Well of *course* he's dead," Amber replied.

"We know that," N/Ice added. "That's why he's been in the same building for so long."

"We don't see why that should complicate things," Rose finished. "Uncle Herkimer's been dead for two hundred and fifty-seven years—more or less."

Melinda Mae sighed. "Mostly more, I'm afraid. It's a good thing your uncle had the sense to leave behind an endowment to pay his lease in perpetuity, or he'd long ago have been out on his decaying ear." She eyed her offspring sternly. "That doesn't excuse the fact that he's deceased."

Rose exchanged a look with her sisters. "Aw, Mom, from what I've heard, Uncle Herkimer still gets around pretty good."

"Pretty good for a really old dead guy," Amber added.

"Good enough to supervise us," N/Ice insisted.

"Yeah," Simwan added, feeling that he needed to contribute a few words to the argument. "It's not like he has a regular haunting gig, or something. I imagine that he's home most of the time."

It was clear that in spite of her increasing fatigue, Melinda Mae was less than convinced. There ought to be some truth in what the kids were saying ¾ but the Truth was missing. She was starting to feel it in her bones. "That's just it: He's home most of the time. And if I know you kids, you won't be. Of course," she added, arguing with herself, "there really wouldn't be much point in going to New York if all you were going to do was hang around somebody's apartment." Once again her gaze fixed on her son, who found himself fidgeting uncomfortably under that unflinching maternal stare. "Museums, hmm? Since when did you develop such a deep interest in higher education Simwan?"

He thought fast and, somewhat to his surprise, found himself with an immediate answer. "It was the Egyptian exhibit at the Met this past summer, Mom. We couldn't go, but I found the online catalog and went through it backward and forward and upside down. It was really fascinating."

At the head of the table, Martin was nodding reminiscently. "That explains all the sacred scarabs we found running around your room in September. At least they took care of the cookie crumbs and leftover pizza you forgot to pick up." Ever so slowly, the instinctively resistant but now weakening Melinda Mae continued to lose ground. "How would you get around the city on your own? You know Uncle Herkimer couldn't take you. Not during the day, anyway."

"We'll be fine." Doing his best to keep a lid on his eagerness, Simwan looked at his equally excited sisters, then back to his parents. "I've read up on it. The subway's easy to use, so are the buses, there are cabs, and if we get stuck somewhere we can always simul a fragin."

Martin Deavy looked up over his coffee cup. "Now Simwan, when was the last time you simuled a fragin?"

"I know the spell," he insisted. "I can teach it to the girls, too."

"That's a hoot," Amber remarked. "*You* teaching *us* something."

"Hoots call for a different spell," N/Ice put in, missing her sister's point entirely.

Martin looked over at his wife. "It would be good for their development. The New York schools have already had their break, so the kids would largely have the city to themselves, kidwise, for the week. And you'll be able to get some rest." He tried to cheer her. "They can help old Herkimer decorate for All Hallow's. You know he'd be glad to see them again. Dead relatives don't get many visits from kids, let alone live ones."

"I just don't want ours to end up in a similar condition," Melinda Mae murmured worriedly.

"Nothing's going to happen to us, Mom," Rose insisted forcefully. "It's not like you're sending four *Ord* children to the city."

Whether Rose's observation swayed Melinda Mae or she was simply too tired to argue it was impossible to tell. Turning to her husband, she moderated her tone slightly. "You really think they're ready for something like this, Martin?"

Deavy père surveyed his expectant litter. "Like I said: It would be good for them. It would be good for you. It would be good for Herkimer. Asmotheles knows he has room enough to put them up for a week, though I wouldn't vouch for the conditions."

He set down his coffee cup. It tried to sneak away, but he grabbed it and settled it firmly on its disapproving saucer. "I think it's time for the kids to show some responsibility. I believe they can take care of themselves, and they'll have Pithfwid to look after them." Leaning to his right, he located the family cat where it was lying contently by one of the baseboard heaters. "Isn't that right, Pithfwid?"

The cat looked up, yawned, flashed fur that was at present a mind-bogglingly vivid blend of cerulean and pink with gold highlights, and declared indubitably, "Meow," before putting his head back on his paws and closing his eyes anew.

"There, you see?" exclaimed Martin, straightening in his chair. "Also, there's one more thing that I think needs to be taken into consideration in deciding this." His attention returned to the children. "I believe this may be the first time ever that Simwan and his sisters have ever agreed on anything."

She finally gave in. "All right, then. I'm missing the Truth and I *could* use the rest."

Simwan and his sisters could barely contain their delight. To look at them, one would have thought they really were going on a vacation, instead of planning to wrestle the stolen Truth away from a thief of indefinite dimensions and unknown powers. "But you be sure to pack the right clothes, and gear, and charms. You'll all be on a strict allowance. This trip is all about improving your education and experience, not shopping."

Screaming and yelling their delight, the coubet disappeared upstairs as both Amber and N/Ice took off in pursuit of Rose, their feet pounding on the wooden steps.

That left Simwan holding the proverbial bag, faced with the prospect of dealing with any remaining questions from his parents by himself. Which, now that he thought of it, might have been exactly what his entirely too clever sisters had intended in collectively fleeing the table.

"We'll be fine," he asserted as the receding storm that was the sound of his sisters taking cover in their room finally faded from earshot. "I'll watch out for the girls, and we won't do anything stupid." *Dangerous, maybe,* he thought to himself, *or potentially fatal, or maybe crippling. But not stupid.*

"All right then." Taking another sip of her coffee, his mother peered over the rim of the cup at him. "You'd better get up to your room and start laying out what you want to take. If you and your sisters are going to do this, you'll want to be on your way as quickly as possible. No point in going if you don't get going, as my far-too-many-times-removed great-grandfather used to say when he was working as a deckhand for Odysseus."

Traveling light enabled them to pack fast. Being a guy, Simwan's backpack, when full, weighed considerably less than those of his sisters, who insisted on taking what limited makeup their mother would allow in addition to things they actually needed. To satisfy her, each of them had to take at least one new book with them, to read on the train and during the "slow" moments none of them felt they would experience.

A bit of a traditionalist, Rose chose *Mrs. Brackenwraith's*

Primer for Young Sorceresses—Level III. Amber opted to take both volumes of the newly published *Asian Enchantments and Hexes—Skeptical Inquirer Supplemental Publication*. N/Ice settled on *Albert Einstein's Universe—A Handbook for Transdimensional Tourists (Young Adult edition)*. As for Simwan, at the last minute he remembered to download his dad's copy of *A Metaphysician's Manual for New York City—Where to Stay, Where to Eat, Where to Invoke* onto his tablet. And all four of them, naturally, had their music with them.

It was cold but clear when their parents drove them to the train station the following day. To Simwan, the crisp morning air felt as if he were walking toward an open refrigerator that stayed a foot or two in front of him. He was glad of his heavy jeans and lined leather. If the Crub felt it was still being followed, it did not choose to place any obstacles in their way. Leastwise, Simwan mused, not yet.

His mother, thankfully, did not cry as for the tenth time she checked to make sure each of them had their bags. To his alarm, she looked drawn as well as tired. Clearly, the sooner the Truth was returned to Clearsight, the faster she would recover. It had been the responsibility of his family for thousands of years, and its disappearance from its storage space in Mr. Gemimmel's drugstore was wearing on his mother mentally as well as physically.

"Now, girls," she told the bright-eyed, attentive coubet, "you listen to your brother. And Simwan," she reminded him, "you listen to your sisters. And all of you listen to Uncle Herkimer and do what he tells you." By now all out of "We wills," they just nodded. Lights flashed on the platform. The ten o'clock train was not nearly as long or as full of morning commuters as its predecessors. As they boarded, Simwan saw what he thought might have been a tear or two in his mother's eyes. She really didn't look well. Good thing she didn't know the real motivation behind their trip. Then there would have been more than tears, and not necessarily in their favor.

Moments later, the train was accelerating away from the platform. At last, the Deavy clan was on its way: himself, his sisters, and Pithfwid, snuggled inside his innocuous, hard gray plastic pet carrier. While the cat fumed at having to travel in so degrading a fashion, he was enough of a realist to accept the need. As the train rattled along the track, Clearsight was soon left behind. Full of expectation and adrenaline, the girls giggled and chattered excitedly among themselves. As they gossiped and conversed, they listened to music on their tablets. There were only three other commuters in the car: a young couple leaning against each other in the first row, and near the back, an overweight salesman intent on snatching a few winks as he reclined across a row of empty seats. All three Ord travelers were asleep, catching up on their slumber until the time the train pulled into Penn Station. They ignored the children who had boarded outside Clearsight, and the children ignored them. Simwan thought it time to lean over and address the occupant of the pet carrier that was sitting on the seat next to him, close to the window.

"Pithfwid, are you okay in there?"

The carrier rocked slightly as its sole inhabitant shifted his position. "Other than the affront to my pride, yes, Simwan."

Pulling out his wallet, Simwan checked its contents. There was his dad's Aether Express card (don't leave your reality without it), which he was only supposed to use in emergencies.

Filling out the wallet was his school ID card, his driver's permit (an invitation to suicide in Manhattan), several other forms of identification including one that was completely invisible except to those non-Ords who knew how to read it, and money. The latter was a combination of his savings (the girls had their own) plus cash his parents had given him to pay for minor daily expenses. There weren't a lot of bills, but they were unusually compliant. Properly prodded George Washington, for example, would willingly surrender his place to Ben Franklin, or Ulysses S. Grant, or whichever presidential portrait (and corresponding denomination) might be required at the time.

As the train rolled on, he practiced murmuring the appropriate words and dragging his fingers over a sample bill, altering images and numbers and other relevant factors until he felt he had a feel for everything from singles to hundreds. As his dad had always told him, a person had to know how to be flexible with their money. Just for fun, he called forth on the paper the face of Woodrow Wilson, and spent several minutes studying the resultant hundred-thousand dollar bill. It would be fun, he knew, to use it to pay for a meal at McDonald's and then ask for change.

Though he was traveling with all his sisters plus Pithfwid, he felt suddenly alone. While the cat was napping, he knew that the girls would welcome him into their conversation. Trouble was, he could guess the subject matter without even having to listen in: boys, the latest clothes, boys, popular music, boys . . . All things being equal, he decided that he'd rather be stuck in a self-induced coma.

Picking up his backpack off the floor, he dug through the outer layer of clothes until he came to his tablet.

He'd brought along a couple of titles. One was science fiction. Many of his Ord friends at school favored fantasy, but when your own life is someone else's fantasy, it's hard to get into literary interpretations of far more mundane material. But he liked the science in science fiction, so he scrolled to the James Lawson novel and opened it to where he'd left off.

It passed the time until they crossed into New Jersey. The salesman and the couple forward had stirred briefly a few times, but for the most part remained fast asleep. As the train ducked into the tunnel that snaked beneath the Hudson River, Simwan stowed his tablet, crossed his arms over his chest, and tried to ignore the babbling of his sisters behind him. Their inane girl-girl-girl conversation was as enthusiastic and mind-numbing (to a sixteen-year-old boy) as it had been when they had first stepped onto the train.

It grew dark inside the car as the train rumbled through the tunnel under the river. Minimal overhead illumination came on automatically. The girls' voices seemed to grow even louder as the tunnel closed in around them. Simwan was already planning how they were going to get from Penn Station to Uncle Herkimer's apartment building when the unlatched door to the pet carrier popped open and Pithfwid stuck his head out.

"Hey," Simwan exclaimed in surprise, "we're not there yet." He glanced around anxiously, but none of the other three passengers was even awake, much less looking in his direction. "Get back inside."

"I smell something." The cat's ears were erect, he had his head tilted back, and he was sniffing the air vigorously. Suddenly, his eyes widened and he shouted, "I call on the Deavy coubet!"

"Ssshh! What's the matter with you?" Putting out a hand, a startled Simwan tried to push the emerging cat back into the carrier. "There are Ords here!"

In response to the cat's cry, the girls had ceased their playful conversation. Three heads appeared over the seats that formed the row where Simwan sat.

"What is it, Pithfwid?" Rose was suddenly all serious.

"Problem, quandary, dilemma?" Amber demanded to know.

N/Ice wasn't looking at the cat. Instead, she found her attention drawn to the window that looked out into the dark tunnel. Except—the dark tunnel wasn't entirely there anymore. It was dissolving, dissipating, fading away before her eyes.

In its place was the bottom of the Hudson, ton upon ton of black river water, on the verge of collapsing onto the last car of the train. The car that held four Deavy offspring, one Deavy cat, two dozing lovers, and one recuperating salesman.

–VI–

As the last of the tunnel appeared to disintegrate and the first thrust of cold dark river surged silently toward the side of the now isolated car, the Deavy girls automatically linked hands. Their delicate but strong fingers entwined in a manner that would have looked to an outsider as if every one of their girlish knuckles had been forcefully dislocated. Two sisters linking would have been insufficient to stem the incoming tide. Three might well have overreacted clumsily. But a coubet—a coubet was just right.

"Water rush and water flow, brindle back the undertow! Hold the line, sew it fine, stitch it up with aqueous twine!" In perfect sisterly unison they chanted and sang, muttered and mimed. "Station far, station near, bring us to the station dear!" Drops of water began to bead on the car's windows as it continued to rattle along its lonely way through the tunnel that had ceased to exist. Theirs was the last car of the train, Simwan remembered.

Looking out the tightly shut front door of the car, he could no longer see another in front of them. Whatever malevolent, diabolical force had placed them outside the railroad tunnel and under the Hudson had also separated them from the other cars and the engine. Which meant that somebody knew the Deavy offspring were traveling in it. Somebody, or something, that wanted them dead. There was little doubt in his mind as to its identity. *How did the Crub know it was being pursued?*

He would worry about that later. Right now his full attention was focused on helping his sisters ensure that their car emerged from beneath the river dry and in one piece. Thus far the linked, rhymed spelling of Rose, Amber, and N/Ice had been equal to the task. The interior of the car remained watertight. It continued to move forward, even in the absence of an engine.

A distinct aura surrounded the girls now, a pale fuzzy nimbus that flared brightly each time they spoke a new rhyme, voiced a new charm, murmured a new mantra. They were throwing off energy as freely and easily as new words. At the front of the car, the dreaming couple dozed on. In the back, Mr. Reluctant Traveling Purveyor of Frivolous and Overpriced Auto Accessories grunted in his sleep and rolled over, dreaming blissfully of commissions as prodigious as his waistline.

None of them noticed the absence of the rest of the train, or the ominous shapes that were starting to emerge from the dark damp that now enveloped the isolated, solitary car.

The fish arrived first: big, ugly, snarling monsters of the deep baring long, sharp teeth. Perch and bass threw themselves against the car windows, trying to shatter not only the glass but the spells that held them back. Now it was Simwan's turn to move to the defense of himself and his sisters. Raising his arms and hunching his shoulders, he stabbed his fingers at one group of Piscean predators after another, spinning in his seat to defend both sides of the car. It was not all that different from the video games he liked to play, except that in this case he was manipulating magic instead of buttons and a joystick.

With each jab of his fingers, with each gesture that was accompanied by a suitable word of power or two, the attacking fish were driven back, away from the submerged but miraculously still airtight car. Or in some cases, depending on the words he used, the fish were transformed. Fried, usually. Sometimes in butter, sometimes in oil. As he fought frantically to stave off the assault, Simwan whispered silent thanks for all the time he had spent helping his mother and sisters in the kitchen. Flash fried, or broiled, or steamed, or poached, bass and perch and trout and even a farrago of ferocious flounder foundered in their repeated attempts to break through both window glass and tautly murmured spells.

The more he invoked, the fewer the creatures who assailed the car. Gradually, in ones and twos, they began to break off the onslaught, to fade away into the darkness of the river. Soon the water around the car was devoid of all but the usual river denizens: small fish and bits of drifting garbage. He was almost ready to settle back down into his seat when something vast and glowing appeared off to the left-hand side of the car.

It was coming straight toward them. On the seat by the window, Pithfwid stood up on his hind legs, his front paws resting on the bottom of the glass as he stared through the scratched and battered transparency and sniffed intently. Then he let out a yowl and ducked back into his cat carrier.

All at once, Simwan found himself somewhat fearful. "Pith-fwid, what . . . ?"

By now he could make out the shape that loomed beyond the window. The nearer it came, the faster it seemed to move. It was heading right for the car. His eyes widened. His sisters, still actively chanting to hold back the insistent pressure of the river and maintain speed, didn't notice it. The other sleeping passengers didn't notice it. Unless there was a submarine lurking somewhere in the immediate vicinity, no one else noticed it.

Simwan sure noticed it. It's pretty hard not to notice a giant squid.

In the Hudson River?

Whoever was trying to stop them from getting to Manhattan, Simwan realized anxiously, was really going all out.

What kind of incantation would stop a giant squid? Living as he did in the woodsy countryside of eastern Pennsylvania, he did not have much occasion to deal with oceanic monsters like *Architeuthis*. River bass and trout and catfish were one thing, but giant squid? In the course of his specialized, after-school homework he *had* been required to study many diverse creatures that sported tentacles. Was there a useful spell there? Urgently, he tried to think if he had ever watched his mother prepare calamari. No doubt his aunt Free, who lived up the coast just north of Boston, would know all sorts of appropriate spells for dealing with such a threat. But Aunt Free wasn't here. It was just him and Pithfwid and the girls.

One long tentacle thrust out and slammed against the car, rocking it violently. Behind him, Amber paused in her chanting long enough to let out a soft moan of concern. The break in the coubet's concentration interrupted the dike spell long enough to allow a brief gush of water to seep in under every one of the car's windows. N/Ice and Rose tightened their fingers in Amber's, restoring her resolve and restrengthening the coubet. The flow of water was shut off, but Simwan knew he'd better do something, and quick. Swallowing hard, he raised both hands over his head, all ten fingers pointing toward the rampaging squid. It hovered now right outside the windows, tentacles uncoiling. If it got a good grip on the car, Simwan realized, it could probably yank it right off course in spite of everything the girls could do.

Spell, spell—what was the proper intonation for the incantation? It didn't matter. He was out of time, and would have to improvise as best he could. Thrusting his stiffened fingers in the direction of the monster squid, he opened his mouth and began to chant.

Radiance burst through the window, causing him to blink and turn away. It flooded in through all the windows, the illumination in the interior of the car shifting with astonishing abruptness from dim to bright. The squid shot away, fleeing back to the benthic basement from which it had come. Shaking his head, Simwan rubbed at his light-shocked eyes and peered outside.

The water was gone. So, for that matter, was the tunnel. He was staring at a concrete wall covered with graffiti. Other tracks sidled up to the one their train was on like so many male snakes courting a female. The fronts of old buildings appeared behind the spray paint–smeared wall. Of modest dimensions at first, they quickly became taller and more massive, newer and more impressive. Cars, taxis, buses, pedestrians, streetlights, street vendors, street chaos manifested themselves as he stared. He looked forward. Another car rattled from side to side in front of theirs. They were once more part of an ordinary, everyday commuter train.

They were also out of the tunnel. They were in Manhattan. They were safe.

Letting out the longest single exhalation of his life since he had first competed in the school steeplechase, Simwan slumped in his seat. From the plastic pet carrier, Pithfwid ventured, "I love seafood, but not when it has eyeballs bigger than me."

Something struck Simwan simultaneously on the top of his head and his right shoulder. He nearly jumped out of his seat, but the contact had come not from tentacles, but from the balled-up hands of his sisters.

"Way to go, Simmie!" Rose was laughing and tousling his hair. Angrily, he turned in his seat and swatted her hand away.

"Scuba lessons—I want scuba lessons!" declared Amber as she leaned over the seat back next to his and affectionately patted Pithfwid's carrier.

"*In vivo mares mysterium*," N/Ice murmured solemnly as she tried to insert a Wet Willy into her brother's undefended right ear.

"Sit *down*, all of you!" he snapped as he whirled in his seat and pulled away from them. "How can you laugh about it? We nearly got killed!"

"Drownded," Amber agreed with mock solemnity.

"Seriously saturated," Rose admitted as she gazed out the window while still leaning over the back of the seat in front of her.

"Operative word is *nearly*, big brother," N/Ice pointed out.

"Might as well laugh now. Grab the opportunity when it's presented to you. Can't laugh when you're dead."

"I bet *you* could." Rose quipped back. "I bet you'd cackle like a laminated lamia throughout all eternity."

Her sister took a halfhearted swing at her. "When eternity gets here, we'll see about that. She who cackles last, cackles best!"

"Get yourselves ready." Simwan did his best to appear stern and in charge. "When we get off the train, we want to look like we know just what we're doing and exactly where we're going. That's how Dad said we need to act to avoid attracting the attention of the sleazy types who hang out in big train stations." Woe unto any type, sleazed or otherwise, he thought, who might have the misfortune to draw the attention of the Deavy coubet. But he didn't say that, of course. He needed to keep his outrageous sisters in line. Especially now that it was apparent they were being tracked. The Crub must have left minions at every Hudson River crossing to watch out for them since there was no way to predict just how they'd come into Manhattan.

The girls behaved reasonable and proper as the train pulled into the station. Not because their disposition had grown any less rowdy or their nature had become suddenly subdued, but simply because the effort of holding back the Hudson and dealing with the underwater assault had sapped at least a little of their otherwise irrepressible energy. Striving to look ten years older than his sixteen, he led his sisters off the train and onto the platform. Lights, signs, and the single direction being taken by the passengers exiting the cars in front of them eliminated the need for him to ask questions. All the Deavy progeny had to do to find the exit was go with the flow. The fact that his sisters had hooked them up to a different train going to a different station mattered not a whit. All that mattered was that they had arrived safely in Manhattan.

The young couple in the front seat of the car who had slept through everything awakened as the train pulled into Grand Central. While the woman stretched and yawned, her paramour rose to remove their luggage from the overhead storage rack—and promptly slipped and fell. Picking himself up off the floor of the car, he paused to stare at the hand he had used to try and break his fall. It was covered with slime and fragments of unrecognizable plant matter. A hasty inspection showed that more of the same unidentifiable goo inexplicably coated the walls and floor of the car. Muttering about the lack of maintenance on the commuter line, the traveling pair hefted their luggage and exited the car while actively discussing the letter of complaint they intended to write to the train company's management.

At least they did better than the salesman who had slept the entire journey in the rear of the same car, who upon rising promptly stepped on an almost-dead carp and nearly threw his back out. Propelled by a combination of fear and bewilderment, he too hurried to be on his way. Unlike the younger couple who had preceded him, however, he had no intention of complaining to the company, lest someone inquire about the nature and origin of the hangover he had been sleeping off. It was to this he attributed his arrival at Grand Central when he had been certain, absolutely certain, that he had originally embarked for Penn Station.

Neither his puzzlement nor that of the young couple who preceded him were anything compared to that of the train's engineer, who swore on his twenty-two years in the industry that he had been assigned four cars and not five. Nor could anyone explain how a commuter car from Pennsylvania and New Jersey headed for Penn Station had ended up riding tail-end on a midday commuter line out of Long Island traveling in the opposite direction. By the time confusion reigned supreme, the only individuals who could have answered those many questions had long since departed not only the train but the station.

"Wow!" Setting aside any hope of acting cool, Simwan tilted his head as he took in the immense enclosed space that was the main hall of Grand Central Station. Less concerned about whether any onlookers thought them in charge of themselves or anything else, the girls spread out slightly to marvel at their surroundings. The slight dispersion was enough to remind Simwan of his responsibilities.

"Stay together. Amber, get back here!"

"I just want to see!" she called back to him as she dragged her wheeled backpack in the direction of one art-filled corridor.

Rather than challenge her loudly, Simwan chose to follow her lead, hauling her sisters, his own backpack, and the awkward cat carrier with him. The fact that they had arrived at Grand Central instead of Penn Station did not trouble him. According to what he had read in the guidebook, there were several exits from Grand Central. Since they intended to take a taxi to Uncle Herkimer's apartment, one way out was pretty much as good as another, just as their place of arrival would make no difference to how they eventually reached their final destination.

As he and Rose and N/Ice trailed the excitable Amber, they

had time to observe that the massive, venerable old station was a meeting place not only for daily commuters of the Ordinary kind, but for all manner of travelers. One would think, for example, that the insurance company workers and office drones and hurrying executives would notice that the large man in the dun-colored overcoat had two heads: a sight unusual even in New York. But the secondary skull was as invisible to the hordes of Ords as a beggar in front of Bergdorf's.

At least the two-headed traveler was more or less (more, in this case, Simwan decided) human. The presence of other-worldly creatures indiscernible to Ords but perfectly visible to him and his sisters was enchanting. Chain-clad giants trod the polished stone floor, delighted at having a place to meet that was both safe from the chilly weather yet sufficiently expansive to allow them to move about without having to bend to clear low ceilings. A tour guide led a group of wide-eyed loup-garous across the center of the station, pointing out highlights of the historic architecture as they walked. Or rather, loped, since Simwan knew they were anything but your usual clutch of French package-tour visitors.

On a coffee break, a clutch of harpies occupied an upper corner of the main hall. Over lattes and laughter, they discussed the latest doings on Wall Street: what aviation stocks were doing well, which airlines were in trouble, the weather back home in Greece and Turkey, who was disemboweling whom—the usual morning tittle-tattle. They wore the latest uptown fashions—though only the upper halves of the perfectly tailored suits and blouses they had purchased, of course.

Leaving the contrary giants and cappuccino-sipping harpies

and curious loup-garous behind, Simwan and his sisters entered one of the access corridors that led to the street outside.

They spotted a snack shop equipped to serve both ordinary and more knowledgeable visitors. Located in an alcove on one side of the busy access way, it offered cold and hot drinks, sandwiches, sushi boxes (no calamari, Simwan was relieved to see), burgers, and desserts. The girls were immediately drawn to the snakezel bin. Ords ordering from the display cases had access only to the usual giant pretzels. They were unable to see the half-foot long serpents that twisted and coiled around the metal serving spears on which they had been skewered.

"I want a diamondback!" Rose exclaimed, nudging Simwan's free arm.

"Stripes for me." Amber eyed the bin hungrily. "I think they're spicier."

As he set down the cat carrier and reached for his wallet, Simwan eyed his third sister. "N/Ice, you're not hungry?"

"Not yet," she told him. "But I could use a drink."

The short-sleeved proprietor, a slight fair-haired immigrant from Atlantis, did not question their requests. Anyone who could see the snakezels coiling and writhing within the serving bin was by definition sufficiently adept to deal with one. Using a pair of special tongs, he removed a twisting, hissing diamondback from the container and placed it within a large piece of appropriately enchanted wax paper. On contact, the snakezel suffered instant petrification, freezing in the shape of the less exotic pretzels with which it had shared a home only a moment before.

"Y'want mustard wid dat?" the proprietor asked Rose.

"Sure. Also frankincense and myrrh."

The young blond émigré smiled and jerked a thumb toward a nearby shelf. "Over there with the other condiments." Fishing out a striped snakezel, he passed the sleek solidified snack across to Amber. "What you want on yours?"

"Just sea salt, thanks." Taking the wax paper handful, she bit into the snakezel with gusto, starting at the head.

In addition to the snakezels, all four of them ordered drinks: cold mead for Rose and Amber, a coke for Simwan, and for N/Ice a tall glass of imported schweel, which managed to be both hot and cold at the same time. As they headed away from the snack booth, the pet carrier rocked insistently in Simwan's grip.

"Hey, what about me!"

Leaning toward the box, Simwan whispered tightly, "Cats don't eat snakezels and they don't order drinks with ice."

Reluctantly acknowledging the truth of that statement, Pithfwid urged them on. "We can't stand around gawking all day. Better get to your uncle Herkimer's place and check in. You know your parents will be waiting to hear that you've arrived safely."

"Aw, Pithfwid," Amber protested, "can't we just walk? There's so much to see!"

"Indeed," the cat replied, drawing a seriously startled look from a passing six-year-old firmly attached to his mother's hand. "There'll be plenty of time for that later. Check in first. Get me something to eat. Then we have work to do. Put out feelers in search of the Crub." As he finished, a pair of feelers emerged from his ears and promptly set out across the street, looking like a pair of fuzzy black worms training for the hundred-meter dash. Ords did not see them, of course, but the pair did have to deal with a brace of persistent pigeons. They made it safely across the street and disappeared into a welcoming drainage grate when one of the pigeons, overly fixated on the unusual prey, ended up ornamenting the windshield of a speeding delivery van, thereby contributing much to the ongoing irritation and bad language of its bilious driver.

–VII–

By a Foulness ye shall know Him. Also by his home address."

That was the thought that was in Jekjik's mind as he zig-zagged his way toward the entrance. It looked no different from any other drain in Central Park: a decorative round steel grate that covered the terminus of a small concrete drainage ditch, almost completely hidden by trees and grass. Only someone educated in the ways of the city would know that it led to realms beyond the imagining of the urban engineers who had designed and built the system.

Making sure he didn't catch his large, fluffy tail in the grate, Jekjik squeezed through one of the several gaps and dropped down onto the service ledge that paralleled the deeper, wider ditch. He was thankful it had rained hard last week. The flush of fresh water had scoured the tunnel clean of the more mephitic muck with which it was often filled, and the stench that still lingered was tolerable.

Even so, he had to catch and hold his breath several times. A resident of the trees, he was never comfortable underground. Occasional squeaks and scritches marked the movement of those who were. Despite invitations to do so, he did not stop to chat with any of them. He was already late. A bearer of bad news was never welcome. One who was also tardy was apt to receive the full force of his master's displeasure. Jekjik shuddered, his tail quivering. He had considered making a run for it, only to discount the notion out of hand. For one thing, the presence of man and his grinding, crushing works throughout Manhattan made attempted flight to the suburbs suicidal. For another, trying to avoid the attentions of the Crub when he demanded your presence was more than foolish.

There were worse things, Jekjik knew as he scampered onward, than dying.

The deeper he plunged into the depths of the New York City sewer system, the darker and danker it became. Fading and hesitant, light from above grew intermittent, then nearly absent. Fortunately, like all his kind, Jekjik could see extremely well in the dark. Where overhead light was lacking entirely, occasional clumps of phosphorescent fungi that clung to walls and ceiling supplied a pale, eerie glow. Eventually, he had penetrated far enough into the secret places to pass not just rats and roaches, but Other Things.

He was not sure how far he had descended when he came upon the first ools. Sluglike in shape and sluggish in manner, they were creatures to be avoided. Arising from the bubbling, fermenting sludge that collected in the deepest, filthiest, most stagnant corners of the sewers, they were largely hydrocarbon based. Set alight, an ool would burn with the ferocity of a gallon of kerosene. They fed by enveloping their prey, then forcing extensions of themselves down the throats of their unfortunate victims until they suffocated on the choking mire. Not a pleasant way to die. Jekjik found himself desperately wishing for the cool clear skies and swaying treetops of the great park that was his home. But that refreshing, open landscape lay far above his head now. He could not go back until he had delivered his report.

The tunnel down which he had been running abruptly opened up into a sizable underground chamber. More than a hundred and fifty years ago it had been a collection, distribution, and clean-out nexus for several sewer lines. Long since abandoned in favor of larger, newer culverts, it was aboil with rodents of every shape and size. In the enclosed space their continuous, combined squealing and squeaking was deafening. Suppurating slime and bloated fungi hung from the ceiling. At the far side a podium of sorts had been constructed out of fragments of human detritus. A steady stream of rodents carried food to the podium, and other things.

Flanking both sides of the throne that dominated the center of the podium was a compilation of the eclectic: all of it scavenged or stolen. A gold diadem set with green diamonds rested on the skull of a long-dead philosopher. Spanish doubloons lay scattered among the corpses of dead pixies whose tiny bones had been gnawed bare *raw*. A wand of pure silver inscribed with symbols in ancient Mandarin lay propped up against an Ashanti idol. The eyes of the idol flickered, indicative of the life trapped helplessly within. There were brooches and bracelets, teeth from unnatural beings and frozen howls waiting to be released, spirit capsules and disembodied bejeweled tongues. Lying indifferently to one side of the pile and waiting to be moved to the storage area that held the bulk of the hoard was a certain small, inconspicuous, ancient blue bottle, still intact and filled with its precious contents.

The throne that rose up from the piles of scattered booty consisted of an ivory pedestal that had been looted from a still-undiscovered tomb in ancient Hellas. Lying prone on his sprawled-out belly atop the pedestal-throne, his legs spraddled out to the sides, was the Crub.

Though currently no more than twice the size of the rodents who made up his personal ratinue, the Crub was, Jekjik knew, capable of more impressive expressions of self. Such demonstrations of power were not appropriate for a location like the sewer nexus, where the ability to race rapidly down often-narrow tunnels was paramount. But the implication, the perverted promise, was there. This potential was not nearly as intimidating to supplicants as was the Crub's stare.

It was cold and unblinking, as dank and rank as the sewer surrounds. Presently, it was focused on Jekjik. He would rather have been anywhere else, but he was not, there being no point in trying to run from the Crub's reach. The servant had been summoned to inform. With luck, he would also be given time to explain.

Sniffing the rancid air, whiskers twitching, his host looked down at him. The voice of the Crub was deceptively soft and cloying, each sentence lingering like wet Kleenex on the hearing of those within its range.

"How went the intercept of those who follow?"

In spite of himself, Jekjik stammered. "The—the intercept—went well, Master."

The Crub considered. "I perceive that you are being truthful, but incomplete. Do elaborate. Do you mean to say that those who follow have been destroyed?"

"No—no, Master. Many were the hurdles that I conjured in their path. Each of these, I am ashamed to say, was shunted aside. It was my feeling that had I been dealing with but a single follower, or perhaps two, they would now be slowly dissolving in the toxins of the river bottom. But there are four of them. Or three. Or possibly even five. To this moment I am not sure which is correct. Whatever the actual number, their ability to work together was remarkable, their knowledge of the Ways and Callings impressive. I suspect that both accomplishments are born of inculcated persistence and a righteous family."

The Crub's upper lip curled back, exposing dark, sharp teeth. "I can admire the former while despising the latter. So, at least I have a better idea now of what comes. Three or five or four individuals of knowledge would constitute an unpresumptuous threat. Three or five or four bound by blood are another matter entirely." He brooded. "I perceive a distinctive relationship between what was taken, one or more who remain behind, and those who follow."

After allowing for a pause of respectful silence, Jekjik hazarded a hope. "Then Master recognizes the dimension of the menace that I strove to deal with, and does not blame me for failing to call it to account?"

"Hmm . . . what?" Behind the Crub, a hairless fleshy tail inexplicably struck sparks from the stone that supported the ivory throne. "No, Jekjik. Not realizing the binding nature of those who follow, much less their skill in the Ways, you could not be expected to be prepared for or equipped with the means to challenge them efficiently."

The visitor exhaled a barely perceptible but heartfelt sigh of relief.

"However," the Crub continued, "that does not excuse you."

Jekjik tensed up all over again. "Forgive me, Master, but I am confused. If I am not to be blamed for preventing these followers from reaching the kingdom, then what is it that I am not excused for doing? Or for not doing?"

"Why, isn't it obvious?" declared the Crub, quietly ominous as he leaned down and forward from his prone position on the pedestal. "You have forgotten to bring the customary gift." One claw-tipped paw gestured to take in the noisy, malodorous surroundings. "You know full well that each time one is granted a formal audience, those who serve are expected to bring me a gift. Those who are present must present a present."

It was true, Jekjik realized in sudden shock. In the rush to deliver his report, he had forgotten to acquire and bring along a gift. In the absence of this expected homage, he tried to offer an explanation.

"I thought it was more important than anything else that Master be informed of the status of the followers, with whom he was so concerned. Next time," he added hastily, "I will bring two presents."

"Your swift rationalization commends you," the Crub murmured unemotionally. "Commends—but does not excuse." Sitting back on his haunches, he raised both front legs. "I forgive you your abject failure to halt the enemy. Clearly, you do not possess the necessary skills. But forgetting to bring a gift—that is unpardonable." While whiskers stiffened and tail stirred lightning from a low-lying haze of methane gas and oils, the right paw gestured to its right, the left paw to its left. Aroused and alerted, the ratainers of the Crub pulled their muzzles out of masses of decomposing dog food and began to inch forward.

"No, Master—please! I have a mate, I have a family!" Consumed with sudden horror, Jekjik started to back rapidly away, nearly tripping over his considerable tail in the process.

Spinning around faster than any human could manage, a wide-eyed Jekjik bolted for the nearest tunnel. The Crub's bodyguards caught him before he reached the first yawning opening. One clamped slavering jaws firmly on the squirrel's tail while the next dug its claws into Jekjik's back. In less than a minute, half a dozen of them had swarmed the unfortunate servant. His small, pitiful screams were horrible to hear. They rose even above the surging babble that filled the chamber and echoed off the walls of peeling metal and crumbling stone.

From his position atop the throne, the Crub observed the actions of his ratainers with a mixture of approval and distaste. Approval for the speed and efficiency with which they had carried out sentence. Distaste for table manners that were deplorable even by the standards of rodental etiquette. It was a shame to lose one as knowing in the Ways as Jekjik, the Crub mused regretfully. But to forget to bring a gift, regardless of circumstances . . . It was an oversight that could not be overlooked. No matter. So, those who had followed had succeeded in entering the kingdom. Very well. The closer they came, the more in the way of horror and awfulness the Crub could place in their way.

One last time the Crub raised his eyes to peer in the direction of the late Jekjik. Not much left of him now but a few bones, with those being snapped and crunched between strong jaws so that their owners could get at the sweet marrow within. The awkward episode only confirmed what already should have been known.

Never send a squirrel to do a rat's job.

"There's another one!"

Amber was pointing excitedly down the street. Like her sisters, she had excellent vision, and had spotted the empty taxi that was heading their way before anyone else.

"Not that one," came a voice from within the pet transport.

Frowning, Amber put her hands on her hips and turned to look at the gray box. "Why not? What's wrong with it?" Overhearing, a passing insurance broker favored her with a look of confusion. Noticing the man's reaction, she reacted testily. "What are *you* looking at?"

Quickly picking up his pace, the man hurried on his way. Anywhere else, he might have been inclined to have had a word with such a blatantly disrespectful young girl. But not in New York, where children younger and less well turned-out than the four standing on the sidewalk sometimes concealed weapons of a distressingly adult nature on their persons.

"It's another Ord taxi," explained the voice from within the depths of the cat carrier.

"Pithfwid's right." Standing on tiptoe to see over the heads of the opposing rivers of preoccupied pedestrians, Simwan continued to search for appropriate transportation. "It's yellow, like most of the cabs in New York. Some of the other ones are green, some white. Dad said to be sure and look for one that was pale. 'Behold a pale taxi,' he told me. Said it would be cheaper, save time, and we might learn some stuff from the driver."

"There's one!" shouted N/Ice elatedly, being the first to spot it because she was more than a little pale herself.

As the three girls hailed the cab and Simwan bent to pick up Pithfwid's carrier, the vehicle worked its way across the line of traffic and pulled up to the curb. It looked exactly like any other taxi on the busy street: bright yellow, with a rectangular illuminated plastic sign on top and appropriate inscriptions on the sides indicating how much its driver could charge. But if you had been trained to look closely at such things, and shut one eye just so, and squinted at it just right, it took on the appearance of a jellyfish that had been stretched out and dunked in stiffening preservative preparatory to mounting: just a faint outline whose interior, including bench seats and trunk and meter, were clearly visible through the supposedly solid sides.

"Hisss!" whispered the driver as he leaned toward them.

"Excuse me?" Simwan dropped his backpack onto the floor and slid into the front seat with Pithfwid's carrier on his lap.

The driver looked startled, glanced into the backseat where the three giggling, excited girls were settling themselves in and wrestling for space, then eyed his front-seat passenger carefully.

"I mean, where to? You're from out o' town, ain'tcha?"

Simwan nodded. "Pennsylvania."

At this the driver grinned, showing rather more teeth than was normal. Also bigger teeth. Also sharper teeth. "Got Knowledge?" A faint white horizontal line appeared just above his mouth.

"Some," Simwan admitted modestly. "My sisters and I are in town to visit our uncle." He gave the address.

"I know where dat is. Nice neighborhood on the Lower East Side, near da bridge." Sticking his head not out of but through the driver's side window, he yelled at a passing delivery truck that had nearly taken off his side-view mirror. "Hey, ya smelly spawn of da Unnamable, watch where you're goin'!" Pulling his head in, without any damage to the rolled-up window, he smiled anew at his passenger.

"Sorry for da language, kid, but dis is New Yawk. You don't stick up for youself here, you might as well be drivin' in Hell." Hands on the wheel, he depressed the accelerator and pulled away from the curb.

"Are you a demon?" N/Ice inquired politely from the backseat.

"Well, sure. Whattid ya think? Dat some Ord would be drivin' a cab like dis?" Affectionately, he reached out to pat the dash to the right of the wheel. "Thoity million miles on 'er and she's still runnin' strong. She's got a top-drawer engine enchantment, but more dan dat, I was smart when I bought her license. Paid for a warranty dat covers me throughout all dimensions Now and Forever. 'Cept for da after-market accessories I added on myself, of course."

"Uh, I don't want to tell you your business, sir," Simwan spoke rapidly as the vehicle careened crazily toward a momentary gap between pedestrians, "but aren't we heading straight for the side of that really tall, really solid-looking skyscraper?"

"Appearances can be deceivin', kid. Especially in New Yawk." Gripping the wheel with both hands and prehensile tail (the latter having slid out from beneath the driver's seat), eyes wide and expression maniacal, the cabby sent them hurtling straight toward a towering wall of stone, steel, and glass. Behind Simwan, the girls shrieked in delighted anticipation. Simwan just closed his eyes.

Only to open them again an instant later. Still accelerating, they were racing *through* the building. Occasionally, they would also pass right through an Ord, who would pause briefly and alternately blink, wince, belch, or otherwise react reflexively to the momentary unusual intestinal disturbance they could feel but not see.

Wheels screeching silently, the cab slid sideways, throwing Simwan against the door on his side and the laughing, squealing girls against one another. Simwan didn't see what the driver was fighting to avoid because he was too busy hanging onto the cat carrier (from whose darkened interior arose increasingly acerbic comments of displeasure regarding the violent turn their taxi ride had taken) and staying upright on his own seat.

"Shortcut." Exposing pointed, six-inch-long fangs, the driver grunted at Simwan, then yanked sharply on the wheel again to steer clear of what appeared to be a small volcano erupting molten mercury. "I tell you, dis city ain't no place for da faint o' hearts."

Shrinking back in his seat as they plunged into the nebulous interior of what appeared to be another solid, impenetrable building, Simwan could only agree. The Deavy coubet, meanwhile, acted as if they had been given a free pass to ride all day on a multi-dimensional roller coaster. Their enchanting (if not enchanted) shrieking and giggling filled the cab as it careened from one seemingly fatal encounter to the next. From within his cat carrier, an irritated Pithfwid snarled something about spilling newly carbonated milk, but otherwise kept to himself.

That left Simwan free to be alternately relieved and terrified, depending on the route the cab happened to be taking at that particular moment and the apparently solid objects at which their driver continued to insist on hurling it. Then, almost as soon as the wild ride had begun, they were back out on a normal street again. Second Avenue was also full of traffic, but in contrast to the jam they had left behind, it was manageable traffic.

"Sorry 'bout the detour," the cabbie apologized. "Dere's a dead dragon blocking da intersection up at Thoity-thoid Street and I'm damned if I was gonna wait around for Spectral Removal to show up and haul it away. 'Course," he added pleasantly, "it wouldn't really ha' mattered that much 'cause I'm already damned anyway."

Eventually, they reached the far Lower East Side, down near the Manhattan Bridge, and found themselves in one of the oldest parts of the city. Here, where the East River flowed past the Brooklyn Navy Yard on the other side from Manhattan Island, remnants of the great city's nautical history and financial future were to be found.

The girls had gone silent. Heads tilted back, necks craning, they strained to see the fronts of the old apartment buildings that rose several stories high on either side of the constricted lane. Save for a brace of imps pushing a cart piled high with fresh fruits and vegetables and a cable installer truck parked outside one building, there was a notable absence of other vehicles. Shut out by walls of brick and chiseled stone, even the sun seemed to have taken a bye.

Emitting a grunt of satisfaction, accompanied by a match-size flicker of flame from between his otherwise tightly clamped lips, the driver slowed and stopped at one curb. In places where the concrete was cracked and buckled, weeds and grass broke through, announcing their imperfect but determined attempts to recoup the land for a paved-over Nature. On the surrounding structures, crows and ravens, sparrows and pigeons staked their claim to nesting spaces in a profusion of nicks and crannies and rooftops. Few were the windows that were not masked from within by thick shades or heavy curtains. A shadowy silence hung over the street, a quietude that affected even the air, which did not move. An old newspaper page that was skittering down the center of the street was doing so on its own, too impatient to wait for a following breeze. This was a neighborhood that had been overlooked by the ages.

Turning to Simwan, the driver extended a hand. The expectant open palm was rough-surfaced and covered with scales, not skin. "Yous won't find dis street on no regular map o' da city. That'll be ten lucks, please."

For a moment, Simwan wondered if they had been brought to the right address. Eyeing the stolid buildings that constricted the street like a Sphygmomanometer around a bare arm, it didn't look as if anyone lived in any of them. On the other hand, he decided, if the cab driver had wanted to cheat them, he could have continued driving around Manhattan for another hour without his young passengers being any the wiser.

Digging out his wallet, he handed the driver two bills: a dollar (for a tip), and a ten-luck. Reflecting the nature of the unique currency, the face on the front of the latter was that of an older, happier Alexander Hamilton: one who hadn't died as a result of wounds suffered in his duel with Aaron Burr. In the currency of another place and time, Hamilton had lived on—a fact reflected in the knowing wink the face on the bill gave the driver as Simwan passed him the note.

Pulling his head and tail back inside the taxi, the cabbie pulled away from the curb and drove off, disappearing around the next corner. Or maybe he disappeared before he reached the corner. Simwan couldn't be sure. Turning, he put the cat carrier down on the crumbly, ancient sidewalk and together with his sisters, stood studying the building that loomed before them.

Constructed of brown brick the color of weathered wood, it boasted narrow curtained windows and touches of decorative gray granite. The pair of stone gargoyles that served as downspouts for the rooftop drain were just that: inert stone. In contrast, Simwan was sure that the pair of windows that fronted the small area that was visible below street level had blinked at him at least once. According to the information his parents had given him, Uncle Herkimer lived on the top floor. That meant a better view, more isolation from any street noise (assuming there ever was any noise on this street, he mused), and cleaner air. Picking up his backpack, he slipped the shoulder straps over his arms, hefted Pithfwid's carrier, and started toward the dozen or so wide stone stairs that led up to the building's front door. Chattering among themselves, his sisters followed, lamenting the neighborhood's apparent absence of any boys older than themselves. The nonappearance of any other type of human being did not particularly concern them.

The front door opened into a small alcove. Embedded in one wall was a single row of metal mailboxes. Inspecting them briefly, Simwan was unable to decide if they were made of weathered, blackened brass or true gold that had been disguised to look like weathered, blackened brass. The other wall boasted a somewhat haphazardly written list of residents and a built-in intercom. Befitting his location at the top of the building, the top of the list featured the name they were looking for: J. Herkimer. Simwan pressed the small, square black button opposite the name. Within the wall, something buzzed. There was no reply. He buzzed once more. Again, nothing.

Behind him, the girls crowded close. "Let me try," offered Rose. Stepping aside, Simwan let each of them take a try at the button. The buzzer-bell worked fine, but no voice responded from the speaker set into the wall.

"Pick me up."

Doing as Pithfwid requested, Simwan lifted and awkwardly held the front end of the cat carrier so that it was facing the wall speaker. From within the carrier came a peculiarly modulated yowl that to a non-Ord would have sounded no different from any other feline yowl. It sounded only a little different, and was equally incomprehensible, to Simwan and his sisters. But there was an immediate response from the speaker.

"Well why didn't you *say* so?" rattled a voice from within the wall. Listening to it, Simwan wasn't sure if it was the speaker or the voice that rattled. It didn't matter. It was the fact that they had finally roused a response that was important. "Marty and Melinda Mae's kids—I've been expecting you, already."

The high, narrow double doors that blocked the entrance to the interior of the building promptly swung aside, opening inward, groaning and squealing alarmingly as they did so. Once more a voice issued from the speaker.

"Don't mind the doors. It's their job to scare off nosy sales-people. Everybody should have a job, even a door, yes? Come on up."

The girls ran toward the broad central stairway that extended itself slightly to greet them. Simwan followed more slowly. He was tired from the trip, from the effort of battling the evil that had tried to drown them beneath the Hudson, from the responsibility of looking after the coubet, and from the less than tranquil taxi ride they had suffered from the train station. It would be good to relax for a while. He was also looking forward to sitting down and chatting with his uncle Herkimer. Even if he was dead.

-VIII-

The condition of the hallway reflected that of the apartment building as a whole: somewhere between decrepit and spotless. Certainly, it was quiet as they started up the wide, carpeted stairs. Dead quiet, Simwan decided. But it was not deserted. Occasionally, sounds loud enough to be heard reached the ascending Deavy brood: the muted mutter of televisions, the hum of people conversing behind tightly closed doors, the muffled chatter of a pet parrot. On the second-floor landing, a door opened and a hand emerged to place a bag of trash outside. The trash was ordinary but the hand was not. It was bright green, covered with large dark blotches and warts, and boasted six fingers that terminated in long, curving nails. Of the owner of this singular appendage they saw no more than the hand and the olive-skinned arm to which it was attached.

The third floor reverberated to the beat of fugitive music. Also to the footsteps of a diminutive elderly lady wearing a tutu;

shiny white, cut-off top ballet slippers; and a harried expression. Hefting what looked like a butterfly net but wasn't, she was huffing and puffing as she chased the music around the central stairwell. As the Deavys looked on, the woman swung and swiped the net back and forth until it finally collapsed around something invisible to them but clearly not to her. Firmly holding the mouth of the net closed, she hurried past them, breathing hard.

"Terrible sorry; 'tis I." She held up the choked-off white mesh net. Neither Simwan nor his sisters could see anything inside, but the frantic jerking and twitching of the gauzy material clearly indicated something was trapped within. Each time the net heaved, a different discordant melody rocked the hallway. "'Tis a pirate recording, you see," the little old lady explained, "and as such, 'tis ever attempting to flee its proper venue. Sometimes it gets out, and the neighbors rightly complain." Lowering her voice, she sidled closer. Gesturing with a nod of her head, she singled out a door identified as 3C by the large brass letters that had been screwed to the wood.

"MY DEAR MISS DALAPILLY! HAVE YOU SNUCK-ERED DOWN THAT BLASTED TUNE YET?" The entire building seemed to tremble.

"Yes, sir, yes I have, sir," Miss Dalapilly piped up nervously. Tightly clutching the net holding her recaptured music, she proceeded to abandon the young visitors to the stairs and to their fate as she vanished into the apartment marked 3F.

Taking her comments to heart, the Deavys resumed their climb, making sure to keep their voices down and to step lightly on the carpeted stairs. Thankfully, no further tectonic rumblings were forthcoming from the mysterious depths of apartment 3C.

The top floor proved to be smaller than the four they had already passed. Saddled with the task of hauling the cat carrier, Simwan reached the landing a little out of breath. Burdened only by their backpacks, the girls were in fine fettle. Though they took care to kick the blue-blossomed fettle out of their way, other weeds and wildflowers growing out of the floor threatened to impede their progress toward the floor's only door. Unlike those fronting the apartments on the three levels below, it had only the number 5 attached to it, with no appended letter.

"Uncle Herkimer lives in a penthouse. Cool," declared N/Ice. Standing next to her, Rose observed that there was no doorbell. In its absence, she reached out and grabbed the heavy ring of the brass lion's-head doorknocker.

Snarling, the golden-hued lion head bared its brass teeth.

Simultaneously startled and miffed, Rose yanked her fingers back sharply. "Hey, quit that! No biting. We're relatives."

"Oh, sorry," growled the doorknocker. "I thought you were selling cookies. Those Girl Scouts somehow sneak through all obstacles in their quest to make a sale. Please come in." Emitting an appropriate grinding groan, the door swung inward.

The front room of the penthouse was larger than they expected, with a high, vaulted ceiling. The far side of the room was dominated by a quintet of tall, narrow windows that were presently blocked by heavy, dark curtains bound together with thick gold cords. Enough sunshine leaked in around the sides of the curtains to illuminate the room with diminished but adequate light. There were a couple of overstuffed eighteenth-century couches upholstered in azure blue damask, together with matching chairs, a slim-legged writing desk, and a pair of massive walnut armoires. The floor was covered with a huge carpet that might have been Persian, Berber, or Lemurian. Woven into it were fanciful images of plants and animals that no longer existed, might never have existed, or existed only in the minds of whoever had labored over the weaving. The ceiling was frescoed with stars, clouds, and a full moon that seemed to shine with a silvery internal light of its own.

Simwan's attention was drawn to a full suit of standing French armor mounted on a wooden base. The girls cooed delightedly over an oil painting in a heavy frame that depicted a young woman on a swing. A second glance was not necessary to note that the ropes of the swing were not attached to the tree in the painting. To right and left, open doorways led to other darkened rooms. Silence weighed on them like a goose down comforter on a cold winter's night. It was broken by the squeak of the door closing behind them. Sticking out of it and corresponding precisely and in proportion to the lion's-head doorknocker on the other side was the body and rear end of a male lion, rendered in brass. The tail continued to twitch back and forth and one foot to scratch the other until the door was completely shut.

A familiar feline voice came from within the plastic cat carrier, which a relieved Simwan had set down on the carpeted floor. "Someone's coming."

Footsteps that were hushed yet distinct drew the Deavys' attention to the open portal on their right. As the sounds came nearer, Simwan could hear them, too. Slow, steady footpads whose noise was muffled by thick carpet. Next to him, the coubet ceased their chattering. A figure appeared in the doorway.

It was less than a foot tall. No wonder its footfalls had made so little noise.

It had four legs and no arms, oversize pointy ears, no hair, and a short, naked tail that wagged back and forth like a runaway ballpoint pen. Like the rest of the figure, the tail was a mottled, sickly green color.

A disbelieving Amber gaped at the apparition. "Uncle Herkimer—you've become a *dog*?"

The primordial Chihuahua trotted into the room. "I *beg* your pardon. I am Señor Nutt. A friend of your uncle's. A very old friend, in every sense of the word." The small black nose tested the air, wrinkling distastefully. "Ugh. I smell cat."

From within the depths of the pet carrier an appropriate response was swiftly forthcoming. "Drop the last word and the accuracy of your observation becomes indisputable."

"Cut it out, Pithfwid." Crouching next to the carrier, Simwan unfastened the latch. "If we're going to be guests, you're going to have to get along with *everyone* who lives here."

"Hmph. Oh well. It can't be any worse than that time I was trapped for two days in the Sworl of Solemn Stinks just outside the Golden Gates of Azgremal." Stepping delicately, Pithfwid emerged from the cat carrier and glanced perfunctorily at his surroundings before his gaze settled on the diminutive canine standing before him.

"Not only dead," the cat sniffed disdainfully, "but bald as well."

"Unburdened by an unnecessary coat," the Chihuahua responded brusquely. Advancing, it cautiously and with obvious reluctance touched its nose to that of its feline visitor. Sparks flared from Pithfwid's tail, but that perpetual-motion appendage bottled up only slightly. From the greenish dog came the faint odor of essential preservation.

"You're cute." Crouching, Rose patted the animal on its head. "You're dead too."

"Naturally," admitted the dog. "Quite ironic, in a way. Instead of digging up bones, another dog dug up me. Your uncle took me in, and we've been together ever since. I've actually been dead considerably longer than Herkimer. I have Aztec ancestors, you see. I come from a noble line of canines that stretches all the way back to the dire wolf."

"How the mighty hath shrunketh." Pithfwid had wandered off and was sniffing the furniture. Encountering a spot that Señor Nutt had sprayed, he drew back sharply, his nose offended. "Or stunketh, depending on the particular sense in use at the moment of revelation."

"Nephew Simwan!" a slightly louder voice suddenly exclaimed, "and the whole Deavy coubet! How wonderful to see you, and all grown up, too!"

All eyes turned to the doorway that had brought forth the dead dog. Standing framed in the portal was an old man. Taller and skinnier than their father, he had tufts of white hair growing from the sides of his head. Also from his nostrils and ears, the sight of which the four visitors determined to ignore. Clad in a tattered but still serviceable shirt of maroon silk, matching dark pants, and hand-made Spanish loafers, he sported a gold skull earring in his left ear and heavy rings on several fingers. Spreading his arms wide, he welcomed them warmly—until his right arm fell off at the shoulder.

"Drat." Reaching down, he picked up the disarticulated limb and forcefully jammed it back into its momentarily vacant socket. "That's the trouble with being dead. Maintenance."

"Uncle Herkimer!" Delighted, the girls rushed into his welcoming arms, careful not to press the less securely attached right one. He managed a hug without losing any other body parts, then released them and stepped forward.

"And Simwan." Unexpectedly alert eyes, though blotchy with age and migrating cataracts, brightened at the sight of the young man standing next to the cat carrier. Slipping off his backpack and letting it slide to the floor, Simwan extended a hand.

Herkimer took it firmly. The grip came down, as expected, on the side of clammy and cold. Yet Simwan did not feel distanced. This was his uncle, after all. A close relative, not simply some strange zombie. When Herkimer withdrew his fingers, Simwan waited politely until his uncle was looking the other way before wiping the slime from his hand.

"It's so good to have company." Glancing down, Herkimer added, "Isn't it, Señor Nutt?"

"Aye and arf. It is good to have company." The dog was keeping a wary eye on Pithfwid as the presently indigo and white-spotted cat continued his methodical inspection of the furniture. "Though only time will tell if the company is good."

"Now, now, Señor N," Herkimer admonished him, wagging a cautionary finger at the dog. "You two need to be friends. I'm the only one allowed to do any mournful howling around here." Raising his gaze, he smiled at Simwan and the girls, displaying an astonishing array of ragged, broken, stained, and inlaid teeth the mere sight of which would have been sufficient to send even the most stalwart orthodontist fleeing in terror from the sight.

"Come this way, children, and I'll show you to your room. Only one for the five of you, I'm afraid. I don't get much company, so I only ever have one room ready for guests."

Simwan's concern vanished as soon as he saw where they were expected to stay. Like the rest of the apartment, it was much larger than he expected. There were three beds. This suggested that two of the girls would have to double up, but N/Ice volunteered to sleep in the air above one of the beds, thus allowing Rose and Amber to each have their own. A padded window seat promised Pithfwid plenty of comfort as well as a view of the street below from beneath the bottom edge of the gold-fringed curtain. Many of the blood-red tiles that walled the attached bathroom were broken or chipped, as was the matching red bathtub-shower, but Herkimer assured them that the water that emerged from the penthouse's pipes was clear and clean, and that if it was not hot enough, he would have a word with the building's devil of a custodian.

"We'll be fine," Rose assured him as she tossed her backpack onto one metal-framed bed.

Herkimer mustered an affectionate smile. "I'm just happy to see you, my nephew and nieces, and to have some company for a little while." A ghostly green, partially decomposed hand fluttered in the direction of a distant cabinet. "See? I even have television. No cable or satellite, I'm afraid. Just what the building's roof antenna can bring in. But this is New York. There's plenty to watch."

"You watch TV?" Simwan asked as he looked around for Pithfwid. Where had the cat gotten himself to? He hoped their pet was not eating Uncle Herkimer's canine companion, though he didn't think dead dog was much to Pithfwid's taste.

"Not much else to do when you're deceased," Herkimer told him, "though I think I'm more alive than some of the stuff that's on these days." He took a step backward. "I'll let you kids unpack. When you're through, come into the kitchen and we'll discuss how you're going to spend your vacation."

As soon as he was gone and N/Ice had sealed the door, the Deavys gathered around Rose's bed. She was already talking on her cell phone, which, surprisingly, still functioned on the out-of-the-way street.

"Hi, Dad. Yes, it's me, Rose. We're here at Uncle Herkimer's and just settling in." A pause, then, "Yes, the train ride was very—entertaining." Nearby, N/Ice and Amber had to stifle their reactions. Simwan just stood and shook his head silently.

His sister's expression fell and he was immediately concerned.

"Oh. Oh, Dad." The look on Rose's face as she glanced up at her siblings told them more than they needed to know. "Well, tell her we all love her, and that we'll be home soon. Bye." She terminated the call and sat quietly.

Amber took a step forward. "What is it, Rose? What's wrong?"

The other girl swallowed. "Mom's in the hospital. But she says not to come home just yet. There's nothing we can do. The stupid Ord doctors don't know what's wrong with her, of course. Dad said he's going to insist that somebody come down from Boston to treat her."

"It won't matter." N/Ice's expression, like her tone, was grim. "Mom needs to have the Truth close to her." She looked at her brother. "We have to get started looking for it right away."

"In the morning." Despite being as worried as his sisters, Simwan knew it was incumbent on him to provide rational, sensible instructions. "We're all tired from the trip, we just got here, and we're liable to do more bad than good if we try to go stumbling around the city while we're exhausted. Agreed?"

Troubled but understanding, the two-and-a-half of them nodded.

"Are we going to tell Uncle Herkimer why we're really here?" Rose wondered aloud as she put her phone back in her pack.

"We can't," Simwan declared firmly. "He's a really sweet dead guy, but he's liable to tell Mom and Dad. If we're going to get back the Truth, we have to be able to operate without parental controls."

"Yeah," agreed Amber. "You know Mom." She proceeded to perfectly mimic Melinda Mae's voice. "'No invocations, no summoning in front of Ords.'"

"'No levitating,'" added Rose with mock solemnity.

"'No slip-sliding between dimensions,'" finished N/Ice, with a certainty that only the sole twelve-year-old girl in Washow County, Pennsylvania, who thought Stephen Hawking's books were travel guides would have.

Simwan nodded. "As far as Uncle Herkimer and Señor Nutt are concerned, we're all here on break, to enjoy the city, have a good time, and help him get ready for All Hallow's. Not that we can't do all that, too," he added, "but our principal task is to return the Truth to Mr. Gemimmel's store."

"Well, the Truth isn't worth anything on an empty stomach." Slipping off the overstuffed bed (without pausing to contemplate what it might be stuffed with, and ignoring the slight, disturbed moan that came from deep, deep within the depths of the mattress as she took her leave), Rose headed for the door. "I'm starving! Let's see what Uncle Herkimer has to eat."

"For sure," agreed Amber eagerly. "We haven't had anything to eat except snacks since we left home this morning."

It was only by coincidence that the yapping and yowling they heard happened to be coming from the kitchen. Both cries were oddly distorted, though at first Simwan could not identify the origin. As he and the coubet entered the cooking area, the source quickly revealed itself.

Initially, it was impossible to tell whether Señor Nutt was chasing Pithfwid, or the other way around. Both were moving so fast that they were little more than a couple of blurs: one pale green and black, the other ebony tipped with crimson. They crisscrossed the limited dimensions of the curtain-darkened kitchen like a pair of runaway electrons, streaking across not only the floor but the table, chairs, appliances, walls, and even the ceiling.

"Stop it, you two!" Simwan shouted. "Pithfwid—Señor Nutt; quit fighting!"

The pair of streaks halted abruptly—on the ceiling. Rose had to step aside as drool from the tongue-lolling, heavily panting, upside-down Chihuahua dripped to spatter on the floor. A few feet in front of the dog, Pithfwid hung downward, his claws dug into the plaster. An indication of the speed at which the cat had been traveling, tiny wisps of smoke rose from the vicinity of his paws.

"We're not fighting," the cat announced.

"Indeed." Señor Nutt's oversize, pointed ears cocked downward in the direction of the upward-staring visitors. "We are merely engaging in a little friendly inter-species exercise." Turning his attention to Pithfwid, he added, "I thank you for the workout. Most of the time I am reduced to chasing my own tail for exercise. Not only is that particular activity inadequate for the purpose to which it is put, but the resultant tornadic vortex, albeit on a small scale, tends to play havoc with the furniture."

"Don't mention it." Grudgingly, Pithfwid added, "For a dead dog, you move pretty well."

"Compliment noted. May I say that your skill at running through objects as well as around them is unprecedented in my long experience?"

"Look," an exasperated Simwan told them, "I don't care if you two are going to argue, fight, or work out a formal dance routine, but do it on the floor, will you? You're liable to mess up Uncle Herkimer's ceiling."

Señor Nutt let out a small yip of disdain. Nevertheless, he promptly relinquished his foothold on the ceiling and dropped. At the last possible instant he twisted himself completely around, to land gently and right-side up on all four feet. Completing a successful four-point landing of his own, Pithfwid went entirely pink, sat down, and began licking one overheated paw.

Meanwhile, N/Ice had moved to the refrigerator. It was a surprisingly massive affair, its stainless-steel, double-doored front suggesting a commercial rather than a home model. The hum from its powerful compressor was deep and steady. The oversize unit was obviously maintained in markedly better condition than the ancient, dirty white electric stove and mold-encrusted sink that comprised the remainder of the major kitchen appliances.

"I'll have tuna, if you please," Pithfwid volunteered helpfully as Simwan tugged open the left-side door.

A hard young man to shock, the senior Deavy present nonetheless stumbled backward in astonishment and let out a small yelp of surprise.

Though the bulb inside the refrigerator had long since burned out, there was ample light in the room to show that there were no shelves. Occupying the entire compartment was a single solitary figure. As the girls came closer for a better look and Simwan held his ground, the figure's eyes snapped open to regard them.

"Just taking a little nap." Uncle Herkimer lowered the arms that had been crossed over his chest. Stepping out, he closed the door behind him and stretched slightly.

"You sleep in the refrigerator?" Amber asked him, slightly wide-eyed.

"Well, of course." Herkimer smiled. "How else do you think I keep this long-demised body in shape? I tell you, in July, there are those in this city among the living who would dearly love to do likewise, if only they could get around the awkward business of needing to breathe. As you know, I don't have that problem."

"Then where do you keep your food?" N/Ice leaned forward to peer into the empty, lightly padded refrigerator compartment.

"I don't have that problem, either," he told her.

Putting her hands on her hips, Rose regarded her half a sister. "Well, *duh*! I mean, he's dead."

N/Ice was defiant. "That doesn't mean he isn't interested in a snack now and then, just for memory's sake."

"Not really." Herkimer moved toward the table and folded his crumbling corpus into one of the old chairs. "Food's not much fun when your sense of taste has been gone more than a hundred years, and being a ghoul never really appealed to me." He shook his head distastefully. "All that moaning and wailing and bawling mournfully in the middle of the night. Too much like politics." He brightened. "But there's a nice neighborhood market a couple of blocks away, in the direction of the South Street Seaport. You can buy whatever you want there and cook it here." He indicated the monolithic fridge. "Plenty of storage room on the other side."

"So we'd keep our food in—with you?" Amber considered the prospect. "Eewww—that sounds great!"

"And this is New York," Herkimer reminded them yet again. "There are interesting places to eat on every block, on every street. Just be careful that anything you buy hasn't been dead too long. As non-Ords, you'll be offered all sorts of exotic dishes. Some of them with food on them."

"We'll be careful, Uncle Herkimer." Drifting upward, a dreamily diaphanous N/Ice fell to an examination of the kitchen ceiling where Pithfwid and Señor Nutt had been gamboling. "A little glue and a simple blending spell and I think I can fix this."

Amber made a disgusted noise. "The only blending spell you know is the one Mom showed us for Socratic mousse."

Her sister peered down at her, defiantly. "So? I happen to think it will work for wallpaper, too. The constituent organic components . . ."

While his sisters energetically debated the merits of paste-summoning and ceiling repair, Simwan settled himself into a chair next to his uncle. Fiddling with his left ear, which was threatening to fall off at any moment, Herkimer smiled through horrifically bad teeth.

"So, nephew, what do you kids want to see first? The Museum of Natural History? The Metropolitan Museum of Art? The Empire State Building? The Efferwhere of Sensorlium? Or maybe you'd like to go shopping? There's always Macy's, though I guess that'd be more for the girls. You—you'd probably like the Shop of All Worlds. I'm told there's a really nice little restaurant next door: Mirabilis Southwest. Specializes in Tex-Mex-Hex." Folding his moldering hands, he rested them on the table. "Myself, I never was big on spicy food."

"That all sounds great, Uncle Herkimer. But first . . ."

"But first," Señor Nutt piped up from next to him, pausing in his race with Pithfwid, "there's something I have to know. Something that's intrigued me ever since Herkimer told me who was coming to visit."

An uncertain Simwan braced himself. Had he and his sisters overlooked something in the course of their careful planning? Something this uncanny dog had sniffed out? "Uh, sure, Señor Nutt. What is it you need to know?"

"How did your parents ever come up with a name like Simwan for a nice boy like yourself?"

Simwan sighed. It wasn't the first time he'd been asked that question, and he doubted it would be the last. "It was all an accident. The name, I mean: not me. As I was told it, the nurse attending the ward where they put me after I was born was from the Old Country. Nobody ever said which Old Country. The story is that she was always kind of hard to understand at the best of times, and not real careful with her magic, and on that night she'd had a lot to drink. Whenever anyone came to visit and to see the new Deavy baby, she got kinda confused when she was trying to point me out, and kept saying, 'Someone's right there for you. Someone's right there in that bed.' Intentionally or not, she enchanted the name right onto me. The Ords who ran hospital administration were unsure about it, but by then it was too late, and you have to keep in mind that this was rural Pennsylvania. There's lots of unusual ethnic names in rural Pennsylvania." He shifted his backside on the kitchen chair, trying to ignore the subtle, crawling movements within the seat.

"After that, the name kind of stuck. I say 'kind of' because my parents couldn't just name me 'Someone.' I mean, how would that work out? People would be looking for 'someone,' and they'd invariably come after me. Or a person reporting a crime wouldn't be able to identify the perpetrator, so they'd say 'Well, all I know is that someone did this,' and the police would come looking for me." Tired of having to tell the story of his name yet again, he found himself using one finger to trace circles on the tabletop. He would erase them later.

"So my parents settled on Simwan, which sounded enough like the name the nurse had imprinted on me not to cause confusion, but different enough to keep me from having to deal with constant misunderstandings all my life."

As the explanation lapsed, Herkimer took over again. "Now then: back to your vacation. Where do you want to go and what do you and your sisters want to see first?"

Simwan considered how best to reply. He and the coubet had already decided that they couldn't tell their uncle why they had really come to New York. Just as they had when they were convincing their parents to let them make the trip, they had to pretend that they were there to sightsee, and get educated. At the same time, Uncle Herkimer had been so accommodating and so sweet that it pained Simwan to have to lie. He had an idea.

"Actually, we're not really sure. I guess what we need to do first is check everything out and then make some decisions." He made a show of scrutinizing his surroundings, even though he knew what he was about to ask for was not likely to be found in the kitchen. "Do you have a guidebook?"

"Why certainly!" Herkimer rose, tottering no more than usual, and beckoned for Simwan to follow him into the front room. "Your parents didn't send one along with you?"

"I have the *Metaphysician's Manual for New York* on my tablet, but that's not exactly the same thing as a regular tourist guidebook. It's mostly about the right places for a visiting non-Ord to sleep, eat, and invoke."

"Quite so. Well, let's see what we can scare up."

As the two of them entered the front room, a pair of streaking shapes rocketed past Simwan's legs, one on either side. A pair of very small sonic booms followed in their wake.

"Señor Nutt, Pithfwid—don't you two break anything, now!" Herkimer shook a warning finger in the general direction of the two disappearing streaks as he approached a bookcase filled with moldering, cobweb-clad tomes. "Pets—I tell you, sometimes I wonder if they're worth it."

Simwan was struck by a sudden thought. Fortunately, it was a small, relatively soft thought, and so left no mark. "Where does Señor Nutt sleep?"

"On the other side of the refrigerator, of course." Bending low, his back creaking audibly with the effort, Herkimer studied a shelf of books, using an index finger to move from one title to the next. "But don't worry—he won't eat your food. He doesn't eat any more than I do, and his bed doesn't take up any more space than a frozen pizza. Ah, here we are." Pulling out a slim, blue-bound volume, he passed it to Simwan.

It was exactly what his uncle had promised: *A Compleat and Thorough Guide to All of New York City, Including Its Boroughs and the Surrounding Countryside*. Simwan flipped to the back of the title page. It required an effort not to smile.

"Uncle Herkimer, this was published in 1869."

"It was?" Taking the book, Herkimer squinted at the small print. "Dear me. Well, I don't get to bookstores much anymore. Or any other kind of stores, for that matter. What to do, what to do . . ." Resting his chin in his right hand (to keep his head from falling off) he pondered the conundrum for a moment, then nodded knowingly.

"I suppose you can go buy a current guidebook. Or download one. That might be best. Or even better, you can put any specific requests to Mr. Everywhere."

Simwan made a face. "Mr. who?"

"Mr. Everywhere. Old friend of mine. Not dead. Just kind of immortal."

Wondering how someone could be "kind of immortal," Simwan thought rapidly. "He knows New York?"

Uncle Herkimer laughed. Though it was more of a deathly, hollow cough, there was no mistaking the genuine delight in it. "Mr. Everywhere knows New York, London, Rome—he's a wandering city boy, he is. Likes the fast life, the night life." Moving to the desk, which dated from no later than the Federalist Period of American furniture, he put pencil to work on paper. "I'll give you directions on how to find him. Just tell him your interests and he'll tell you where to go and how to get to them."

"For *any* place in New York?" Simwan's tone was hesitant as he continued to query his uncle.

"Anyplace," Herkimer assured his nephew. "Anything you want to see, Mr. Everywhere will know about it."

A hopeful Simwan watched his uncle's dead fingers wrestle with the recalcitrant pencil. If he and his sisters were lucky, maybe "anyplace" even included the hiding place of the Crub. It had better, he thought.

From the tone of Rose's conversation with their father, and while he did not want to add any more gloom to what was already a serious mission, it seemed to him that their mother might be running out of time.

-IX-

When he finally awoke and looked at his watch, which he had left facing him on the nightstand, Simwan was startled to see that it was already after eight o'clock in the morning. Recalling the gravity of his mother's condition and the need for speed, he blinked away reluctant sleep and started to sit up—only to be struck square in the face by something large, heavy, and relentless. It was followed by another of its kind, and another, all assaulting him with obvious intent to smother. Still only half awake, he fought back furiously. He relaxed his efforts only when the laughter started to penetrate his panic.

Irate, he flung out both arms and shouted "ALAMAK!" The heavy pillows, stuffed with feathers plucked from reluctant lyre-birds, were flung aside to reveal his mischievous two-and-a-half sisters already mostly dressed, drifting near the foot of his bed and laughing at him.

"Did you *see* his face?" Amber could hardly contain herself.

Rose was pointing. "Brother, you looked like the Crub itself was in bed with you!"

N/Ice, for her part, was laughing so hard she kept flashing in and out of existence.

"All right, all right. Very funny." Trying (and failing) to ignore their laughter, he slid out of bed and starting jamming his legs into his pants. "Get yourselves together. We've got a long day ahead of us and no time to waste."

Being male, it took him far less time to get ready than it did his sisters, so their considerable head start meant the four of them were all more or less prepared to leave at about the same time. They slipped out of the apartment quietly, not wanting to wake Herkimer or Señor Nutt. Simwan took charge of the apartment key their uncle had left out for them. Only Pithfwid had to be reminded to keep his voice down as they stepped out into the hall and started for the central stairwell.

When outside his carrier, the Deavy cat was obliged to travel on a leash lest his free-roaming presence upset some felinophobe Ord. Even though no leash or line could restrain or hold him if he wished otherwise, he resented even the appearance of such a restriction. Necessity, however, demanded that he bear indignity with dignity. Manhattan was not Clearsight, and its inhabitants held different feelings about the wisdom of letting animals run "loose."

"Take it easy," Simwan told him, gripping the leash a little tighter. "Slow down."

Pithfwid complied, albeit reluctantly. "I just don't want anyone to get any wrong ideas about who is leading whom."

It was on the second floor that they encountered the two dwarves and the leprechaun crossing the hall. The trio's attire differed as dramatically as did their appearance. All three looked to be about the same age, though with the leprechaun it was hard to tell.

"I'll bet he dyes his whiskers," Amber whispered to N/Ice as she nodded in the direction of the stunted, green-clad, red-haired resident. In contrast, the two dwarves positively flaunted their graying tufts. They were dressed more casually, in jeans and cotton shirts. One wore a leather bomber jacket while his companion was clad in a more tasteful full-length winter coat. London Trog, Simwan guessed, having seen the attire advertised in one of the numerous odd magazines to which his parents subscribed.

"Top o' the mornin' to ye," the leprechaun called out to the cluster of Deavys as they descended the stairs. "I heard old Herkimer had relatives a'visitin'."

"Good day," added the dwarf in the leather jacket politely. Lost deep in thought, his companion did not offer a greeting.

"Where are you off to?" N/Ice was nothing if not direct.

The dwarf pointed to the far end of the hall. "Number 2B. Waltzinger's place. It's our weekly poker game."

Passing the Deavys, the fey trey reached the end of the hall. Glancing over his shoulder, Simwan could just see a massive, coal-black hand covered with rocklike nodules opening the door to apartment 2B. The treelike fingers gripped the door high up, near where it met the lintel, which made him wonder just how large the occupant of that particular apartment might be.

Though the day remained overcast with low clouds, it was amazing how quickly the light seemed to brighten once they had walked a couple of blocks from Uncle Herkimer's street. All of a sudden there were people everywhere: well-dressed men and women hurrying to and fro, teenagers traveling in small barking packs, children clinging onto the hands of their parents or nannies or older siblings, looking for all the world like commuters hanging onto the overhead straps inside a subway car.

Ords, all of them, Simwan saw. Ordinary people, living ordinary lives, ignorant of those who had access to special abilities and unique knowledge dwelling among them. Those like himself, and his sisters, and the cat leading them on his leash. He did his best to take the measure of everyone who passed him on the sidewalk. Though it was possible to overlook a non-Ord, it was uncommon. Finding themselves outside what appeared to be a nice, clean, inexpensive restaurant that served breakfast, Simwan led them in. It was busy, which he knew was a good sign. Much as the girls might dislike letting their big brother always take the lead, their mother had impressed on them how important it was for them to do so in order to mollify the cultural expectations of ignorant Ords.

"Four for breakfast, please," he told the young woman in charge of seating customers.

She started to escort them to a table, then halted. "You can't bring that animal in here." A finger pointed accusingly at Pithfwid.

It took an effort for the cat not to bristle angrily, much less hold back from turning the hostess into a newt. Instead, he walked up to her and began rubbing himself against her lower legs while purring like a smothered locomotive.

"Please?" pleaded Rose, making her eyes as big and limpid

as possible. "We can't leave him outside. Somebody might try to take him." (Pity the poor person who did, Simwan thought while keeping silent.) "We'll keep him under the table, out of sight. Nobody will see him, or hear him. He's very well behaved," she added, concluding with a lie.

"Well . . ." Hesitating, the hostess looked around for her boss. "Pretty please?" added Amber, making her eyes as mirror-big as her sister's.

Abruptly, the hostess broke into a sympathetic smile. "Come with me, kids. Keep him between you."

She led them to a table next to the long front window, where they could not only watch the endlessly fascinating foot traffic outside, but where Pithfwid could curl up against a wall and out of sight. Simwan, Rose, and Amber ordered omelets and toast and potatoes with onions while N/Ice opted for the waffles. Rose waved a menu in her sibling's face.

"What are you gonna put on waffles here, sis? This isn't home. There's no ambrosia. Just fake maple syrup."

"I *like* fake maple syrup," N/Ice countered. "I didn't expect ambrosia. I know it can't be like home cooking."

It certainly was not, but the food that arrived sooner than expected was tasty and filling. Periodically reaching under the table, Simwan slipped Pithfwid samples from his own plate. A feline of wide-ranging tastes, Pithfwid was content to eat everything that was passed to him, from buttered toast to bits of egg.

When they had finished, Simwan examined the receipt, chose a pretreated bill from the wad in his wallet, spit on it, and passed it three times over the single gold denarius he always carried with him. It took a moment for the avuncular portrait of Benjamin Franklin to appear on the front of the newly enchanted bill. As soon as it had properly solidified, Franklin winked back at him from the face of the bill, then went quiescent.

Uncle Herkimer's instructions for finding Mr. Everywhere had been straightforward. Go down this street, find a place to have breakfast, then continue on to this place, turn right, walk so many blocks, and enter the designated subway entrance.

"But if he's everywhere," Rose had speculated with her wonderful muddle of thoughtfulness and innocence, "why isn't he just here?"

"Even everywhere can't be everywhere at once," Herkimer had explained. "Because if everywhere was everywhere, then there'd be no room for nowhere, and we know that nowhere has to be somewhere, now don't we?"

Rose had left it at that. The subway entrance their uncle had specified would have to suffice.

The stairs were narrow, busy, and no dirtier than they expected. Once below the surface, the omnipresent street noise was drowned out by the echoing clip-clop of many feet, the distant rise and fade of the rumbling subway, and a thickening of the atmosphere that was the result of hundreds of Ords exhaling heavily within a warm enclosed space.

Tiled walls lined with glassed-in advertising boxes split off into two corridors. After a moment's hesitation and a brief caucus, the Deavys chose the tunnel on their right. It soon opened up onto a platform fronting empty tracks. Several dozen commuters waited, sitting on benches and reading or standing and waiting for the next train (most Ords were already at work). The dark mouths of the train tunnel were visible to left and right. Across the tracks, other travelers awaited trains going in the opposite direction. An empty, boarded-up concession booth occupied the center of the platform.

"He's got to be here somewhere." Amber was looking around restlessly, searching the platform and the benches. None of the people who were present looked like someone who could be everywhere.

"Uncle Herkimer said we'd know him when we saw him." Rose had started up the platform, unobtrusively studying the faces of each commuter as she passed.

"That's not much of a description." More solid than usual, N/Ice joined her sisters in scrutinizing the travelers.

They split up, wandering among the largely silent commuters, the girls covertly listening in on several of the stolid travelers who were wearing personal music playback devices in hopes of overhearing something new and interesting. Simwan's seeking was more restrained, constrained as he was by the need to keep track of Pithfwid. Fortunately, there were no other pets on the platform and therefore nothing with which the obstreperous Deavy cat could become embroiled.

Inordinately perceptive, the coubet identified insurance adjusters and office clerks, assistant chefs and oily mechanics, temp teachers and daydreaming librarians, but none who might qualify for the sobriquet Mr. Everywhere. When the next train stopped, everyone who had been waiting got on. Those who emerged shuffled in massed silence toward the two exits. Within moments, the platform was deserted. One by one, the next batch of southbound travelers wandered down to the platform from the street above. And still no sign of anyone who could be Mr. Everywhere.

Then Pithfwid's ears perked up. Not surprisingly, having far more sensitive hearing than any of his merely human companions, it was he who heard the music first.

Simwan felt a purposeful tug on the leash. "What's up?"

Glancing around and back, Pithfwid favored him with an urgent expression but said nothing. He couldn't, now that Ord commuters were repopulating the waiting platform. Simwan allowed himself to be led forward. Behind him, Rose saw what was happening and notified her sisters.

The music was coming from the far side of the tracks. They had to go down a flight of stairs, cross under the tracks, and come up on the other platform. The blank-faced commuters waiting on the opposite side were no different from those they had previously encountered. Only the music was new. It came from a banjo. This battered but still serviceable instrument was being plucked and strummed by a middle-aged man of dubious appearance and unsteady mien. He sat cross-legged on the floor, his back resting against another shuttered concession kiosk, a tattered floral cushion the only intermediary between his flat backside and the cold concrete. A smattering of coins and a couple of bills lay in the open instrument case lying in front of him. He was shorter than Simwan, shorter even than the girls, with jet-black curly hair exploding out from beneath a battered brown fedora and a tangle of a beard in which anything from lice to a small lemur could have been hiding. His brown jacket was open and unzipped to reveal a stained blue and white shirt, and there was a hole near the left cuff of his dark serge slacks.

At the moment, he was playing something wistful. From his music studies, Simwan recognized it as a traditional Bohemian folk lament better suited to a mandolin than a banjo. It seemed an odd selection for a subway busker. Focusing on his instrument, the short, swarthy figure concluded the dirge and effortlessly segued into a Mozart violin concerto. Simwan had never heard Mozart played on a banjo and suspected the man had fashioned the necessary transcription himself. Leaning over, Simwan spoke to the black cat on the leash.

"That him?"

For the nonce, there were no other commuters, or music lovers, nearby. Pithfwid glanced up and nodded confidently. "That's him."

The coubet had gathered alongside their brother. "That's Mr. Everywhere?" Amber was unconvinced. "He doesn't look like much."

"He's certainly not what I expected." Rose frowned as she studied the cross-legged lump of human dishevelment.

"Definitely a letdown," put in N/Ice for good measure.

"How do you know it's him?" Simwan whispered to the cat.

Raising a paw, Pithfwid pointed. "Several reasons. A number of astral axes align in his presence. He stinks of data. And lastly, I notice that his posterior is not actually in contact with that cushion."

Blinking, Simwan crouched down as low as he could without drawing the curious attention of the commuters behind them. It was true: There was a gap of a millimeter or so between the busker's backside and the cushion he was nominally sitting upon.

They were soon standing close to the banjo picker as he shifted effortlessly from Mozart to Mahler. A bit of the *Erlicht* solo, Simwan noted. It was doubtful that Mahler had ever envisioned his sublime music being played on a banjo. Still the player did not look up. Reaching into her purse, Rose took out a coin and tossed it into the open instrument case. Maybe it was the arrival of the money that made the man finally stop playing and raise his gaze. Maybe it was the fact that the coin (albeit a small denomination) came from the original hoard of King Midas. Rheumy brown eyes blinked at them, traveling from coubet to cat to Simwan. Like oil dispersing on a wave, the corneas cleared even as Simwan met the player's gaze.

"Now what would a quintet of such curious aspect as yourselves want with such as me?" His fingers strummed lightly over the strings of the banjo, and this time they seemed to quiver with a special intensity, sending out vibrations not all of which lay within the realm of human ken.

"You are Mr. Everywhere." The way Amber said it, softly and with hope, made it sound like something other than an accusation.

The stocky player chuckled. "Well, I don't know about everywhere, but I'm here, anyway. Everybody has to be somewhere, don't they?" He plucked out a tune. Simwan thought he recognized a paean to Ramses II, usually strummed on a lyre. "Got a request? Want to hear something special?"

"We need some information," he told the cross-legged figure. "Our mother is in trouble and our uncle suggested we query you. He said that if we wanted to find something anywhere in the city, you were the one to ask."

"Did he now? Your uncle must be a person of a certain discernment."

"He is," N/Ice put in, "even if he is dead."

"The dead are full of knowing." The player squinted at her, straining to see better. "My goodness—you're not all there, are you, my dear?"

"You know how it is." N/Ice pushed at her hair.

"I don't know about this 'Mr. Everywhere' stuff you've been told. I'm just a simple busker. I sit here and play my band of Jo, trying to eke out a living."

"If everyone knew who you really were, you'd eke out a living," Simwan countered. "You're Mr. Everywhere, and as such, you can answer our question." He tried to stand a little taller. "In the name of the eternal internal, we ask that you do so."

The eyes that met his own were in no ways wise or rheumy now. "You're pretty sure of yourself, sonny. If I'm who you say I am, then I could be somewhere else right now. I might not be here at all. How then could there be any answer to your question?" As Simwan stared, the figure before him began to fade.

The leash was yanked out of his hand as Pithfwid leaped. Landing on the banjo player's right knee, the cat dug in with the claws on all four feet. Electricity climbed his tail as if it were a miniature Tesla generator, to flicker off and vanish into space. For a fearful instant, Pithfwid started to fade also. Then the cat solidified, his claws clinging tightly to reality, compelling the banjo player to hang with him. Frowning, the forcibly restrained Mr. Everywhere raised a hand to strike the cat.

Pithfwid's eyes flashed with inner fire as he regarded the man whose knee he was grasping. "I wouldn't do that if I were you. Better to stick around awhile."

"It's a rare day when I encounter music lovers so persistent. All right then. Present your query. But be quick about it." He indicated the open instrument case. "I'm not making any money squatting here yakking with you."

Pulling out his wallet, Simwan let fall another blank bill. By the time it came to rest in the yawning black case, it had morphed into a twenty. The player's eyes glittered.

"Well now, that's a sight more welcome than even a well-worded compliment. Your question?" He glanced at the cat still fastened to his knee. "And if you wouldn't mind letting up a mite with that grip, kitty, as I believe you are beginning to draw blood?" Pithfwid responded by relaxing, but not completely releasing, his grasp.

"We're looking for something," Amber informed him impatiently.

"What is it you're looking for, girl-on-the-cusp?"

"It's the Truth, it's in a bottle," Rose told him, "and it is intimately tied to our family. Especially to our mother. It was taken by a resident of this city who is called the Crub."

At the mention of the name, the man's now perfectly clear eyes went wide. His mouth opened and the shock on his face was palpable. Around the Deavys the light grew dim and yellowed, as if the power to the station, or perhaps the world, had been suddenly interrupted. The train tracks on their right, the platform opposite, the commuters waiting behind them—all faded from view without quite entirely disappearing. While the banjo remained unaltered, its owner expanded and diffused, until like a giant ghost he occupied the entire volume of the tunnel except for the place where his questioners were standing. Finding himself suddenly clinging to not much more than air, Pithfwid dropped ten inches to the ground.

An obviously frightened Mr. Everywhere now really *was* everywhere, except for the small space where they were.

As for the rest of the world, it was gone.

-X-

For Bubastis's sake, unseethe thyself!" Pithfwid snapped irritably, looking up at the now gigantic—if diffuse—head of the banjo player where it hovered near the ceiling. "Get a hold of yourself, or I'll have to do so again. And if you leave it up to me, it won't be pretty. I'll draw more than blood this time."

Like a balloon rapidly losing air, Mr. Everywhere collapsed and condensed. As he returned to the size, shape, and density of a human, the light around the Deavys brightened and they once more could view their surroundings clearly. None of the waiting commuters had reacted to what had happened because it had happened outside their ordinary realm of perception. They stood still, isolated, and indifferent as ever, engrossed in their music players, their newspapers, their tablets, and their cell phones.

But the banjo player was breathing hard. "You're telling me that you're looking for the Crub? *Intentionally?*"

N/Ice nodded. "We promised our local druggist, Mr. Gemimmel, that we'd get the Truth back. He was just looking after it for our family, and he feels terrible about what's happened. We have to, so the people in our town will realize what's going on with a proposed development, and feel the presence of the Truth in their lives, and vote to stop it." She dropped her eyes to the pavement. "And so that our mom will get better and be able to get out of the hospital."

"Isn't there something else you can use instead? A right proper enchantment, maybe, or a powder, or a dead serpent's tears?"

Rose shook her head resolutely. "Nope. It's got to be the Truth."

"And the Crub pilfered it," Amber added.

"But—you're just children." On the strings of his instrument, Mr. Everywhere plucked out a sad mad wail of a tune that hailed from the Red Cliffs of Mongolia. "Children against the Crub," he said and shook his head dolefully.

"We're not *just* children," Simwan informed him firmly. "We're *Deavys*."

"Ah-hmm," considered the musician.

"We're not asking you to come with us," Pithfwid murmured cajolingly. "Just to give us some directions. We'll deal with this Crub by ourselves."

The man looked up from where he was once again seated with his back against the vacant concession stand. "Will you now? I suppose it's not for me to say. But the Crub . . ." His voice trailed off. "If I help you, you must swear by all the ancient laws of Mesopotamia that I am not to be held responsible for the consequences. I have my morality to worry about, if not my mortality."

They promptly swore as requested.

When the banjo player began to sing, Simwan realized it was not surprising that he should give them instructions in song. It was his manner of communicating best, without attracting the unwanted attention of anything that might be watching, or listening. To further confuse any possible spies, Mr. Everywhere couched his directions in the form of a most taut tautology.

"Oh, it's wet but it's dry, and as bold as the sky
But the place that you seek is quite dark.
There's no life but no death, just the bilious breath
Of some creatures as slick as the snark.
You've got to go careful, you've got to go quick
You need to be cautious, and wield a big stick.
Not the gods, not the wizards, not even dead Teddy
Will be able to help you, because it's so veddy
Veddy dangerous where you're going, where the BBDT
    is lowing
As it lies in wait for whatever comes by
In that place where the earth and the sky go to die."

Following the conclusion of this euphonious ditty, the coubet caucused, Simwan considered, and Pithfwid committed the portentous verse to memory, at which point Rose turned and said to the somber singer, "That's evocative, and almost pretty, and more than a little bit scary—but it's not real specific."

"Oh well then," responded Mr. Everywhere amiably as he

set his banjo down on his lap, "alternatively, you can take any of the lines going uptown, and get off at Central Park South." He indicted the stairway they had used to cross over to his side. "You'll have to go back to get a northbound train."

"Okay," Simwan noted. "Central Park South. Then what?"

The banjo player's shoulders rose and fell. "I dunno. All I know for sure is that the park is the only place where the Crub is known to have been seen—by those who have lived to tell of the sighting. Maybe you can find someone there who can give you more specific directions." Picking up his instrument, he slung it once more across his lap and prepared to play.

"I don't understand." Amber was no less confused and disappointed than her siblings. "If you're 'Mr. Everywhere,' then shouldn't you have been to the place where the Crub abides, too?"

A smile beamed up at her through the thicket of chin whiskers. "Even Mr. Everywhere can't be everywhere at once, or even at a fraction of once. And the Crub's lair is one where I don't care to go. So there."

"What's the 'BBDT'?" Rose asked curiously, remembering his song.

Abruptly, the light on the platform grew dim. For a second time, the other waiting passengers seemed to fade from view. Reality blurred around the Deavys, as if they were suddenly immersed not in air but in oil. Shapes appeared, swooping and soaring at the farthest range of their vision, as if eager to come closer. Mr. Everywhere looked around apprehensively. When nothing drew near, he leaned forward slightly. There was an undertone to his voice they had not heard before, and it had nothing to do with music. It was as if the itinerant banjo picker was suddenly channeling a voice from the past intent on dispensing the wisdom of the ages.

"The Big Bad Dark Thing lives away from the blue sky, away from the warmth of the sun. Laughter and happiness are its enemies, misery and despair its favored company. It sucks up the light of innocence and crushes small the hopes of young and old alike, squeezing them into little round black balls of ugliness it can then swallow easily, but with no delight. It can't be killed, it can't be swayed, it can't be stopped. It's attracted to bad things done, so it might well be after this stolen Truth itself." Eyes that were now fully alert darted from girl to boy to girl to cat to girl. "Beware, take care. You might not be alone in your search for this taken Truth. You might be having some unwelcome competition for it."

"If this whatever-it-is is also after the Truth, won't it also have to find a way to take it away from the Crub?" N/Ice had lowered her own voice without quite being certain why she had done so.

"If something it has in its possession has drawn the Big Bad Dark Thing to it, then more likely the Crub will be too busy trying to save itself to worry about a little thing like the Truth. Not even the Crub can stand against the BBDT." So saying, he cradled his banjo closer to him, much as a father might cuddle a son, and began to play again. The light on the platform brightened, the outlines of the other travelers again grew distinct, and the sounds of feet shuffling on concrete and the muted clash of competing music players were once more sharp and clear all around them. The things that had been swimming at the range of their vision diminished to nonexistence.

Despite their best efforts, the Deavy brood could not get him

to stop playing long enough to respond to their additional que-
ries. Other travelers began to pass by now, occasionally dropping
a coin or three into the open instrument case. One well-dressed
man spotted the coinage of Midas that Rose had tossed in and
tried to swap it for a quarter, only to draw his fingers back as if
bitten. For a moment he looked as if he was going to say something. Then he thought better of it and continued on his way,
muttering under his breath. Maybe it was the accusatory stare of
the unblinking Deavys that dissuaded him. Or maybe it was the
fact that, despite the coin having no rough edges, the index finger
of his grabby right hand was bleeding slightly.

Simwan tried one more time to entice the musician to
respond to them, but by now Mr. Everywhere would not even
meet his eyes. His body was still present, but it was as if the
rest of him had gone elsewhere, if not everywhere. His efforts
defeated, Simwan turned to his sisters.

"I guess we're going to Central Park."

The girls were not entirely disappointed. The park was on
their list of things to see while they were in New York. This way
they could see it while they were hunting for the Crub, and
recovering the Truth, and saving their mother.

Crossing under and over and up again, they arrived just in
time to catch the next northbound train. The girls insisted on riding in the lead car. From there they could look out its front window and watch the gloriously bright multicolored signal lights
come racing toward the train. Simwan was content to surrender
his place to them, choosing to relax on a seat with Pithfwid curled
up in his lap, listening to the rattle and rumble of the train as it
sped along its track.

It being the middle of the morning on a work day, the train was far from crowded. Most of the passengers had gravitated toward the middle cars, which would save them a few steps to the street once they reached their respective stops. The only other occupant of the front car was a fat man in a heavy twill overcoat and matching hat. He sat near the back of the car reading the *Times*. The dog whose leash the man kept wrapped around his right hand was a plug of a pug: short, tenacious, curious, flat-faced, and bright-eyed. It barked twice in Pithfwid's direction until its owner absently shushed it.

Near Simwan and Pithfwid, the Deavy coubet was laughing and gesturing delightedly as signal light after signal light came rushing toward them, only to sweep past in a blur of green or yellow. Reds were also visible, but off to right or left, signifying tracks that were closed for maintenance or other purposes. From time to time the train stopped to take on or disembark passengers. The front car remained unpopular, which suited Simwan fine.

"Now *that's* different." Rose practically had her nose pressed up against the thick pane of safety glass. Her warm breath condensed against the window, a puff of life. Amber crowded close on one side of her, N/Ice on the other.

"I see it," confirmed Amber. "There are two red lights together, but they look like they're right in front of us."

"They probably are right in front of us," opined N/Ice, "and we're going to go around a curve and miss them."

But they didn't go around a curve. The twin red lights drew closer and closer, until it seemed they were going to smash into the front of the train. The faint echo of mild cursing could be heard coming from the driver's insulated compartment: a security-sealed, windowless alcove immediately to the right of the girls and their window. Then the twin lights shot on past, on the left side of the train, and the way ahead showed normal again. That is, it did until the red lights reappeared. They were quite large: much larger than the usual track signaling lights.

And this time they were not in front of the train, but racing along parallel to it, on its left side.

Something struck the train with a solid *boom*. In the cars behind them, Simwan could hear people scream and curse. Looking back through the window located at the rear of the front car and through to the one next in line, he saw people scrambling to regain their seats. Since the train didn't stop, they assumed that the jolting episode was over and done with, its unknown cause behind them now. To an individual, they were more angry than frightened. The only exception was the heavyset man sitting in the rear of the front car. He was gawking out a left-side window as if paralyzed. His pet pug had jumped up on the hard plastic bench seat. Whimpering piteously, it was trying to force its way between the seat and its master's back.

A hiss came from Pithfwid. Hair bottled, the cat had leaped up to stand on the bench and glare out the window. Spinning around on the seat, Simwan found himself looking directly at the two bright red lights that continued to parallel the train. Except they weren't lights.

They were eyes.

Big now, big as bus wheels, bright fiery red with cup-size inky black pupils, they glowered back at him, full of malevolent intelligence. They were only the highlights of a nightmare head that was the front end of a garish, cylindrical, segmented body a hundred feet long. From each segment thrust a pair of short, pointed, shiny black legs that moved so fast they were little more than a blur. Working in tandem, dozens and dozens of them provided the means that allowed the segmented atrocity to keep pace with the train.

Simwan flinched back as for a second time the monster slammed sideways into the car. More screams from the other cars, accompanied by loud demands for the driver to do something. Emergency stop buttons were pushed, to no avail. Connections between the other cars and the driver's compartment had been damaged. Within that cubicle of isolation the driver frantically studied the readouts on his console and struggled to decide what to do next. Her instruments showed nothing amiss. According to them the train was racing along nicely on its track at its proper, predesignated speed. There was nothing to show that twice now it had nearly been knocked off its rails. External cameras indicated quite clearly that it was alone in the tunnel. Apart from the two inexplicable jolts, all was as it should be. Accordingly, she saw no reason to slow down, much less brake to an emergency stop and back up the entire line all the way to the tip of the island.

It wasn't the driver's fault, Simwan knew. She was Ord and so was her equipment. Neither could detect the gigantic, frothing, centipedelike thing that was hurtling up the tunnel alongside the train, nor could the other passengers. The exception was the poor retired gentleman who had the misfortune to be seated in the same car as the Deavy brood, and who involuntarily and greatly to his distress found himself partaking of their perception.

"Do something!" Simwan yelled at himself as much as at the coubet. Another strong shove might well knock the train off its track and send it crashing into the tunnel walls. By this time the pug's whimpering had given way to steady wailing. Between the sight of those burning red eyes so close to the window glass and the dog's unremitting howling, it was hard to think properly.

What were the right words for disposing of giant bugs? No, that wouldn't necessarily work, he told himself. The monster that threatened the train was buglike but not like any bug he had ever seen. What about the spell his mom used when she wanted to fumigate the basement? It worked for getting rid of ants and spiders and silverfish. Would it work on something this big and relentless? There was always the charm he used to clear his computer of worms, but this was decidedly larger and more powerful than any computer worm.

While he fought to think of something, the beast lunged a third time at the train, throwing its fast-moving bulk against the line of cars. This time, however, Pithfwid was ready for it, even if his humans were not. The cat spat. Lightly radiant, his spittle penetrated the thick window glass to strike the monster square in one of its huge, glowing red eyes. Wrenching back, it let out an ear-splitting shriek that sounded exactly like the whistle of an oncoming train. It was loud enough to penetrate all the cars. Momentarily panicked, the other passengers whirled or strained for a look out the nearest window. Out the right side of the train they saw only the dark, mottled stone of the tunnel speeding past while out the other side it was much the same, except for what some thought was a line of pale, pale smoke hanging in the enclosed space.

Long, curving fangs wiped furiously at the injured eye in an attempt to clean it as the subterranean apparition continued to rocket along parallel to the train. Inhaling until he was twice, then three times his normal size, Pithfwid readied himself to spit again. At the back of the rattling front car the single Ord passenger continued to sit motionless, staring neither to left nor to right. His dog cowered behind him, alternately whimpering and wailing madly.

Then N/Ice was clambering onto the bench seat alongside her brother, between him and the front of the train. While Simwan looked on uncertainly, but knowing from experience not to interfere, she stuck herself *through* the window until she was half in, half outside the speeding car. Leaning into the tunnel, the air rushing past causing her shoulder-length hair to blow wildly toward the rear of the train, she put her thumbs in her ears, waggled her fingers, and made taunting faces at the monster. Enraged, it snapped at her with its fangs. She pulled back sharply and the black, hook-shaped arcs of death scraped only the window. As the apparition resumed trying to soothe the eye where Pithfwid's caustic spittle had landed, she pushed herself through the glass a second time. This go-round she hooked her right fingers into the upper part of her mouth and the fingers of her left hand into the lower, pulled her mouth apart, dislocated her jaw, bulged her eyes, made her tongue three feet long, and wagged it at the creature. One flaming red eye half-shut with pain, the enraged monster struck furiously at her again.

Only to vanish with an accompanying cry of surprise and outrage off to the left, down the side tunnel Rose and Amber had been chanting steadily to prise open for it.

"There!" More than satisfied with her effort, N/Ice drew her extraordinary tongue back into her head, let her upper jaw rejoin the lower, retracted her eyes back into her skull, and sat down on the seat. Raising both hands palm outward, she exchanged congratulatory high fives with her sisters and then a lesser, more decorous hand-paw smack with Pithfwid. She would have swapped similar congratulations with Simwan, except that he had risen from his seat and was heading down the center of the car toward its sole Ord occupant. Well, one of two, if you counted the dog.

"P-p-please," the man was blubbering. Seriously staggered by what he had just seen and experienced, he tried to shrink back into his seat. This squashed the pug that had taken refuge there, causing it to yelp in panic. "Whatever you are, don't hurt me! Please don't!"

"*Simulacrum othway restat*," Simwan murmured gently as he came near. "*Treatis pardonai majestatus.* You saw nothing. You see nothing. You remember nothing. All is as it was. All is as it should be."

It was a good spell. A sound spell. He knew it was because he had once used it on his sixth-grade math teacher, Mrs. Apfelkopf, to make her forget that he had arrived late for a pop quiz. Upon learning of this, his father had used a spell of a different kind on him, one that had nothing to do with magic or math but everything to do with a soon-to-be-sore backside. In the long run, homework, the wincing younger Simwan had quickly determined, was decidedly less painful than using prohibited spells to casually smooth one's way through an Ord world.

The older man's eyes closed and he swayed slightly. While he was eye-closing and swaying, Simwan turned his attention to the poor dog. He didn't have time to do anything about the spreading pool of urine on the seat, but he could calm down the pooch that had peed it.

"Woof," Simwan elucidated reassuringly. "Woof woof, bark. Bark bark, arf, woof woof. Yip."

As soon as Simwan ceased reciting, the man opened his eyes. Blinking and slightly dazed, he cast a tentative look at his surroundings. Nothing was amiss. The quartet of well-dressed youngsters who constituted the entirety of his fellow passengers was still clustered at the front of the car, the three girls (or was it two?) staring out the front window at the oncoming signal lights, the teenage boy sitting quietly petting the leashed cat in his lap as the train slowed on approach to the next station. It was the man's stop. Rising to leave, he hesitated, then felt uncertainly of his coat's hem. When his hand came away damp, he turned to glower and shake a disapproving finger at his stub-legged, snub-nosed companion.

"Bad dog, Lucius. Bad dog!" Using his newspaper (but careful to save the crossword page), he blotted up nearly all of the small pool of urine, and headed for the door. When the train stopped, he disembarked hurriedly, for some unknown reason feeling it was better not to gaze too long in the direction of the children who remained on board.

Within the sealed, locked driver's compartment, a puzzled metro subway employee of seventeen years' experience opened her report file, mulled over what to enter and how to word it, and finally decided to overlook the inexplicable incident altogether. Traveling over the same section of track, the train immediately behind hers was reporting everything normal. If one of the passengers filed a complaint about the two mysterious jolts her train had endured, then and only then would she feel compelled to respond. Otherwise, she decided, there were times in one's life when it was best to pretend that nothing had happened, even when something patently had. Closing the file, she waited for the doors to sound the all clear preparatory to heading uptown to the next stop.

"What do you think it was?" An excited Rose queried her sisters and brother and pet. To look at her, to look at any of them, it was hard to imagine that they had nearly met catastrophe and death in the form of something massive and monstrous that dwelled only in the tunnels and deep places beneath the great city. But then, they were Deavys. And not just Deavys, but two-and-a-half twelve-year-olds and one sixteen-year-old and one very exceptional cat of indeterminate and indeterminable age.

"Not a bug," Simwan declared with certainty. "That was my first thought. But definitely not a bug."

"Maybe it was an *Erdekönig*. An Earth King." Amber had always had a particular interest in all things that dwelled below the surface of the earth. "If they breed here, it would provide an explanation for a lot of the troubles the New York City subway system has gone through since they first started building it."

"Maybe," conceded N/Ice, "but me, I think it was more like a subgrub. If that was a larval stage, it makes me wonder what the adult form is like."

"And what it does," added Rose.

Simwan looked down at the furry ball that was once more curled up in his lap. "Pithfwid?" The girls went silent as the cat raised its head to look at them.

"Personally, I am more concerned about the *why* of the thing than the *what* of it. If Amber is right, then we just happened to board a train that just happened to run afoul of such an extraordinary vileness. On the other paw, if it was something sent by the Crub specifically to look for and then attack us, then that contemptible creature realizes we survived its assault under the Hudson, and also knows where we are now, more or less." At the looks of concern that subsequently appeared on the faces of his humans, he added encouragingly, "*Erdekönig*, subgrub, or something else, I did not get the impression that our assailant was particularly intelligent. I don't think it capable of reporting sensibly back to its master. That is assuming it *has* a master and that its assault *was* deliberate, and not merely coincidental. In the absence of evidence to the contrary, I think we may assume the latter. But while doing so," he warned with a flick of his ears, "we should keep in mind the warning voiced by your estimable and loving uncle. That this city can be a dangerous place." He glanced up at a concerned Simwan. "Based on our experiences of the past two days, the next time we have a long distance to travel, may I humbly suggest that we take the bus?"

The remainder of their ride uptown was unmemorable, which suited Simwan just fine. The underground attack had unnerved him more than he cared to admit, mostly because of what Pithfwid had hypothesized about it potentially having been commissioned by the Crub. The quiet ride gave the cat a chance to nap while the girls resumed their delighted ogling of the tunnel lights ahead. For the duration of the journey all of the lights—green, yellow, red, and otherwise—remained nothing more than signals set along the sides of the track. None leaped out at them; none sprang to the attack. At each stop, preoccupied Ord passengers shuffled on and off, ignoring the youngsters clustered at the front of the first car.

He was feeling a lot better by the time they got off at 59th Street.

Until he realized their next steps awaited them.

-XI-

Simwan felt Pithfwid tugging him forward as they came up the steps to the edge of the area known as Central Park South. Simwan continued to study their surroundings as he followed the feline's lead. "What is it, Pithfwid? You see something?"

"Indeed I do," the cat informed him. "I suggest we pursue our inquiries there." Raising one paw, he pointed. Not far ahead up Fifth Avenue (the wide boulevard that separates the park from the line of hideously expensive apartment buildings to the east), a small cylindrical kiosk stood on the park side, like a nail emerging from an old board. Constructed of brightly painted wood in the style of its nineteenth-century predecessors, it sported a conical roof of green copper plating and slivered side windows of leaded glass. The interior glowed with a sepulchral light that only a very few highly attuned non-Ords could detect. But cats could see it easily.

Pithfwid sounded pleased as he strained once more at the leash. "Just what we need," he told his humans. "An information booth!"

Hundreds of such general merchandise kiosks, of varying shape, size, and architectural merit, dotted the streets of the great city. Save for being possessed of (or possibly by) a shadowy radiance few but cats could see, this one looked little different from any of the others. Yet Pithfwid continued to insist it was an information booth.

Neither Simwan nor his sisters found the sight of the proprietor encouraging. The elderly woman sitting on the single high stool inside the structure wore her gray hair coiled up and back in a tight, no-nonsense bun. The thick glasses perched precariously on her vulturine beak of a nose were prevented from sliding downward by a chain of beads that ran around the back of her neck. She wore a faded, multicolor, buttoned-up sweater embroidered with alpacas and vicuñas. Looking at it, it was impossible to tell if it was a present from a well-heeled relative or a refugee from a thrift store. The sweater hung slightly open to reveal a white blouse beneath. A heavy woolen skirt completed the decidedly lackluster ensemble.

It was left to N/Ice to notice the earrings. At first glance they appeared to be little more than chunks of cheap rose quartz. Mineralogy being one of N/Ice's special interests, it was not surprising that she was the one to identify them as pink diamonds of approximately two carats each. Hot pink being among the scarcest of all diamond colors, and anything over a carat in that color being exceptionally rare, they were as out of place on this plain, hatchet-faced oldster as gold-plated toilet seats in a national park outhouse. In short, they did not jibe: a fact that N/Ice pointed out to her sisters in whispers.

While the girls were discussing the matter of the old woman's unlikely jewelry and without waiting to be invited, Pithfwid jumped up onto the small shelf that fronted the serving window. Instead of being startled, or objecting, the woman smiled and reached out a wrinkled, liver-spotted hand to stroke the cat's head and back. Pithfwid obligingly paced back and forth, purring like the compact dynamo that he was. Sparks jumped from his tail and the fur on his back, crackling like miniature fireworks in the cold air.

"Hello, little kitty-witty. Your wit is part of your kit, I wager." Raising her gaze, she peered over the tops of the thick reading glasses, adjusting their position with her free hand. Her eyes, Simwan noted with a start, were perfectly clear and cataract-free, the color of a glacial tarn, and so pale blue that they were almost white. "What have we here?"

As Pithfwid seemed fully occupied and for the moment disinclined to speak, Simwan looked at his sisters, who looked back at him, which left him with the task of replying.

"My name is Simwan Deavy. These are my sisters: Amber, Rose, and N/Ice—and our cat, Pithfwid."

"Always confusing the possessive," Pithfwid interjected, without adding anything useful.

"Pleased to meet you." Shrewd old eyes flicked from the first youngster to the last. "Given what I perceive about the four of you, not to mention this chatty conniver of a cat that's currently sucking up energy from my fingers, I expect it's only fair and appropriate to give my name." She did not extend a hand through the open window or across the narrow shelf. "I am Trishramenu Syranna sic Glorioso Santarem." As a clap (an applauding clap, Simwan was sure) of very distant thunder rolled and the pedestrians on Fifth Avenue curiously checked the increasingly cloudy sky for signs of rain, she smiled, showing oddly perfect teeth. "You charming dearies may call me the Witch Trish."

The girls were unreservedly—if not literally—captivated. "A real witch!" Rose exclaimed excitedly.

"Here, in New York!" added an elated Amber.

"On the edge of Central Park." N/Ice politely indicated the pink diamond earrings. "I rather think you must be a very rich witch named Trish."

Reaching up with the hand that was not stroking Pithfwid, the old woman jiggled one of the earrings. It caught the muted, cloud-filtered morning light. From the darker depths of the kiosk, pink fire flashed. As it did so, Simwan noticed that the vicuñas and alpacas on the front of the sweater had all wandered over onto the left side of the garment. The finely sewn herd was standing there, staring back at him uncertainly.

"A girl's got to wear *something* pretty when she goes to work, doesn't she?" The Witch Trish's smile changed to a look of mild exasperation. "Where else would you expect to find a witch, if not New York?"

"If you're a witch real and true, why are you working out of this tiny booth, selling maps and bottled water and chocolate bars? You must not be a very good witch."

"N/Ice!" For once both Amber and Rose were shocked by their sister's directness.

"It's all right, dearies." Trish smiled. "I sell other things, too.

Lotions and potions and devious notions. But it's true: I'm largely retired from sorcery. Thaumaturgy's too traumatic. Selling candy and magazines is a lot less stressful." Extending a wrinkled but still soft hand outward, she indicated the traffic on frenetic, frantic Fifth Avenue. "Working here, I get to meet people from all over the world. They come to me and I don't have to go to them." She paused to check her witchwatch. The big broomstick was approaching the twelve and the little one was on the eleven. A small window at the bottom of the watch face kept track of the phrases of the talkative moon.

"We're looking for something," Simwan explained. "Mr. Everywhere told us it might be found in or around Central Park, but he didn't know more than that. He told us we should ask for more detailed information when we got here." Raising a hand, he indicated the sign fastened to the top and front of the kiosk. In addition to CIGARETTES and COFFEE and assorted other promised offerings, it included the word INFORMATION.

"I'll certainly help if I can, dearie." As Trish leaned slightly forward, crossing her wrists in front of her and leaning lightly on the inside edge of the shelf, a broom behind her began to sweep the small floor space. It was only a whisk broom, which doubtless explained why only a mouse was riding it.

Simwan continued with the now usual explanation, finishing with, "We're pretty certain it was the Crub."

Unlike the ever wary Mr. Everywhere, the old woman didn't blink, didn't cower. Just replied knowingly, and somberly. "That's bad. That's very bad. Sweet dearies such as yourselves shouldn't be looking for such as the Crub. It's rumored that it likes children. Preferably with tabasco, and maybe a little salt."

"We're not so easily put on anybody's menu." Amber's reply was short, sharp, and defiant.

Trish chackled amusedly (a chackle being a sound peculiar to a witch that is, of course, half chuckle and half cackle). "My, but you're a tetchy bunch."

"We're *Deavys*," N/Ice explained proudly.

"I can see that nothing I can say is going to discourage you." That said, the witch pivoted around to fumble among her stock before finally turning back to the youngsters. As she did so, she placed a large chocolate bar on the shelf between them.

Carefully, she adjusted the position of the bar on the shelf. From somewhere below it and out of range of their sight, she removed a hammer. "Not exactly a wand of power," she muttered to herself, "but in retirement, one makes do. Step back, please."

With that she brought the hammer down on the perfectly positioned bar, smashing it to pieces with several swift and surprisingly authoritative blows.

"*Causus comida Criollo couverture!*" she intoned. "*Trinitario forestero latudinus, ee conch sanctus, ee localentus Crub!*"

The Deavys crowded closer. The dense aroma arising from the broken bar was almost overpowering. It would have drawn passersby closer to the kiosk had not the children completely blocked the single opening. As carefully as if she was undressing an infant, Trish removed the bar's paper outer wrapping. Peeling away one end of the gold foil that was its underwear, she picked the whole thing up and dumped the smashed contents out onto the shelf. Simwan expected the shattered fragments to go all over the place. They did not. Instead, they lined up neatly, forming letters and numbers.

"Wow." N/Ice was visibly impressed. "Pretty neat trick."

The old woman smiled at her. "It's an ignorant and impecunious fool indeed who doesn't know how much magic lies in a bar of chocolate, dearie." One gnarly finger nudged several neatly broken pieces. "Hmm. East 67½ Street. That's Inner Upper East Side. Not too far from here." She squinted harder at some of the smaller brown fragments. "No specific address, which doesn't surprise me, but there is a name."

Amber read it aloud. "Tybolt the Butcher." She glanced over at her sisters. "That could be taken a number of different ways."

Trish was rubbing her prominent chin with one finger. "Tybolt, Tybolt—I know that name. Does a big business, does this Tybolt. I've never used his services myself, but it's said he can supply product to meet everyone's taste, from the ordinary human to the extraordinary Humungous. Somewhere in between, he might very well do business with the Crub. Or at least with the Crub's minions." She let her gaze rest on each one of them individually.

"If you're still bound and determined to do this, then pay a visit to this establishment. Poke around, make careful with your inquiries, and above all else, be certain you remain at all times on the customer's side of the counter." Her attitude was dead serious now.

"Just cross over Fifth Avenue and head north. You'll have to look sharp to find 67½ Street. It's one of those unexpected, narrow lanes, almost an alley. There are a number of them in the city, and each one is harder to find than the next." Reaching into an inside shelf, she withdrew a folding map of Manhattan and slid it across the counter. It glowed slightly. Simwan decided it was most definitely not an official publication of the NYC Transit Department. "Here, take this. Just in case."

With that mildly ominous observation in mind, and a cheery farewell wave, they took their leave of the helpful witch and the information booth and crossed to the east side of Fifth Avenue before resuming their walk resolutely northward.

None of them, not even Pithfwid, noticed the gust of black stuff that spurted outward and up from an unprepossessing sidewalk vent. Smoke would have dissipated quickly. Soot would have been wafted away on the first substantial breeze. But this was something very different; the first inkling of a different kind of darkness. It had consistency, it had form, it had direction.

Most chillingly of all, it had curiosity.

It followed the Deavys, tracking them and keeping out of sight—an easy enough task in New York, where smoke and soot and all manner of darkness were everywhere to be found.

-XII-

Like a seventeen-year old boy who's just learned that his girl-friend has dumped him for another guy, the sky was trying to weep but could not. Clouds hung heavy over the great city, gravid with moisture but not yet delivering on the threat of rain. It left all the millions and millions of inhabitants, human and plant and animal, a bit nervous and on edge. Whenever a slight drizzle began, the eternal question formed in the minds of the bipedal citizens: to umbrella, or not to umbrella.

Examining the east side of the block slowly and methodically as they paced off its length from 67th to 68th Street, the Deavy clan failed to discover anything resembling a street, or even a service alley. There were numerous entrances to buildings, but no street. Stumped, they paused before the roll-up metal delivery door to an exclusive apartment building.

"C'mon, Pithfwid," Rose urged their cat. "Can't you see a sign, or anything?"

"Yeah," Amber added. "I thought cats could go anywhere."

"Most of us can," Pithfwid retorted. "But first we have to have a defined anywhere to go to. And the kind of sign we need is not the sort that is mounted on a pole." Lowering his nose, he began sniffing along the line where the foundation of the apartment building met the concrete of the sidewalk, looking, for all the world, like a miniature and very oddly proportioned bloodhound as he did so.

Pithfwid halted so abruptly that a momentarily distracted Simwan, on the other end of the leash, was nearly yanked off his feet. How such a normal-size feline could destabilize a far heavier human was something no onlooker could have understood. The Deavys knew the reason, however. Pithfwid was considerably bigger than he looked.

"Got it," the cat murmured with satisfaction. "In any big city, it can be hard to find these little side streets. Half streets are more difficult still. Then there are quarter streets, and eighth streets, of which this city in particular has more than its share."

Simwan and his sisters stared. Pithfwid had stopped and was gazing down a crack between two tall buildings. There was maybe enough space between the massive, towering walls of stone for an agile grasshopper to squeeze through.

"*That's* 67½ Street?" Rose looked dubious.

"That's not even wide enough to be just the ½ part," Amber commented.

The cat looked up at them and grinned. It is a rare and

wonderful thing to see a cat grin. "Come now, girls. Surely you haven't put on *that* much weight?" He eyed Amber's thighs meaningfully. "Although, all that holiday chocolate you've all been eating your way through lately . . ."

"Why you spiteful little *katze!*" An angry Amber reached for the fluffy tail. Pithfwid skipped effortlessly back out of reach, she followed—and both of them disappeared. *No*, a startled Simwan realized. They hadn't disappeared. They'd just gone down 67½ Street. N/Ice was right on their tail—well, Pithfwid's, anyway. He glanced at Rose, then back at the river of pedestrians. Absorbed in themselves, they took no notice of the remaining Deavys. Taking each other's hand, and deep breaths, Simwan and Rose took a step toward the barely visible crack between the two buildings.

Half expecting to smack his nose against unyielding granite, Simwan was pleasantly surprised to find that he had merely stepped onto another sidewalk laid perpendicular to the one he had just left. Letting go of his sister's hand as hastily as if he had been holding onto a burning stovetop, he turned to look back behind him. What he saw was a crack between two buildings. Except that instead of being built of stone, one was made of used brick and the other of green glass. Fish swam to and fro within the glass wall, through which he could see several mermaids busy at ballet rehearsal.

The stories one heard were right on, he mused. You *could* find everything in New York.

East 67½ Street was narrow, but on balance not all that much different from East 67th Street or East 68th Street. Like all good Manhattan streets, it ran straight and true. Traffic flowed in the direction of the East River. Tall buildings lined both sides. The street itself was frantic with taxis, delivery vans, flying carpets of varying size piled high with goods, messenger pixies, elves on smoke break, mounted police on unicorns: all the usual occupants of an active Upper East Side block.

Well, Simwan decided as he took in the scene, maybe a little more than usual.

"We're looking for Tybolt the Butcher," N/Ice reminded them as she drifted alongside, and sometimes through, her sisters. She was already checking out the storefronts that lined both sides of the street. "No wonder the Witch Trish couldn't give us a number."

It was true, Simwan saw as they advanced down the sidewalk. None of the storefronts had any numbers on them, just names. The Deavys walked carefully around the sawhorses and yellow tape that delineated the borders of an excavation in progress. A team of grumbling, grunting trolls was repairing a broken water line. Each wore a yellow hard hat, dirty jeans, and shirts that proclaimed "City of New York—Dept. of Water and Powers." One of the smaller, younger workers leaning on his shovel noticed the Deavy clan approaching and started to whistle through his tusks. Somewhat to the girls' disappointment, he caught himself hastily when he saw that they were way underage, and quickly turned back to his work.

Well behind them now, and unremarked upon, a puff of black smoke oozed out of the crack that led to Fifth Avenue.

The notion that one could buy anything, absolutely anything, in New York was never more apparent than on 67½ Street. Shops sold unusual cooking ware, unique clothing, remarkable furniture, gourmet imported food, and a great deal more. A rambling used bookstore offered not only publications of recent vintage but incunabula, scrolls, delicately painted papyrus, inscribed cuneiform tablets (including the rare paperback editions), and petroglyphs of particular significance. In the window, held in place by a spell that served the same purpose as a paper book jacket did for more mundane publications, was a supposedly lost poem by the famed Sufi master Ismandar. It floated in the air like colored smoke.

Resuming their walk, the Deavys passed more shops. Reaching the intersection of 67½ and Stark Avenue, they paused before the flow of thundering cross traffic, watching the streetlight. Only when it put out a double field of force, holding back the ferocious, snarling traffic on Stark, did they and their fellow pedestrians cross in response to the backlit sign that instead of *Go* or *Walk* declaimed clearly *Hurry or Die*.

And then, there it was, halfway down the next block, nestled snugly in between a hardwhere store—a travel agency for the metaphysically challenged—on one side and a bakery—"No matter who or what it is, we can make flour out of it."—on the other.

"'Tybolt the Butcher.'" Rose read the sign aloud. Her gaze dropped to the leaded glass front window. The display behind it featured a tasteful, even elegantly arranged selection of choice chops, steaks, sausage both cased and ground, bacon, poultry, and seafood. One sign shouted a cut-price sale on fresh calamari, which should have rung a bell in Simwan's memory, but did not. There was also a Grade-A sticker from the City of New York Health Department, a couple of framed reviews (one from the *Alternate Times*, the other from *Rampant Carnivore* magazine), and a small map of the world known and unknown with tiny hovering stars marking the sources of the shop's more exotic cuts.

"I'm getting hungry," Amber announced after studying the offerings in the window. "Maybe they serve sandwiches, or something."

"I'm hungry, too," Simwan admitted. Ordering lunch would give them more time to study their surroundings and decide how best to proceed, as well as providing an excuse for lingering inside.

The interior of the butcher shop was a mix of the ultramodern and the ancient. The slats that made up the wooden floor were thick as ceiling beams and covered with a coating of fine sawdust. "To soak up any errant liquids," the ever-knowledgeable Pithfwid tactfully pointed out. On the other hand, the glass-fronted refrigerated compartments were made of spotless stainless steel, as were the several towering, jammed-together, front-opening freezers that formed a wall near the back of the shop.

Sandwiches were indeed offered, and there was a tall cooler cabinet from which one could purchase sodas and other drinks. There were only three tables near the back of the store, suggesting that the majority of sandwiches on offer were made up for takeout by busy New Yorkers to eat on the run or back at the office. As it was still comparatively early for nearby businesses to break for lunch, all of the tables were vacant.

"Yob, whats can I do for you?" As the goblin—surprisingly clean—behind the counter leaned forward to peer over the case of cold cuts, his slitted eyes traveling from one Deavy to another. "Three of you want to eats the fourth? I can fix." The goblin gaze fell still lower. "Or maybe you wants me divvy up that cat?" Pithfwid bristled, but held his tongue.

"No thanks, we're all eating together," Simwan responded to

the butcher's assistant with admirable matter-of-factness, as if he dealt every day with suggestions for the dissection and consumption of the family pet. Not to mention his sisters. He smiled. "Early lunch." He made an effort to sound as sophisticated as any long-time New Yorker. "Is your glop eel fresh?"

The goblin looked offended. "All our seafoods is fresh. Glop eel caught in Maelstrom and flown in daily from North Sea."

"Then I'd like a glop eel salad sandwich on a Kaiser roll, please. With mayo, hold the fickle." He glanced back at his sisters. Ravenous as they were, they needed no encouragement to add their own orders.

"I'll have sliced roast jackalope on whole wheat toast," Rose put in hungrily.

"Club sandwich with smoked roc instead of turkey," Amber declared, making no attempt to hide her eagerness.

"Bagel with cream cheese, onion, lox, and caperers." N/Ice had the most metropolitan taste of any member of the coubet.

As soon as he finished writing up the order, which appeared as small blood-red lettering floating in the air, the goblin expanded his cheeks like a bullfrog and blew the letters toward a taller, skinnier, slightly yellower version of himself working the back of the shop. That loathsome (but hygienic) entity sucked the drifting words into its eyes, nodded its acknowledgment of the order, and began assembling the requested sandwiches. Having four arms to work with instead of the usual two made the work go quickly.

There being no table service in the butcher shop, they selected their own drinks from the cooler and seated themselves at the table nearest the rear of the establishment. As befitted their individual tastes, Rose chose Coke, Amber opted for Pepsi, N/Ice picked Africola, and Simwan popped a can of Skull-Splitter Kola from the Firth O' Forever bottling plant that was located in a part of Scotland that is not to be found on most maps of the British Isles. As befitted a brewery that also bottled an idiosyncratic variant of Irn-Bru, the national soda of Scotland, the Firth O' Forever's kola had a distinctive metallic aftertaste.

Somewhat surprisingly, the goblin who had taken their order brought it out to them himself as soon as it was ready, balancing all four plates on a single tray. As the girls dug in and Amber picked off choice bits of roc to feed the finicky Pithfwid, the goblin lingered. "You foods okay?"

Dipping a French fry into the pool of ketchup she had squeezed out onto her plate, Rose shoved it into her mouth. This took a certain amount of effort since the French fry was exhibiting a disturbing tendency to try and push back.

"Everything's delicious," she proclaimed honestly. Next to her, N/Ice smiled but did not reply, as she was busy trying to keep the caperers on her bagel from boogieing off her plate.

By way of reply, Simwan chomped down on a mouthful of sliced glop eel salad. It was, he had to confess, well made, though a little heavy on the dressing for his taste.

"Enjoy you foods." Satisfied with their responses, the goblin turned and headed back to his station behind the counter.

From their seats near the back of the shop, the Deavys were able to watch the comings and goings and occasional vanishings of a wide assortment of customers. Clearly, Tybolt's was every bit as popular with the denizens of this singular part of New York as the goblin had claimed. Business was so good and so steady that he and his sisters were taken by surprise when a very short, stocky goblin of especially bilious hue waved his apron like a semaphore to darken the front windows. It then moved to the front door and threw a pair of security bolts. Recalling the well-meaning cautionary words of the Witch Trish ("Above all else make certain you stay safe on the right side of the counter"), Simwan hastily finished the last of his sandwich while quietly urging his sisters to do the same.

Licking salad dressing from his fingers, he rose and walked back to the counter, where he fumbled with his wallet. "Check, please."

Nodding, the goblin wrote out a ticket in the air, puffed out his cheeks, and blew it in the customer's direction. Simwan read the last figure and dodged to his left as the list tried to enter his eyes. It drifted past him to dissolve in the air in the middle of the shop. Handing over payment, he smiled, nodded his thanks for the food and the service, and turned to go.

"Whats, no tip?" the goblin hissed. Pale red eyes glared across the counter from beneath protruding bony ridges.

"Oh, sorry." Pausing, Simwan reached for his wallet again.

"Not moneys," the goblin insisted. It was grinning in a way Simwan didn't like. Glancing uneasily to right and left, he saw that the rest of the store staff had set their work aside to gather together in twos and threes. Some of them still clutched their heavy butcher knives. They were whispering and gesturing in his direction.

"If you don't want money, then how can I tip you?" As he posed the question, Simwan was backing slowly away from the counter.

"Don't want a handful of coins," the goblin told him. "Maybe just a hand. Or two." He gestured behind the increasingly wary young man. "Eyes of young girl also very nice. Make good base for jellied consommé." And with that he leaped right over the high glassed-in counter, brandishing a huge, bloodstained blade in one hand.

Anticipating what was coming, Simwan was ready for him. Stepping back into a karate stance, he uttered a defiant "Hee-yah!" and raised his hands, edge on. As the rest of the store crew rushed the coubet, the goblin who had served them let out a high-pitched shriek and plunged the knife it held straight toward Simwan's heart.

Simwan blocked the blow exactly as he had been taught in Mr. Othmul's class, bringing his left hand up in an ascending chopping motion. There was a sick, slick, shearing sound as the goblin's hand was sliced off cleanly at the wrist. Green blood spurted. Following up on his surprise and advantage, Simwan darted forward, stiffening his fingers and jabbing. His fingertips went right through the goblin's neck. When he drew back his hand in a single sharp, pulling motion, blood the color of pea soup gushed everywhere. Clutching at its throat, the choking, dying goblin collapsed onto the sawdust-covered floor. Simwan eyed it for a moment to make sure it no longer posed any threat, then raced to the aid of his sisters.

All those long hours spent repeating and rehearsing moves in Mr. Othmul's special classes had certainly paid off. Not for nothing had he studied how to combine the traditional moves of Tang Soo Do with everything he had learned while helping his mother cut up vegetables for dozens of Deavy dinners.

ALAN DEAN FOSTER

The girls didn't need his help. As soon as the attack came in their direction, they had risen from their seats and formed a coubet triangle. Standing back to back, facing three directions simultaneously, they cast at the oncoming goblins such a farrago of spells, incantations, charms, summonses, and forthright preteen angst that the poor creatures never knew what hit them.

One found itself turned into a green carp. It fell to the floor where it lay flopping helplessly, fighting for oxygen. Two others were lifted into the air. Slammed together, they became fused at the head. This made it difficult for them to stand, much less attack anything. Seeing what was happening to its cohorts, a fourth goblin tried to flee by leaping back behind the counter. A flurry of force from N/Ice left it diced and sliced and neatly laid out on a platter inside the refrigerated case between slabs of marbled beef and well-trimmed buffalo.

Breathing hard, Simwan emerged from his defensive pose and looked around the shop. All was quiet, the shade-darkened space around them devoid of motion, except that the last of the surviving caperers took the opportunity to flee N/Ice's unwatched plate.

"Trish was right to warn us." Lowering her hands, which tingled from the aftereffects of casting strong magic, Rose walked back to their table, picked up her soda, and drained the last dregs from the bottle. "I hate fighting goblins. They're so predictable."

"WOT'S ALL THIS, NOW?" bellowed a voice from the back of the shop.

Slamming both double doors out of its way so forcefully that one hung broken and loose from its upper hinge, a gigantic figure

174

appeared from the back room. Its yellow-brown flesh was blotchy and scarred from a thousand minor nicks and cuts. The broad flat face flaunted a wart-strewn nose pierced by a single massive metal ring. Hugely protruding ears resembled dead stingrays that had been stapled to the sides of the head. Wild bulging eyes looked down on the startled Deavy brood. A butcher knife the size of a headsman's ax dangled from one massive fist while the tentlike meat cutter's apron the apparition wore was flocked with half a dozen different kinds and colors of blood.

Straightaway appraising the carnage around him, the lumbering ogre threw out a massive, hairy arm and caught Amber, who was still near the freezers, around her neck. Effortlessly drawing her back to him, it held her tightly against his chest as yellow eyes glared out at the rest of the stunned, hard-breathing children from beneath protruding brows that were like ledges formed of granite.

Simwan stared in shock. Any karate moves, even those enhanced by practice in his mom's kitchen, were unlikely to have much effect on the hulking figure that had lurched into the front room of the butcher shop. Rose and N/Ice likewise held back, uncertain how to respond. Any sudden moves on their part and the infuriated monster might snap their sister's neck like a dry twig. With her arms pinned to her sides, the frightened Amber couldn't raise them to work any spells herself.

"Look wot you've done to my staff!" the giant howled in fury and disbelief as it took in the carnage that littered the floor. "*DO YOU KNOW HOW HARD IT IS TO FIND GOOD HELP IN THIS CITY?*"

Holding the enormous meat-cutting knife high in one hand

like the blade of doom itself and clutching the terrified Amber tightly to him with the other, Tybolt the Butcher took the first of several earth-shaking steps directly toward the staring, wide-eyed Deavys.

-XIII-

Frightened as they were both for themselves and their sister, Rose and N/Ice weren't about to let any of them be sliced up and added to the butcher shop's selection of prime cuts. Raising their hands, they prepared to fling what they could at the stout, threatening giant while simultaneously hoping to free their trapped sibling. Tybolt the Butcher was an ogre. Big, menacingly big, he was also no fool. Observing their preparations, he stopped where he was and took stock. "OI, SO THAT'S 'OW IT IS, IS IT? WICKED LITTLE MAGICIANS, BE THEE? NO WONDER YOU MANAGED TO COST ME SO MANY GOOD EMPLOYEES." Grinning evilly and flashing snaggled, broken teeth, he swiftly brought the edge of the enormous chopping knife right up to Amber's neck. Instantly, she stopped struggling. One stiff shove of that massive hunk of razor-sharp steel, an agonized Simwan realized, and Amber's head would go rolling across the floor. He knew incantations for stopping bleeding, and for repairing injured limbs, but he didn't know any spells strong enough to reattach the head of a loved one. From the alarmed looks on the faces of Rose and N/Ice, they didn't either.

"SUBMIT!" Tybolt the Butcher bellowed, pressing the edge of the knife into Amber's neck so that it just barely dimpled her smooth skin. "SUBMIT TO ME NOW, OR I'LL MAKE THIS GIRL'S SKULL INTO A PLAY-PRETTY TO DANGLE FROM ME EAR!"

Simwan looked around frantically, urgently, as if help might materialize simply from the wishing for it. Rose was no less panicked, and N/Ice was crying tears that vanished into elsewhere before they could hit the floor. They *couldn't* give their binding submission. To do so would be to look forward to an unrewarding future as cold cuts in someone else's freezer. But *not* to do so would mean seeing their sister decapitated right in front of them. As he struggled desperately with how to respond, how to reply, Simwan thought he heard something in the silence of the room. It was so subtle and soft as to be nearly inaudible. It barely tickled his ears.

Was that a meow?

He was almost afraid to turn around, almost afraid to do much of anything. But at the moment, the ogre's attention was fixed on Amber's sisters. Glancing around as furtively as he could manage, Simwan found himself the focus of Pithfwid's urgent stare. His fur all bottled up and presently the color of pure silver, Pithfwid was standing next to one wall, the claws of his right rear foot pressed up against it and dangerously close to . . .

It was something Simwan had seen the cat do before. Whether

it would work this time, and have any effect if it did work, he had no way of telling. Not knowing what else to do, he determined to do his part. It couldn't worsen the situation, and it was certainly more promising than doing nothing. He returned his attention to Tybolt the Butcher and the ogre's limp, helpless prisoner.

"If you touch one hair of my sister's head!" Simwan began warningly. "Just one single hair, I'll . . ." His voice trailed off.

Grinning unpleasantly, the butcher accepted the challenge. Using two fingers of the hand that was holding the slablike knife, he fingered one of Amber's auburn tresses and tugged it out straight. She winced and let out a little whimper of pain. The ogre's smile grew wider. At that precise instant, Pithfwid promptly jammed one of the claws on his rear foot into the wall socket it had been concealing, raised the index claw on his left front foot, and stabbed it forward. Simultaneously, the captive Amber reached out in the direction of her pet.

The interior of the shop shook as a single bolt of channeled lightning traveled from the wall socket, through Pithfwid, out his forward-facing front claw, and into Amber's extended fingers. High voltage and low expectations coursed through her. Every one of her hairs stood on end, electricity dancing violently from tip to tip. The powerful charge also raced through her captor. He began to vibrate uncontrollably, smoke rising from his ringed nose and Dumbo-like ears. The huge knife blade quivered against Amber's throat, but did not push inward. Ungrounded by relevant cat magic, he suddenly and slowly toppled forward, like a tree that had just been felled. Amber let out a scream and threw herself sideways. Freed from the ogre's grasp, she just managed to avoid landing on top of the still lethal blade.

Running to her, her sisters strained to extricate her from beneath the smoking, weighty, cleanly electrocuted corpse of Tybolt the Butcher.

"Amber, are you all right?" Rose eyed her sister anxiously, looking her up and down.

N/Ice was so upset she kept blinking wildly in and out of reality. "Amber, did he hurt you?"

Climbing to her feet, the object of their concern blinked once, adjusted her clothing, and then felt gingerly of her shock-straightened hair. Her eyes went wide. "Omigod, omigod—somebody give me a hairbrush! In Aphrodite's name, somebody give me a hairbrush!"

While the coubet fussed and fretted over Amber's explosively straightened coiffure, a relieved Simwan wandered back to where Pithfwid sat quietly, licking his still tingling front left foot.

"That was fast thinking on your part," he complimented the cat.

"Don't be too hard on yourself, Simwan. Everything happened very fast." Whiskers twitched expressively. "A shocking development, to be sure."

Simwan nodded gravely. "Electrifying, even."

"Every dangerous encounter inevitably contains elements of both the negative and positive." Concluding his tongue bath, Pithfwid rose onto all fours, arched his back into a stretch, relaxed, and padded past his human. "Though we have concluded our business with the proprietor of this onerous and odiferous establishment, there still remains the small matter of obtaining the information we came in search of."

"Oh, right," remembered Simwan. "How to find the Crub."

He indicated the dead butcher. "But if we can't get it from him . . ."

"Then we will ask it of his surviving employee," finished Pithfwid as he raised his freshly groomed front paw and pointed, "who is presently cowering behind the far end of the meat counter trying to pretend he does not exist."

Simwan looked up sharply. Sure enough, an apron-clad goblin not much bigger than Pithfwid was peeking out from behind counter's edge. Realizing it had been spotted, it uttered a squeal of dismay and bolted for the front door. Simwan reached into a pocket and withdrew the door key that Uncle Herkimer had given him so that he and his sisters could let themselves back into the apartment if their host had laid himself to rest for the night. Or the day, or a week or so.

"*Seal the wheel!*" the most senior Deavy present yelled.

The goblin leaped and grabbed for the door handle. As he did so, the now glowing key flew from Simwan's fingers and slammed into the center of the door. A burst of subtle radiance radiated from the chunk of molded brass and spread in a circle to all four corners of the portal. No matter how hard the goblin yanked on the handle with both green hands, no matter how ear-burningly he cursed at it, it would not open for him.

A moment later it didn't matter, because he found himself surrounded by three Deavy girls. After what had nearly happened to Amber, none of them were in a mood to be courteous.

"We've got a question or two for you," Rose growled threateningly.

"Yeah. And you'd better answer straight and true. We'll know if you lie." N/Ice flashed an expression that was redder than any blush.

"You especially don't want *me* to lose my temper." A grim-faced Amber extended one hand in the diminutive goblin's direction. "I'm not feeling real sociable right now."

"Pleases, pleases, don't hurts!" Shrinking back against the sealed door, the goblin threw both hands up to protect its face. "You asks what yous wants, I tells you. Anything you wants." Its glance traveled across the room to the large lump of motionless meat that moments before had been its master. Satisfied with the effect the coubet had produced, Simwan stepped forward. "We're from out of town, and we've come looking for the Crub."

"I knows, I knows."

Simwan blinked. The girls exchanged a glance. Pithfwid sighed resignedly. "You knows—I mean, you know?" Simwan replied.

Lowering his hands, the goblin nodded. "Word comes in not longs before you gets here. 'Watch for strange young non-Ords,' it says. 'Means ills for good customer the Crub,' it says. Master Tybolt instructs us take care if we sees such peoples. Instructs we captures such young peoples."

"And do what?" Amber asked menacingly.

Once more the goblin threw up his green, long-fingered hands. "We tolds to keeps you around untils Master comes. Master has standing order for certain kind of sausage, and likes to watch making of."

Simwan leaned toward the cringing goblin. "What was your master's connection to the Crub? How close were they?"

"Not personal close. Only business," the goblin insisted. "Crub's servants steal things in New York proper. Brings them here to trades for scraps and trimmings of rare meats."

Amber nodded understandingly. "Brings them here from where? Where can we find the Crub?"

"In the great park, the Central Park," the goblin told her.

Blowing into an open palm, N/Ice brandished a handful of fire under the goblin's chin. "*Where* in the park?"

"I don't know, I don't know!" the goblin gibbered as it shrank back from that threatening blaze. "I only works front counter."

Amber looked at her sisters. "Well, at least that narrows it down. New York City's a big place, and now we know the only part we have to search is Central Park."

Simwan considered. If the goblin was telling the truth, then contact between the Crub and Tybolt the Butcher was not constant. That meant with a little luck, they might catch it before news spread. Providing, of course, that in the interim it was not informed otherwise.

They hauled the squealing, protesting little creature to the back of the store. N/Ice opened the freezer while Rose, Amber, and Simwan tossed their captive inside. "Waits, waits!" A green arm thrust outward as Simwan prepared to slam shut the heavy steel door.

"What?" he asked impatiently.

A small green head popped out to eye him accusingly. "You still nots leave tip for your sandwiches."

"Get back in there!" N/Ice raised a threatening hand. With a last squeak, the pitiful creature ducked back inside and Simwan and his sisters slammed the door shut, making sure to drop the locking handle into place.

Goblins dealt quite well with being frozen. Eventually, someone would arrive to check on the business and sooner or later open the freezer where the Deavys had chosen to store him. Even as a satisfied Simwan was making sure the freezer door was tightly closed and latched, a rising whine drew everyone's attention.

"Sirens!" Amber yelped. "Police sirens, maybe."

"Someone outside must have heard all the noise and called the cops." Amber hurried toward the front door, still brushing frantically at her hair.

It was time to go. At least now they knew where to look for the Crub, even if it *was* somewhere within the boundaries of one of the country's largest municipal parks. Raising a hand, Simwan stretched it out toward the front door.

"*Steal the feel, unseal the wheel,*" he recited. His enunciation was perfect. His teachers would have been proud.

Once more, the door glowed slightly. The key that had jammed itself into the center flew backward to land in Simwan's hand. Returning it to a pocket, he hurried to join his sisters.

Cautiously opening the door, all three girls peered out, one head above the other. Just as when they had entered, the sidewalks were packed with pedestrians: some human, many not. Although the wail of the approaching siren was louder now, no one on the street paid it any attention. This was, after all, New York, where the sound of a siren was as common as that of the wind. The traffic and its indifference, Simwan saw, would help to slow the arrival of the authorities.

Not that he minded having to answer a question or two. They had responded to Tybolt and his murderous employees in self-defense. It would have to be an addled cop indeed who upon scrutinizing the carnage inside the butcher shop came to the conclusion that a teenage boy, his three younger sisters, and a cat had acted with intent to commit unprovoked mass murder— upon a passel of knife-wielding goblins and their monstrous ogre of a master, no less.

It was just that he did not want to waste the time that would be needed to answer such questions. Also, if they were picked up by the authorities, the police might insist on getting in touch with their parents. He and his sisters couldn't allow that. It would only upset their father and worry their mother, and in her present condition, the last thing she needed was that kind of additional stress.

"I don't see any uniforms," N/Ice whispered tautly.

"Let's go!" Pushing from behind, Simwan and Pithfwid forced their way out. Amber and N/Ice were right behind them. Only Rose lingered briefly, to etch the glowing word CLOSED onto the front door as she pulled it shut behind her.

They strode resolutely onward, even remembering to glance at occasional shop windows, trying to blend into the crowd and make themselves as inconspicuous as possible. Behind them, the complaining screech of the siren steadied. It did not disappear, but it stopped coming closer.

Simwan badly wanted to look back to see what was happening, but forced himself not to. "Sounds like maybe they've stopped outside the butcher shop. If they go in, that ought to keep them busy for a while."

N/Ice had a sudden thought that nearly caused her to blink out of existence. "Oh gosh—what if they find the goblin we left in the freezer? He won't be frozen yet." Unable to stop herself, she turned and looked back.

"N/Ice . . ." Simwan began warningly, "don't—"

"It doesn't matter!" She broke into a run. "They're coming!"

That was enough to make all of them turn. Sure enough, a squad of cops was making its way in their direction. Thankfully, the crowd at this end of the increasingly narrow street was so tightly packed that people and creatures spilled off the sidewalk onto the street and left no room for vehicles. Having been given the description of the murderous children by a decidedly biased—and shivering—goblin, the local authorities were hot on their heels.

"There!" Raising a hand, Simwan pointed excitedly. The crack that separated two tall buildings at the end of the street was now visible just ahead. Panting hard, he broke into a final sprint.

Would their pursuers follow? There was only one way to find out.

N/Ice was first through, effortlessly flattening herself to the thickness of a pane of glass as she slipped into the constricted opening. Rose followed, with Amber right behind her. Just as Simwan took the opposite of a deep breath and prepared to follow his sisters, a heavy hand clamped down on his left shoulder.

"Gotcha! Don't fight it, kid, we only want to—"

A ball of fur swollen to the size of a giant pumpkin landed on Simwan's right shoulder and hissed at the startled cop. Not only was it swollen to the size of a giant pumpkin, it looked exactly *like* a giant pumpkin—or to be more exact, a fuzzy yellow jack-o'-lantern with eyes of blazing brimstone. The sight was enough to make the startled policeman momentarily release his grip.

Release it just long enough to allow Simwan to slip into the opening between the two buildings. Working his way sideways, he scuttled through until he finally lost his balance and fell.

Right out onto Fifth Avenue, where his waiting sisters clustered anxiously around him.

"Simwan, are you all right?" Rose asked uneasily.

"Did they hurt you?" Amber was searching her brother for signs of harm.

"Are you in one piece?" N/Ice asked, knowing that now that they were back in the Ord part of the city she couldn't let herself stretch completely around her brother in the healing arc that was one of her sorceral specialties.

Picking himself off the pavement, he dusted himself off and looked back the way he had come. The crack between the two buildings was unchanged. Putting one eye to it, he could just make out a bevy of blue-clad shapes gesticulating and flailing futilely at the far end. But none were coming through.

Near his lower legs a familiar black shape, tail twitching back and forth, was also peering into the crack. "I think we're safe now," Pithfwid murmured softly. "We're no longer in their precinct."

Relieved at their narrow (in every sense of the word) escape, the four of them turned and found themselves contemplating the thickly treed, mysterious expanse of Central Park that lay across the street.

Across Fifth Avenue, the bold green upthrust triangles of slender evergreens mixed with golden- and brown-leaved deciduous oaks and sycamores that were in the process of sacrificing their leaves to autumn. Somewhere in those thickly treed depths, if the small goblin was to be believed, lay the lair of the Crub. Somewhere in there, they would find the Truth, the means for restoring their mother to health—and quite possibly a number of things they did not want to find.

Pulling out the map Trish had given them, he checked it once, then folded it as best he could and clumsily shoved it back into his pocket. There were spells for many things, he knew, but no one, not even a grand sorcerer, had yet come up with one that would allow a paper map to be easily and correctly refolded once it had been opened.

"We might as well start looking here, at the south end of the park," he told his sisters. "The nearest proper entrance is just down from where we are now, on 66th Street, by the zoo."

Rose immediately clapped her hands together. "Super! While we're asking questions, we can have a look at the animals."

Her brother eyed her sternly. "We're here to look for the Truth, Rose. Not monkeys and bears."

Amber poo-pooed his concern. "If we don't know where to look, that means we need to look everywhere, and consider every possibility. Who knows? Maybe the Crub hides out in the zoo."

"Yeah, right," Simwan agreed sarcastically. "In his own cage, up front and out in the open where everyone can see him. With a big identification sign on the bars. 'Giant Wizard Rat of Evil Mien and Wicked Intent—Do Not Feed or Speak To.'"

N/Ice rested a calming hand on his arm. "Rose and Amber are right, brother. The Crub may not dwell in the zoo, but that doesn't mean those who do are ignorant of his whereabouts. Remember what Aunt Grace told us once: 'It never hurts to ask the monkey.'"

Seeking support, Simwan looked down at the cat sitting quietly by his feet. "Pithfwid?"

Wise yellow eyes peered back up at him. "It might help."

Outvoted, Simwan gave in with a sigh of resignation. "All

---

right—we'll start searching at the zoo." He wagged a warning finger. "But no casual gossiping with the animals; some Ord might see us."

"Deal," declared Rose.

"We'll only talk to the monkeys," Amber added.

"Better yet, we'll let you do it, 'cause you'll have instant rapport," N/Ice finished.

"I suppose I could—hey, wait a minute." He frowned as the deeper import of his half-a-sister's maybe-compliment started to sink in. But it was too late for him to voice a comeback—the Deavy coubet was already racing for the crosswalk at 66th Street. All he could do was hurry and follow Pithfwid, grinding his teeth as he did so.

The crowd on the street had momentarily thinned when something black and nebulous oozed out of the crack that barely separated two towering apartment buildings. It looked like a lost patch of smoke. Passing by, an elderly man in overcoat and hat paused curiously. He thought it peculiar that instead of rising, the smoke puff seemed to be hovering in one place, unaffected even by the occasional blast of wind. Warily leaning toward it, he took a single, cautious sniff.

His eyes bulged and began to water. Despite the chill midday air, sweat immediately broke out on his forehead and cheeks. Both hands clutched at his throat as he began to choke. Alarmed at the sight, other concerned pedestrians stopped and tried to render what aid they could as the man collapsed to the pavement, kicking and twitching. Pulling out their cell phones, two women dialed 911.

Seconds later the unfortunate businessman's back arched in

a rictus of pain. Stepping out of the rapidly gathering crowd, a male nurse just starting his lunch break immediately began to administer CPR. None of it mattered. By the time the paramedics arrived, the man was dead, his heart stilled for good.

With all of the attention focused on the dying businessman, no one noticed the feathery tendrils of what looked like black smoke drifting lazily across Fifth Avenue in the general direction of Central Park.

-XIV-

Between the chilly, damp, breezy weather and the fact that it was nearly noon on what was still a school day in Manhattan, the Central Park Zoo was largely empty. A few couples, children accompanied by single parents or nannies, and the occasional tourist were the only people other than employees that the Deavy brood encountered as they paid to enter. In the distance, the Delacorte Music Clock, with its activated mechanical animals, was just finishing up playing "A-Tisket, A-Tasket." As the youngsters passed through the entry gate, the clock launched into an appropriate tinkly version of "Ding Dong Dell."

Once inside, they headed for the habitat that was home to a troop of white-faced langurs. Larger than Pithfwid but smaller than N/Ice, the primates were active, intelligent, and curious. After making sure that any other visitors were out of earshot, Rose leaned as far forward as she could to offer a mature female a handful of peanuts. Seeing this, several other adults and curious infants gathered around. Palm out, the troop's lead female chittered excitedly at the Deavy girls.

"Don't push," Rose instructed the chattering younger monkeys, careful to employ the correct dialect.

"Oh, well, that makes it easier," replied the senior female in words the Deavys knew well. She swiveled around on her backside, her long tail flicking out of the way. "Hey, didn't you hear what the human said? No shoving in back!" Accepting the peanuts from Rose, she swallowed some while passing the majority along to her squabbling relatives. "Where do you cultured kids hail from?"

"Clearsight," Amber told her. "Pennsylvania."

The langur matriarch nodded as she shelled a peanut. "Any Kandy there?"

The three girls exchanged a glance. "We don't have any candy," Amber replied apologetically. "Only peanuts. But if you want candy . . ."

"No, no, sister no-tail." The langur exposed sharp white teeth. "We're *from* Kandy. It's a district in central Sri Lanka. Since you can speak proper langur, I was just wondering if you knew anyone from home."

Simwan shrugged diffidently. "We don't get out of Pennsylvania much."

"Too bad. You'd like Kandy." She held up an empty shell. "Nice nuts. Thanks. Something I can do for you?"

Leaning closer to the bars, N/Ice lowered her voice until it was barely audible. "Someone's stolen the Truth, and we're looking for it."

The langur nodded knowingly. "Someone's always trying to steal the tooth. That's why it's kept under guard in Kandy."

Simwan sighed. "Not Buddha's tooth. The *Truth*. It was stored in a bottle in Mr. Gemimmel's drugstore and we've come to get it back. The Crub stole it."

Abruptly, the monkey habitat went as silent as it had ever been, as silent as on the day when its reconstruction had been finished but before its denizens had been transferred back in. In fact, for just an instant, the entire zoo went dead quiet. None of the other human visitors remarked on the astounding coincidence because none were trained to pay attention to such things. But the Deavys noticed it. Darn right they did.

After what was after all only a second or two, bellows and cries, chirpings and hootings, barking and growling resumed—though with an undercurrent of unease only the most sensitive could detect. Simwan noticed the subtle change, and it caused him to scrutinize his immediate surroundings with more concern than previously.

Not coincidentally, every one of the other langurs had fled, disappearing among the rocks, trees, and ravines of their habitat. Only the matriarch remained, facing the visitors who had uttered the unmentionable name. She eyed them up and down from beneath her bushy white brows, her manner and tone deadly serious and anything but monkey-comical.

"You're either very brave or very stupid children, and I can tell that you're not stupid. One doesn't speak lightly of the Crub, much less go looking for it."

N/Ice straightened and, confident no other visitors were looking in her direction, emitted a brief golden flash. "*We* do. We promised to get the Truth back, we *have* to get the Truth back, and we're going to follow through on our promise."

"To save our woods, restore the health of our mother, and preserve our town," Amber underlined.

The senior female scratched her head, then her butt. "You are really determined, aren't you?" She sighed sadly. "Yes, I can see that you are. A pity. It's so rare to find humans one can talk with. Most of the time we don't even try; we just sit back and laugh at their antics and at the silly faces they make. It's enough to make one wish the whole species would just devolve." Leaning forward, she stuck her face between two of the bars.

"If you insist on pursuing this to what is likely to be an unhappy end for every one of you, I will go ahead and tell you where you can find the Crub." She looked around apprehensively. "But I don't want my tribe brought into it, understand? Anything you hear, you didn't get from me."

Simwan nodded gravely. "Understood."

"All right then." The matriarch sat back. "But it's going to cost you. Go over there, empty that, and bring the contents to me."

It took them a few minutes to drain the peanut dispenser of its entire stock. As soon as this had been transferred to the langur habitat, one double handful at a time, the senior female once again moved as close to her new confidants as the metal barrier would permit.

"Hearken to me, balding cousins. The Crub dwells underground, in a deep, terrible place somewhere in the upper reaches of the park. I don't know exactly where, except that it lies to the north of the Reservoir. Never been there myself. They don't let us out much. In fact, they don't let us out at all. But there have been some mice come through this way, and the occasional snake. They're always looking to steal food from the different habitats. Occasionally we corner one, and in return for not eating it, we use it to catch up on the news."

Simwan quickly fumbled for his map. The girls crowded around as he ran a finger over the lower half. "See, we're down here, in the south end of the park." Pushing his finger up the map, he quickly located the huge reservoir, moved on to the park's northern boundary. "We can just go back outside and take a bus up to 110th Street. When we get off, we'll be on the park's northern boundary."

The matriarch was shaking her head, her words slightly slurred because her mouth was full of freshly shelled peanuts. "Huh-uh, humans. Won't work that way. If you go that route, all you'll see is what Ord-folk see: just the park and its proper Ord places. According to what I've been told, the only way to get to the Crub's den is to follow a Path of Singular Significance straight through the park from south to north. There are parts of the park that Ords never see, never experience, and can't get to. The lair of the Crub lies in one of them."

Simwan nodded slowly. "But you don't know exactly where in the northern section it resides?"

"Afraid I can't help you there." Rising on her hind legs, the matriarch picked up a double handful of peanuts and started to walk away from the barrier. "Like I said, they don't let us out. So I've never been on that path myself. And if I could, I wouldn't, and you shouldn't." Looking back over her shoulder, she left them with five final words. "Watch out for the testudines."

"Hey, wait! Come back," Amber yelled. Their sole source

of information ignored them as the primary primate sauntered languorously in the direction of her offspring and a quiet place to munch what she had scooped from the hoard. As soon as she was out of easy biting range, the mob of drooling langurs who had been tensely awaiting her departure descended on the remaining peanuts. Howls and screeching pierced the air as shells, nuts, and not a few hanks of fur flew in all directions. The excessive commotion drew the attention of a frowning zoo-keeper, persuading the Deavys to leave lest they be questioned about the disruption.

Wandering around the zoo, they debated how best to proceed.

"'A path of singular significance,' she called it." Rose was so deep in thought she didn't even glance up at the pair of tall, time-killing young men who passed them headed in the other direction.

"All we can do is head north and keep a lookout for visible signs and symbols," Amber pointed out reasonably.

"And invisible ones, maybe," suggested N/Ice.

"We'll find it." Simwan felt it incumbent on him to be posi-tive. "If the monkeys could pick up that much information with-out even leaving their habitat, then we ought to be able to do better, since we can go anywhere in the park that we want to."

"That's right." Amber's spirits rose. "And once we've found this Crub's burrow, we'll step on in and take back the Truth."

"And leave its owner with a firm warning never to return to Clearsight," Rose concluded staunchly. "Right, Pithfwid?"

Pithfwid nodded. "Well, let's get going. The Truth comes only to those who seek it."

With their everyday, run-of-the-mill black cat trotting along between them, the Deavy coubet and brother exited the zoo through its front gate.

Then the weather turned and they were forced to take shelter halfway between the zoo and the Rumsey Playfield. Tired of being pushed and shoved up against one another, the irritated clouds overhead had set to arguing violently. The result of their infighting was a cold, steady rain that came down hard as the Deavys ducked for cover beneath one of the many weather shelters that dotted the park.

In the northeastern United States, thunderstorms were most common in the summer, but were not unknown at other times. One was passing overhead now. Bursts of lightning illuminated the park grounds and thrust the trees into skeletal relief. By this time, anyone with any sense had fled for the safety of anywhere that wasn't exposed to the elements. The storm was violent enough to make Simwan wonder if it had been summoned forth by the Crub itself. But while lightning crackled all around them, none of it struck near the simple three-sided shelter under which they were huddling.

It was not long before the embedded storm cell moved off to the northeast and the downpour gave way to light, intermittent rain. While sufficient to keep most would-be joggers and bicyclists indoors, it was not nearly bad enough to prevent the Deavy offspring from continuing on their way.

Most Ords had some idea where lightning went (into the ground) and what subsequently happened to it (it dissipates). But it took sharp-eyed non-Ords like the Deavy coubet to spot what happens to the thunder. Like the lightning that gives it birth, thunder almost always rolls away to fade into the distance.

Only the occasional rare outburst takes the shape of a disarmingly small plant. Very rarely did an Ord ever accidentally stumble over a thunderweed.

N/Ice was especially adept at locating the sudden, explosive growths. They tended to appear in the midst of dense clusters of other vegetation, locales that made them even harder to find. Having picked a small bouquet, she amused herself by giving each gray-green branch a liberating kiss before tossing it into the air.

"Will you quit that?" Pulling one of her music player's earplugs from her ear, Rose snapped at her sister.

By way of reply, N/Ice stuck out her tongue, kissed another thunderweed, and tossed it high into the sky. At the apex of its arc, it dissolved away in a clap of rolling thunder. An Ord standing that close to such a detonation would have been deafened. Not so for the Deavys. Some of the learning games they had engaged in when younger were louder than any dissipating thunderweed.

Rose and Amber only relaxed when N/Ice had tossed away the last of the blooming thunderclaps.

To get to the central part of Central Park, they had to pass between two bodies of water: the Lake, as it was straightforwardly known, and the much smaller Conservatory Water. Though it was hard to make out shapes through the damp mist that alternated with the light rain, Simwan thought he saw only a couple of other hardy (more likely foolhardy) individuals. One was exercising a horse. The other, some rich resident's thoroughly miserable-looking servant, was walking a pair of dogs. The twin poodles pulling at their respective leashes were clad in designer rain gear that the speculating coubet quickly decided held higher price tags than the entire clothing budget for the average family of four.

One didn't see such displays of blatant ostentation in rural Pennsylvania. This being none of his business, Simwan had decided to ignore the dogs and their owner when the two pampered pooches began to snarl and drag their sopping-wet walker in his direction—and in Pithfwid's.

The cat ignored them until they were very close. Straining at their restraints, they snapped and snarled, eager to take a bite out of the lone black cat.

"I'm terribly sorry." The poor servant charged with walking his master's pets struggled to hold back the dogs and prevent them from assaulting the youngsters' cat. He yanked hard on the two leashes. "Don't worry about it." Simwan raised his voice slightly to make himself heard above the rain. "Happens all the time."

While the servant was focused on Simwan and Simwan was looking back at the servant, Pithfwid finally deigned to recognize the snarling dogs with a glance in their direction. It was a fleeting glance, very brief indeed. For barely a second or two, unseen by the walker, the cat's eyes trebled in size and turned bright crimson, the vertical pupils flashing both fire and threat. Simultaneously, a remarkably deep yowl emerged from Pithfwid's throat. Half of this lay below the range of human hearing—right where the growl of a hungry jaguar might be.

The two poodles backed up so fast they skidded on the wet pavement in their haste to take cover behind the legs of their handler. Distracted from the apology he was delivering to Simwan, the man looked down at them and frowned uncertainly.

"That's odd. What's got into them?" He bent toward the dogs. "Mitzy, Fritzy—did you see something?"

The dogs were paying him no attention. Thoroughly cowed, they stayed bunched up behind his ankles, trembling and whimpering, their eyes half bulged out of their heads as they stared at the former object of their curiosity.

"Shadows in the rain," Simwan theorized aloud even as he threw Pithfwid a cautionary look. The cat ignored him, blandly innocent.

"Yeah, I suppose."

"Have a nice day." Simwan smiled as he herded his sisters away.

As soon as they were alone again in the park, Simwan gazed disapprovingly down at the cat. "That wasn't very good manners, Pithfwid. What if the Ord had seen you?"

"He didn't," the cat replied brusquely. "And I *was* mannerly. Dogs are conceived uncouth. Anyway, it's not like I bit somebody's nose off. I just put the fear of felinity into them."

"Look!" Rose was pointing.

They were coming up on the Conservatory Water, with the more extensive expanse of the Lake just visible through the rain off to their left. At this rate, Simwan decided, they would reach the northern portion of the park well before nightfall, with a chance to locate and enter the Crub's lair before their quarry suspected they were so close. That was assuming, of course, they encountered no delays.

Unfortunately, the first of these was waiting for them just ahead.

A group of them.

-XV-

A dozen shapes were visible off to the left of the Conservatory Water. Some of them, in twos and threes, huddled close together in conversation, as if proximity to one another could stave off the falling rain. A couple stood off by themselves, discussing unknown thoughts and vistas. What drew Simwan's attention and put him and the coubet instantly on alert were the two teenage girls who were playing catch. It wasn't their activity that alerted him. There was nothing overtly suggestive, much less threatening, about two girls playing catch.

It was the fact that instead of a volleyball, or a football, or a soccer ball, they were playing catch with a basketball-size sphere of ball lightning.

Now, the distinctive phenomenon known as ball lightning is not necessarily lethal, or even especially dangerous. But it is not something commonly found on a playground, not even in a city like New York. It was also not something suitable for a game of catch between two teenagers.

At least, not between two *Ord* teenagers.

"Hey, check it out," a screechy, high-pitched voice declared ahead of them. Simwan had stopped, but it was too late to try and go around the group or to retreat without being seen. He and his sisters had been spotted.

Coalescing like a large family (or a small army), the dozen teens who had been idling in the mist started toward the Deavys. Simwan did not have to warn his sisters to be ready for trouble. At their feet, Pithfwid bristled slightly while doing his best to give the appearance of an ordinary housecat.

It was only as they drew near, emerging clearly from the mist, that Simwan saw that while the members were all more or less female, some were decidedly not girls. There was the one with the long brown tail and pointed ears, for example. And a duo of others who really were *others*: No more than five feet tall and stockily built, they had leathery skin that appeared distinctly leprous in the rain-muted, reduced afternoon light. That did not prevent them from wearing eye shadow and lipstick, or neck-laces and earrings. Not all of the earrings, Simwan noted, were attached to earlobes. Then there were the leather-and-denim–clad, chain-wearing individuals who sported jewelry in even odder places. One had a set of alternating gold and silver rings encircling the very distinctive elephantine trunk that protruded from the center of her face. Another lit a cigarette by breathing on it. The gang smelled, Simwan decided, as distinctive and unpleasant as it looked, though the rain helped to mitigate the group's aroma.

The tallest member came sashaying directly toward him, halting barely an arm's length away. Though taller than Simwan, she weighed considerably less. Her body was more than slender. It was positively serpentine, an impression that was reinforced by the hypnotic side-to-side swaying of her upper torso. Ears that were almost invisible against the sides of her head—nearly disappearing beneath her shoulder-length blond hair—slitted eyes, and a flat, tiny nose completed the image of a female who was more *serpens sapiens* than high school cheerleader.

"Well, well, what have we here?" she hissed calculatingly. Dismissing Simwan with contemptuous indifference, she turned her lidless stare on the coubet marshaled next to him. "A babysitter and his three—or is it two—charges?" She ignored the cat at her feet as she indicated the gang clustered close behind her. "These are the Ictis. I'm Zamandire Gosht. Who the hell are you?" She flicked a glance skyward. "Kinda wet out for nurseys to be walking their babies. Whatsamatter? The cartoon channel off the air?"

No doubt the lanky leader of the gang was used to her appearance and attitude intimidating those she challenged. She had never previously, however, encountered any Deavys.

"All the cartoons seem to have been moved to the park," Rose replied without missing a beat.

You could see the tension ripple through the gang members. Doubtless used to having their way, and scaring off anyone and anything that got in their path, it was clear that they were as unused to defiance as they were to sarcasm.

Zamandire slithered right up into Rose's face, having to bend low to all but butt noses with Simwan's uncowed sister. "You got a mighty big mouth for such a little twerp. If you're not real care-ful, someone might make you eat those words."

"I don't like eating words," Rose replied, unperturbed. "No nourishment, and too many of them taste bad." She smiled delib-erately. "I'm very fond of *snake*, however. Our mom usually serves it ground up and mixed with cashews and water chestnuts."

Simwan readied himself. For an instant, it looked like Zaman-dire was going to jump right down Rose's throat. Then the gang leader grinned and drew back.

"What a smarmy little big-mouth you are. You look just like your sisters. Triplets, are you?"

"We're a coubet," clarified N/Ice. "Two-and-a-half. And you're right. Each of us is just like the other."

"So if you want to have a go-round with any one of us," Amber finished, "you'd better be ready to round-go with all two or three of us."

"That's very confusing." Reaching into a pocket of her long black jeans, the gang leader withdrew what looked like a knife but was more akin to a fancy letter opener. Its black lacquer finish was covered with arcane oriental and Arabic symbols. "If you're all the same on the outside, then you should look exactly the same on the inside, right?"

Simwan started to bring up his arms, only to have Rose firmly push his hands back down. "No, big brother, you stay out of this." Her attention returned to the muttering, hissing, growling gang members. "This is a girl fight."

"Don't be ridiculous, Rose," he shot back. "A fight's a fight, this isn't the Clearsight Junior High playground, and these aren't the rough-playing girls from the Wilson Memorial soccer team."

Something pushed up against his ankles and meowed. Looking down, he saw Pithfwid play-acting at kitty-normal. Only the cat's penetrating gaze hinted at the depths within. The look was full of meaning, which Simwan reluctantly comprehended. Hesitant and a bit bemused at seeing the cat side with the coubet, he obediently stepped back.

Amber's right hand had slipped into her purse. "We don't want any trouble. We're just taking a walk in the park."

Zamandire nodded slightly. Slightly, because her head seemed fused to, rather than mounted atop, her neck. "Only a walk, hmm? Well then, I suppose we might let you go. Just kiss my foot, turn around so I can kick you a good one, and go back the way you came."

Rose had also dipped one hand into the purse she carried. "I don't mind kissing your foot, but we can't go back. We have to go north."

"North?" The leader of the Ictis looked back at her gang in mock surprise. "But you can't go north. Because you're south of us, and to go north, you'd have to go through us." She tightened her grip on the cryptically inscribed letter opener.

"You mean, like this?" Without waiting to see what mischief the letter opener might portend, N/Ice leaped forward.

Sprang would be more like it. Even Pithfwid would have been hard put to match N/Ice's pantherish leap. Still, it wasn't quite fast enough.

Exhibiting the flexibility of a wire cable, Zamandire bent her torso out of the charging girl's path. Shooting past the tall teen, N/Ice found herself entangled with a pair of hot-tempered gang girls. Not only hot-tempered, but hot to the touch. Flames sprang from their fingertips and their lips as they did their best to ensure that the audacious visitor would get singed for her impudence. Flying through the air, N/Ice did a complete flip that Mrs. Sanders, the Clearsight Junior High gymnastics teacher, would have scored at least an eight, and landed on her feet. Her landing was transparent, and so, for the moment, was she. Clutching at her, the finger-flames of her assailants went right through the sometimes there, sometimes not-there member of the coubet.

Having reached into their purses, Rose and Amber withdrew . . . lipsticks. Amber's boasted one of those silly, foolish names so beloved by girls from eight to eighty. Something like "December Japanese Plum Blossom." Rose's was darker and more orangey. As to any guy, they all looked red to Simwan. But the lipsticks carried by the Deavy girls were more than mere mouth paint.

Wielding the chain that she had been wearing as a belt, one of the Ictis lunged straight at Rose, swinging the heavy metal links like a whip. Seeing her coming, Rose brought her lipstick up and thrust it forward. A stream of thick, glowing crimson (or maybe December Japanese Plum Blossom) shot forth from the tip: a fluid that in consistency and power fell somewhere between blood and napalm. The attacking gang member parried the flow with her swinging chain. The red fluid struck the metal—which promptly melted, falling to the ground as a ropy mass of hissing slag.

The gang member reacted to this in an entirely reasonable manner. Eyes wide, she halted where she was, considered the molten, rapidly solidifying remnants of her steel belt, looked up at the defiant twelve-year-old confronting her, and started to back off.

A trio of girls was closing on N/Ice. One as blocky and thick-set as the polished stone from which she appeared to be chis-eled (and maybe was) lumbered toward N/Ice as her companions tried to cut off any line of retreat. N/Ice appraised the three of them, took a deep breath, and ran. Not backward, not to flee, but straight ahead. Smiling nastily, the stout female figure before her extended both massive arms expectantly. As soon as N/Ice was within reach, they slammed together, grabbing.

To grab nothing but air.

N/Ice didn't go around the female creature. She didn't slide between those heavy legs, or leap over the short, flinty hairdo. Instead, she went right *into* her assailant. And didn't come out the other side.

Stunned, the chunky gang member looked down at herself. Her expression was one of utter disbelief. Her companions stared at her as if she had suddenly taken on the aspect of a really bad date. Slowly, carefully, the blocky girl began feeling herself. She did so hesitantly, as if afraid of what she might find. Then her face started to turn green. Really green: bright green like lime Jell-O. Her cheeks bulged. She began to sweat pebbles that tumbled and clinked off her face to fall noisily to the ground. Clasping both hands to her middle, her mouth opening wider than seemed possible, she suddenly and explosively threw up.

What she threw up was N/Ice. Standing on the wet ground before the now deathly queasy gang member, N/Ice shook her-self, made a face, and spoke without looking at anyone in particu-lar—least of all any of her three assailants.

"Yuck! I've spent time in some really icky places, and some really icky people—but that was just gross!" As she finished, the girl whose body she had temporarily inhabited keeled over backward, rolled onto her stomach, and continued upchucking the remaining contents of her digestive system. N/Ice watched for a minute, then turned to face the other two girls.

"At least you two look halfway human. I wonder what the other half is like?" She took a step toward the nearest of the two gawking gang members. Immediately, and wisely, they turned and ran, disappearing into the rain.

Confronted by Zamandire, Amber held her ground, waving her own lipstick before her and using it to trace defensive patterns in the air. The gang leader jumped back and forth, searching for an opening, only partially aware that the rest of her gang was having rather more trouble with the other two twelve-year-old park visitors than anticipated. Slowly, threateningly, she opened her mouth, to reveal a pair of incisors much too long and sharp to belong to any human. Reaching up with both hands, she proceeded to remove them, plucking them from the roof of her own mouth and twirling them like drumsticks in her supple fingers. An apprehensive Simwan knew immediately what they were. Ord gang-types might carry switchblades. Zamandire Gosht had access to switchfangs.

Striking as swiftly as any cobra, Zamandire leaped and stabbed with one blade. Amber jumped backward and parried with a sweep of lambent orange-red from her lipstick. Almost immediately, the gang leader threw herself forward, bringing the other blade down with as much force as she could muster. Amber quickly brought her lipstick around in front of her. Red-orange flow and glistening fang clashed and locked. Grinning, much bigger and heavier than Amber, Zamandire Gosht pressed down, using her weight to force the fang-blade closer and closer to the smaller, younger girl's throat. Grimacing, Amber struggled to push back, to hold the bigger girl off.

Despite what he had been told, Simwan started to rush forward. Something tripped him before he could advance more than a step toward the two combatants. Lying on the wet grass, he looked back in surprise. Pithfwid was standing there, wagging one paw back and forth and shaking his head.

Slightly frantic now, Simwan looked up just in time to see Amber, who had starred in her dramatics class at school and who had done a wonderful job of feigning imminent collapse, bring up a knee sharply to catch the conquering Zamandire right under the chin she had brought conveniently close. The gang leader blinked. A stupefied expression came over her face. Still holding onto both blades, she straightened unsteadily, rocking back and forth on both feet. Brushing herself off, Amber approached and, with a single deliberate motion, thrust the lipstick she was holding directly at her wobbly nemesis. A burst of red-orange shot from the end of the faux gold case to strike Zamandire directly in her open mouth.

There was a flash of red-orange light, sufficiently brilliant even in the dim, rain-swept light of afternoon to force Simwan to turn momentarily away. When he looked back, a three-foot long snake lay twisting and writhing on the grass right where the gang leader had been standing. As he and his sister stood gazing down at it, a wailing cry came from overhead. Though the Deavys did not know it, the hawk that appeared out of the rain to snatch up the snake in its claws and carry it off was something of a local celebrity. Whether it and its mate would be able to handle this particular meal was another matter. They could hear Zamandire Gosht yelling and protesting as her serpentine form was carried away into the clouds.

The fight was over. Relieved, Simwan moved to rejoin his victorious siblings.

"Nobody messes with the Deavy sisters!" Rose proclaimed proudly as she walked up and gave N/Ice a congratulatory pat on the back. Her hand went right through her kinswoman.

"Sorry, sis." N/Ice promptly went solid and returned the embrace.

That was when Simwan saw one of the lingering gang members pull a gun. The girl was standing a goodly distance away, but that didn't lessen the threat posed by the weapon. Especially since it glowed with an unholy reddish light. She was in the process of aiming it at Amber, who was still standing on the spot where the hawk had carried off her transmogrified tormentor.

There was no time to analyze, no time to think. Reaching down, he picked up a fist-size rock, laid on it as hasty an enchantment as ever he had uttered, and threw it with some force. Before she could get off a shot, the gang girl with the gun saw the rock coming toward her. She promptly jumped to one side. The rock shot past, missing her by a good couple of feet. It then proceeded to curve around in a tight, neat arc and retrace its path. Letting out a bleat of alarm, the girl turned and ran, dodging and twisting with a nimbleness that was more than human. It didn't matter. Appropriately commanded and admirably committed, the rock followed the girl's every twist and turn. A minute or so passed, by which time the rain and mist had swallowed up both girl and stone. The echo of a dull *thunk*, however, was sufficient to assure Simwan that the thrown stone had finally found its intended target. Sure enough, no sign of movement showed itself through the steady drizzle, nor did any gunshots ring out above the sounds of rain falling on grass and pavement.

Amber was putting her innocent-looking lipstick back in her purse. No wonder, Simwan mused as he walked over to rejoin her and the others, his sisters and their friends often spoke of good makeup as being a girl's best friend.

"I remember people back home in Clearsight who had been to New York always talking about how nice it was to take a walk in Central Park," Rose ventured as the Deavy clan reunited, "but they just have no *clue*."

They resumed their trek northward. The girls' rehashing of the fight gave way to the realization they were all more than a little thirsty.

"Hot chocolate." Amber eagerly searched the mist-shrouded trees for signs of a concession stand.

"Tea with sugar," countered N/Ice. "First blush, like Mom prefers, and only the tips." Thinking of her hospitalized, Truth-starved mother caused her expression to drop.

"Coffee with cream," declared Simwan manfully. Having voiced his preference, he then joined his sisters in looking expectantly at Rose.

"Actually," she responded a little defensively, "I kind of feel like ice cream."

"Ice cream?" Amber's disbelief was magnified by a desire to express her astonishment. "In *this* weather?"

Rose pushed out her chin. "I *like* ice cream."

"Oh well," N/Ice observed diffidently, "each to their own. Maybe with *hot* fudge."

And none of them noticed the smoke that wasn't curling just off the path. . . .

The concession stand was in the park but not of it. It was no bigger than any of the thousands of other portable, rollabout food carts that populated the streets of Manhattan. In addition to the usual giant, hot, soft pretzels and the less common churros dusted with cinnamon sugar, it also advertised drinks. That was what the three thirsty Deavys were looking for, and they made a beeline for the cart.

A colorful striped awning shielded the proprietor from the rain while the heat from the pretzel and churro warmers kept the temperature comfortable in the cart's immediate vicinity. In his late middle-age, the proprietor looked to be of Middle Eastern or perhaps Pakistani origin; plump and seriously mustachioed, he wore his floppy cap like a helmet against the autumn air.

"A slow day and a damp one," he told Simwan in response to the question that hadn't been asked. "What can I get for you kids?"

N/Ice pushed to the front, drawing frowns from her less aggressive sisters. "Tea! Hot tea, with sugar. First blush, brewed with the tips only."

The cart operator's expression underwent an abrupt and remarkable transformation. Suddenly, he was no longer a jaded, overweight vendor of fast food. His eyebrows rose and a gleam appeared beneath that hinted of experiences and knowledge gleaned from sources even more exotic than the streets and avenues of central Manhattan.

"Oho! What have we here? A connoisseur, and one both young and pretty, at that!"

"She's not pretty," put in Rose quickly. "Just pushy."

"Ah, but," observed the proprietor sagely, "she looks just like you. So if she is not pretty, then you must also be not. . . ."

"Maybe a little pretty," a chastened Rose hastened to correct herself.

"They both look like me," Amber hurried to add.

"You are all pretty." As the Deavy coubet stood there in the drizzle, the cart's owner seemed to have grown in wisdom and stature before their very eyes. No more a vendor of cheap snacks and paper-cupped drinks, he had been subtly transformed into a potentate of potions, a purveyor of the purest potations. "Except you, of course, young sir," he told Simwan. Leaning forward to peer down over the front of the cart, he added, "And you too, oh architect of a wicked tail."

The man turned to a speed boiler capable of brewing either tea or coffee. "First blush, tips only, you said." As his fingers performed sleight of hand with water and infuser, he cocked one shrewd half-closed eye in her direction. "Plantation? Altitude?"

Out of her depth now, and aware that her sisters were watching her, N/Ice gulped and mumbled hesitantly, "Surprise me."

The proprietor nodded. Water began to boil, though Simwan could not see how the brewing machine was powered. Batteries? Or something less . . . ordinary? The soft, pulsing yellow glow that came from somewhere within the machine itself seemed to suggest the latter.

213

"Nepal? Sri Lanka? Darjeeling? Assam?" He was smiling encouragingly.

Feeling less intimidated, N/Ice smiled back. "Darjeeling, please."

The man nodded. Whisking fingers through the air like a magician feeling for invisible cards, he produced a half handful of tea-leaf tips. Blowing on them to add moisture, he then crushed them in his fist, brought the result close to his nostrils, inhaled, and nodded with satisfaction. Into the water they went, a small pot of water that had come to a steady boil unnaturally fast. Without pausing, he turned his attention to the other girls. "Ladies?"

"Hot chocolate?" inquired Amber tentatively.

Another small pot was filled with milk and brought to another preternaturally rapid boil. The round-faced operator eyed her expectantly. "All Criollo single-origin cocoa, of course. Plantation?"

Amber exchanged a look with N/Ice, then turned back to the kindly snack master. "Surprise me," she replied, echoing her sister.

By the time the man's attention came around to Simwan, the combined fragrances from the two pots—one light and delicate as the finest perfume, the other thick and cloying as the memory of a particularly intense kiss—threatened to overwhelm him. He could barely gasp out, "Coffee, with cream and sugar."

"What kind—no, let me guess," the man murmured, catching himself. "You want me to surprise you."

"Why not?" was all Simwan could murmur.

Rubbing the heavy stubble that landscaped his cheeks and chin, the proprietor studied the teen standing before him while

214

Rose and N/Ice immersed themselves in their tea and cocoa. "Let me see, let me see. You look to be a sturdy type, well read and reasonably athletic, but not overpoweringly physical or overpoweringly confident." He gestured conclusively. "Yes, I think a nice Jamaican Blue for smoothness, with a touch of Goroka to give it a little kick." Having concluded his caffeinated analysis, he busied himself with the brewing machine that seemed capable of turning out just about any kind of exotic libation one could wish for. Once again, he seemed to draw the basic ingredients for the chosen brew out of thin air.

When Simwan accepted the steaming paper cup, the aroma rising from the dark liquid within threatened to send him into a swoon. He would have uttered "Wow!" except that he was too busy drinking.

"And what for you, last little miss?" The proprietor smiled encouragingly at Rose, who had been silent until now. She looked simultaneously embarrassed and rebellious.

"Actually, I'm not thirsty. I'd just like a scoop of ice cream. If you've got any."

If her sisters and brother expected the man behind the cart to recoil, to demur, or even to laugh at this request, they were mistaken. He merely nodded. "To everyone, her likes and dislikes, her large tastes and little defiances. Why *not* ice cream?" Turning away, he bent to open a small cooler and began to fumble within. "I am afraid my selection today is somewhat limited. The weather, you know. I only have vanilla, chocolate, mint, frankincense, acajou, rambutan, Hanuman-nut, Loki-scramble, and everyberry." He poked a little farther into the cooler. "Oh, and pismashio."

Simwan lowered the astounding coffee from his lips and frowned. "Don't you mean *pistachio*?"

The proprietor looked up and smiled. "No, pismashio."

Simwan really wanted to have a taste of that, but Rose disappointed him by ordering everyberry. Nodding agreeably, the cart owner dug into the depths of the cooler and scooped out a big ball of something blue and red and purple and—Simwan discovered that he couldn't quite identify the exact color of the paper cup's contents. It wasn't his fault. The color kept changing even as he looked at it, and the transformation wasn't an artifact of the afternoon light, which was pretty consistently drab. In contrast, the contents of the cup all but smoldered with a continuously shifting inner sparkle.

Accepting it, Rose used the accompanying plastic spoon to dig in. Sipping at their own astonishing distillations, Amber and N/Ice crowded close around their sister.

"What's it taste like?" N/Ice asked with unconcealed interest. "Strawberry?"

"Yes," Rose admitted as she smacked down spoonful after spoonful. "Strawberry."

"Looks more like raspberry to me," Amber countered.

"Yes, raspberry," her tastebud-transported sibling agreed.

Simwan sensed that they were in the presence of something special, dessert-wise. "Blueberry?" he inquired. "Blackberry?"

Rose nodded enthusiastically, but only between tastings. "Uh-huh. Blueberry. Blackberry. Also marionberry, loganberry, juniper berry, query berry, and every other kind you can think of."

"Wow." N/Ice pushed closer. "I wanna taste."

"Me too!" Amber crowded Rose's other side.

While the coubet clashed over their sister's unexpectedly diverse scoop of ice cream, Simwan noticed that the affable proprietor had set a small bowl in front of Pithfwid. The cat took one look at the dish's ivory-hued contents, settled himself comfortably, and started lapping away. Clutching his coffee, Simwan moved closer to the cart and to the radiant warmth of the pretzel heater. He nodded in the direction of the contentedly consuming Deavy cat.

"What did you give him?"

"Fresh Devon clotted cream. I thought he deserved something nice, too. " The man rubbed at the back of his head, scratching his scalp through the floppy cap. Looking on idly while the girls squabbled for samples of Rose's everyberry ice cream, Simwan did his best to make conversation. "Your stuff is good. I mean, really, really good. On a sunny day you must get a lot of customers."

The man shrugged. "Some days are good, some are slow. Location is everything in this business. Baghdad in the time of the caliphs, now *that* was truly good for the coffee business. And outside the grand mosque in the days of Suleiman the Magnificent I hardly had time to chat, so busy was I brewing. Or for the Soongs—that was a proper dynasty, I tell you. As for the Mak-ah, of all the rulers of Chichen-Itza, they were the ones who were serious about their hot chocolate." He winked conspiratorially.

"In the same way, I could tell as soon as your first sister asked for her tea that you five were not your usual stroll-in-the-park family." He glanced meaningfully upward. "Young travelers such as yourselves must have a very important reason for being out on a gloomy, wet day like this."

Though instantly on guard, Simwan had the feeling he could trust this omniscient vendor of snacks. "We're looking for someone who took something that belongs to our family and was being looked after by a friend."

"I see. Well, don't tell me about it. If you don't tell me, then I can't tell anyone else, no matter how they put the question to me." He gestured at Simwan's cup. "Want a refill? Half price."

No fool even at his age, and realizing that if he lived to be two hundred he might never taste coffee this good again, Simwan immediately agreed.

"What do I owe you?" he finally remembered to ask, as Rose's shrinking scoop of ice cream was reduced to its final four flavors.

"Hmm." The proprietor considered. "Three drinks, one coffee refill, one ice cream, single scoop." He smiled down at Pithfwid. The cat was sitting back on its haunches and using a paw to clean its face and whiskers. Glancing up at the man, he put the paw over his mouth, burped a delicate compliment, and methodically resumed his grooming.

"That's a dollar each. Four dollars, please. The cream for the kitty was a gift because I like cats. They have gourmet taste buds, don't you know, and many've been the time I've asked a cat to check an ingredient of mine to see if it had gone bad.

Simwan looked stunned. "That's all? Four dollars?" He indicated his sisters, who were dumping their empty cups into the plastic trash bag that was clipped to one end of the cart. "For—everything?"

The man smiled as he took the five-dollar bill from Simwan and made change. "I get more joy out of seeing special customers like yourselves enjoy something than I do from the selling of it. You can put a price on someone else's food, but not on their pleasure." Leaning over the center of the cart between the pretzel and churro warmers, he lowered his voice. "Keep heading north, beware the Reservoir, and you should find the one you're looking for."

"What?" Startled, Simwan started to reply—only to find himself staring into the trees and bushes. The snack cart, with its wondrous cornucopia of smells and lights, was gone. As was its smiling, all-knowing, mysterious operator. Around Simwan and his sisters all was quiet again except for the feathery fairy patter of falling rain. Even the air seemed thick and muffled.

"Good ice cream," a cheery Rose finally proclaimed into the silence.

"Best tea I ever had," confessed N/Ice. Turning away from the place where the cart had been, she started northward into the middle reaches of the park. Her sisters flanking her on either side, their rapid-fire conversation turned back to the plot of a certain TV show and the possible paths its central storyline might take in the coming weeks.

Simwan happened to look down. Four black streaks on the path's pavement indicated where the snack cart's tires had rested only moments earlier. Even in the rain, the streak marks looked as if they had been made by flame and not rubber. As he stared at them they began to fade, washed away by something considerably less prosaic or obvious than running water. Each time a bit of blackness disappeared, it was in a flash of splintered light, like a cheap Fourth-of-July sparkler flaring out.

He felt a pull on his end of the leash he was holding. Pithfwid was looking up at him and tugging with some urgency. Turning away from the dissipating wheel marks, he followed coubet and cat into the mist. His thoughts should have been on the way ahead, but they were not. After all, he was only sixteen. So instead of concentrating on what threats and dangers might yet lie before him, all he could think of was the phenomenal coffee he had imbibed, Amber's remarkable hot chocolate, N/Ice's narcotizingly marvelous tea, Rose's everyberry ice cream, and the special gift the cart's operator had affectionately placed before Pithfwid. All that, and one last, lingering regret.

I should have bought a pretzel, he told himself. No telling what *that* might have tasted like.

-XVI-

As the Deavys approached the middle portion of the park called Cedar Hill, they saw nothing out of the ordinary. The intermittent rain and drizzle had given way to a cloying fog that seemed more appropriate to San Francisco than Central Park. Though no other afternoon visitors were visible, any number could have been present just out of sight, swallowed up by and hidden within the hovering mist. It dampened not only vision but sound, rendering the ceaseless hum and honk of traffic on Fifth Avenue barely audible. That was one of the great virtues of the park: It provided a refuge from the sounds as well as the sights of the great city.

A certain number of those sights were not visible to the vast swarm of Ords who called Manhattan home. The proper perceiving of these concealed places of interest was the province of those who had been trained to look a little more carefully at things, to probe a little deeper than their ordinary friends and neighbors. Though still young, every one of the Deavy brood had acquired that ability. So it was that they all saw the Bruise at the same time.

It occupied the west-facing side of a hill that was topped by red cedars. In place of wet green grass, a wide swath of dull brown and sepia showed where a broad swatch of growth had been severely damaged. To a passing Ord, everything would have looked normal. Only Simwan and his sisters saw the hurt underneath as they drew near. The vegetation here had been wounded, though by what unnatural force they were unable to tell.

Halting at the edge of the injury, Rose gently extended one leg and lowered her foot down onto what to an Ord would have appeared to be grass no different from that growing anywhere else in the park. A feeble, faint moan rose from the ground and from the brown, half-dead grass blades that immediately recoiled from her foot, in obvious pain. She quickly stepped back.

"Something bad happened here." Peering warily into the smothering fog, Amber saw nothing that could be construed as threatening. Whatever had damaged this hillside was no longer present.

Kneeling, N/Ice ran her fingers gingerly through the nearest strands of scruffy turf. Even the weeds that poked hopeful heads up above the grass showed signs of injury. "Whatever did this has moved on." Still crouching, she tried to take in the full extent of the damage. "I don't see any indication that this lawn is going to recover properly any time soon." Straightening, she wiped moisture from her fingers. "At least, not without help."

"Well, it's not our business," Simwan murmured halfheartedly as he started to look for a way around the damaged hillside. "We can wonder about it, but we can't linger." He glanced skyward. Though the fog blocked out all but a suggestion of sunshine, he knew from his watch that the day had already sunk well into afternoon. They still had a long way to go to reach the area where the Crub might be found.

His sisters eyed one another. As usual, their communal compassion exceeded their collective common sense. "We can't just leave it like this," Rose implored him. "The ebb and flow of life here has been hit hard."

Amber nodded. "Mom always told us to help living things whenever we could, 'cause that's a good that always comes back to you."

"She told *you* the same thing," N/Ice finished as she stared meaningfully at her brother.

Rolling his eyes, Simwan looked down at Pithfwid for support. "What do you think?"

The cat considered the feebly moaning hillside. "Personally, I'm just as happy in dirt as on grass. But you can't eat dirt. And if we lend assistance—assuming we can actually do anything for this dreadfully bruised bit of earth—those we help might in turn be able to narrow our course."

Simwan made a face as he gestured at the hillside. "This is *grass*. You can't talk to grass."

Eyes that were the color of cut amethyst stared up at him. "Speak for yourself. All living things have ways of communicating." Lowering his gaze, Pithfwid looked past him. "If you girls want to give it a try, I see no harm in making the effort. But be quick about it."

That was enough for the coubet. While Simwan simmered, reduced to watching his watch and bemoaning the loss of ever-diminishing daylight, the girls debated how best to proceed. Healing spells were discussed, revivifying enchantments gone over, rejuvenation magicks analyzed. In the end, it was an impatient Pithfwid who finally suggested a possible course of action.

"A couple of dump-truck loads of good-quality fertilizer would seem the best answer, but only to Ords." Waving a paw, he indicated the fog-swept hillside with its stand of red cedars brooding helplessly on the heights. "What's needed here most of all is the kind of cleansing innocence that will wash away the foulness that has so badly bruised this piece of earth." The cat regarded his trio of female humans. "I know it will require a great effort on your part, but do you three think you can muster up a few moments of innocence?"

Taken aback, the girls eyed one another uncertainly.

N/Ice looked toward the patch of tormented turf. "I'm not innocent. But I remember what it is. I swear that I do." She eyed her sisters, each in turn. "If we can remember it, we can bring it back—if only for a little while." She smiled softly, hopefully. "We can at least try." She held out her hands.

Rose took one, Amber the other. This time forming a line instead of a circle, the three sisters advanced as gingerly as they could, stepping out onto the anguished vegetation. As their feet contacted the injured growth, the moaning from below grew louder. But it was restrained, as if the grass and flowers and weeds were aware of what was intended, and were doing their best to stifle back their pain.

Forming a circle on the wounded hillside, the girls sat down as carefully as they could and crossed their legs. Still holding hands, they lowered their heads toward one another until they were nearly touching. The sisters exchanged a single long, lingering glance. Though no words were spoken, the concurrent communication was complete. Simultaneously, they closed their eyes and began to murmur softly in unison.

Standing on the healthy grass that bordered the Bruise, Simwan looked on with a mix of admiration and affection. Sure, he and his sisters fought all the time. And sure, as the only guy, when it came to arguments or discussions he was always outnumbered. But that didn't mean he didn't love them, and even occasionally think highly of them. As visiting aunts and uncles and elderly cousins were fond of pointing out, even among the small and tightly knit population of non-Ords, the Deavy coubet was something special.

They were exhibiting that uniqueness now.

Often brash and bratty, irksome and chatty, the coubet underwent a gradual, subtle transformation as profound as it was inclusive. Touches of gaudy, trendy makeup faded away, to reveal underneath complexions as pure as polar snow. Rose's blond hair turned to pure gold, Amber's became auburn, N/Ice's metamorphosed to silver. Not gray, as an Ord onlooker would assume, but true silver, chased and chaste, as untarnished as that to be found in any royal crown. Their contemporary attire vanished, replaced by floating capes of white laced with gold: capes that fluttered and soared like the wings of the wandering albatross—and this in the complete absence of wind.

A torus of bright radiance appeared above their heads, its

nexus hovering at the exact midpoint between them. Pure white at first, it changed with the slow, solemn chanting of the sisters to a pale, then to a darker green: a lambent emerald hue as profound and mysterious as the color of the deepest rain forest. When it had achieved the intensity of green fire, the three Deavy siblings raised their heads, opened their eyes, and gazed at it fixedly. Rose's eyes had assumed the blueness of a New Orleans funeral march played in January rain, Amber's had turned as dark red-brown as the heart of cocobolo, and N/Ice's . . . N/Ice's eyes were like the overhanging brow of an Antarctic glacier where it gazes out onto the Southern Ocean.

Amber murmured something. Rose added to it. N/Ice swirled it all together into a single cohesive command. The green torus flashed, expanding outward in all directions at once, forcing both Simwan and Pithfwid to look away momentarily. Shattering into a million billion miniscule particles, the turbulent, roiling greenness sifted to the ground where it was gratefully absorbed by dead and dying grasses and other desperate vegetation.

Capes vanished, to be replaced once more by jackets and jeans. Blond curls and familiar eyes were once more the order of the day. The girls rose and started back down the slope to rejoin Pithfwid and their brother. All around them, comforted by the mist and reassured by the coubet's magic, the hill was rapidly regenerating. Healthy green grass replaced dead brown stalks. Weeds reasserted their grip on the soil and fought their way upward. Bunches of flowers erupted like rainbow popcorn. The sisters had done a good thing. Nearly overdone it, Simwan decided.

It was going to be a puzzled landscape worker indeed who

sometime in the course of the following week stumbled across a clump of Peruvian ground orchids sprouting amid a patch of dandelions.

"*Much* better." Rose hiked the strap of her purse higher on her shoulder. Her flaxen hair had regained its previous chic, garish tinting.

As they made their way away from Cedar Hill and toward the eastern edge of Turtle Pond, they were illuminated by a few moments of sunlight. Forcing its way through the October cloud cover, the sudden glow warmed them as well as their surroundings.

They continued walking while, overhead, the clouds had once more quietly come together, shutting out any view of the canyonlike skyscrapers that walled in the park. Along with the rethickening of the atmosphere came the threat of renewed rain. Mimicking Pithfwid's actions, if not his actuality, Simwan checked the very real timepiece on his right wrist.

"It's getting late, and we haven't even made it halfway through the park. I don't want to go back to Uncle Herkimer's and have to start all over again tomorrow morning."

Somehow Simwan knew that this might be their only chance to find the Truth. And save their mother.

And they went on.

-XVII-

The undergrowth in the vicinity of Turtle Pond was much thicker than anything the Deavys had previously encountered in the park. With its weeds and reeds, its dense bush rows, and the many trees that overhung the narrow winding path that was leading them northward, it was a haunting reminder of the beloved woods behind their house back home in Clearsight.

Though the familiar look and smell of the place made them all momentarily homesick, it served as a useful reminder of why they had come to New York: to recover and bring back the Truth so that the ordinary citizens of their hometown would no longer be blinded by the unctuous lies and flashy multimedia presentations of the would-be developers, and would realize anew why they needed to get out and vote against the proposed mall and its related urban expansion. Without the Truth, the Deavy's town, their home, and their mother might not survive.

On the map of the park that Simwan carried, Turtle Pond was not a particularly daunting patch of water. But the map was an Ord map, and they were advancing through a landscape that was a swirling, mist-shrouded jumble of Ord and non-Ord reality.

So they were surprised but not shocked to find that Turtle Pond now extended all the way across the park from west to east. Or maybe it was just that the recent rain had raised the pond to such a level that it had overflowed. However, it was not the water that held up their advance. It was the Pond's namesakes.

Now, it was not unreasonable to anticipate encountering turtles in a place called Turtle Pond. One might even expect to find them if looking beyond the boundaries of the Pond itself. A wandering turtle here, a couple of feeding turtles there. What brought the Deavys to a halt were not a turtle here and a couple there, however, but dozens of them. Hundreds, even. Some were not moving while others rushed about at frantic velocities that approached two miles per hour. Simwan could have hopped around the fastest of them on one leg. Backward.

Except that he could not get around them because they were stacked on top of one another, in some places as high as a hill. In others, only a couple of turtles blocked the Deavys' path. But those couple might consist of Galápagos or Aldabra tortoises: enormous animals weighing hundreds of pounds. Calling on her studies in Mrs. Coulter's Biology class, Rose reminded her siblings that all turtles and tortoises could bite. Some, like the Mississippi alligator snapping turtle, had jaws that could snap a broomstick in half. Or a misplaced arm.

Though they searched to left and right, they could find no opening of any kind in the solid wall of turtles, tortoises, and terrapins. As usual, it was left to Pithfwid to point out the obvious.

"Let's talk to them," the cat suggested, retreating a few cautious steps as one mud-coated muck mauler threatened to snap in their direction.

Simwan scrutinized the hard-shelled, slow-moving wall that blocked their path. "Okay. Which one?"

"Pick an old one. Turtles and such live a long time. An old one should be a wise one."

Rose was nodding sagely. "That makes sense." She paused, staring at the hundreds of creatures piled high in front of her. "Uh, how do you tell an old turtle from a young one?"

"Look for the gray hair." No one was ever half as amused by Pithfwid's humor as was Pithfwid himself. "Oh, botheration—I'll sniff one out."

They settled on a truly antediluvian wood turtle, wood turtles being reckoned among the smartest of their kind. It was an undistinguished-looking individual, with a typically turtlish gray, diamond-patterned shell and a neck of no great length. Together, they formed a circle around the wood turtle, who was patrolling slowly along the base of the turtle wall.

Halting, it started to turn around, only to see an expectant N/Ice blocking its retreat. With Rose on its left and Amber on its right and Simwan and Pithfwid crouching down in front of it, their cornered subject had nowhere to go. Nor was it likely to break into a sudden sprint and dash off between someone's legs. Settling on Pithfwid as the instigator of its confinement, it emitted a short, challenging hiss, then relaxed. Simwan decided that more than anything else, its response smacked of bored resignation. Its first words confirmed this view.

"All right. What d'ye great clumsy mammals want of me?" It reserved particular scorn for the encircling humans. "Me name's MacCunn, I'm visiting from Nova Scotia, and I've no time for childish shenanigans."

"We won't keep you long, then," Simwan assured him. He indicated the endless wall of Testudines that was blocking the way. "We just need to get into the northern half of the park."

Its head swiveling from side to side on its muscular neck, the wood turtle eyed each of the Deavys in turn. "Then why don't ye just take an uptown bus?"

Amber shook her head. "We can't. To arrive at where we have to get to, we have to go through the park. Through each and every manifestation of the park. If it were as simple as just traversing the Ord version, we wouldn't be talking to you right now."

The turtle MacCunn considered. "Och, that do make good sense, it do."

"So how do we get through?" Straightening slightly, Simwan indicated the armored wall. "We don't want to hurt any of you, and we don't want to get hurt ourselves. Can we just ask your relatives to temporarily move aside so we can pass? Or could you maybe ask them for us?"

"Canna make it happen, boy," the turtle told him sorrowfully. "'Tis not in me power. The wall represents all that is I and me kind. Only the King o' the Pond can call for a breach in the barrier. Ye'll have to talk to 'im."

"Where do we find this 'King of the Pond' who can let us pass?" Pithfwid asked politely.

"In the pond proper." Turning as slowly as steamed broccoli on a lazy Susan at a Boy Scout picnic, the wood turtle gestured to the west. "I can show you, if you like."

"We would like," Simwan replied. "But in the interests of exspeediency, and if you don't mind . . ." Bending, he carefully picked up their reluctant guide, holding him firmly with both hands.

A contented MacCunn voiced no objections to this more rapid mode of travel. It was a short walk to the edge of the main pond anyway.

A complex chorus of croaks and ribbits greeted them as they arrived at the edge of the lily pad–pocked, reed-fringed expanse of dark water. Among the occasional raindrops, dozens of pairs of bulging, spherical eyeballs stood out, peppering the pond's surface like so many glistening marbles. Turtle Pond was as hospitable a home to hundreds of frogs as it was to the hard-shelled reptiles that had given it its name. There didn't appear to be more than a turtle or two in the actual pond, however. The majority had gathered to form the smelly wall that stretched off to east and west. Incapable of perceiving the barrier, Ords could walk right through it. Not the Deavy brood, however. Being a non-Ord, Simwan reflected, had its drawbacks as well as its advantages.

Well, this shouldn't take too long, he decided. Gently, he set the wood turtle down at the edge of the water. "How do we find this King of the Pond?" he asked.

MacCunn raised a foot and pointed. "Be ye blind as well as half daft? He's right here in front of ye."

All four Deavys, plus Pithfwid, scanned the ground, the water, and the dense reeds and brush beyond. Other than the undergrowth, they saw nothing but dozens of frogs and the occasional off-duty turtle.

"I don't think I'm blind," Amber observed, "but I don't see anything that looks especially kingly."

MacCunn had already lumbered halfway into the water. "I tell ye, the one ye seek is right here under your very eyes. Dinna ye know the legend?" By way of illustration, he proceeded to whack the frog closest to him with one front leg, sending it spinning out of the shallows and onto the mud. Dazed, it lay on the bank and struggled to collect itself. "A beautiful damsel kisses a frog, and it turns into a king." By this time the turtle was completely submerged except for its head and the back of this shell. "I've done what I kin for ye, and that's all I kin do. Not being a beautiful damsel, I canna do your kissin' for ye."

The Deavys studied the still-stunned frog that was numbly stumbling from side to side on the bank at their feet. It was palm-size, dark green with black spots, and decidedly slimy-looking. Rose looked at Amber. Amber promptly turned to look at N/Ice. N/Ice, in turn, focused her gaze expectantly on Rose. Simwan, being anything but a beautiful damsel, felt much relieved. "Rock, paper, scissors," suggested Amber half-heartedly. "It's the only fair way."

"All right. But still . . ." Unable to think of a better way out of the slippery conundrum with which they had been presented, Rose unenthusiastically agreed to the process, as did N/Ice.

Simwan looked on as his sisters stuck out their right hands and counted down to a hesitant but unavoidable one-two-three. Rose was the loser, having gone with rock, while both her sisters had materialized paper. For a moment, she thought of throwing the rock she had conjured at one of the frogs. That wouldn't do, of course. She had to kiss one, not whack it unconscious.

"Go on," Amber encouraged her sister.

"Do it," a more solid-than-usual N/Ice urged.

Swallowing hard, Rose knelt down and picked up the frog. Whether because it was still stunned from the smack MacCunn had given it or because it was otherwise disoriented, it did not try to hop from her hand. As her sisters, Simwan, and a mildly interested Pithfwid looked on, Rose brought the squidgy creature toward her face.

"Oh, yuck!" she muttered. "I don't know if I . . . I can't . . ."

Though Simwan rarely played Big Brother, he did so now, eyeing Rose sternly. "Quit stalling."

"Oh, all right!" his sister snapped at him. "Blither it all, anyway." And with that she brought the frog up to her face, puckered her lips, closed her eyes, and kissed it square on the mouth.

"Eeww . . ." Amber's expression wrinkled up like a week-old onion. "She *did* it."

"Yuck squared," commented N/Ice succinctly.

Opening her eyes, Rose blinked. A soft, surreal golden glow had begun to envelop the frog. It began to bloat, to expand in her hand. Very quickly it grew too big and too heavy for her to hold. Bending, she set it down on the damp soil and stepped back. As the Deavys surrounded it, the cylinder of light rose, taller and higher, until it was greater in width than any of them and taller than Simwan.

As the pulsing glow began to fade, a shape became visible within the dying radiance. It was a man of middle age: bearded, powerful of bearing, and chiseled of face. His head was crowned by a symbol of office: a tall, gleaming white hat that . . .

A white *hat?*

The last of the luminous casing vanished. The man stood there, regarding them querulously. All was silent for a long moment, until Amber finally observed, with more than a hint of uncertainty in her voice, "You don't *look* like a king. Not even of a pond."

"King? Who's a king?" The man had a pleasant voice and a strong European accent. "I'm Tartelli, the baker. Who are you?"

"We're the Deavys," Simwan explained. "We were told that in order for us, as non-Ords, to proceed on our chosen path through this park, that we have to ask the King of the Pond—this pond—to order the turtles barring our way to make a portal for us." More than a little annoyed, he glanced at the surface of that mysterious body of water, but the wood turtle was nowhere to be seen. There were only frogs. "The one who instructed us said that a beautiful damsel—in this case my sister Rose—should kiss you to turn you into the King."

Looking apologetic, Tartelli shook his head regretfully. "I'm just an enchanted baker. Are you sure you were told to kiss *me?*"

Simwan hesitated, eyed his sisters. "Well, no, maybe not. What MacCunn said was 'A beautiful damsel kisses *a* frog, and it turns into a king.' "

Obviously wishing to be helpful, the baker nodded knowingly. "I see. *A* frog. Not *the* frog, or *this* frog, or even *that* frog. Just *a* frog."

"He said that it was right here in front of us," Rose objected, still wiping furiously at her lips with the back of her left hand.

"Well?" Turning, Tartelli indicated the pond behind him. As ever, it was chock full of frogs. "I think your helpful turtle friend was just using me as an example."

"Do *you* know which one is the King of the Pond?" A touch of desperation colored N/Ice's query.

"I'm afraid not." The baker sighed regretfully. "We're most of us here separately enchanted, you see. And even to other frogs, most frogs look pretty much alike." He smiled at Rose. "That was a very nice, innocent little kiss, by the way. I'm sorry I'm not the one you want." Stretching, he tilted back his head and surveyed the cloudy sky. "It's nice to be human again for a little while, but frankly, I'd rather be a frog. Catching bugs is a lot easier than baking pies, and I don't have to get up early in the morning to get to work."

Simwan seized on just four of the enchanted baker's words. "You said 'for a little while.'"

Tartelli lowered his arms. "Oh yes. Unless accompanied by a suitably complex fixing spell to make the restoration permanent, the effects of a damsel's kiss only affect the relevant enchantment for a short while."

"So," Amber was thinking aloud, "how *do* we find the King?" Based on what the helpful Tartelli had told them, she was afraid she already knew the answer.

She was right.

"Trial and error, I'm afraid." He shrugged his white-clad shoulders. "If you're serious about it, I suggest you get started. You don't want the effects of your kisses to start wearing off before you've found the one you seek."

"OH YUCK!" Though all three Deavy sisters exclaimed it in harmony, it did nothing to take the edge off the method all three were going to have to employ.

Standing back and looking on, Simwan almost felt sorry for them. He was able to temper his concern by remembering every nasty trick, every practical joke, they had ever played on him. Together with Pithfwid, he stood under a tree and watched as the girls removed their shoes and socks, rolled the legs of their jeans up to their knees, and waded out into the chilly, murky, shallow pond. One at a time, they would scoop up a frog, bring it up to their grimacing faces, and kiss it. Glow after towering glow repeatedly illuminated the mist and drizzle as enchanted amphibian after enchanted amphibian was provisionally restored to temporary humanness.

It was a tiring, boring, exasperating task: one in which Simwan was glad he did not have to participate. Frustration mounted in tandem with the increasing number of transformed frogs. Through the magic of their kisses the busy, and increasingly numb-lipped, Deavy coubet brought forth from the depths of the pond enchanted policemen, firemen, a dry cleaner, a couple of street musicians, a Coptic priest, several thoroughly bewildered members of Genghis Khan's Golden Horde, a Polish tailor from Krakow, assorted sailors who had been lost overboard from their respective vessels, marooned, or who had overdosed on assorted alcoholic stimulants, and the entire basketball team of the town of Bantaral, Paraguay, who had been lost in a plane crash in the lowland jungles of the Amazon.

An attack of unrepentant nausea finally forced Amber to the sidelines, where Simwan did his best to comfort her while her two sisters osculated valiantly on. Rose was beginning to stagger herself when the thirtieth (or maybe it was the fortieth) entity she had brought back to humanness regarded her with a mixture of uncertainty and sternness and declared loudly, "Who disturbs King Thadd, and with a maidenly kiss summons him to resume this shape?"

Not sports shorts or fireman's coat, but rather regal robes draped the handsome, impressive figure. The crown that adorned his high-browed forehead was more of a crownlet: short on jewels and workmanship, but lustrous with gold beads and hammered plate. His eyes were dark and penetrating, his nose majestic, and his neatly trimmed beard ever so slightly flecked with gray. As the self-proclaimed king proceeded to lick the memory of Rose's kiss from his lips, a newly alert Simwan thought the revealed royal tongue a bit long. "I summon you," a greatly relieved (because she would not have to kiss any more frogs) Rose informed him. Gesturing with one arm, she added, "I, Rose Deavy, and my sisters, Amber and N/Ice, and our lazy good-for-nothing-except-making-jokes-about brother, Simwan, and our most estimable cat, Pithfwid."

The King of the Pond looked around. Already, policemen and musicians, sailors and basketball players, were periodically reverting to their previous batrachian bodies.

"No ordinary kisses can suspend such strong enchantments."

"We have to travel to the north end of the park, and to find what we seek there we have to travel *through* the park. Certain parts of its reality that are closed to Ords are open to us, and vice versa." Turning to his right, Simwan indicated the wall of turtles that cut through the middle of the pond. "This barrier of Testudines is one of the versas. We *have* to get through. To do that we were told to put the request to you, as King of the Pond, to grant us passage."

"And rightly so," the monarch of the muck agreed. "The question remains: Why should I?" He inspected Simwan up and down. "I do not know you. I do not know, or care, about your purpose in crossing the park. It has nothing to do with me, or with my realm." Extending and raising both arms, he gestured expansively. "The Pond is a dominion unto itself, clear and clean and devoid of the illnesses that infect both the ordinary and non-ordinary worlds. We enchanted who dwell within it delight in having as little as possible to do with either."

This wasn't going as Simwan had hoped. "Please, Your Majesty. You don't understand. If we can't continue our journey, then we won't be able to fulfill our quest. If we fail in that, terrible things are going to happen in the town where we come from, and maybe beyond. Our mother . . ." He had a sudden burst of insight. Or maybe it was just one of those occasional sharp, unexpected pains that sometimes stabbed him behind his left eye. He'd know in a moment.

"A stream runs behind our house, on our property, and there are ponds there, too. Every year both are full of frogs, and if we can't go on with our journey, that stream is going to be diverted and those ponds are going to dry up, and *all those frogs are going to lose their homes.*" He paused to let that sink in and then added for good measure, "*Thousands* of them."

The king looked appropriately stunned. "That sounds like a truly catastrophic event. But," and he brought his face closer to Simwan's, "how many of those frogs are enchanted folk? For that matter, how do I know that any of them are enchanted?"

Stuck for an answer, Simwan tried to stall by looking thought-ful. This resulted in him adopting the expression that tended to make Ords frown at him and pretty girls giggle and point. It was not what he intended.

It was Rose who came to the rescue. Like the rest of the cou-bet, she was not intimidated by much of anything. Certainly not by a mere king.

"As far as my sisters and I are concerned, *all* frogs are enchanted!"

Straightening, the sovereign of slime eyed her sternly—and then broke out in a wide grin. An exceptionally wide grin that, given its source, was to be expected.

"A wise response. Not necessarily a knowledgeable one, but wise. In truth, all frogs are enchanted. I suppose I should not be surprised by your reply, since you and your sisters are also enchanting."

Almost old enough to blush at such a compliment, Rose did the next best thing by turning away so he could not see her face.

"Very well." Splashing quietly and carefully through the pond, the king faced the slowly shifting wall of turtles and tortoises. "I'll cede you the path you seek. But it will cost you."

One hand dropping reflexively to his side, Simwan felt of his wallet. The pocket demon within stirred slightly, then went back to sleep. Would an enchanted king see the ruse inherent in enchanted currency? "We're just four kids visiting the city. We don't have a lot of money."

"Money?" The now outwardly affable king smiled through his beard. "What would I do with money? If it was wealth that I wanted, I would have found a way to stay human." His attention shifted back to the coubet. "What I would like is another kiss. From each of you, if you please."

The girls exchanged a glance. "Okay," agreed Amber readily as she stepped forward. One by one, she and her sisters planted firm but chaste kisses on the king's face, choosing their angle of delivery and site of contact as carefully as any bomber pilot targeting an objective.

N/Ice was last. She didn't even wipe her lips when she stepped back. "That wasn't so bad," she murmured. "I thought it might be slimy."

"Or beardy," added a reflective, and slightly conflicted, Rose.

A look of fond remembrance washed over the king's countenance like watercolor on a white board. In addition, there appeared a dampness at the corner of one eye that was no lingering manifestation of his present condition but rather a sincere reflection of something long lost and almost forgotten.

"So much time passed," he murmured, more to himself than to his audience. "Innocence and beauty. Friendliness and warmth." Hauling himself back to the present, he looked down at the coubet and smiled. "I get a lot of tongue, but nary a true kiss. Thank you for reminding me of what it is like, and of the deeper meanings that it holds."

Simwan could not keep from asking the question that had been bothering him ever since Rose had applied her initial, restoring kiss. "Why go back to what you were? Isn't there some way for you to remain a king, or at least stay human?"

The tall, dignified figure peered down at him. "Do you think enchantments are so easily broken? Nothing against the effectiveness of your siblings' young lips, lad, but to permanently break such a powerful spell would require the attention of one who is older, more deeply attuned to the individual who is I, and of royal blood herself." He sighed heavily. "Perhaps one day she will come. If not, well, I am still a king. Small, green, and uncloaked, perhaps, but a king nonetheless." Turning to face the living barrier, he started to raise his hands.

"Wait." Simwan had one more question. "If in your enchantment you take the form of a frog, how is it that you can command turtles?"

The king looked back him without lowering his arms. "We water-folk have all manner and variety of arrangements. That is what happens when you have much in common with another kind besides simply sharing the same living space."

Reaching into his regal coat, he withdrew something small and stringed. Simwan could not see it clearly, but he could hear the sharp, precise notes that reverberated through the afternoon air as the king ran a couple of fingers across the concealed instrument.

That was all it took; a few plucks on a magic twanger, and the wall of turtles began to fall. Well, not fall, Simwan corrected himself. A portion of the barrier simply dispersed in two different directions, slowly and with considerable deliberation. The large turtles that formed the foundation lumbered ponderously to one side or the other while their smaller relations slid or tumbled clear.

"There you go." Slipping his mysterious, unseen little instrument back inside his coat, the king stepped off to one side and extended an inviting arm northward. "Hop to it."

As soon as all of them had passed through and were making

their way to the other side of the extended pond, they turned to wave farewell to the king. Standing in the gap, flanked on either side by turtles stacked ten feet high like so many four-legged building blocks, the very solitude of his temporarily restored humanness adding to his nobility, King Thadd waved back. Behind him, soldiers and bakers, ballplayers and musicians, all the enchanted who had been provisionally brought back to their human selves by the coubet's energetic kisses, were shrinking. Within a few moments, the watery surrounds were once again dominated by a counterpoint of chirruping and croaking.

"That wasn't easy." Stepping out of the shallow water on the far side of the pond, Amber bent to roll down first one pants leg, then the other. "Kissing them all."

"Could've been worse," N/Ice pointed out. "I don't see any sign of warts."

"He was a nice king." Rose, who after all had been compelled to deliver herself of not one but two kisses to the man in question, wore an expression Simwan had never seen on his sister before. "I wonder if he'll still be here and still be enchanted when I grow up."

"Forget it, girl," Amber chided her sternly. "It wouldn't make any difference. For one thing, you've got no royal blood in you."

"Hey," Rose shot back as she turned on her sister, "it's not like I'd want to *marry* the guy, or anything." Her vociferous demurral notwithstanding, vestiges of that unprecedented expression hinted at returning. "But I bet he'd be an interesting date."

"You know," N/Ice put in, "we never even thought to ask him what he'd been king of. Before the Pond, I mean." Alarmingly, she showed signs of embracing the same expression that had come over Rose. "I think you're right, sis. In a few years, it might be really interesting to come back here and talk to him again. And maybe try a different kind of kiss."

"Well," murmured Amber, "there's only one way to decide for sure."

Her sisters eyed her uncertainly. "How's that?" wondered Rose.

Amber's expression cracked, though to her credit she never quite lost control. "We'd have to take a Thadd poll."

Simwan shook his head despairingly as he watched Rose and N/Ice chase their sister across the slight grassy rise ahead of them. Thankfully, the rain had let up again, though it was still cloudy and damp. Behind him, the turtle barrier had vanished, lost in the mist and the rising up in its wake of the ordinary part of the park.

"Sisters," he muttered. "When they're not fighting with me, they're fighting with one another." He looked down at the cat pacing him. At the moment, Pithfwid had chosen to appear golden brown with patches of white. "Do you think they can stop being little girls long enough to deal with something as grim as the Crub?"

"Separately, your chattering siblings are children on the cusp of adulthood. Together, they are a coubet. Those are two very different things," the cat reminded him. "Children would have no chance against such as the Crub. A coubet—now that's something else entirely." He glanced backward. "A good thing indeed that we are once again on our way. That confrontation was no less difficult for me than it was for your sisters."

Simwan looked uncertain. "Why was it difficult for you? You didn't have to kiss any frogs."

"No, but I did have to struggle to mind my manners. I happen to be very fond of frog legs, and I suspect that had I made a meal of one of the king's subjects, he would have been much less inclined to grant us safe passage."

Simwan nodded understandingly. He could not quite sympathize with the cat, however, because he had never eaten frog legs. That was one more unforeseen consequence of their recent encounter.

Now, he never could.

-XVIII-

The appearance of more Ords than they had encountered since they had first entered the park was, in its perfectly ordinary, unspectacular way, comforting and reassuring. Though the mist and light rain continued, the vast flat expanse of the Great Lawn allowed the advancing Deavys to see a fair distance in any direction for the first time since they had left the vicinity of the zoo. Ignoring inviting side paths and suggestive signs, the Deavys struck out straight across the lawn. Heading north and very slightly west, they deviated from their chosen course only once, so that everyone could take a long draught from a public drinking fountain. Possibly the signs of normality all around caused them to relax more than they should have. Or maybe the fog that suddenly dropped over them like a blanket of wet soot was enough by itself to shut out the non-ordinary part of the park. Whether the fog was responsible, or whether they had entered into another, subtler variation of the landscape, it was impossible to tell. One consequence soon became obvious, however. Regardless of the cause, exercising Ords and their attendant pets, spooning couples, and puffing joggers were soon once more lost to sight, swallowed up by the returning mist.

After a short but brisk walk they found themselves on the paved walkway that bordered the vast expanse of the Reservoir. Looking like a cloaked, seated statue, an old woman was feeding stale popcorn to sodden pigeons. Otherwise the area fronting the water, like most of the park on this cold, damp October day, was devoid of visitors.

The decision to take a short break to rest and catch their breath was a unanimous one. There were benches of concrete and wood and metal to sit on, and the fog had lifted sufficiently for them to see partway across the perfectly flat body of water that was by far the largest such expanse in the park. Shining through the misty overcast like a sheet of unrolled steel, it spread out before them. The Reservoir occupied about a sixth of the park's total area while even the Ord version extended nearly from one side to the other, east to west.

Choosing one bench, N/Ice glanced to her right to make sure none of the Ords were looking in their direction. She need not have concerned herself. The few joggers were steadily passing in and out of sight; the old lady was intent on her voracious avian friends. Cupping both hands together in front of her mouth, N/Ice inclined her head toward her palms and uttered a short, sharp, simple spell. A flush of radiance appeared in the bowl formed by her hands, the light shining pale red through the narrow gaps between her fingers. As she pulled her palms apart, she puckered her lips and blew gently. Impelled forward and down by her breath, the ball of pale yellow light she had called forth struck the concrete bench and sank into it like butter melting into a hot baked potato. The luminance dissipated rapidly, taking with it all the moisture that had accumulated on the bench's back and seat.

The girls promptly sat down on the freshly dried bench. Since the coubet backsides took up its entire length, Simwan was left standing. He didn't mind. As a big brother of all sisters, being left out was just something he had gotten used to. Pithfwid had no such problem. With three warm, comfortable, girlish laps to choose from, he selected one and jumped possessively up into Amber's.

After calling up a few thousand ants to clean the dirt off their clothes, the girls—and Simwan—felt refreshed as they walked up to the edge of the concrete barrier that held back the deceptively tranquil body of fresh water known as the Reservoir. Simwan stood quietly studying the gray expanse. It was too deep to wade, as they had done at Turtle Pond, and it extended nearly from one side of the park to the other. Somehow, they had to get across.

Movement drew his attention away from the beckoning water. The freshly cleansed coubet had come up alongside him. For all their noisy bravado, the girls were once again waiting for him to make a decision.

"We have to get across," he told them, reiterating what they already knew, "but the prospect scares me. Remember what the nice old guy with the snack cart told us."

Rose repeated it aloud. "'Beware the Reservoir.'"

Her brother nodded somberly. "If his warnings are as well made as his drinks, I don't think we should take the chance."

Amber spoke while surveying the empty expanse. "Then what do we do?"

Turning, N/Ice gestured at the walkway that traced the Reservoir's southern boundary. "There's more park to the west of the Reservoir than there is to the east. One thing I remember from the map is that the park's main bridle path runs south to north on that side." Her tone was hopeful. "We could follow it. It could be the Path of Singular Significance that the senior lady langur told us to take."

Simwan was unsure. "I dunno. She also told us that to get to the Crub's lair we should follow on *straight* through the park. That's pretty much what we've been doing." He gestured westward, into the fog and drizzle. "If we turn off to the left now, we won't be going straight anymore."

Rose was deep in thought as she kicked idly at the pavement with one foot. Finally, she looked up and declared, "Well, straight on or not, I'm still pretty dry in spite of the rain, and I'm sure not going for a *swim*."

"Me neither." N/Ice sounded just as defiant as her sister.

Despite the misgivings he felt over the looming and seemingly unavoidable change of direction, Simwan was not ashamed to be outvoted. Their parents had raised them to live side by side not just as brother and sisters, but also as a small democracy. In the event of a tie, Pithfwid was available to break any deadlock. Simwan eyed his remaining sibling.

"Amber?"

"I think we should take to heart what the man with the snack

249

cart told us: to beware the Reservoir." Even in the mist-diffused light of late afternoon, her unblinking eyes shone like discs of polished slate speckled with gold dust.

Simwan chose not to argue. For one thing, he couldn't think of a better course of action. Nor did he particularly fancy stripping off *his* clothes and going for what promised to be a cold, cold swim, either.

But as they started westward along the gently curving pavement, he could not get the monkey's admonition out of his mind. For the first time since they had left the zoo, they were no longer proceeding northward, were no longer heading straight toward their goal.

He just had to hope that in spite of that, they would still get where they were going.

-XIX-

It was early evening when they reached the place where the paved walkway that bordered the south reaches of the Reservoir intersected the main bridle path. All manner and kinds of trees lined the heavily forested route, which was much wider than any of the merely pedestrian walkways they had encountered since entering the park. Though covered only with gravel and hard-packed earth, it was expansive enough to accommodate a truck. Except for park maintenance vehicles, however, no machines were allowed on the path. Only horses, riders, and pedestrians.

Simwan's map showed the path winding its way along most of the length of the park all the way from south to north. Snaking its way between the west side of the Reservoir and Central Park West, it seemed to offer easy access to the park's north-ernmost reaches. As they stood studying the route, a couple of Ord joggers came boinking past, their faces frozen in the familiar grimace common to all such creatures whose chosen activity is mistakenly marketed as fun. Watching them labor past, heading south, Amber shuddered at the prospect.

"Ever see one of those things smiling?" she commented.

Rose shook her head sadly. "Not once. Not ever." Glancing skyward, she stepped out onto the path. The cloud cover that had been present all day made it hard to judge the time by the movement of the heavily obscured sun. So she dispensed with tradition, and checked her watch. "We'd best hurry."

"Okay," agreed N/Ice, "but no matter how late it is, I'm not jogging."

Omnipresent fallen leaves crunched like stale potato chips beneath their feet as they set out on the path. Gold, brown, and every shade in between, they formed a colorful carpet beneath the children as they made their way northward. They encountered no more joggers. Simwan was not surprised at the absence of riders. Even to a non-equestrian like himself, horseback riding in the rain didn't seem like it would be much fun.

They had progressed maybe halfway around the Reservoir when Pithfwid came to a stop. Surrounded by fallen and falling leaves, the cat had halted in the middle of the path. Now he was lying prone, stretched out full-length on his right side on the hard, wet ground. Hands on hips, a disapproving Amber frowned down at him.

"I know cats need a lot of sleep, Pithfwid, but this really isn't the time or the place for a catnap."

"Shut up," he hissed curtly.

The sharpness of his retort stunned everyone. Pithfwid could be brusque, he could be aloof, but he was rarely impolite. It suggested that he was really irritated—or that something ominous was afoot.

That was when Simwan noticed that in addition to being sprawled full-length on the ground, Pithfwid's head was firmly pressed to the earth. He was listening to something not only with his right ear, but with his entire body. Trying to divide his attention between cat and path, Simwan knelt beside him and whispered.

"What do you hear, Pithfwid? What do you feel?"

A pause, then: "Vibrations. Coming toward us. Growing stronger."

The girls had gathered around to gaze down at the cat. "Horses and riders?" Amber finally asked.

"Yes—but not what you think." Springing sharply to his feet, Pithfwid whirled and sprang forward—back the way they had come. It was the first time since they had entered the park that the cat had retreated so much as a step. "*Run!*"

Reflexively, everyone looked north, up the bridle path, even as they complied. From infancy, they had each and every one of them learned to pay attention whenever the cat said "jump." He never did so unless there was a good reason for it, such as the time baby Rose had been caught prodding a wasps' nest to try and coax out the pretty-colored creatures dwelling within, or when a curious four-year-old Simwan had tried to stick his fingers into one of the wall sockets in the Deavy house. There were no wasps' nests visible on the bridle path, or open sockets, but Simwan knew that something serious had alarmed the cat, and that was enough to persuade him to break into a worried sprint.

N/Ice had declared that she wouldn't jog—but she had voiced no such compunction about taking flight. They raced back the way they had come, following Pithfwid, occasionally looking back over their shoulders. Nothing was to be seen behind them for several minutes.

That did not mean there was nothing to be heard.

The grunts that came out of the increasingly dark mist were low and terse, loud and deep. They suggested the approach of something large and powerful, and more than one of whatever it was. Above the rhythmic grunting could be heard high-pitched speech of a kind that was alien to Simwan. It sounded at once familiar and yet completely foreign: the sounds guttural and the words unintelligible, as if someone was reciting a half-known language backward and upside down. Both grunting and growling were closing quickly. He tried to run faster. The girls kept up with him (who knew that all that soccer practice would have a practical payoff?), while Pithfwid had to slow his pace to keep from leaving them behind.

The bridle path was reserved for the use of pedestrians, joggers, and horses and riders. Listening to the earth, Pithfwid had acknowledged the approach of the latter—"but not what you think." Straining to see back through the gloom and the mist, Simwan's eyes widened as the reason for the cat's cryptic comment finally thundered into view.

The mounts were goliaths of their kind, but there was nothing equine about their features. They were true giants. Naked of body and blunt of face, they came pounding heavily down the bridle path on all fours, chomping on metal bits forged to fit mouths not equine, but human. Their hands and feet were oversize and callused from running, and they galloped with a ferocious dullness in their eyes that shouted their lack of intelligence.

This was in direct and incontestable contrast to those astride the saddles that straddled the broad human backs. Hoofs jammed into stirrups, eyes blazing, long snouts exhaling streaks of condensation in the chill air, the five riders held their respective seats despite the heavy, damascened, silver-hued armor they wore. They carried swords and lances, and their manes and tails snapped in the wind.

"*Madoon!*" Pithfwid yelled back as he led his humans onward. "Among their kind, the horses ride the people instead of the other way around!"

This bizarre recognition inspired a number of questions in Simwan, but when a spear plunged into the earth off to his left and entirely too close, he decided to save them for later. Right now he needed all the air his lungs could gather just for running.

Then Rose stumbled.

She didn't make a sound, though she went down hard. Her sisters and brother were at her side in an instant, helping her up. Gravel and dirt fell from her recently cleansed clothes as she struggled to resume running. But despite her best efforts, the most she could manage was a fast limp. Simwan didn't think anything was broken, but a sprain would be almost as incapacitating. It didn't appear serious, but it did not have to be. It did not have to stop them, all it had to do was slow them down.

The intersection where they had stepped off the paved walkway and onto the bridle path loomed just ahead. If not for Rose's injury, they would already be there. Helping his sister along, Simwan felt as if he could feel the fetid, sour breath of one of the

Madoon's mounts warming the back of his neck. He expected to be cut by a sword or pierced by a lance at any minute. He couldn't afford the time to look back. Grimacing in pain, Rose limped along as best she could between him and N/Ice. He heard Pithfwid yowl: a mixture of alarm and defiance.

The screams of the mounted Madoon split the mist-filled air. To Simwan, they sounded like shouts of anger and frustration, not triumph. Despite struggling with the burden that was his sister, he risked a look back.

Amber had halted directly in front of the onrushing giants and their mutant equine riders. She could have cast a spell, if she'd had enough time. She might have laid down a challenge to their pursuers, if she'd known what language to use. She could even have tried to delay them by fighting (all the Deavy children had received schooling in the martial as well as the magical arts), if only she'd had access to a weapon. But she had neither enough time, nor the right words, nor anything more lethal than a nail file in her possession. Yet despite every deficiency, and Simwan's initial fear that she would be trampled underfoot by the onrushing giants, she had somehow managed to stop them in their tracks.

That was why the Madoon were screaming at their suddenly contrary, balking mounts. These had abruptly come to a standstill. Instead of continuing the pursuit to finish off their intended prey, they were picking and grabbing at the ground. Sharp whips and harsh words had no effect on the saddled giants. Ignoring their Madoon masters, two of them had started fighting with each other. Encompassing Madoon and mounts alike, general confusion now held sway.

Supporting Rose between them, an exhausted Simwan and N/Ice reached the intersection and turned off back onto the paved walkway that marked the southern border of the Reservoir. Pithfwid was already there. By the time one of the Madoon finally managed to regain control of its mount and resume the chase, Amber had succeeded in rejoining her siblings.

"Keep running!" Simwan yelled as he started to lift Rose from where she had taken a seat on a park bench, not even bothering to dry it first this time.

Pithfwid forestalled him. "It's all right, Simwan. Just as the bridle path is intended for the use of riders and mounts, so pedestrian walkways are forbidden to them." Tail bottled, ears flared forward, the Deavy cat defiantly held his ground.

Instinctively, Simwan positioned himself between his injured sister and the charging Madoon. Red eyes opened wide, nostrils flaring, it glared down at him as the giant it was riding turned sharply leftward—and reared up on its legs, pawing at the air with both heavy, unshod hands. As it dropped back down, the Madoon thrust its sword threateningly in Simwan's direction— but that was the extent of its approach. Pithfwid was right: The Madoon and their mounts were restricted to the use of the bridle path, and could not leave it. With a furious whinny of rage, the horse-faced rider yanked on the reins it held in its other hoof and whirled around, galloping back to rejoin its equally frustrated companions.

Breathing hard, Simwan wiped sweat and rain from his face as he watched the quintet of bloodthirsty Madoon retreat northward, back the way they had come, until the monstrous and unnatural shapes of both human mounts and their equine riders had once more been swallowed up by fog and drizzle. Turning, he found Amber.

"How did you get them to stop? What did you use?" He shook his head in undisguised admiration. "I never saw anyone in the family, not even Grandpa Morregon Deavy, work an enchantment so fast."

"That's because it wasn't an enchantment." Amber looked slightly embarrassed. "I didn't have time to speak one even if I could've come up with something appropriate. I just happened to have something in my purse that I thought might work, so I threw it at them."

Pithfwid frowned. "'Threw it at them'? What in the name of all the Ten Lives did you have in your purse that was capable of halting a posse of Madoon in its tracks?"

Amber essayed a shy smile. "Candy. Lemon drops, and cherry drops, and lime and grape. I had just enough time to whisper a few words, a quick and simple enhancing spell. I thought if the candy colors were flashy enough, they might distract the Madoon for a moment or two. But what happened was that the giants saw them, and they went right for the candy. Just like horses after sugar cubes." She turned thoughtful. "Have to remember that the next time I'm troubled by pesky giants. Who knows? Maybe it would work on trolls, too."

N/Ice came toward her sister. Anticipating that one Deavy sibling was about to deliver a compliment to another who had just saved all their lives, it was evident that Simwan had momentarily put aside what he knew of his little sisters. N/Ice's face as she spoke was flushed, and not from the cold.

"*You* had *lemon* drops and you didn't share them with *us*?"

Amber was immediately both defensive and defiant. "Hey, I was gonna! I was just waiting for the right time, that's all."

"Oh yeah, *sure* you were," N/Ice shot back, looking like she wanted to take a poke at her sister. "Like, maybe *never*."

"Knock it off, you two!" Simwan turned back to his one sister who was not participating in the spat. Seeing where their brother's attention was directed, Amber and N/Ice set aside their argument as speedily as it had flared and moved to help attend to the third member of the coubet. Rose had rolled up the left leg of her jeans. Drawing near, N/Ice and Amber bent to examine and gently feel all around the edge of the very visible bruise on the bare, pale flesh.

"It's not broken," N/Ice observed, confirming Simwan's hasty original diagnosis.

"Wrong *time* for a sprain," Amber decided.

Rose was fighting back tears as she leaned forward to inspect the injury. "Well, all I know is that it hurts like crazy."

"We can do something about that." Digging into her purse, N/Ice brought forth several small containers. Selecting one, she put the rest back and opened the cap on the tube she had chosen. Squeezing it from its base, she forced about two inches of what appeared to be glowing gingery dust out onto her sister's injured leg. While she recapped the tube and tucked it back into her purse, Amber began tenderly rubbing the dust into the bruise. She had to work fast because a breeze threatened to catch the dust and swirl it into the air where it would disperse. Simwan eyed N/Ice questioningly.

"Oxide of orangeium," she informed him. "I remember Mom using it on me when I fell off my bike and banged up my right ankle."

Amber looked up at her sister. "You wouldn't have banged it up so bad if you hadn't been riding ten feet off the ground."

N/Ice made a face. "Hey, that's where the bike wanted to go. You know how ornery bikes can get if you just restrict them to riding on the street. Once in a while you have to give them their headlight."

Rose sat back and closed her eyes. "It feels better already."

N/Ice nodded knowingly. "That's one reason I chose this. I remember that it works real fast. Mom said it's good for contusions, deep cuts, bloody noses, scrapes, bee stings, and that it's really good on Oreos. Makes them taste just like Dreamsicles."

"Can you stand?" Simwan was watching his sister closely. If she couldn't travel at a reasonable pace, they would have to give up the quest—at least for the day—and go back to Uncle Herkimer's. They could try again when Rose's leg was better, but by then the Crub might have found out how close they had come to tracking him down. It could take appropriate steps to see that the Deavy brood had a much harder time of it next time they tried to cross the park. That is, Simwan thought, if they were even allowed a second chance.

And there were other factors to take into account. Uncle Herkimer might not be so willing to let them out on their own if he felt they were going to be gone long into the night. Or the New York weather might take a turn for the worse.

No, their best chance, their best opportunity to succeed in their quest, was to keep going, to press on. If they could. He dreaded having to choose between his sister's health and that of their mother.

Fortunately, N/Ice had chosen her medication well. With the

oxide of orangeium working magically on the bruise, Rose was soon not only able to stand but insisted she could run again if circumstances demanded it. Her leg was sure to be sore for a while, but she was adamant that she could manage.

"I can even run away from those awful Madoon again if I have to," she insisted stubbornly.

"You won't have to do that." Simwan was staring in the direction of the bridle path. "Because we're not going to risk running into them again." Turning to his right, he let his gaze rove out across the steadily darkening expanse of the Reservoir. "We'll find another way north."

Amber protested immediately. "I told you, brother—I'm not going swimming. Not in *this* weather." Her sisters were adamant in agreement.

"There are ways of crossing open water that do not require individual immersion." Having hopped up onto the concrete wall that held back the Reservoir, black- and azure-striped tail switching emphatically back and forth, Pithfwid stood staring in the same direction as Simwan, the cat's bright blue ears erect and alert.

N/Ice joined him, resting both palms on the concrete and leaning forward as she stared out across the basin. "It's smaller than an ocean but bigger than a pond. A boat is what we need."

"We could try the path on the east side of the park," Rose suggested.

Pithfwid shook his head. "There's bridle path to be crossed there as well. Too dangerous now that the Madoon know we are here. If they want to track us down, they'll be looking for us to try something like that." The cat turned bright indigo eyes on

Simwan. "I won't say that we're well and truly trapped, but our options have definitely narrowed. I think at this point we can do one of two things: We can go forward, or we can go back."

Silence ensued, broken only by the lonely, far distant honk of a truck horn or the mournful wail of a city siren. At that moment, they might as well have been as far away from the bustle of Midtown Manhattan as a plateau in Qingzai. Simwan looked at his sisters. The coubet eyed him back.

"We can't," Amber finally declared. "If we don't bring the Truth home with us, Mom—Mom might not . . ." She couldn't finish. She didn't have to.

"We've come too far and we're too close to give up now," N/Ice added resolutely.

Rising from the bench, Rose gingerly put weight on her injured leg and smiled determinedly. "Remember what Gramma and Grandpa always told us. Deavys don't run. Besides, if we keep on, maybe I'll get the chance to kick some Madoon tail."

From his perch on the edge of the concrete barrier, Pithfwid looked expectantly up at Simwan. "Well, boy? What say you?"

The girls were staring at him, waiting. "Like I have a choice," he finally muttered. "Like living with these three, I've ever had a choice." He turned his attention to Rose. "You're sure now, about being able to walk okay, and run if you have to?"

She nodded and, to emphasize her confidence, jumped. Not too high, but convincingly enough. "And I can kick with the *other* leg."

"Okay, then. What about Uncle Herkimer?" He cast a meaningful glance skyward. "It's starting to get dark. Should we give him a call?"

The coubet considered. "Better not to," Amber decided. "He might ask us to come back to the apartment. Then we'd have to tell him we can't, or lie about what we're doing. If he doesn't hear from us, we won't put ourselves in that position. It'll be all right. Uncle Herkimer knows we can take care of ourselves, even in a strange city. He knows that we're Deavys."

"Even knowing that we're Deavys, he still might start to worry a little if it starts to get really late," Rose put in, "but by that time we should have recovered the Truth and be on our way back to the apartment."

"We'd better be," N/Ice added grimly. "It's cold and it's wet and it's dark." She eyed the cloud-filled, mist-swept sky. "And it's only going to get colder and wetter and darker."

"All the more reason we need to get to the Truth as fast as we can," Amber observed quite sensibly. She started pacing the edge of the Reservoir, searching the water, the paved walkway, and the grass-covered ground they had recently traversed. "There *has* to be a way to cross."

It took them less than five minutes to find a boat. It was a nice boat. A straightforward one, with a single sail and boom, virtually no rigging, and a rudder to steer with. Perfect for their purposes, with only one drawback.

It was only a foot long.

Simwan scanned their immediate surroundings. Though the fog and mist had lifted slightly, his range of vision was correspondingly limited by the increasing darkness. There was no one to be seen: not on the pathway, not in the direction of the distant, dark hulk that was the art museum, not on the Great Lawn behind them. The child who had presumably forgotten the toy craft and left it behind after a visit to the park was probably on his or her way home, if not already there. They might be lamenting the loss, or like so many Ord children, indifferent to it, knowing that if they moaned and wailed about it loudly and often enough, their despairing parents would simply buy them another.

It was, most certainly, the only boat in sight. Rapidly running short of both daylight and time, the Deavys mulled it over long and hard.

"We could shrink ourselves to fit," Rose suggested, none too usefully.

"What, and have some oversize goldfish slurp us up for supper?" Amber argued.

"There isn't enough space on it to hold even one of us." N/Ice was gazing intently at the little wooden craft as it bobbed up and down against the interior of the Reservoir wall.

"'One of us'? There isn't enough room on it to hold one of my *shoes*," a disappointed Simwan pointed out. He glanced at Pithfwid.

"I see what you're thinking," the cat responded. "You can just forget it. While I might be able to sail that toy across the Reservoir, and while I could conceivably go after the Truth myself, that would mean leaving you four behind. I promised your parents I'd keep an eye on you. So you can skip the line of thought you're presently tripping down. Through success or failure, we're staying together." Raising one paw, he gave it a dainty lick. "I don't trust you kittens not to get into trouble if I'm not around to look after you."

By now all three girls were eyeing the model sailboat attentively. "Well," Rose finally declared, "if we're not going to make ourselves smaller, I suppose we have to try and make the boat bigger. Big enough to hold all of us."

"It doesn't have to be a perfect job." N/Ice was encouraging. "We're only going to sail it through part of Central Park, to the edge of North Meadow. It's not like we're sailing to Byzantium."

"Ephesus," Amber put in. "I'd rather be going to Ephesus."

"North Meadow." Simwan knew how easily his sisters could be distracted. "We're going to North Meadow. Ephesus can wait. What do you think? Can you guys do it?"

Amber was gazing fixedly at the toy vessel. "We don't need to conjure something new. We just need to make this one bigger."

"And maybe a little nicer," N/Ice added. "It's awfully plain."

Simwan saw the warning signs, heard the hints, but by the time he thought it might be appropriate to say something about them, the coubet had already bent to work.

As the sister possessed of the steadiest grip, Rose leaned over the concrete wall and held the toy as motionless as she could, gripping it by the stern while pointing its miniature bow out into the water and simultaneously uttering unfamiliar provisos. Amber stood on her left, working her fingers along with her words as she vigorously thrust both in the boat's direction. On Rose's right, N/Ice was bending forward and waving her hands back and forth over the sides of the little craft, murmuring softly under her breath. Simwan stood back, out of the way, watching and wary lest something go wrong.

True to their word, none of the girls had ever done much work with boats before, there not being much cause for them to do so while attending a landlocked school or living in a land-locked town. As they waved and intoned and gestured, he felt himself tense. A wary Pithfwid took temporary cover behind his lower legs, his vivid violet eyes widening slightly as he observed the coubet at work.

Something was happening, anyways.

A ball of light began to emerge from the water, swelling and intensifying in time to the sisters' steady sing-song. No, not from the water, Simwan saw. From the boat. Concerning the toy itself, the light soon grew much too bright for him to look at directly, even when he squinted. As the soundless golden globe continued to expand, lines began to appear within it. The girls were wholly into their work now, having entered into a trancelike state that was half theurgic, half sisterhood, and all coubet. As was usual during such times of powerful application, Rose and Amber remained firmly grounded while N/Ice could not keep from rising several inches off the ground.

Shafts of light like lambent ropes trailed from their fingertips as they wove the words and conducted the magic. Within the golden sphere, distinctive lines continued to solidify. Shading his eyes, Simwan found that he could now make out the first glimmerings of gunwales and tiller, mast and sail. It was the same toy ship they had found, greatly enlarged and doubtlessly more than a little transformed. How much more transformed he would find out in a moment or two.

The coubet's steady susurration slowly faded away, leaving the only sound the slight plinking noise produced by accumulated moisture falling to the ground from nearby branches and benches. As the girls went quiet, the golden sphere dissipated swiftly, the waves of light melting into the welcoming wavelets of the Reservoir. In their wake stood the model sailboat, enlarged enough to carry them all and, as Simwan had expected, more than slightly altered from its original design. Approaching, he looked it over from stem to stern, shaking his head critically. Pithfwid leaped lithely up onto the Reservoir barrier to study the result of the coubet's combined effort.

"Girls!" Simwan made a disgusted sound. "Honestly, can't you fix *anything* without overdoing it?"

A tad embarrassed, Amber looked over at Rose. Rose lowered her gaze as she glanced at N/Ice. N/Ice did her best to face down their big brother.

"Look, we've never modified a boat before. We've done ponies, and bikes, and skateboards, and even helped Dad with the car, but never a boat." As this threadbare reasoning sounded feeble even to her, she hastened to add, "Besides, this *is* New York."

At least it *looked* seaworthy, Simwan decided reluctantly as he stepped up onto the concrete barrier that held back the waters of the Reservoir. As Pithfwid made the short jump onto the boat's deck, Simwan extended a hand back toward his sisters. Still favoring her left leg, Rose accepted his offer of assistance without hesitation. A moment later, and they were all aboard.

Since no one else seemed inclined to take the position (or the responsibility), Simwan sat down in the stern and draped his right forearm over the hardwood tiller that controlled the rudder. As soon as he straightened it out, the boat began to move forward, away from the wall and out onto the gray expanse. As was to be expected, progress was smooth and steady, since there was virtually no wave action. The only sense of motion was forward.

With the fog once more snugging in around them and the

inexorable advancement of evening, he could see nothing in the way of landmarks. Not even the western or eastern boundaries of the Reservoir, much less any of the concrete and steel and glass towers that ringed the park. He was not concerned. North to south, the Reservoir was only ten blocks in length, extending from 96th Street to 86th. They were crossing a portion of north Central Park, not the North Central Pacific. It was pretty much impossible for them to get lost.

He peered off to the west. There was no sign of angry Madoon patrolling the distant bridle path, or of recreational Ord riders. Reality had become too stable for the former, too late and damp for the latter, he decided. He allowed himself to relax, his right arm resting lightly on the tiller, holding the magically modified craft on its steady northward heading. The watery tranquillity offered an opportunity halfway through their quest to take it easy for a moment or two. If only his sisters hadn't, in the course of their otherwise estimable exertions on behalf of critical toy boat renovation, decided to go and overdo things. The ostentatiousness of their work risked drawing dangerous attention. Fortunately, it did not appear as if there had been anyone around to bear witness to the results. So far, anyway.

Why don't you just relax? he chided himself. This *was* New York. With all that implied and promised, as N/Ice had defiantly put it. What were the girls doing, after all, but having a bit of fun with their magic? He took a deep breath, let it out slowly. Of all people, when charged with making the model sailboat suitable for use, he more than anyone ought to have expected his sisters to go a little—overboard.

What more was wanted than what they had produced? As well as hewing to a steady course, the enlarged toy boat floated sufficiently high in the water to keep them nice and dry and well above any shallow patches. He did not understand how this could be so, given the apparent weightiness of its transformation. Idly, he wondered which of his sisters had succumbed to the notion of making the hull solid gold. Probably Amber. Of them all, she was the one most prone to garishness.

Though daylight was fading and the heavy fog reduced the ambient light still further, Simwan still found himself having to squint occasionally when a stray shaft of light bounced off a diamond fitting to temporarily blind him.

"Really now," he asked N/Ice, and by inference her sisters, "even for New York, don't you think that as a piece of fey this is maybe a little bit over the top?" With a wave of his left hand he indicated the boat's interior. "I mean, come on now: diamond bolts and silk sails?"

"Hey," Amber protested from where she was relaxing on the silken center bench, "like N/Ice said, we've never worked with a boat before, y'know?"

Since they could no longer see the southern edge of the Reservoir, Simwan felt it reasonable to assume they were at least halfway across. Though there wasn't much in the way of wind, or even a breeze, he kept the boat moving steadily forward by sculling back and forth with the rudder. There being neither current nor wave action, their situation was comparable to going for a peaceful sail in a bathtub.

They landed on the far north shore of the Reservoir without incident. Night made the air seem colder, though in fact there was as yet little change in the temperature since it continued to be moderated by the heavy cloud cover.

Their first order of business upon setting foot on dry parkland was to retransmogrify their sturdy but entirely too flamboyant little craft. It wouldn't do to have some idle Ord runner come jogging along the path that paralleled the Reservoir's north shore and stumble upon a full-size sailboat fashioned of gold and platinum and precious stones. Awkward questions might be asked. If more than one Ord happened across the craft, fights over discovery could well ensue. Worst of all, lawyers could become involved. Having determined to recover the Truth, the Deavys were not about to leave behind a creation of their own that would invariably generate less of that rare and valuable commodity.

Once again Simwan was able to stand back and play spectator as his sisters proceeded to deconstruct their magic. Gold vanished, platinum evaporated, silk turned back to cotton, and within a couple of minutes their garish vessel had been reduced to its original size, shape, and status. They left the toy craft there, by a bench, with nothing to indicate the remarkableness of the short but eventful journey it had just concluded. Hopefully, its young owner would return and recover it.

Their fight with the Madoon and the stress of crossing the Reservoir, coupled with the lateness of the hour, had left everyone famished. The north shore, however, proffered no invitingly illuminated, convivial snack wagon of the kind that had supplied drinks and nibbles to them prior to their watery crossing. There was nothing in the way of an evening restaurant or fast-food booth, nor did the rolling reaches of the North Meadow that lay spread out before them offer guarantee of anything more nourishing.

To the west lay the Upper West Side and the temptation of upscale neighborhood bistros and fast-food eateries. But getting there would mean having to recross the Bridle Path, a prospect no one cared to contemplate. To the east lay the culinary environs of the Upper East Side. But leaving the park meant, as they had already determined, having to abandon their search and start all over again another day. There was nothing for it, it was decided without argument, but to press on.

But not until something had been done to alleviate their hunger.

Simwan didn't argue. As badly as he wanted to hurry onward to the Crub's lair and maintain as much of an element of surprise as possible, he had to admit that to rush into what could be a potentially serious situation on an empty stomach was downright foolish. In the absence of restaurant or pushcart, they would have to find a way to feed themselves. Remembering the stories Grandpa Deavy used to tell of crossing the Tibetan Plateau on foot in the company of only a single Yeti, Simwan decided he and his sisters would find a way to get by.

That didn't mean any of them were happy about it.

"I'm cold." Rose flopped down on a nearby bench, her scrunched expression illuminated by the soft glow of the overhead streetlight. "And my leg hurts."

"I want a hamburger." Amber pulled her coat tighter around her upper body and tugged the lip of her hood further down over her forehead. "With everything."

N/Ice could not keep from commenting. "Better be careful

what you wish for. This being New York, no telling what you might get on a hamburger if you ask for it with 'everything.' In Australia, you'd get it with a slice of beetroot and a fried egg."

Rose and Amber looked at each other and, in perfect unison, responded with a heartfelt "Eewww!" Simwan had to smile. His sisters might be cold and wet and discouraged, but they still had the energy to complain. Clearly, there was no lack of the traditional Deavy spirit among the tired, damp expedition.

"Come on," he urged them. "We've dealt with everything else that's come our way so far. *Surely*, we can manage dinner."

N/Ice lowered her gaze warningly. "By 'we,' I take it you mean *us*? You're not implying, are you, big brother, that we twee three should be responsible for conjuring up dinner just because we're *girls*?"

Simwan met her gaze evenly. "You've tasted my cooking, both Ord and otherwise. Are you *sure* you want me involved in scaring up our supper?"

"Don't provoke him, N/Ice," Amber interjected hastily. "Remember that time when Mom and Dad were out and he tried to make marshmallow crispies for all of us?"

Rose nodded in remembrance. "Yeah, and he confused the spell for egg whites with the one for a certain other kind of powder, and ended up making them with cement instead of marshmallow."

"Fine, then." N/Ice was convinced, if not necessarily mollified. "*We'll* figure out something for dinner." Suddenly, she brightened. "Actually, I think big brother may already have helped."

Her sisters eyed her uncertainly. "How do you mean?" Amber asked.

"He said something about 'scaring up' supper." Rising from the bench, she turned to gaze out across the misty, dimly lit expanse of the rolling North Meadow. "Maybe that's just what we ought to do. Can you imagine how many cookouts and picnics and barbecues people have scarfed down in this place?" She turned back to face her sisters. "All we have to do is call up their ghosts."

"What good will it do to call up the ghosts of deceased picnickers?"

"Not the ghosts of the *picnickers*, silly." N/Ice's fervor warmed the air around her. "The ghosts of their *food*."

Amber blinked. "I didn't know food could leave behind ghosts."

"Well, not all food." N/Ice wavered slightly in her conviction. "Just food that goes unappreciated. A fried chicken that doesn't get eaten, for example, perishes unfulfilled. In that case, the chicken died for nothing. Or take a hamburger that just gets a bite taken out of it and is thrown away. Somewhere, somehow, a steer died to give birth to it, and all that beautiful cud-chewing life is just wasted. I imagine it's also true for vegetables that are cooked but discarded."

Simwan found that his appetite, which moments earlier had begun to verge on the all-consuming, was fading rapidly. "I dunno about this," he muttered uncomfortably. "I mean, eating ghost food . . ."

"Better than eating food intended for ghosts. It's bound not to be very fattening." Rose was thawing to the idea. "And since it's already been prepared, we wouldn't have to do any cooking." She smiled at her other sister. "You might even be able to get your hamburger."

"How do you 'scare up' ghost food?" Amber looked questioningly at N/Ice.

Finding herself on the spot, N/Ice straightened and declared with more assurance than she actually felt, "I've heard that a good chef always knows how to improvise. So that's what we'll do: We'll improvise."

Once more, the girls linked hands. Instead of chanting in unison, they allowed N/Ice to take the lead. She did so with inspiration born of appetite. Simwan didn't catch all the words—Amber, for one, sing-songed something about N/Ice being "the hostess with the mostest toastest"—but he was right there when the ectoplasmic egg salad sandwich materialized out of nothingness. It was only half visible and half solid, but it was undeniably an egg salad sandwich.

He was not surprised that it was the first specimen of ghost food to come forth in response to the coubet's chanting. If he had been at a picnic where hamburgers and hot dogs and barbecued ribs were sizzling on a grill and someone had offered him an egg salad sandwich, he would have thrown it away uneaten, too. Present circumstances being somewhat different, however, and having not eaten anything since lunch at Tybolt the Butcher's, he snatched the spectral sandwich out of the night air before it could drift away or dematerialize and unhesitatingly took a big bite out of it.

As expected, there wasn't much to it. The lettuce in particular had little substance and less taste. But the faint, or in this case ghostly, tang of egg salad was unmistakable. Chewing something so insubstantial was almost an afterthought, and it slid down his throat without much effort on the part of his teeth and jaws. Once settled in his stomach, however, it felt right at home.

He finished the sandwich as other wraithlike nourishment started to materialize in response to the coubet's spell-cooking. Only when the girls felt they had called forth sufficient sustenance did they release one another's hands and scramble for their share of the drifting, itinerant bounty.

As the last of the lonely lunch meat faded back to nothingness, they cleaned themselves as best they were able and headed out across the damp greensward that comprised the gentle rolling hillocks of the North Meadow. They were in the northern quarter of the park now: the home stretch of their quest. Surely, Simwan felt, it could not be long before they encountered someone or something that could point the way straight into the Crub's lair.

Turns out he was right.

Unfortunately.

-XX-

By now they were—all of them, coubet, cat, and boy—mightily encouraged. They had made their way northward through most of the park and must surely be closing in on their quarry. True, dusk had fallen (or more accurately, given the steady mist and drizzle, seeped), catching them out later than they originally planned. But having made as much progress as they had in the course of a single day, Simwan was feeling more and more confident they would be able to catch the Crub by surprise. With luck, they would recover the Truth and be out of the park and back in the Ord part of the city before the repulsive thieving rat-thing knew what had hit him.

It was dreadful dark out on the meadow. A group of Ord youngsters would have huddled together uneasily and hurried toward the nearest well-lit paved pathway. Not the Deavys. They were not afraid of the night. There is a very real difference between being wary and being intimidated by something. Simwan was alert, but he was not scared. From time to time the coubet would break into a skip and a song, though they kept their voices down. Any hint of moon was pillowed behind the persistent rain clouds. Patches of denser fog danced and ebbed around the advancing Deavys like waltzing wraiths. The appearance of sentience was a coincidence only. Fog did not think. A foog, now—that was a different matter entirely.

"I smell something." Slightly in the lead, N/Ice slowed her pace until she had fallen back between her sisters.

"Take more baths," Rose suggested snidely.

Ordinarily, this response would have provoked an ancillary comment from Amber as well as a suitably snotty comeback from N/Ice, but this time neither girl replied. That, in turn, piqued Rose's interest as well as that of their brother.

"I smell it, too." Head tilted slightly back, Simwan sniffed at the damp night air.

What he was smelling was all wrong. It smacked of something burning. Aside from the fact that there was no source in sight, the odor was all wrong for where they were. He struggled to identify it. It did not arise from burning newspapers or cardboard, as might have been expected if a couple of resident tramps had built an illegal campfire somewhere nearby. It did not reek of charcoal, as it would if a bunch of college students were toasting marshmallows around a fire-filled metal barrel. There were no overtones of pasteboard or plaster, wallboard or cured wood, so it couldn't be coming from a burning structure.

It took him a few more minutes before he could place it. More than anything else, the burning smell reminded him of the special desserts they enjoyed on their all-too-infrequent visits to Great-Aunt Erica's house up in the mountains of Vermont.

Cherries Jubilee.

Or maybe it was more like Bananas Foster. Or Crepes Suzette. It bothered him that he couldn't identify it precisely. Strawberries Romanoff, maybe, or Baked Alaska. In addition to adding to his ongoing frustration, these particularly toothsome remembrances were making him even hungrier. Then it hit him. What all those splendiferous desserts had in common. They were all *flaming* desserts. *That* was what they were smelling. Burning alcohol. As the pungent tickle in his nostrils intensified, he found himself looking around more and more anxiously.

Then the girls let out a simultaneous scream, Pithfwid threw sparks as he yowled a warning and jumped backward, the ground erupted in front of Simwan, and though they could not immediately identify the thing that emerged from the bowels of the earth directly before them, of one thing they were all right away certain. It was not a forgotten dessert.

If it *was* a dragon, it was surely the most peculiar representative of its kind Simwan had ever seen. Not that he had actually *seen* more than a dragon or two (there was that time several years ago when the family had vacationed in China), but they had been part and parcel of his after-school studies ever since he was old enough to peruse the special books in the family library. Yet what else could it be but a dragon?

The gaping mouth was huge and lined with appropriately vicious-looking, hooked teeth—but the jaws narrowed almost to a point. The eyes were set low down on the skull, which was as smooth and aerodynamic as the business end of a guided missile.

For a moment, Simwan thought the apparition was wingless. Then the wings—two pairs, not one—extended from where they had been folded flat against the creature's flanks. Instead of being dark and bat-leathery, they were veined and iridescent, like those of an immense dragonfly.

The four of them were also each twenty feet in length. Fully unfolded, they beat the air like long, thin propellers, lifting the rest of the coiling, twisting, muscular body completely out of the ground. Slim fore and hind legs were tipped with talons so gracile they looked as if they had been manicured in one of Fifth Avenue's finest beauty salons. Except for the iridescent wings and red eyes, it was a bright, shining silver all over, as chrome-hued as the hood ornament on a luxury car.

If ever a dragon had evolved to commit both butchery and ballet, the beast hovering high in the moist night air before them was it.

Struggling to remember the right spells, Simwan forced himself not to run. This dragon might not be as physically impressive as some, he told himself, but it would be very fast, very quick. They would have to deal with it directly, and without panic. He could tell from the tempo of its wing beats that there would be no second chances.

"WHO TRAMPLES UPON MY SLEEP IN THIS PLACE OF REFUGE?" it hissed like a braking locomotive.

Amber spoke up immediately. "We're sorry. We didn't know it was a place of refuge."

Rose nodded swift agreement. "We thought it was North Meadow."

"ORDS CANNOT BE EXPECTED TO KNOW—EVEN

THOUGH I SPORADICALLY RISE UP TO SNATCH THE
OCCASIONAL SLOVENLY ONE. *YOU* HAVE NO SUCH
EXCUSE." The arrow-shaped head flicked toward them on the
end of its long, snakelike neck. "YOU REEK OF LEARNING.
AS SUCH, YOU SHOULD KNOW BETTER." A long, triple-
forked tongue flicked out to almost touch N/Ice. She held her
ground with remarkable poise. "WHEN CONSUMED, YOU
WILL HAVE THE FLAVOR OF KNOWLEDGE, THOUGH
NOT OF WISDOM."

The great tapering jaws parted to expose razorlike rending teeth
as a burst of white-hot flame shot forth from the depths of the cav-
ernous maw. The fire was tinged with pale blue and smelled of—it
was the bright, sharp stink Simwan and his sisters had detected just
before the creature had surfaced. The aroma of flaming alcohol,
rather than the expected and more customary burning sulfur.

This was a different dragon indeed.

As it swooped toward them on gigantic dragonfly wings, however, its tastes were plainly of the traditional kind. Being boiled in
alcohol instead of sulfur would not matter to the boilee, Simwan
knew. As the girls hastily linked hands, he threw up both arms
and tried to assume one of the more defiant sorceral stances he
had practiced. A long white beard and massive, crystal-crowned
staff would have rendered the pose more impressive, but he
could only work with what he had. At least, he reflected as he
prepared to defend himself and his sisters, his acne had receded
during the past year.

"Drakon begone, firedrake shake! I command you to flee! Go
back to the depths that gave you birth!"

Semi-transparent wings beat close before him and the

arrowhead-shaped skull was so close he could smell the creature's body odor as well as its alcohol-fueled breath. Nearby,
Pithfwid was doing something ineffective with his paws while the
girls were chanting softly and intently, but to no apparent effect.

The head turned slightly to its left and a great blood-red eye
fixed on Simwan's own. "KNOWLEDGE, NOT WISDOM. THE
IGNORANCE OF YOUTH. YOU WILL BE LESS FILLING,
BUT HAVE MORE TASTE." The svelte yet powerful jaws
started to part once again.

"Wait!" A desperate Simwan threw up both arms anew. "By
the Laws Draconian, I demand to know who it is that threat-
ens!" There, he thought, finding that he was sweating profusely
despite the chill and damp. That should buy them a little time,
if nothing else.

Affronted by the conceit, the dragon-thing drew itself up to
its full height, which was very impressive indeed, and extended
its four wings full out to left and right into the mist, and they
were equally impressive.

"I AM SLYTHROAT THE SLAUGHTERER. KNOW,
CHILDISH INTERLOPERS, THAT THIS ISLAND HAS
BEEN MY HOME FOR LO ON THRICE THREE THOU-
SAND YEARS, AND THAT I DO NOT SUFFER CALCU-
LATING INTRUDERS TO PASS MY PLACE OF REST
UNBIDDEN." Swift as a striking mamba, the sharp-pointed
skull struck forward and down until it halted less than a yard
from Simwan's face. It was all he could do to hold his ground
and not flinch. "I DO, HOWEVER, SUFFER THEM TO BE
SUPPER. OR IN YOUR INSIGNIFICANT INSTANCE, AT
LEAST TO BE APPETIZERS. PREPARE YOURSELVES!"

It was then, most unexpectedly, that Pithfwid stood up on his hind legs and pointed with one paw. "*Now* I know you! You're the wyrm—the wyrm in the Big Apple!"

Annoyed by the interruption, Slythroat jerked his head around to his right to focus on the Deavy pet. "IN YOUR CASE, CAT, YOU ARE LESS EVEN THAN AN APPETIZER. YOU BE NOT EVEN A MORSEL. BARELY, I SHOULD SAY, A LESSEL. BUT I WILL NOSH YOU NONETHELESS, ALONG WITH YOUR LARGER COMPANIONS."

Dropping back to all fours, a now gray-furred Pithfwid sauntered boldly forward. Simwan looked on aghast while the girls ceased their ineffectual chanting. The cat was not much bigger than one of the dragon's hind talons. He could have made a bed of just one of the creature's gleaming chromelike scales. Now he strutted back and forth just below that steaming cauldron of a mouth as if he had not a care in the world.

"The wyrm in the Big Apple. I knew I'd seen you somewhere before."

Slythroat's lids dropped lower over his glaring eyes. "ALL CATS SPEAK IN RIDDLES. BUT I WOULD HAVE AN EXPLANATION BEFORE I BITE."

Halting directly in front of the looming, lethal skull, Pithfwid stopped pacing and turned to face the dragon. "This is truly your home. At night you can go where and whence you wish. But like so many of your kind, you are nocturnal and need a place of safety to sleep out the daylight. You abhor sunshine, yet cannot bury yourself deep enough in this crowded place to avoid the attentions of humans." He shook his head sadly. "So many humans, these days. Times are different than they used to be."

The great, fiery head bobbed slowly up and down in agreement. "AT LAST—A LITTLE WISDOM I HEAR FROM THE SMALLEST OF YOU. BUT THOUGH YOU SPEAK TRUTH, IT WILL SAVE YOU NOT." The toothy mouth parted in a white shark smile that was half Dracula, half Cheshire Cat. "WHEN I AM AWAKENED, I WAKE UP *HUNGRY*."

Pithfwid did not appear in the least intimidated. "You want to know where I've seen you before? It was in a picture, in a book. A picture of the place where you sleep during the *day*, in full view of the humans who have swarmed over your ancient home. You are at once always visible to them, and yet they never recognize you for what you truly are. It is this hiding in plain sight that helps to keep you safe in a place and times of such tumultuous change." Turning, he glanced first at Simwan, then at the coubet.

"Slythroat the Slaughterer may sleep here in this ground through the night—but during the daylight hours he takes his ease as part and parcel of the exterior of the topmost floors of the island building called Chrysler. He is as one in spirit with its many architectural decorations, and his natural coloration blends perfectly with the structure's aluminum crown." He looked back at the fire-breathing monster hovering in front of him and his humans.

"I wonder: Has this always been your natural appearance, or when the building went up did you adopt an art-deco look the better to blend in with your daytime hiding place?"

Drawing back his head, Slythroat let loose a blast of blue-tinted flame that washed directly over the cat. The girls screamed anew and N/Ice had to hold Rose back to keep her from running forward. Simwan's eyes grew wide with shock. But when the conflagration faded, Pithfwid still stood, apparently unharmed by the fire. Turning his head to his left, he grinned over at a stunned Simwan.

"Did you ever notice?" the cat purred as he used his tongue to groom his still unburnt gray-blue coat, "that when it is mined from the ground, raw asbestos has exactly the same color and consistency as gray feline fur?" Returning his attention to the equally startled dragon, he spoke sternly.

"Harken unto me, Slythroat the Stutterer. We Deavys have no quarrel with you. We're sorry if we interrupted your rest, and we would have asked permission to pass if only we'd known you were here. You can go ahead and eat my companions—"

"Hey, wait a minute," an alarmed Rose began.

"—but you can't eat me. Not in my present configuration. I'd give you one horror of a bellyache. Or asbestosis. You'd end up spitting me back out. Then I'd find a way to reveal your place of daytime rest. Not to the Ords, who do not believe, but to the enemies of your kind, who would be delighted to happen upon a dragon caught asleep out in the sunlight, and would take it apart like a Christmas goose."

For a moment, Simwan thought that in spite of Pithfwid's warning, Slythroat the Slaughterer was going to charge and live up to his surname. Then, all at once, the bravado (if not the steam) seemed to go out of the dragon. It settled to the ground on all fours, slumped to its belly with its great iridescent wings flapping forlornly at its sides, and dropped its head to the wet earth. A tiny, thin seep of smoke emerged from one corner of its snaggle-toothed jaws to rise rather despondently before dissipating into the night sky.

"WISDOM FROM THE SMALLEST," it rumbled disconsolately. "I *HATE* WISDOM FROM THE SMALLEST."

Without another word, Slythroat extended his left front foot. Neither dragon nor cat could properly grip the other's paw, so Pithfwid settled for placing his own against the tip of one of the dragon's sharp talons. The resultant contact represented a meeting of the minds as effectively as it did that of bodies.

"We'll be on our way now." Pithfwid lowered his paw. "And no hard feelings."

"THERE BE NONE." Reeking of flames barely held in check and the heady smell of smoldering alcohol, the dragon smiled down at the infinitely smaller, but notably wiser, feline. "I KNOW THAT WERE SIZE AND SITUATION REVERSED, YOU WOULD HAVE DONE THE SAME HERE AS I."

"Not really," Pithfwid demurred. "I don't much care for the taste of snake. Not even if it comes pre-heated." With that, he started northward, following the sprawled-out length of the dragon. Hurrying to catch up with him, Simwan leaned low to whisper to his feline companion. Pithfwid listened, nodded, then turned to shout back at their scaly former adversary.

"One last thing. We've come a long way and have overcome many dangers in our quest. We seek the return of something that was taken from a friend of ours. It resides in the possession of a miserable creature called the Crub. That's where we're headed. Or will be, if you can help us refine our route."

Looking toward its tail end, the massive head drew back slightly from the four youngsters and one feline. "THE CRUB! YOU DON'T WANT TO GO THERE. BETTER TO FORGET THAT WHICH WAS TAKEN FROM YOU AND GO HOME."

Raising its gaze, the dragon stared up into the mist-shrouded night sky. "AS I MYSELF WILL WITH THE COMING OF THE DAWN."

Simwan took a couple of steps backward, in the direction of the head that had turned to consider them. "We can't do that." Gesturing with one hand, he indicated the coubet. "We're Deavys. I realize that probably doesn't mean anything to you, but it means a lot to us, and to those who know our family."

"IF YOU MUST KEEP ON, KEEP ON IF YOU MUST. THAT WAY"—the great head rose high and gestured north—"LIES THE LOCH. WHERE IT BECOMES THE RAVINE, BENEATH THAT YOU WILL FIND THE ENTRANCE TO THE LAIR OF THE CRUB." Quadruple iridescent wings thrust outward and began to fan the air. Simwan blinked as droplets of water were flung in his face by the force of the dragon's wing beats. He felt as if he were standing at the entrance to a car wash.

"LOOK FOR THE TWINNED TREE," the dragon advised them as it rose into the air. "OPPOSITE AND DOWN AND UNDERNEATH LIES THE WAY IN. DESCEND THERE AT YOUR PERIL. MYSELF, I WOULD NOT DO IT."

Having delivered himself of both instructions and a warning, Slythroat the Slaughterer ascended until they could barely make out the dragonesque silhouette soaring among the low clouds. Then he folded his wings to his sides and dropped, plunging earthward at speed sufficient to surpass the best efforts of a peregrine falcon. Simwan started to run, only to relax when he saw that the dragon was not aiming for them. Spinning faster and faster, round and round like the bit of a drill, Slythroat struck the crest of the low hillock from whence he had initially emerged to confront them. In an instant he was gone, having bored straight back down into the subterranean hiding place where he slept during the night. The wyrm had burrowed back into the Big Apple's core.

They stood there staring at the silent hillock for a moment longer. When it was evident that the dragon had no intention of putting in a reappearance, they turned as one and resumed their northward trek.

"Isn't a loch a Scottish lake?" Amber wondered aloud.

Rose started uneasily. "I hope we haven't wasted all this time tramping through the wrong country."

Reaching into a pocket, Simwan brought out the small map of the park and unfolded it. The girls gathered around as he pointed to markings in the darkness.

"It's right here. The Loch is a stream that runs from the Pool to a much bigger lake called Harlem Meer. I guess whoever laid it out thought it would be nice to give it a Scottish name."

I hope we're ready for this, he thought, since the task was enough to intimidate a dragon. He found himself suddenly wishing that their parents were with them. Martin Deavy was an accomplished wizard, and Melinda Mae had a master's way with witchy words. *They* would know how to deal with the likes of the Crub. But their parents weren't present. Their dad was back home in Clearsight, confident in the knowledge that his offspring were having a swell time visiting New York, taking in the sights and enjoying the city while he dealt with his own worries. Their mom was in the hospital, seriously weakened by the absence of the Truth. If only they knew.

Simwan visualized the Deavy den, with its home electronics

and roaring (occasionally simpering) fireplace, shelves of books, comfortable couches, and thick carpets. He pictured his sisters clustered off in a corner chattering about some arcane figment of girl stuff, his father sitting in his favorite chair reading a book while the pillow supporting his head and neck looked over his shoulder, his mother avidly attempting to conquer the latest video game. Himself following this or that sport on the TV while the stack of homemade cookies in front of him was methodically reduced in stature. It was a warm, familiar, comforting image. He wished he could inhabit it instead of just envisioning it.

Turning his head away from a brief gust of wind, he blinked rain out of his eyes. Nearby, his sisters yammered on incessantly. To look at them and listen to them, one would never know that they were about to risk their lives to recover something as intangible—but invaluable—as the Truth. In spite of all their persistent put-downs, Simwan discovered that he was as proud of the coubet as a big brother could be of three constantly nagging, needling, nosy younger sisters. He could, if pressed, even confess to loving them.

But not out loud, of course. And certainly not in front of any of his friends.

They were fortunate in that their chatter allowed them to temporarily take their minds off their mother's condition and the serious work that lay ahead. Unlike the coubet, Simwan had no brother to confide in. He did, however, have a cat—though if queried Pithfwid would immediately have seen to the reversal of the possessive.

"That was something, back there." He gestured behind them,

through the drizzle. "I've never heard or seen pictures of a dragon like that."

Pacing alongside, Pithfwid replied thoughtfully. "Very different," he agreed. "For a voracious, fire-breathing, befanged, taloned, carnivorous giant mutant flying numinous reptile, he wasn't such a bad sort at all." The cat glanced up at Simwan. "You could invite him to your next party. I'm sure he would be a big hit at the dinner table."

Simwan made a face as he searched the dimly lit expanse of meadow that stretched out before them. "Sure he would—as long as he restricted himself to cooking the food and not the guests."

-XXI-

It was not only dark when they finally reached the Loch, it was late. As the Deavys silently worked their way through the trees and down to the water's edge, Simwan found himself wondering if Uncle Herkimer was aware of the lateness of the hour, of their continuing absence, and if he was worried. No time for that now, he told himself grimly. They dared not call their uncle lest he ask where they were and what they were up to. If not already at the Crub's front door, surely they were knocking at the gate. More than anything else, he needed for his mind to be clear, his physical and mental reflexes sharp, and his senses alert.

The Loch was different from anything they had previously encountered within the park. Not for nothing, Simwan saw, was this section called the Ravine. Deep, dark, and mysterious during the day, it was transformed at night into a geologic interloper from another planet. With its dense brush, overhanging branches of mature ash and maple and oak and hickory, hidden forest floor flowers peeking out from among the goldenrod and spurge, it looked like a strip of green-walled water that had been lifted whole and entire from somewhere in the oldest, deepest part of the Adirondacks.

For the second time that day they found a part of the park reminding them of home, of the woods near the Deavy homestead in eastern Pennsylvania, and by inference, the reason they were here in the middle of the night picking their way through bushes and thickets that clung to their clothes as if desperately trying to keep them from penetrating any farther.

"Don't go in there!" the oaks seemed to be silently whispering.

"Go back where you came from," the maples were all but shouting.

Though they heard the warnings voiced by the trees, the Deavys pressed on until they had reached the edge of the creek itself. Grasses and weeds had cobbled together enough mud to form transitory islands in the middle of the stream. The persistent clamor of a small waterfall could be heard but not seen. Hemmed in by the banks of the ravine and with nowhere to go, fog pressed in closer around them than it had anywhere else. Gently descending mist made it difficult for them to see one another, let alone locate the singular growth the dragon had described. Somewhere out in the stream, a frog croaked. It was too late in the year and too cold for frogs to be about, the Pond they had crossed being an enchanted exception. Evidently, no one had informed this particular amphibian. Though in no wise especially informative, the sound was a welcome indication that normal life existed in the otherwise oppressive creek bed.

"What now?" Both Rose's voice and attitude were uncharacteristically muted.

Aware that his sisters were once again looking to him for direction, he nodded and gestured downstream. "We'll head that way, toward Harlem Meer." He squinted into the fog and damp. "As long as we can see both sides of the brook, we'll be okay. If we don't find what we're looking for before we reach the lake, we'll just have to turn around and retrace our steps upstream to the Pool, where the Loch originates. Everybody keep a sharp lookout as we go."

"As opposed to a dull lookout?" Amber kicked at a dead branch as she turned and started walking. Simwan didn't mind the mild belittling. So long as his sisters managed to sustain their usual high level of sarcasm, he knew they were all right.

At first the going was easy enough, where a narrow but well-maintained path followed the course of the stream. But soon they encountered places where it did not. Here the Deavys had to clamber over rocks made treacherous by the constant damp, and push their way through thickets that had been left to grow wild. In one place the combination of foggywet weather, poor lighting, and an absence of any clear trail was so rough that they nearly missed what they were looking for. Pithfwid and Simwan had walked right past it (in Pithfwid's defense, the cat's line of sight was considerably closer to the ground than those of his humans) when N/Ice called out.

"Hey, hold up, you guys. I think this might be it."

Turning, Simwan and the cat retraced their steps. To Simwan's relief, there was nothing ambiguous about the ancient oak N/Ice had found. "Look for the twinned tree," the dragon

Slythroat had instructed them. Joined by her sisters, she stood gazing at a pair of trunks that thrust separately upward from the moist soil, only to meld together several feet above the ground to form a single bole.

"This has to be it." Rose was stroking the conjoined trunk with the flat of her palm, lightly caressing the weathered bark.

"I think you're right." Simwan could not imagine finding along the length of the Loch another tree that better fit the dragon's description.

"Assuming it is," murmured Amber as she turned from the tree to study the flowing stream opposite, "where do we go from here?"

"Remember the rest of the dragon's words." Rose repeated them aloud. "'Opposite and down lies the way in. Descend there.'"

"'At your peril.'" Amber added the final words that her sister chose to eschew.

Having tiptoed down to the water's edge, Pithfwid finished lapping up a drink before sitting back on his haunches to study the riparian riddle that lay set before them. "'Opposite and down lies the way in. Descend there.' Clearly, our scaly acquaintance meant for us to find the entrance opposite the twinned tree. And downward." His fur having turned a forest green checkerboarded with black, he leaned slightly forward. "I see nothing on the opposite bank that suggests an opening of any kind."

"Maybe it's hidden under a big rock," N/Ice suggested.

"Or a big spell," Rose added as she contemplated the far shore.

Simwan had been doing some hard thinking of his own.

ALAN DEAN FOSTER

Perhaps it was the extensive esoteric reading he had done in his parents' library. Or maybe it was all the video games he'd played. For whatever reason, moreso than the girls he found himself taking the dragon's directions literally.

"Slythroat didn't say the way in lies *across* and down. He said *opposite* and down. And in."

His sisters eyed him uncertainly. "Brother," exclaimed Amber, "I'm not sure I see the difference."

He proceeded to elaborate. "If the dragon had said 'across,' then the instructions would be unmistakable." He nodded at the far side of the creek. "We'd have to look for an entrance over there somewhere. But he didn't say across. He said 'opposite.' Opposite and *down*." With one hand, he gestured at the gunmetal-gray, running water. "I think the way in does lie opposite this tree, but *under* the water."

"That's crazy," Amber insisted immediately.

"That's stupid," added Rose without hesitation.

"That's—wicked," ventured N/Ice rather more thoughtfully.

Pithfwid had already lowered his gaze, redirecting his attention away from the far bank and back to the stream itself. "What it *is*, contentious coubet, is an interesting notion. What better place to hide a hidey-hole from the casual view of Ords and the more perceptive sight of non-Ords than beneath flowing water itself?"

Amber frowned. "Wouldn't it flood? I mean, even if there's an airtight door of some kind, or a vacuum spell, what's to keep the creek water from pouring in every time somebody wants to go in or come out?"

"An interesting question to go with the interesting notion,"

Pithfwid admitted. "Hopefully, we'll come up with an interesting solution." He tilted his head to peer up at Simwan. "Boy, I am possessed of paws that will soothe, and claws that will kill, but I must confess yet one more time to the lack of opposable thumbs. Give me a hand here, please."

Unsure of what the Deavy feline had in mind but knowing from experience never to question it, Simwan knelt beside Pithfwid. The cat then proceeded to direct Simwan to do something that was patently impossible. Even if some sorcerer *had* patented the idea, it still seemed an outrageous defiance of all laws both natural and unnatural. But wasn't that what the Crub was all about, Pithfwid pointed out when Simwan questioned his instructions? Defiance of laws?

"This is crazy," Amber muttered.

"It isn't going to work," N/Ice murmured with conviction.

"Aren't we wet enough already?" Rose concluded.

"Go on. Do it." Pithfwid's unblinking stare was locked on Simwan's eyes.

Oh well, Simwan thought as he reached forward and down. Regardless of whatever eventuated if he followed the cat's instructions, it was unlikely to hurt. Extending both arms he reached out and, doing as he had been instructed, grabbed at the glistening edge of the water.

Just as Pithfwid had predicted, it lifted up easily in his hands, like a shimmering, wet blanket.

The cat examined the perfectly inexplicable phenomenon as though it was something he encountered every day. "'Under the water.' Your presumption turns out to be spot on, boy." Lowering himself back onto all fours, he started forward. "Opposite the twinned tree and down lies the way in. So sayeth Slythroat the serpent. Come along, now, kittens."

Utterly ignorant of exactly what he was doing and how he was doing it, Simwan lifted the side of the creek higher to make room enough for his crouching sisters to slip underneath. When the last of them had disappeared, he joined them below the manifest impossibility.

Though they scrambled down into the depths of the creek bed, the underside of the water remained just over their heads. Looking up, Simwan could see the occasional dark shape of a fish or salamander swimming past. Once, he reached up and stuck a finger into the underside of the stream. It came away wet.

"What kind of spell is holding it up, and away from us?" Rose stumbled downstream, careful not to trip on any of the small rocks or clutches of pebbles underfoot.

"A really strong one." From time to time N/Ice would drift upward until her head vanished into the underside of the creek, only to reappear moments later dripping wet down to her neck. "Somebody around here knows how to handle water."

Handle was the right description, Simwan mused as he made his way downstream along the dry creek bed. Hadn't he "handled" it when Pithfwid had directed him to lift up the water's edge?

They had gone maybe half a mile when a dull, greenish glow caused them to slow. Sister pressed close against sister, sister moved nearer to brother, while Pithfwid hunkered low against the water-worn rocks and licked his lips, his tail switching back and forth, his ears aimed expectantly forward like miniature radar scopes.

They had found the Way In. And it was blocked.

Before Simwan had lifted up the edge of the stream so they could slip underneath, they had wondered how an opening located below it could avoid being flooded. Now they saw that there were two reasons. First, the Way In was not located under the water—it was situated *under* under the water. And second, it was tightly plugged by something that not only prevented any water from entering, but kept *anything* from entering.

A hoofin.

It was a full-blown, unmentionable, Four-G hoofin, too: green, glowing, gross, and grotesque. Its bulbous backside effectively stoppered the entrance. Three great protruding black eyes dominated the high, oval skull. Half a dozen red horns erupted from its swollen head. A narrow, questing trunk probed the air under the creek while the too-wide mouth almost split in half the puke-yellow head. Mucus drained from the oversize, scalloped ears and the tip of the trunk while green drool dribbled from one corner of a mouth that was filled with needlelike teeth. It squatted in the entrance gurgling unpleasantly to itself, the three round black eyes closed as it dozed on duty.

The hoofin was a nightmare. Traditionally, about seven on a scale of ten. Not sufficiently frightening to cause a heart attack, but plenty scary enough if it invaded someone's dreams to cause them to wake up screaming. Seen outside a dream, it was no less frightening than if it had been encountered during slumber. It was also arguably much more dangerous in this state, because it could invade the awake.

That was what made it such a perfect sentry, Simwan realized. In the event of trouble it did not have to raise the alarm itself. All it had to do was enter the mind of an intruder and cause it to start running around in circles shrieking uncontrollably as it tried to escape. They had no choice but to approach it with care and caution. With its fat butt plugging the Way In, their quest would end right there and then unless they could find a way to dislodge it. Preferably without sending any of them running and screaming.

He was trying to think of a spell that might work when N/Ice stepped out from behind the cover of the rocks and started forward. Flashing the fearless demeanor of a decidedly downsized pre-adolescent Valkyrie, his sister eyed the menacing shape of the hoofin and declared in a voice both cocky and unafraid, "This one's *mine*."

"Are you sure, N/Ice?" Rose asked worriedly.

"Be careful, sis." Despite N/Ice's declaration of confidence, Amber too was preparing herself for battle. "You know what is said. Anyone who tries to targle a hoofin and fails risks encountering that nightmare every time they fall asleep." She cast an anxious glance her brother's way. "What do you think, Simwan?"

That's right; put it all on me again, he thought resentfully. "It's N/Ice's call. With her being half girl and half dream herself, maybe she is the best equipped of all of us to tangle with something . . ."

"Targle," Rose quickly corrected him. "Targle with."

"Targle *and* tangle," Simwan growled irritably. He turned his attention back to his half-a-sister. "N/Ice, I don't know any spells for targling a hoofin." He looked embarrassed. "I've never studied how to deal with anything more advanced than a Two-G nightmare."

She smiled up at him, then over at her sisters. "Don't worry. Just watch me." She turned back to the squatting, sputtering hoofin. "I'm going to targle the hell out of it."

An approaching Ord would have been spotted and bathed in total, mind-numbing horror long before it could have been able to reach the hoofin. But N/Ice was no Ord. Furthermore, she was exceptionally quick, a quality Simwan attributed to all the upside-down running around she did with her sisters on the ceiling of their room (that and soccer practice). When it finally did catch sight of the onrushing Deavy sister, the hoofin reacted with a mixture of surprise and outrage. So startled was the nightmare that it pulled itself out of the opening as it turned to confront her charge.

The path to the Way In was clear. If N/Ice could distract the hoofin for just a couple of moments or two, Simwan saw that there was a good chance he and Pithfwid and his other two sisters could duck inside. Beyond appraising the possibility, he never gave it serious consideration. Deavys stayed *together*, no matter how critical the quest, no matter how grave the danger.

Heedless of anyone or anything that might be near enough to overhear, Rose and Amber were suddenly out in the open, wildly cheering on their sister.

"Go get it, N/Ice!" Amber yelled.

"Targle its ears off!" Rose bellowed as forcefully as she could.

Simwan added nothing. He couldn't. He was too concerned with what might happen to his sister if she failed. A hoofin was no childhood bad dream. It was a mature, developed, full-formed nightmare that, once it got a hold on you, would never let go. The third volume of the *Field Guide to Dreams* described it as a kind of mental malaria: leaving for a while only to return later again and again at full strength to torment the sleep of the afflicted. So while Amber and Rose formed a passionate cheering section of their own, urging on their sister's efforts, Simwan found he could only watch and worry.

As for Pithfwid, he sat motionless, staring as only a cat can stare, utterly intent and unblinking. Cats did not cheer—at least, not out loud. But there was no question that he was as concerned for N/Ice's safety as were her human siblings.

The hoofin was no slouch (a slouch being only a One-G nightmare), but speed and quickness were not its forte. It was charged with staying in one place, guarding an entrance, and making sure only authorized visitors were granted admittance. With the speed and unexpectedness of her attack, N/Ice had already accomplished the task of getting its butt removed from the Way In. That wouldn't matter if she failed to finish the job, Simwan knew. In that event, the hoofin would simply resume its stance as guardian of the Way In. Or rather, resume its seat.

The ugly trunk straightened and tried to curl around her neck. Demonstrating the agility of a legendary female samurai (and the lessons she had learned in ballet class), N/Ice spun clear of the thrust. Rising into the air, she stabbed one hand, fingers extended, in the hoofin's direction. A burst of white lightning (the non-imbibable kind) shot from her fingers to strike the nightmare square between its middle eye and its trunk. Stunned, the hoofin staggered backward, but quickly recovered. Letting out a moan terrifying enough to stun the soul of the most resistant Ord, it reached for her with long, flexible arms that ended in powerful grasping fingers. In an instant of no significant moment, Simwan noted that the nightmare had dirty fingernails.

Flipping parallel to the ground, N/Ice spun clear of the clutching hands. This time she delivered a double burst of energy straight to the center of the hoofin's body. Shocked, it started to tremble, then to shake violently. Eyes wide with realization, Simwan shouted a warning as he dropped flat onto the dry, pebbly creek bed.

"Look out! It's gonna blow!"

A second (or maybe three) later, there was a bright, silent explosion as the nightmare blew apart. Bits and pieces of fear flew in all directions. As he covered his head with his hands, one of them struck Simwan on the right shoulder. It was a small fear, but quite intense. It caused him to whimper loudly for a moment or two before it dissipated.

As the rest of the flying fear faded, he scrambled to his feet and ran forward. The hoofin had been well and truly targled, all right, but—there was no sign of his sister.

"N/Ice! N/Ice, where are you? Are you okay?" As Amber and Rose closed the distance behind him, a small black-and-gold streak shot past them all: a linear feline.

Pithfwid found her lying on her back at the first bend in the creek bed. She was sitting up slowly, one hand resting against her forehead. Her anxious siblings crowded around her, eager to offer their support.

"Are you all right?" Rose fretted as she put a comforting arm around N/Ice's back to help support her.

"Did it hurt you anywhere?" Even as she posed the question, Amber was examining her sister from head to toe, searching for indications of any injury.

"Here," Simwan said simply as he extended a hand.

Taking it and partaking of her brother's strength, N/Ice was able to stand. Unsteadily at first, but stability returned as swiftly as her poise. One hand still felt of her head.

"Wow. I wasn't expecting quite so explosive an outcome." She winced, then blinked several times. "Part of it went right through me."

"How was it?" Amber asked anxiously.

N/Ice regarded her sister. "It burned." She touched one hand to her left temple. "Up here. Like when you're having a really bad dream and you realize it's a dream and you want more than anything, anything else, to wake up but you can't. Then it was gone."

"Well, you sure as heck targled it good," was Rose's admiring compliment.

"Targled it right out of existence," Amber observed. When nothing was immediately forthcoming from their brother, the two sisters eyed him reprovingly.

"Uh, seriously good work there, N/Ice," Simwan hastened to add. All eyes promptly shifted to the one member of their group who had yet to comment.

Pithfwid sat cleaning his eyes with a moistened paw. "Spiffy," he declared with finality. "Now let's get a move on before something worse than a hoofin shows up to investigate."

With the Way In now unguarded and unblocked, they had no difficulty entering, though they had to bend low to do so. "Descend" had been the directive from the dragon Slythroat, and descend they did. The angle of descent was constant but not steep, and the way ahead lit by the limited but intense light from the tiny button flashlights each Deavy carried attached to their keychains. Additionally, an intermittent, eerie green glow emanated from phosphorescent moss and fungi growing on the walls. The color of this natural eldritch light would have immediately spooked an Ord. It only reminded the Deavy sisters of different shades of holiday lipstick. When things grew unbearably dark, they formed a single line and just followed N/Ice.

At first Simwan thought they had entered an abandoned service tunnel of some sort. As they descended deeper, he saw that they were not in a tunnel proper but a large-diameter tube of some kind. A huge pipe, or conduit. It was the smell that finally identified their noxious surroundings.

They were in the sewer. Not *a* sewer, but *the* sewer. The sewer system of New York City, perhaps the most extensive and elaborate in the modern world. For the next half hour, their greatest danger lay not in encountering hoofins, or dragons, or anything else magically monstrous and malevolent, but in slipping on the damp, sucky surface underfoot. And in throwing up. A good thing, he thought as they continued to make their way downward, that they were all wearing sturdy walking shoes. Trying to descend the greasy, stinking conduit in sneakers or sandals would have been like trying to skip down Mount Everest on greased skis. They would have slipped and slid downward, right into—who knew what.

He had no doubt but that they were about to find out.

Though there was constant dripping from the slime growing on the ceiling and sides of the pipe, and a steady trickle underfoot, the dirty water never rose more than halfway up the sides of their shoes. Designed to carry away heavy downpours and fast-running snowmelt, Central Park's industrial-strength sewerage and drainage system was not strained by the day's drizzle and mist.

Long before they had hiked a respectable distance and descended to a considerable depth, they encountered various forms of sewer-dwelling life. Mostly insects, though the outlines of larger shapes could be seen moving about in the darkness. These vanished as soon as the Deavys approached. It was left to a fairly large rat to halt, stand up on its hind legs, and challenge them.

"Sayyy . . . who are you lot, and what are you doing down here?" Using one paw, the husky rodent gestured behind him. "This is restricted territory down here."

"We work for the Department of Water and Powers," Simwan improvised with commendable speed. "We're just in the middle of finishing up an inspection."

Cocking its hairy head slightly to one side, the rat squinted past him. "Since when does W&P run four people on a pipe inspection?" Rodent eyes narrowed suspiciously. "And you look awfully young to be carrying out inspections for *any*body, much less a city department."

"You know humans." Rose mustered a smile. "It's hard to tell anything about us in the darkness."

"I can tell that you're younger than any human sewer workers *I've* ever encountered. Besides, this part of the system never gets inspected. It's why the Master chose it for—" The rat suddenly broke off, as if aware that he might have said too much. "Anyway, every W&P worker I ever saw was an ordinary, and you bunch are surely anything but Ords. Proof of it is that we're having this conversation."

"We're just being polite." Amber mimicked her sister's smile. "We mean no harm."

"Uh-huh," the rat muttered. "And I'm secretly a mink in drag." Dropping back to all fours, it started to back away. "You know what I think? I think you don't belong here. I think you come with spiteful intentions. I think—I'd better warn the Master." When Simwan took a step forward, the talkative rodent scampered back well out of reach. Now it was its turn to smile, unpleasantly.

"Don't think you can catch me. You can't even stand up straight in here. Better you turn around and hightail the tails you haven't got back the way you came. Because if you're still here when the Master hears of it, there'll be—"

An incredibly swift, agile shape currently colored dark green with a black ruff around its neck suddenly burst from behind Simwan's legs. Catching sight of it, the eyes of the hitherto self-assured rat threatened to pop out of its head.

"Mother of muck—there's a *cat* down here!" It whirled to flee.

Then Pithfwid was on top of it, and its eyes *did* pop out of its head. With Pithfwid's assistance, of course. Without the use of any magic that might give their presence away, employing those means and methods familiar to every feline since the beginning of time, the dark green streak utilized teeth and claws to tear the noisy, meddlesome rat into long, bloody strips. Soon silence reigned once more in the depths of the tunnel.

As the Deavys filed past the shredded corpse, Rose looked down and wrinkled up her nose. "It's good that you killed it before it could give warning, but do you have to *eat* the filthy thing?"

From where he was crouched on all fours and feeding energetically, a bloody-muzzled Pithfwid paused to look back up at her. "I'm hungry. Just a quick snack. You like your chocolate and your pretzels and your cookies. I happen to like rat. So do some humans, I might point out." Turning his head to one side, he spat out a small, bloody bone. "I believe in this very city they are referred to by the famished as 'roof rabbits.' The great empire of the Incas subsisted largely on guinea pigs, which they raised—"

"Sorry I asked." One hand covering her mouth, Rose picked up her pace.

They bumped into only one other querulous subterranean sentry, who was likewise dispatched—though not consumed—by the efficient Pithfwid. Shortly after this second encounter, the pipe that had been serving as their thoroughfare merged with another into a third, much larger underground channel. The ceiling of the old stone conduit—nineteenth century, Simwan estimated—was as flat as the floor, and high enough to allow them to continue onward without having to walk hunched over.

"How much farther, do you think?" N/Ice whispered aloud. "I don't feel like walking to Westchester."

Rose leaned close and kept her voice down as she responded. "Don't be silly. We know the lair is somewhere here in the north end of the park, and the park isn't *that* big. The entrance we found was pretty much in the middle. So we ought to be getting pretty close."

"Close to what?" Amber kept shining her tiny but bright light into dark corners and recesses. The beam picked out crawly things she chose not to try and identify further. "How do you suppose this Crub lives? There are no little houses down here, no hollow walls."

"The Crub's a rat," Simwan reminded her. "It'll live like a rat."

Pithfwid had taken the lead. Now he stopped and raised a warning paw. "Hush! I hear noises, and ratversation. A lot of it." The paw made repeated gestures floorward. "You are all of you great bipedal ape-things entirely too visible. I think from this point on it would be better if you belly-crawled."

The girls immediately objected. But Pithfwid was insistent, and eventually they gave in to his reasoning. They absolutely refused to belly-crawl, however. A compromise was reached, which resulted in them proceeding forward on hands and knees.

"Ew—" Rose began, but this time Pithfwid cut her off sharply.

"And no *ewws*," the cat advised her. "From here on, we hold to silence unless it is wrested from us forcibly."

Several times they clicked off their lights and froze in place as more rats scampered past. Simwan thought sure the patrolling rodents would smell the intruders, until it occurred to him that in this underground world of enormous stinks, even a perceptive rat would have trouble separating one smell from another.

Having already passed a wide assortment of rubbish that had been washed down into the drains, they were not surprised to find the way ahead nearly blocked by a pile of garbage that reached almost to the ceiling.

"Wait here." While his humans remained behind, Pithfwid darted through the gap between the conduit wall and the towering trash pile. He was back in less than a minute. "Come quickly: I've found it."

"The way onward?" Simwan made no attempt to hide the

concern in his voice. They had been traveling underground for nearly an hour. His feet were tired, his eyes were tired, his lungs burned every time he inhaled a mouthful of the torpid, malodorous air, and unlike the cat, he could not find energizing sustenance in the rodents who occasionally raced past them. He yearned for a cold drink, a hot late-night meal, and a warm bed. Though he did not ask, he knew that his sisters were just as drained.

Just as drained. Sometimes he wished he could just turn off the tap to his thoughts.

"No, not the way forward," Pithfwid replied calmly. "Something else. Something better. The Truth. Or," he added in a slightly more subdued tone, "at least maybe the place where it has been dumped."

"Dumped?" Simwan eyed the cat, who had gone pink with green squiggly lines running all through his fur.

"That's what I think I'm seeing. That's why places like this are called dumps."

It was then that a suddenly hopeful, excited Simwan found himself studying the trash heap that nearly blocked their way in an entirely new light.

–XXII–

When the last Deavy had squeezed through the opening between the towering garbage pile and the wall and all four of them had trained the beams of their compact flashlights onto it, the reality of what Pithfwid had spoken became immediately clear.

They had emerged into a huge square room whose aged, moss-coated, masonry walls rose nearly three stories high. Some sort of drainage collection point, or overflow chamber, Simwan decided. In addition to the pipe from which they had exited, three other conduits emptied into the large chamber. Like the one that they had just exited, two more were drain tunnels. Entering the dark depths at a sharper angle than the other three, the fourth doubtless led still deeper into the city's sewer system as it carried the collected flow of the first three onward to the complex that treated sewage before it reached the sea.

High up on the walls, parallel streaks left by ancient water lines indicated the heights to which especially heavy flows had risen. Superseded by newer, better-designed drains, it was clear that the sewage and water levels in this old collection area had not filled to such depths in a very, very long time. Any water and debris that still came in was funneled out very quickly. There were even a few dry places on the stone floor, further testament to how little wastewater actually reached it.

One such dry area, elevated slightly above the rest of the floor, was occupied by the "dump" that had attracted Pithfwid's attention. That the pile reached almost to the chamber's ceiling was a tribute to the cooperative efforts of untold thousands of rats slaving down through the decades to accumulate one of every imaginable kind and shape of object they thought might be of interest to their master. There was no rhyme or reason, no direction or apparent purpose, to the contents of the collection. Empty tin cans lay stacked alongside pilfered handbags stamped with names like Gucci and Hermès. Watches seemed to be a particular favorite of the legions of rodential thieves, perhaps because they could be easily carried between thick incisors. There were wind-ups and digitals, cheap knock-offs and elaborate fakes, Japanese and Swiss and American makes. A genuine Patek Philippe glittered next to a Rulex, the latter a specialty of Chinese counterfeiters.

Confirming the intelligence and dedication, if not the taste, of those who had accumulated it, there was not a single duplicate item in the pile. No two watches were alike. No two plastic bags. No two tin cans. Each and every component of the enormous mass was unique and distinct from the piece of junk, or small treasure, lying next to it.

"It's clear this Crub has no taste," Rose commented succinctly as she joined her sisters in beginning an intensive search of the dumbfounding pile.

Picking up and discarding a small bottle that turned out to be half full of the cheapest perfume imaginable, Amber could only shake her head in agreement. "How are we ever going to find the Truth in all this junk?"

"Well for one thing," Pithfwid observed as he clambered over the lower slopes of the pile, occasionally sticking his nose in where he wanted it to belong, "the Truth is a fairly recent addition. So if it's here, it should be somewhere on the outside of the hoard, or at least pretty close to the surface. Pity there's only one of me. I can usually smell the Truth from a good distance away."

"Oh, so you think you're the *only one*?" Leaning toward the conical mass, N/Ice proceeded to commence her own olfactory inspection of the accumulated refuse. Given some of the smells that were emanating from the festering mound, she would have preferred to hold her nose while doing so—but that, of course, would have effectively negated her efforts.

As for Simwan, while his sisters sniffed and searched and Pithfwid probed deeper and deeper into the pile, he kept casting worried glances in the direction of the other three dark, gaping tunnels. Noticing that his human's attention was being repeatedly diverted, Pithfwid let out a soft yowl. "What are you looking for so anxiously, boy?" He indicated the trash mountain. "I know this doesn't look like much fun—and it isn't—but come and help us search anyway."

"I'm looking for guards." Despite Pithfwid's entreaty, Simwan's gaze remained focused on the other openings. "If this is the

Crub's personal stash, I'd expect there to be some guards around. Or at least a lookout or two."

"Why?" Pithfwid was honestly puzzled. "As at least one recently demised, and moderately tasty, rat told us, no humans come this way. And what rat or vole, mouse or troll, would dare risk incurring the wrath of its master, the Crub? His reputation is sentinel enough to deter any would-be thieves from thinking of thieving his thievery."

That did make sense, Simwan decided. Maybe he was obsessing over nothing. Turning away from the looming mouth of the nearest conduit, he dove wholeheartedly (though not literally) into the knoll of plunder, using both hands to inspect and then cast aside item after grimy item.

Their task was made easier by the fact that they knew exactly what they were looking for, and that its appearance was sufficiently distinctive to distinguish it from the bulk of the accumulated rubbish. The small bottle of pale blue Roman glass would stand out in sharp contrast to bolder modern relatives designed to contain the spirits of such as Jack Daniels and Hiram Walker.

Still, the search was proving to be a difficult one indeed. For one thing, they had to be careful when moving an item not to dislodge the mass of packed junk lying immediately above it. Despite their caution, after imprudently pulling out one long-necked wine bottle, Rose found herself buried up to the thighs by a small avalanche of stuff. She could feel her face burning as her sisters enjoyed a laugh at her expense. Unfortunately, her embarrassment caused the rest of her to generate similar heat, to the point where Simwan had to remind her to calm down lest she set alight the flammable portions of the booty piled before them.

He checked his watch. Appropriately enough, they were coming up on midnight. The witching hour. Wiping sweat from his brow with the back of one hand, Simwan reflected that all he wanted at that magical time of day was to espy a certain small bottle. Flying horses and philosopher's stones and the lamps of imprisoned djinn he would look for another time. Besides, nothing, no matter how seemingly important or valuable, was worth much without the Truth to back it up.

It was when he was on the verge of compiling a modified drink spell with Amber's assistance in order to call up a six-pack of cold root beer instead of a flagon of mead that Rose let out a whoop of triumph and raised one sweaty, grime-stained arm. In her fingers was clutched the precious, long-sought-after bottle. Caught in the combined light of their tiny flashlights, it cast an unmistakable radiance of its own: the light of Truth.

"Got it!" she exclaimed triumphantly.

"About time." Grumbling, Pithfwid began carefully picking his way down from the crest of the rubbish mountain.

Relieved and relaxed for the first time since they had plunged into the under-underwater entrance to the sewer system, Simwan grinned teasingly at the cat. "What's the matter? Irritated that you didn't find it first?"

Raising his head, Pithfwid peered up at him and licked his nose. "Personally, I could care less. Cats have their own truth, you know, and humans entirely too little of it. That, and the need to restore your mother's health, are all that allow for my interest in wishing to have it returned to you."

"Oh," mumbled Simwan, properly abashed. The knowledge that their quest was virtually over perked his spirits. "Well, anyway, we've got it back." He turned toward the conduit from which they had emerged. They had a long, smelly hike ahead of them to get back to the surface. The sooner they got going, the sooner they would be able to pop into a corner market and buy whatever cold drinks they wished, without having to worry about spelling them into existence.

He was nearly at the tunnel entrance when he noticed that the girls were hanging back. "Come on, what are you waiting for? Let's move it."

"In a minute, brother." Rose was sorting through a plate-size pile of jewelry she had assembled. "There's so much nice stuff here that's just going to waste."

"We won't be long." N/Ice was modeling a shoulder bag that looked like it had just come off the rack at Bergdorf's.

"Waste not, want waste." Amber leaned toward a small, intact nineteenth-century mirror as she tried to adjust a delicate and very bright diamond necklace around her throat.

One paw raised off the floor, Pithfwid was peering into the dark, dank conduit and sniffing intently. "Humans and their decorative baubles! Myself, I'm perfectly content with a dead mouse." He looked back up at the increasingly anxious Simwan. "This is not a department store, and no place to linger."

"I know, I know." Turning, Simwan pleaded with the coubet. "Okay, each of you take *one thing*, and let's get out of here."

"Race you to the surface!" N/Ice yelled. She darted toward the tunnel—only to halt well short of the opening. And not because she had decided to wait for her kin.

The opening was already occupied.

"Race?" The voice that oozed out from inside the conduit was rich and oily, like that of a self-centered operatic tenor who had just polished off six courses of a particularly fatty meal. "Can I participate?"

N/Ice retreated slowly, backing up as a dark, hairy, muscular shape emerged from the opening. It regarded her and her siblings with eyes the color of the blood of its victims. Sharp claws click-clacked metallically on the stone underfoot and pointed teeth gleamed in its jaws. Both ears were inclined forward while a naked, fleshy tail trailed on the ground behind the rest of it like a stalking snake. Flanking the Crub were his personal ratainers, each of them lean and strong and smiling as they flashed teeth that had been whetted to daggerlike points. Their expressions were eager and hungry as they fanned out around both sides of the tunnel opening. As Simwan watched, the flow of murderous rodents kept coming and coming, until they had formed a perimeter around the interior of the entire garbage chamber. There were at least a hundred of them, with more spilling out of the conduit every minute.

First to spot the arriving ools, Rose nearly gagged at the sight. The steaming, sluglike black shapes had no eyes or ears and no limbs. One end terminated in a round opening of a mouth from whose center projected an equally black proboscis that wiggled and twisted like a worm. The other end terminated in depravity. Having arisen out of the muck and mire, they stank of interminable corruption. Even Pithfwid, who was rather fond of rooting through trash, felt the gorge rise in his throat as the hideous, stinking shapes humped and coiled their way forward. After the ools, it was almost a relief to see scattered platoons of ferrets and snakes among the Crub's entourage.

Concealed behind her sisters, Amber had slipped her cell phone out of her bag and had proceeded to dial 911. Discouragingly but unsurprisingly, it failed to pick up a signal so far below ground and in the midst of so much evil.

"Never mind," declared the Crub when no reply was forthcoming in response to his request. "There isn't going to be any race. Because the race is over." Eyes like rubies flicked from one wary Deavy to the next as the rat's voice thickened. "This race is over, and you lost. After the race, of course, comes the celebratory meal. You are all invited. In fact, I can say with assurance that you will be the center of attraction."

The small bottle containing the Truth lay securely buttoned up in one of Simwan's jacket pockets. Whatever happened, he knew he had to be careful to keep it intact. If the bottle cracked, the Truth, as was all too often the case, had a way of leaking out and fading away.

"We're just tourists," Rose essayed, "out for a night-time walk, and we lost our way."

Amber mustered a smile. "Just let us go and we won't bother you anymore."

"Yeah," added N/Ice. "I mean, it's not like we knew anybody *lived* down here."

The Crub shook himself. Droplets of muck and bits of decaying meat, fetid memories of his most recent meal, flew from his wirelike fur. "I agree that you have most certainly lost your way. Do you think me dumb vermin, like the rest of your fast-breeding, bipedal kind? I know you. You are those who tracked me through the woods. You are those who have battled and defeated every one of my minions' attempts to keep you from coming here. And on top of all that, in addition to all that—you are thieves." Raising a paw, he indicated the necklace draped around Amber's neck, the bag hanging off N/Ice's shoulder, the ring that sparkled on Rose's finger.

"You're hardly the one to be speaking of thievery." Trying to keep an eye on each of the hundreds of rats and ools and other creatures in addition to the Crub itself, Simwan gestured accusingly in the direction of the mountain of recovered rubbish. "Look what *you've* stolen."

The Crub smirked—an unpleasant thing to see in a rat. "Some things found, some thrown away, some . . . borrowed. When one has lived as long as I, amusement becomes the essence of existence." For a second time the raised paw pointed—this time straight at Simwan. "Since I have so few encounters with it, I thought the addition of a little Truth to my world and the removal of some of it from yours would be entertaining. And so it has proven to be." The Crub took a step forward. "After all, it has brought you to me, and you promise to provide much amusement—for as long as you can be kept alive. I can promise you it will be for a long time. There are all manner of ways to make sure someone dies slowly." Teeth flashed.

"Your Truth-loving mother, for example. I wouldn't want you to die before receiving the delicious knowledge that she has preceded you in death. I am told by my minions who keep track of developments in that region that she is very, very ill indeed."

Rose exploded. "Nasty thing! Nasty, filthy thing!"

"Wicked creature," Amber added. "Better you should have stayed beneath the ground and not soiled the surface with your presence."

"Impious offshoot of an honorable race." Her voice having suddenly deepened so that she sounded considerably older than her twelve years, N/Ice was raising her arms in the direction of their adversary. "Hie back to the depths that shelter you! Return to the foulness in which you lie!"

White light erupted from the fingertips of the hand that was not holding the tiny flashlight. For a long instant, the vast stone chamber was illuminated as if by a hundred strobe lights. For an extended moment in time, everything within—priceless trash heap, moss, water, Crub, ools, rats, other servants of the master, and Deavys—was outlined in stark black and white. The rats and ferrets and snakes hissed in collective dread while the ools curled in upon themselves like worms exposed to bright sunshine. Even Simwan had to turn away from the radiance.

It struck the Crub foursquare on his chest, between his front legs. The force of the light blasted aside the thick fur there as if the spot had been struck by a bullet and washed over the chunky rodent shape like the shampoo electric.

The last of the light clung to the tip of the Crub's tail as if reluctant to let go. With a diffident glance and a sharp flick of that naked appendage, it was sent flying harmlessly into the darkness. Blood eyes turned back to the watching Deavys. Wild rat-jaws creased upward in a carnivorous smirk.

"I am not bothered by white light. I am not affected by insults. I am not even," he added with obvious relish as he locked eyes with Simwan, "troubled by would-be witches and sorcerers. I thrive on such diversions. I welcome whatever attacks you can mount. They only make me stronger." He began to advance toward the youngsters: slowly, deliberately, unhurriedly.

"Violence stiffens my resolve, as your spines will stiffen in death. I will indulge my teeth in the soft parts of your bodies."

The Crub charged.

The shrieking and squealing and howling that filled the chamber was terrible. Hundreds of ravenous rats and other rodents poured out of all four of the great drains, filling the open space with their cries and screams, their eyes like thousands of points of shifting, darting red light: crimson stars set in a mad, swirling galaxy of horror. The Deavys fell back into the soundest defensive formation they knew: back to back, hands upraised, each of them facing a different point of the compass.

They fought back as fiercely as they were attacked. N/Ice continued to fling the white light of purity in all directions. While the Crub might be too strong, or simply too mean, for it to affect him, it froze rat after other rat in its tracks, turning their fur and faces stark white. Hands crossed at the wrists, Rose barked out the fleeting, terse charms that were her specialty. Lifting half a dozen rats at a time, she utilized words of power and maturity to hurl them against the masonry walls. The ferocious but small bodies smashed into the unyielding stone and, their backs broken, fell to the floor where bodies had already begun to accumulate in piles of bleeding, twitching bone and fur. Amber flung profound enchantments left and right, catching those rats that leaped high and spinning them in such tight circles that they spun themselves into non-existence.

As for Simwan, he made it his task to pick off the ools. They were faster than they looked, slithering forward with their wide sucking mouths agape. Choosing to respond with the simplest bit of applicable magic he could remember, he called forth the chopping spell that his dad had once taught him to use when bringing in winter firewood. Slashing outward and down while alternating both hands, the edges of his palms became extensions of an imaginary ax. Each time he slashed out, an ool died. Chopped in half, or thirds, or little-bitty pieces by Simwan's spell, each black segment continued to writhe and thrash with a horrible lingering half-life long after it had been sliced and diced.

Pithfwid was an ebony tornado. So swift was the Deavy feline, so fast did his lithe form and teeth and claws slash, that the silver stripes with which he had recently invested his fur could not keep up. They kept darting around the roaring chaos that had enveloped the chamber, struggling to catch up to the rest of the cat, streaks of shadow forever fated to remain one step behind the shape that cast them.

With N/Ice flinging light, and Rose lobbing rats, and Amber spinning one rodent and ferret and snake after another into self-consuming oblivion, and Simwan chopping up slinking, stinking ools like they were so many eels in a Danish fish market, the air was full of blood, rat feces, and flying, dismembered rodent bodies. Had all the professional exterminators in the Northeast been brought into play, they could not have accomplished half so much destruction so swiftly, nor with such efficiency. And all the while, Simwan was careful not to jostle the precious bottle that lay tucked in the padded depths of his jacket pocket.

Awash in the carnage of his followers, the Crub hesitated. As ratainer after broken ratainer, ool after oozing ool, chattering mice and moaning voles and fulminating ferrets were flung around and past him to shatter against the walls and ceiling, freeze in their tracks, or compact into nothingness, his ruby eyes bled fury. Already, he had been deprived of the pleasure of watching his prey perish slowly, picked to pieces by his adoring minions. And while his armies continued to pour into the chamber, their numbers were not infinite. Not every rat in New York bowed to the Crub's command. Not every rodent and ground-dweller heeded his orders.

It had been clear from the very beginning that the offspring of humankind who had first pursued him through the forest and onward into the city and now here, to his very secret place itself, were different. Special. Non-Ords. The Crub growled to himself. It was not, after all, so very surprising. It was even, to a certain extent, to be expected. Humans were not the only species to be divided into those who were ordinary and those who were Something More.

Of his kind, the Crub was the pre-eminent example of Something More.

Simwan was the first to see what was happening. He was able to steal a long enough glance to perceive the transformation because the waves of attacking rodents flowing toward him had begun to subside somewhat. Over by the entrance to the conduit that led back to the surface, a greenish glow had appeared and was intensifying even as he stared at it. It expanded and ballooned, obscenely swollen by the thing it cloaked. Reaching out with one hand (and careful to use the back, non-edge generating part of it), he tapped Rose, who was nearest. She alerted Amber, who in turn took a moment to grab N/Ice by the shoulder and give her a warning shake.

"ENOUGH OF THIS! THE TIME FOR CHILDREN'S PLAY IS *ENDED*. THE TIME FOR RENDING IS HERE!"

Enveloped in ichorous, sickly green light, the Crub had contorted and distorted into his full self. To left and right, he was flanked by the similarly transmogrified dozen of his most trusted ratainers, his personal bodyguard. At the sight of these who had been horrifically transformed, even the rodents who were the Crub's allies scrambled frantically to get out of the way.

Simwan was not ashamed to admit that he was frightened. Ferocious rats he could handle. Biting mice and nibbling voles he could deal with. Snapping weasels and striking snakes he could defend himself against. There were spells and enchantments for dealing with such nuisances. But this . . . this . . . As the Crub and his horrifically mutated dozen servants began to advance, he saw his sisters continuing to do battle with the rest of the underground army. *He* stayed where he was: in the forefront. Being the big brother, that was the place Providence had designated for him. Swallowing hard, he readied himself to do battle with the likes of that which he had never encountered before, not even in a book.

Holding true to prior proportions, the Crub was still twice the size of the next largest of his closest followers. Only now, the master of the sewers was as big as a bear. A rat the size of a bear. Through the intervention of magic most malign, he had metamorphosed into something much more, and much, much worse, than what he had been before.

Already awful jaws had lengthened and expanded until they now comprised fully a third the length of the Crub's body. The hurried and unnatural growth had spawned massive muscles behind the head and jaw, creating a huge hump just behind the distorted skull. Feet and claws had likewise undergone disproportionate growth, so that they now resembled talon-tipped shovels. Even the Crub's fur had changed, turning from dark brown and semi-silky to a thick, tangled mass of kinked strands that were more like wire than hair. Flanked by his most trusted fighters, he advanced slowly and deliberately toward the eldest Deavy.

Simwan struck out as he backpedaled, but whereas previously his charm-enhanced hands had cut into the foe with comparative ease, now his blows only slid off the thicker, tougher fur and skin of his mutated assailants. A panicky glance behind him showed that he was approaching the north wall of the chamber. Soon, he would be unable to retreat any farther. Though his sisters saw what was happening, their attention was wholly occupied by the hundreds of screaming, squealing, fighting rodents that separated them from their brother. They were too far away, too engaged, too busy to help.

He bumped up against the cold, clammy stone wall. He was out of room, out of options, out of ideas. Out of time. Looming before him, the Crub sensed his prey's helplessness as he lapped up the young man's fear.

"OVER NOW," the monster rat rumbled ominously. Nearby, his most trusted fellow killers snarled and squealed in anticipation of the rending and tearing that was to come. "YOU SHOULD HAVE LEFT BAD ENOUGH ALONE. YOU SHOULD HAVE STAYED HOME. NOW, YOU ARE FOOD." Powerful, perverted muscles tensed as the abomination of Nature bared obscenely distorted jaws and prepared to leap.

"Just a minute, now. *If* you please."

His back pressed up against the wall, a startled Simwan looked to his left. A pair of mismatched shapes were emerging from a different tunnel than the one he and his sisters had used to access the Crub's lair. One figure straightened while the other did not have to. Surprised beyond measure, Simwan could only gape.

"Uncle Herkimer?" His eyes dropped to the second figure. "Señor Nutt?"

Wagging his tail as he took the measure of the ongoing battle and continuing rat butchery taking place before him, the tiny dog barely glanced in Simwan's direction as he replied. "No," he exclaimed tartly. "We're the *other* dead guy and his Chihuahua."

Uncle Herkimer's hollow yet perceptive eyes focused on the massive, disbelieving shape of the Crub. "My, but you are every bit as disgusting a creature as I supposed. Be a good monstrosity and be off with you, now, to whatever unclean place you dwell within, and leave my nephew and nieces alone." Broken teeth and cracked lips curved into a genial smile. "They're on holiday, you know."

Stunned by this casual presumption, the Crub hardly knew how to react. Nor was the abrupt and unexpected appearance of the Deavys' uncle and his dog the last of the surprises in store for the master of the sewers.

From atop a pile of dead and dying rodents rose a questioning shout. "Hie, dog! What are you doing here?"

Craning to see, Señor Nutt replied, "I thought that being a cat, you would obviously need some help."

"Help? Who needs help?" By way of punctuation, a vole came flying out of the flickering light to land at the Chihuahua's feet, its furry back broken. "But if you've nothing better to do," Pithfwid went on, "I grow bored with this interminable slaughter.

You could, in your small, insignificant way, perhaps help me put an end to it a minute or two sooner."

"Insignificant?" Señor Nutt puffed himself up, which on the face of it did not result in very much of an expansion. He continued to puff, however, and as he puffed he grew. A cloud of luminous gold sparkles appeared and glittered around him, illuminating the transformation. Bigger and stronger, more and more thickset he became, until when he finally stopped puffing he stood nearly as tall at the shoulder as the crouching Crub. A flabbergasted Simwan recognized what his uncle's pet had become. Not all the books he read were arcane tomes from his parents' library. Others he had perused online, or read in school. Paleontology, for example, was a subject that contrasted nicely with his father's lexicon of real imaginary beasts.

Señor Nutt, the Ur-Chihuahua, had transformed into a dire wolf.

With a snarl that reverberated around the three-story chamber, the newly fashioned agent of canine chaos sprang forward into the line of the Crub's personal bodyguards. The first snap of the monster wolf-dog's powerful jaws nearly bit one in half.

From his location atop an ever-growing knoll of destroyed rats and other creatures, Pithfwid observed the canine metamorphosis. "Hmph. Is that the best you can do? Mere dog stuff." Taking a deep breath, he similarly began to swell. And swell, and inflate. His paws expanded to the size of hubcaps, the muscles in his shoulders and back grew corded and knotted, tufts of hair appeared at the tips of his ears, and his teeth—his front canines grew and grew and grew until they were six, seven, nine inches long.

There came a roar that loosened some of the mortar holding together the aged, slime-coated building stones and shook dust from the ceiling. Those fighting rodents and snakes and ools who were in a position to witness the dramatic, dynamic, and explosive transformation of the Deavys' cat either collapsed on the spot as fear stopped their hearts, or scrambled desperately to flee. For the first time in their miserable collective lives, they saw something that frightened them even more than the Crub.

Crouching low, tail switching back and forth, bolts of miniature lightning crackling from its toes and tail, the violet-eyed black sabertooth tiger crossed the room in a single jump.

Amber, who had been standing closest to Pithfwid, took a moment out from her lethal rat-spinning to marvel at the wondrous transformation before returning to the methodical slaughter at hand.

"Oooh—*big* kitty!"

Shards of torn rodent filled the chamber like a red snowstorm as dire wolf and sabertooth tore into the army of rats and mice and voles and ools. The screaming and squealing that resounded throughout the room rose to new heights of horror.

Seeing the destruction that was being wrought among his followers, the stunned Crub realized that utter defeat was imminent. It made no sense. Apocalypse in a bottle. Who could fathom the workings of the human mind, be it Ord or Otherwise? They were not rat-ional. Had he known that taking the pretty, sensitive thing would lead to such disaster, he would have left the stupid notion on its shelf in the obscure store in the even more obscure town where it had been stored. Now it was too late. Too late for anything.

Except revenge.

As the very much metamorphosed Pithfwid and Señor Nutt rapidly whittled down the numbers of the Crub's surviving ratainers, he advanced deliberately on the one human who was still cornered against a wall.

"STUPID MAN-APE! ALL THIS DEATH AND DIFFI-CULTY OVER A LITTLE TRUTH AND ONE PITIABLE BIRTH MOTHER."

"It's not *your* birth mother," Simwan shot back defiantly. "Why—why did you take it, anyway?" Even though faced with impending death, Simwan could not keep from asking the question that had bothered him ever since he and his sisters had first learned the identity of the thief who had broken into the depths of Mr. Gemimmel's store. "Of what use is the Truth to you?"

"NOT I, NOT I. IT WAS THE GOINGS-ON IN YOUR COUNTRY. NEWS OF THE PROPOSED DEVELOPMENT THERE REACHED EVEN TO THE CITY. MORE DEVEL-OPMENT WOULD MEAN MORE NICE, FILTHY, OVERLY DENSE HOUSING. MORE DENSE HOUSING MEANS MORE FERTILE GROUND WHERE MY KIND CAN THRIVE AND PROSPER AND MULTIPLY." The Crub took another ominous step toward him. "TO MAKE THAT HAP-PEN, THE TRUTH NEEDED TO BE REMOVED FROM YOUR COMMUNITY. IT WAS PLACED THERE TO HELP YOUR KIND. I STOLE IT TO HELP *MY* KIND."

Desperately, Simwan tried to think of a spell to fend off the mutated monstrosity that was padding inexorably toward him. Even one of his mom's kitchen knives would be welcome, but he had paid no attention to the relevant enchantments. Kitchen utensils were "girl stuff." How he wished for a sharp-edged, well-honed length of steel girl stuff in his right hand now!

Seeing what was happening, an alarmed Uncle Herkimer tried to make his way to his nephew's side. But there were still too many fighting rats, too many heaped-up bodies, blocking his path. All he could do was shout a redundant warning.

"Look out, boy! Beware the brute!"

"ALL DIE, ALL! BUT I TAKE ONE WITH ME!" the Crub screeched as it started its leap. Too late, Pithfwid saw what was happening and turned to intervene. But the grown-up throwback cat had been swarmed by dozens of desperate badgers and rats and snakes and ferrets. Señor Nutt's angle of approach was blocked by flying or fallen corpses. The coubet was similarly occupied. In those critical seconds it would be left to Simwan to defend himself.

And he had nothing to fight back with.

–XXIII–

At the last possible instant he remembered what reposed in his jacket pocket. It seemed far too small and insignificant to make a difference. But it was all he had. Fumbling beneath the pocket's flap, he pulled out the small bottle of Roman glass, tugged off the stopper, and flicked a portion of the contents in the direction of the charging Crub. A small bit of what the bottle contained flew outward. It was slight but very bright, as is characteristic of the Truth.

The pinch of particles struck the Crub in mid-leap. A startled expression came over his distorted, bloodthirsty face: a look of utter surprise, and of something else.

Fear.

The brown body went instantly white—and then it began to disintegrate. Thick muscle became thin haze, then brown wisps, and with a final cry of despair and fury, dissolved away into nothingness. Instead of fang and claw, all that reached Simwan was a putrid breeze. Then, even that was gone. Just as it had been, the Crub was no more, no more was the Crub.

With the demise of their master, the remaining rodents who had been battling on his behalf let out a collective squeak of distress and scattered, vanishing into the four tunnels. Within moments the only rats that were left in the chamber were dead ones, or pieces thereof. Surveying with evident satisfaction the slaughter piled high around them, Pithfwid and Señor Nutt proceeded to shrink themselves back to size, reclaiming their respective everyday appearances.

"A fair evening's butchery," observed the Chihuahua calmly. He glanced in the direction of the restored Deavy cat. "I am compelled to bow to the efficacy of your alter."

Pithfwid was methodically cleaning his whiskers. "Where most enemies are concerned, usually the changed appearance is enough to accomplish the necessary task. I try not to maintain the shape for too long. I worry about the possible carry-over of toothache."

Making his way over and around the considerable heaps of dead and rended rodents, ools, ferrets, and other ground-dwellers, Uncle Herkimer rejoined his nephew. The hand that clapped down on Simwan's shoulder was cold and clammy, but welcome nonetheless.

"That was fast thinking, my boy."

Fighting to keep his fingers from shaking, Simwan restoppered the precious bottle and replaced it in his jacket pocket. "I had to do *something*. Dad and Mom always taught us that if we ever found ourselves in a tight situation and there was nothing appropriate at hand to fight back with, to go with whatever was available." He patted the pocket where the bottle resided safely once again. "It wasn't a *lot* more than nothing, but I guess it was enough."

Wisdom regarded him out of dead eyes. "A little truth goes a long way. The Crub had to face all that he was, without his pretense of power and strength. And it destroyed him. He could not, in the end, face the truth of what he really was. Now let us make haste to leave this place. Even to a dead man, it reeks of evil."

They were joined by the coubet. The girls were drained, their clothing stained. Their clothes would not have looked out of place in the back room of the shop of Tybolt the Butcher, but their smiles were, as always, radiant.

"What a messy business," N/Ice observed distastefully as she stepped over a pile of sliced-off rat tails.

"Sloppy work," agreed Amber as she kicked aside a pile of dismembered ool segments.

"Major ick," concluded Rose while squishing her way through a mass of slippery entrails.

"How did you find us, Uncle?" Simwan asked his deceased but nonetheless lively relative.

Even in death, kindliness and concern shone from Uncle Herkimer's distorted, decomposing features. "When it turned dark and suppertime passed and you still hadn't returned to the apartment or called in, I started to get worried. So Señor Nutt and I decided to go looking for you."

"But how did you *find* us?" Amber reiterated. "I tried to call you and couldn't. I mean, this is *New York*."

Herkimer smiled knowingly at her. "When you've lived and

331

been dead in the same place for as long as I have, you learn how and where to ask the right questions." He patted her on the shoulder and, much to her relief, did not bend forward to give her a reassuring kiss. "Now, children, let us leave this hellish hovel. You must all be quite hungry by now."

"Actually," declared Pithfwid as he touched his tummy with a paw, "I'm kind of full. It's hard to destroy a couple of hundred rats and other wandering meat without inadvertently devouring a few samples of one's paw-work."

"Well, *I'm* hungry." Rose's ready avowal was echoed by her brother and sisters.

"Not a problem," Uncle Herkimer assured them. "This is Manhattan, where after midnight even four blood-smeared youngsters and a dead man out for a stroll can find something to eat." He started toward the drainage tunnel that led back to the Loch and the Ravine. Simwan and his sisters followed. All were very much content with the work they had done that evening and confident in the knowledge that they, as well as the Truth, were once more safe and secure.

If only.

It came coiling unhurriedly into the room out of the drainage tunnel in front of them: a dense, slowly expanding black cloud that had grown thicker and much darker with the passage of time. It looked like a cloud of fluffy ink shot through with strips of darker, purer blackness. No words issued from within its dismal depths; no threats were spewed, no hollow sighs resounded. Only an occasional faint, malevolent moan drifted forth, to die as a fading whisper in the still, decaying air of the chamber.

Uncle Herkimer told them to get back. He did not have to.

Simwan and his sisters knew immediately what it was. You could feel it in the air—a kind of tenebrific tingling, as if instead of just a hand or foot your entire body was going to sleep. Despite the fact that the cloud gave off no perceptible odor, Simwan felt suddenly nauseous. Just being in the vicinity of the curling, coiling miasma made his stomach jump. Señor Nutt growled softly as he retreated while Pithfwid hissed challengingly. The fur on the cat's back and tail was standing straight up, and the little sparks that shot forth from the tips of the hairs were brighter and more intense than usual.

The Big Bad Dark Thing skulked stealthily into the chamber of death and spread out, flattening itself against the wall pierced by the tunnel from which it had emerged. Where it made contact, even moss and mold shriveled brown and crinkly, lost its grip on the damp stone, and died.

Still retreating and without taking her eyes off the expanding specter, Amber whispered to her uncle. "What—what does it want?"

Herkimer had his left arm extended out sideways in front of her and her sisters, as if that might somehow serve to protect them. "It wants to kill you. It wants you to die."

"But why?" Rose was at once fascinated and repelled by the dark entity that continued its steady seepage into the chamber.

"Because it hates what you are, what you represent. Light and laughter, pleasure and knowledge, promise and hope, innocence and virtue." Herkimer glanced briefly at Simwan. "And truth. Most especially the truth that is youth. Usually, it appears only in nightmares, where it does less harm. Other times it shows itself just before the moment of death. Ords can sense its presence but rarely see it. That you can do so only angers it that much more, and makes it all the more determined that you should breathe your last."

Reacting to the presence of the Big Bad Dark Thing that hated Truth, the contents of the bottle buttoned up in Simwan's jacket pocket had grown hot, threatening to burn his skin. He forced himself to ignore the rising temperature. Having just routed the Crub, he was not about to give up the Truth to a threatening black cloud.

"How do we fight it?" Remembering how he had defeated the master of rats, he put his right hand over his heart. Through the material of his jacket, he carefully fingered the now radiant bottle sequestered there. "With the Truth?"

"It will take more than the Truth to cast out the BBDT." Uncle Herkimer continued to shield the coubet with his decomposing body. "Unlike the Crub, it knows itself, and so does not fear the Truth. It will . . ."

The chamber went away. No, Simwan corrected himself as he fought to keep his feet, it had not gone away. The wall behind them remained unaffected, unchanged. But everywhere else, everything else—the ceiling, floor, the other three walls, had been . . . replaced.

An immense glowering sky filled with the darkest thunderclouds Simwan had ever seen surged and boiled above them. Thunder boomed and lightning crackled all around. Black lightning. Even so, each sinister flash provided enough of a glow to enable them to make out their surroundings. That made no sense, he reflected. You shouldn't be able to see by the flash of black lightning. But nothing else they were seeing made any sense, either. Beneath them enormous waves rose and broke, their spectral crests crashing against bottomless troughs. Though the wind howled like the one nor'easter he and his sisters had lived through, they remained motionless, hovering high above the tormented sea and beneath the angry sky.

Before them and bloated to gigantic proportions, the Big Bad Dark Thing raged and seethed. Its amplified moaning mixed with the wind to create a shuddering in Simwan's ears. He wanted to clap his hands to the sides of his head to try and shut out that horrible wailing, but he dared not. Now, of all times in his short life, he needed to concentrate, to focus, and to listen to Uncle Herkimer. Wise, old, deceased Uncle Herkimer, who of them all was the only one who might have the knowledge to . . . He looked to his right.

Uncle Herkimer was gone.

He nearly fainted from panic. Only the long hours of training he had undergone at home and at camp—listening to his parents, paying attention to his teachers and tutors—kept him sane and conscious. For the first time in his life, he found himself thankful that he had been assigned homework.

Uncle Herkimer was still there. He had simply darted behind Simwan faster than the eye could follow, to whisper something to the girls. As Simwan backed up, somehow motivating himself to move through the air, the coubet joined hands to form a circle. White light began to envelop each of them: Rose, Amber, and N/Ice, and to spread out around them. As the brilliant sphere of illumination fully enveloped them and continued to expand, the moaning from the immense rumbling mass of the BBDT rose to a skirling howl of outrage and fury. For an instant, it seemed as if it was going to draw back, to flee.

Then it swept forward, and struck.

As the dark, fiery-eyed mass descended toward them, Uncle Herkimer suddenly went stiff as—well, as a board, anyway. "Throw me!" he yelled heedlessly.

"What?" As a measured response, Simwan was immediately aware, the one he had vocalized was singularly lacking in usefulness.

"Throw me, boy, throw me!" In lieu of being able to raise either of the arms that had frozen to his sides, Uncle Herkimer was forced to rely on the urgency in his voice. "Use the right spell!"

The right spell? Simwan frantically plumbed the depths of his knowledge. What was the right spell for throwing one's dead uncle at a boiling mass of onrushing evil? Or for that matter, what was the right spell for throwing him at all? There was no time to delay, no time to ponder. No time for careful consideration.

At school he had excelled in the track events, less so in field. But under Coach Mankewitch's tutelage, he had sooner or later taken a shot at everything from the pole vault to the shot put. His lanky form, coach and student had jointly decided, was more suited to the high jump.

And to the javelin.

Murmuring under his breath what he hoped was the appropriate enchantment while simultaneously seeking comfort in the warmth of the coubet's expanding circle of light, Simwan bent slightly, picked up his stiffened relative on his mother's side, and heaved him as hard as he could straight in the direction of the oncoming Big Bad Dark Thing.

Uncle Herkimer struck the exact center of the oncoming,

frenzied black cloud—and vanished within. For a moment, nothing happened. For a moment, Simwan feared that a fate worse than death had befallen their uncle. Then a strange thing happened.

This was, even in the context of everything that had preceded it on that long, remarkable day, a profound understatement.

The Big Bad Dark Thing seemed to contort in upon itself. It twisted and coiled, writhed and convulsed. Behind Simwan, the coubet's singing rose to a fevered pitch. It was an old, old song: from the Traditions, from the Revelations of Otherness. A simple song, but one of great power. So strong was it that its effect was not even dampened by the discordant, high-pitched counterpoint being supplied by one howling dog and one yowling cat.

> "Lis-semay, lis-semay, drifting along the Appian Way
> Stir the pot, word the chant, shove aside the sycophant
> Put it down, put it down, deep where the Earth doth roil
>   and frown
> To make sure no harm comes to us, lodge it in the heart
>   of Vesuvius
> Keep it there, make it stay
> As you did for the Greeks at brave Thermopylae."

There was an explosion of light and darkness. Out of it came . . . calm. Above them, the clouds grew quiet. Below them, the heaving shadowy seas subsided. Then both vanished, up and gone away, as if they had never been.

They were back in the sewer chamber. Breathing hard, Simwan knew it was so, because breathing hard, he could not escape the putrid smell of the hundreds of rodent carcasses that surrounded him and his outraged nostrils.

Of the Big Bad Dark Thing, there was no sign.

He and his sisters and Pithfwid, not to mention a frantic Señor Nutt, had a bad moment when there was no sign of their uncle Herkimer. Then they spotted him on the far side of the room. He was lying on the corpse-strewn stone floor, one hand holding his head as he struggled to sit up. They were all at his side in a moment: Simwan looking on with concern while the girls fussed and cooed over their no-longer stiff (well, no longer ramrod straight, anyway) uncle. Leaping onto his lap, Señor Nutt rested his front paws on the dead man's chest and began anxiously licking the moldy, decaying face.

Perhaps predictably, Rose muttered, "Eewww."

Accepting a sextet of helping hands from the girls, Herkimer rose unsteadily to his feet. To be fair, he was unsteady most of the time, but at present he was certainly a bit more so than usual. Espying Simwan, and with Señor Nutt panting happily at his feet, he tottered over and clapped his nephew firmly on the shoulder.

"That was as fine a piece of uncle throwing as ever I've experienced, my boy, and I've been tossed around by some of the best! Many are those who would have thought too long about complying with my request. Sometimes even a wizard has to act without thinking."

"What—what happened?" were the first words Simwan could think to mutter in response.

Peering ceilingward, Uncle Herkimer continued to rest a thankful hand on his nephew's shoulder while pointing with the other. "I told you that the Big Bad Dark Thing knows itself. Well, I know myself also. I didn't think it could swallow me and handle that. But I needed someone else to set me in motion."

After giving Simwan's shoulder a parting, affectionate squeeze, Uncle Herkimer drew back his hand and for the second time in less than an hour, started toward the dark opening of the conduit that led to the surface. This time, nothing came frothing forth to contest his passage.

Simwan and the girls followed close behind, with a talkative Pithfwid and an argumentative Señor Nutt bringing up the rear. His sisters were already quarreling over which cleaning spells they were going to employ to cleanse themselves and their clothes. They couldn't just head back to the apartment without doing something about their appearance. Passing Ord pedestrians who happened to catch sight of the three blood-soaked girls and their brother were liable to do anything from faint on the spot to run screaming into the street, while a patrolling policeman would take one look at them and might well assume they were the survivors of a bomb attack, or maybe the worst incident of gang warfare in the history of the city. His sisters' squabbling left Simwan free to chat with his uncle.

"You said you didn't think the BBDT could swallow you, could handle who and what you are." He searched the ghastly but lovable face of his relative as the latter lurched onward, having to bend low so that his dead head would not be knocked clean off by the roof of the tunnel. "I don't understand what happened. Just *who* and *what* are you, Uncle Herkimer?"

The dead man smiled down at him. "I guess your parents haven't told you much about me, eh?"

Simwan shook his head. "As far as the girls and I know, you're just Uncle Herkimer. On our mother's side."

A renegade maggot spilled out of one ear as Herkimer nodded understandingly. "You must have seen my mailbox when you arrived at my apartment and rang the bell. Do you recall the nameplate?"

It was not the explanation Simwan had expected. He tried hard to remember. In his defense, it had been somewhat of a long day.

He brightened. "J. Herkimer."

His uncle smiled anew. Suddenly he did not look so old, or so slow, or even quite so dead. Simwan had a brief, bracing glimpse of the great and powerful sorcerer his uncle (on his mother's side) had once been, lo those many centuries ago.

"The *J,* " Uncle Herkimer told his nephew, "stands for Justice. And like I told you, my boy, for it to be effective in combating evil, it inevitably needs someone to set it in motion."

-XXIV-

Though little short of Armageddon could have topped their first day in New York for sheer excitement, it must be added that the Deavy offspring had a wondrous good time afterward as well. Mailing the Truth home to Mr. Gemimmel (via Express Harpy) resulted in the joyous news that their mother had made an astonishingly swift and complete recovery and had been discharged from the hospital that very same day. All Hallow's Eve was especially memorable, with each of them dressed in a different outfit as they wandered up and down this Manhattan street and that. Their costumes drew a good deal of favorable comment from admiring Ord celebrants, though none could surpass the stream of compliments lavished on Uncle Herkimer, even though he had only gone out as himself.

By and by the week went bye-bye, and they had to return home to Clearsight. Their parents were pleased and duly impressed that their offspring had successfully experienced the big city more or less on their own, and that contrary to their mother's concerns and in line with their father's prediction, they had encountered no trouble whatsoever in the course of their visit, no trouble at all. To the children's delight (and great relief), Uncle Herkimer conveyed nothing to counter this perception.

As soon as a convenient opportunity presented itself, the Deavy siblings bicycled back into town and paid their respects to Mr. Gemimmel, who in turn showed them where he had carefully returned the Truth to the empty space on the special shelf in the far, far back of beyond that was located at the rear of his pharmacy. Not long after, a special election was held to determine the fate of the proposed new town mall and its ancillary property development. Much to the surprise of the developers and the town council and the highly paid lobbyists who had pushed for its approval, the proposal was soundly defeated—so soundly that a run-off vote or recount was deemed unnecessary. The puzzled pollsters who had been predicting passage of the amendment to the county's planning and zoning code that would have allowed the development to go ahead had apparently been wrong all along. Just as many of the voters later admitted they had been from the start. The anti-development group led by Melinda Mae Deavy held a lowkey party to celebrate its defeat.

Life thereafter did not necessarily proceed smoothly, however. Much to Melinda Mae's disgust, Pithfwid continued his regular habit of bringing home dead mice and the occasional low-flying pigeon and depositing their battered carcasses on the Deavy front steps. With the resumption of school following the holiday, Simwan once more found himself subject to the taunts, pranks, and general teasing of the coubet.

It wasn't fair, he fumed on more than one occasion. Other young wizards-in-waiting only had to suffer the assaults of dragons and demons, of threatening trolls and grotesque ogres and evil sprites. Those threats, at least, were understandable. Whereas he, who had done nothing to deserve so miserable and patently unfair an adolescence, was forced to deal on a daily basis with nasty, spiteful, mocking little sisters.

All two-and-a-half of them.

About the Author

Alan Dean Foster is the author of more than 120 science fiction and fantasy novels. His books include the Spellsinger Series, the Pip and Flinx Series, and numerous Star Wars and Star Trek novelizations. In addition to creating imaginary worlds, Foster travels extensively throughout the world. He has camped in the South Pacific, scuba dived on unexplored reefs, eaten fried piranha in the jungles of Peru, and filmed great white sharks in Australia. In addition to writing and traveling, Foster likes to hike, bodysurf, and powerlift. He and his wife live in Prescott, Arizona, with their troupe of cats. Needless to say, the cats rule the house.